The Hidden Blade

SHERRY THOMAS

This is a work of fiction. Names, characters, places, and incidents are the product of the author's imagination or are used fictitiously. Any resemblance to actual events, locales, or persons, living or dead, is purely coincidental.

The Hidden Blade © 2014 by Sherry Thomas
Edited by Tiffany Yates Martin

Cover design © Frauke Spanuth
Print Edition 1.0

*To my dear friend Flora, with whom I spent
some of the happiest hours of my life reading
and talking about our favorite wuxia stories*

One

The Photograph

Peking
The twelfth year of the reign of the Tung-chih Emperor (1873)

THE FOREIGN DEVIL STARED AT YING-YING.

He was the size of her thumb, yet she had trouble holding his gaze. She looked away from his eyes. In the fading photograph, his strangely tight-fitting garments were the brown of eggs cooked in soy sauce, his white skin the color of weathered bamboo. His nose protruded proudly, like the prow of a foreign-devil warship. Thin, colorless lips twisted into a half sneer.

His hair was a darkish shade, cut short, parted on the side, and combed slick. He had neither beard nor mustache, but the same hair that grew on his head extended down the sides of his face almost right to the corners of his lips, like a forest throwing out two spurs of itself down the slope of a mountain.

He did not stand straight, but rather leaned to one side, his left foot propped on a stool, one black shoe gleaming. To the other side of the stool, a woman sat with her profile to Ying-ying, head bent, a large book open on her lap. She wore a ridiculous contraption: her sleeves the size of rice sacks, her skirts a tent large enough to sleep two.

What stupid, impractical things the foreign devil women wore.

Ying-ying's breath caught in her throat. She leaned in closer. She had been distracted by the clothes, but the woman was no foreign devil.

It was Mother.

In her shock Ying-ying almost didn't hear the footsteps coming into the courtyard. She tossed the photograph into its redwood box and shoved the box under Mother's fox fur-lined winter cape.

Dropping the lid of the great trunk, she dashed out to the study and settled into her chair just as Mother's maid came through the doors of the front room. The rooms were stretched against the wall of the courtyard like cubes of lamb on a shish kebab, in one straight row.

Ying-ying grabbed the writing brush she had left resting on the ink stone and pretended to smooth out excess drops of ink against the rim.

"Bai Gu-niang studying so hard?" The maid, Little Plum, teased her gently as she went past. Bai was Ying-ying's family name, gu-niang the respectful address for a young lady. "Little girls as pretty as you don't need to know the classics."

"Has Boss Wu left already?" The silk merchant had arrived only half an incense stick ago.

"They are still drinking tea—he hasn't even had his apprentice bring in the wares yet. Fu-ren sent me to fetch her new fan. She wants to see if Boss Wu has something that will go with it." The servants referred to Mother as fu-ren, her ladyship. Little Plum paused as she located the desired fan. "But she did say to tell you she will expect at least five sheets done when she returns."

Ying-ying moaned. "My wrist will hurt all night."

"Amah will give you an herbal compress." Little Plum laughed as she sauntered out.

Ying-ying was back in the bedchamber in a second, digging through the trunk again.

Nosing through Mother's rooms had become a clandestine hobby of late. It had started when she had been tasked to fetch a supply of paper for Mother's ink paintings. In the study cabinet where she had found the paper, she had also come across a collection of curious ink stones, some big as a plate, others small enough to fit into her palm. Her delight in the ink stones led her to discover troves of vermilion-stained seals, packets of incense from Japan, and a dozen tiny spoons used for ladling water onto the stone to facilitate the grinding of the ink stick.

It had been most natural, after she had exhausted the study, to move on to Mother's inner rooms. There she peeked at Mother's jewels of jade and pearls and sniffed her tiny pots of rouge and powder.

But she had never unearthed anything like the contents of the redwood box.

There were other items inside: an oval ivory bauble that did not seem to be a hair ornament, a flexible jewel-encrusted band of gold, a small booklet that had been cut and sewn by hand, with each page devoted to two strange symbols, sometimes identical, sometimes not, and a sheet of paper with foreign writing on it.

It was the photograph, however, that drew her, like a toddler to the edge of a deep pond.

Mother was concubine to a very important Manchu. Everyone addressed him simply as Da-ren, great personage. He was a prince of the blood and an uncle to the current emperor, but he was not Ying-ying's father.

Who her father was she did not know—and did not ask. Harsh rebukes, received during the earliest years of her childhood, barely remembered but deeply ingrained, made her forbear from ever raising that unwelcome question.

Yet she had always pondered, when she had nothing else to distract her.

And now here was this man, by whose side Mother sat all trussed up in a foreign devil costume, as meek as an oft-fed rabbit.

But he was a foreign devil. A foreign devil! She shuddered. Greedy, bloodthirsty creatures they were, coming from their savage lands with their terrible manners and their blazing cannons. She had even heard whispers that they ate babies.

No, whoever this man was, he was no more blood relation to her than Da-ren.

However, as she raised her head, she saw her own eyes reflected in a small standing mirror on Mother's vanity table. Her irises were not black, nor even brown. Rather, they were a deep, opaque gray-blue, the color of a desolate sky about to unleash a great storm.

She gasped—there was another face in the mirror.

"Put everything back," remonstrated her amah.

How did Amah come up to her without her detecting anything? A curtain of ceramic beads hung in the doorway. The beads clinked whenever anyone passed through. And Ying-ying had keen ears, rabbit ears. She could hear a door open and close three courtyards away.

"I was just looking for a handkerchief," she lied as she buried the redwood box in the depths of the trunk.

She was pulled up by the shoulder. Amah pointed to her chest. "What's that?"

It was her handkerchief, snugly tucked at the closure of her blouse, one corner artfully peeking out.

"Don't go poking where you have no business," Amah warned. "Now go practice your calligraphy."

MOTHER WAS NOT ENTIRELY PLEASED with Ying-ying's output. She frowned as she examined Ying-ying's copy of a great ancient

7

calligrapher's work. Ying-ying resigned herself to the criticism to come. Her characters, alas, always looked somewhat undernourished.

Mother, on the other hand, could do marvelous things with a brush. The couplet on either side of the study doorway she had written herself: *The lamp shines gently in the quiet mountain room; steady rain falls upon the cold chrysanthemum bloom.* Each character on the gold-speckled rose paper was manifest elegance, the strokes measured and meticulous, the balance immaculate—flawlessly, decorously beautiful, just like Mother.

In fact, the entirety of her home was a reflection of her. In paintings, a beautiful woman was never surrounded by too many things; a few choice blossoms and a dancing willow branch set her off perfectly. And so it was with Mother. Her rooms, with their graceful but spare furnishings, formed a comely but muted backdrop for her, whose exquisiteness reigned unrivaled.

To Ying-ying's surprise, Mother didn't say anything as she handed the calligraphy sheets back. Only then did Ying-ying notice that she looked wan despite the rouge on her cheeks.

"Little Plum, help me to bed," Mother called. Then, to Ying-ying, "Tell your amah to make some more of that cough potion for me."

Mother's tiny feet made it difficult for her to walk, but she managed to turn her wobbly progress into something almost like a dance, a sprig of peach blossom swaying in the wind. Ying-ying always liked to watch her walk.

But as soon as Little Plum reached her chair, Mother began to cough. She twisted her torso to one side, dropped her head delicately, unfurled her handkerchief as if it were a flower bud come to bloom, and made almost no noise at all. Her handkerchiefs were once pink or yellow, but since the coughing started, she carried only those of deep red, so the droplets of blood wouldn't show.

One of Little Plum's cousins had died the year before. First he coughed; then he coughed up bits of blood; then he coughed up rivers of blood; soon there was nothing any doctor could do for him. Ying-ying had heard it all in the kitchen, between visits from Little Plum's relatives.

She hurried out to find Amah.

In the next courtyard, along the north-facing side, Amah had fitted out a small room expressly for the purpose of brewing medicinal potions. The far end of the room was taken up by a *kang*, a raised brick

8

platform so arranged with flues that a small brazier placed inside could warm the whole of it. There were *kangs* in a great many rooms of their dwelling. Ying-ying slept on one. Mother thought them ugly and had those in her rooms dismantled. But Mother was a southerner. According to Cook, southerners valued appearance above comfort, even health.

The rest of the room was arranged almost like an apothecary's. Ceramic jars of dried herbs and flowers crowded the shelves that lined the walls. A bench next to the *kang* held clay pots and lidded bowls. Amah sat in the center of the room before a tiny potbellied stove, already making the requested potion, judging by the bitter aroma wafting in the air.

"How do you know she needs it?" Ying-ying took a stool and sat down next to her.

Amah gave Ying-ying a woven straw fan so she could make herself useful. As Ying-ying fanned the flames, Amah stirred the bubbling brown stew of loquat leaf, bellflower root, licorice, and ginger. "It's the fourteenth. Da-ren comes in two days. She always wants to dampen that cough before he comes."

They settled into a busy silence as Ying-ying found a suitable rhythm to her fanning. Like Mother, Amah was from the south. But unlike Mother, who quite intimidated Ying-ying with her great beauty and equally impressive talents, Amah posed no discomfort. She was as plain as a common moth, though she kept herself trim and neat. And *her* talents Ying-ying simply adored.

Amah could capture any insect. In spring she gathered butterflies. In summer she caught fireflies and crickets, and made sure Ying-ying's room was free of mosquitoes. Her hands, rough and round-fingered, were nevertheless extraordinarily skilled. She wove animal figures out of reed, sculpted tiny people with bits of colored dough, and from old sticks of candle she carved mock seals for Ying-ying, with titles such as "Princess of the Fragrant Garden," or "Muse by the Pomegranate Blossom."

But what the grown-ups most appreciated was her expertise in medicinal herbs. She knew a remedy for every common ailment: tree peony for Cook's female problems, fenugreek for Little Plum's stomach pains, cloves and camphor for Mother's backaches. When Cook's water-carrier brothers visited in the kitchen, she'd give them a formula of angelica and ephedrine for their joints. Should Little Plum's aunt drop by, she had just the thing—red peony—for her patchy skin.

In addition, she maintained a greenhouse of sorts, a crude contrivance half dug into the ground, with a low mud wall and slanting frames covered with Korean paper. In the dead winter months, with the addition of a tiny smudge stove, she was able to produce fresh flowers for Mother's coiffure and green herbs for Cook.

"It's almost done," Amah said, giving the brew one last stir.

Ying-ying fetched a bowl. Amah poured nearly to the rim and covered the bowl tightly.

Ying-ying ventured to speak something of what had transpired earlier in the afternoon. "You won't tell Mother, right?"

"No," Amah answered without looking at her. "But what you did was still stupid."

Ying-ying blushed. "I wasn't stealing. I just wanted to see what she had."

"Don't go around digging in other people's things," Amah said darkly. "Dig long enough and you'll always find things you wish you hadn't."

On her way to Mother's rooms with the potion, Ying-ying chewed over Amah's words. Amah had seen the photograph—how could she not, materializing directly behind Ying-ying? If so, did what she said just now confirm the worst of Ying-ying's suspicions?

Was the foreign devil her father?

Two

The Rift

Sussex, England
The thirty-sixth year of Queen Victoria's reign (1873)

"LEGEND HAS IT THAT THIS is the key to a great treasure," said Herb, lifting up the tablet of translucent white jade.

The tablet was about six inches long, four inches wide, and barely a quarter inch in thickness. Upon it a bas-relief goddess danced, her back arched, her eyes closed. To either side of the goddess were characters in intricate Chinese script. But whereas the goddess was all billowing sleeves and trailing ribbons, the words—to Leighton Atwood's untrained eyes, at least—gave an impression of solidity and wisdom.

There were other antiques at Starling Manor—suits of armor from the War of the Roses, tapestries that predated the Renaissance by hundreds of years, and, according to family lore, a jewel-encrusted goblet from which Queen Elizabeth once drank. But here in the library, in the midst of a collection of six thousand volumes, there was only this single artifact from faraway China, kept in a special display case near Father's favorite reading chair.

Herb held the tablet toward the light of the chandelier. The tablet seemed to glow from within, a soft, rich radiance. "Mutton-fat jade, they call it, for its density and creaminess."

He returned the jade tablet to its glass-topped display case and glanced at Father. "A rare and beautiful thing, would you not agree, Nigel?"

The tropical sun, Leighton often thought, must be something like Herb, an entity of unfailing cheer and warmth. Which made it all the more disconcerting to hear the prickliness in Herb's tone.

"Of course I agree," Father answered, his words placating—and slightly anxious.

Father was often anxious, but never when Herb was around. With Herb he was just...happy. It was impossible to be anything else in Herb's company, or so Leighton had always thought.

Until now.

"Would you not tell the legend behind the jade tablet, old chap?" asked Father. "Leighton always enjoys hearing it. Is that not so, Leighton?"

"Yes, sir," answered Leighton, all too aware of the note of uncertainty in his own voice.

It was usually Leighton who asked to hear the legend, and Father who teased that he must have already heard it dozens of times.

Herb turned toward Leighton. He had a lanky build, blond hair, and a deceptively young face that sometimes made Leighton forget that he was not a youth but a grown man of twenty-seven, far closer in age to Father's thirty-two than to Leighton's not-quite eleven.

"The legend," Herb murmured. He smiled, a rueful, almost apologetic smile, as if he sensed the uneasiness he had caused Leighton. "All right, the legend. Tell me, Leighton, where did Taoism originate?"

Father untensed. Leighton released a breath he had not known he was holding. "In China."

"And Buddhism?"

"India."

"Which means..." Herb prompted.

"That for China, Taoism is indigenous, whereas Buddhism is an import," said Leighton.

"Exactly," said Herb. "Toward the latter years of the Tang Dynasty, there was a Chinese emperor who strongly favored Taoism. The Taoists who promised him elixirs of immortality urged him to promote their religion and suppress the practice of Buddhism, which they viewed as a foreign upstart.

"The Buddhist monks of China began to fear that their monasteries would be demolished and their wealth seized. Such wealth—a mountain's worth of silver ingots, Buddha figures of pure gold, not to mention priceless paintings and calligraphic scrolls."

At this point Father would usually—and with great affection—ask Herb how much he had embellished the story. Herb would reply that he had added no sensational details, as the story had come to him already feverishly embroidered.

But tonight Father only listened, a glass of whisky clutched in his hand.

His attention seemed to gratify Herb, who smiled again. "Well, such valuables must not fall into the emperor's greedy hands. So from all over the land the monks gathered under the guise of a great scriptural congress, while secretly moving the riches of their cloisters."

Leighton imagined squat wagon carts stripped to the bone, in order to not leave deep ruts that would give away the weight of the heavy load they carried. There would also have been palanquins in which the venerable abbeys of the monasteries purportedly sat, carried by the strongest monks. Except only gold and jade rode inside the palanquins; the venerable abbeys, in their plainest robes, dusty and road-weary, walked alongside the humblest of initiates.

"Under the cover of night, everything was unloaded into a huge cavern. Then the cavern was carefully sealed, so that it would not be found by the emperor's soldiers or other thieves and pillagers," Herb went on. "The monks were sworn to secrecy. And three jade tablets were made and entrusted to the three seniormost abbeys, for the day when it would become either safe or necessary to find and reopen the cave.

"Almost immediately the legend took root. It was said that grown men shaved their heads and took vows with the sole purpose of trying to locate these jade tablets in the inner sanctums of the greatest monasteries. But time passed—generations, then centuries.

"From time to time stories would crop up of a lucky goatherd who stumbled upon an ancient silver ingot in his path, something that might have been dropped by the monks in their hurry. Others believe that the treasures were ransacked ages ago, much as the pyramids of the pharaohs had been emptied by tomb robbers, leaving behind only pits of vipers. But still others remain convinced that the treasures are exactly where they had been concealed long ago, and if only all three of the jade tablets can be reunited, the treasures too can be found."

The longcase clock in a corner of the library gonged the hour. Ten o'clock. When Mother was home, Leighton was expected to be in bed with the lights out by nine. Father, on the other hand, allowed him to stay up until the first yawn.

Leighton did not in the least feel like yawning, but he did so anyway—he could sense when the grown-ups wanted to be alone.

"Am I putting you to sleep?" asked Herb, smiling, his hand on Leighton's shoulder.

For a moment everything felt all right—the storm clouds receding, the sun shining in the sky. But then Leighton sensed it again, the underlying tension in the room.

"I'm just tired."

They had rowed for hours that afternoon and walked even longer in the rolling hills that surrounded Starling Manor. Leighton was not actually tired—he could have hiked for miles more—but no one questioned his claim.

Herb shook Leighton's hand. "Sleep well, my dear boy. And may all your dreams be marvelous."

LEIGHTON WAS NOT AFRAID of the dark—he did not believe in monsters under the bed. All the same, he did not like to lie awake, staring into the blackness of the night.

It was easier to believe that all was well when the sun fell upon his face. That afternoon, atop a hill that gave onto a wide field of poppies in bloom, Leighton had felt buoyantly happy as he listened to Herb and Father discuss how long it would take to return home. The air had been crisp—almost a little warm; the sky had been pale but blue; and Mrs. Thompson's apricot jam had never tasted so good, in a sandwich made with sturdy bread and fresh butter churned only that morning.

But now, as night stretched on and on, he saw that even then Herb had been a little impatient. He also saw that it was odd for Father to have taken them rowing and hiking the moment Herb had stepped off the train. Leighton hadn't minded, because he loved to be outside. But would Herb have preferred to spend the afternoon resting at Starling Manor?

Why hadn't Herb said anything? His presence was what made his visits such highlights, not whether they traipsed over the downs or sat inside and played card games.

It was almost as if Herb and Father could not speak frankly to each other.

Leighton pushed aside the bedcover and sat up. He didn't want to think about it anymore. The idea of either Father or Herb with a chest full of words they could not say...

A stomachache was preferable any day of the week.

In the library, Herb had created a special nook for the books and magazines he brought Leighton, everything from penny dreadfuls to *The Count of Monte Cristo*—and lately scientific romances by Jules

Verne. Usually Leighton would discover new books only after Herb's departure, but tonight a book he had already read would do. Anything would do.

Light seeped out from beneath the doors of the library. Were Father and Herb still up? It was almost midnight. Leighton climbed up one floor to the solarium: There was another way into the library.

The manor, built by a man who believed himself hunted by mortal enemies out for vengeance, had a number of secret passages. Some had been bricked over by later occupants, but others had been left alone.

Leighton slipped into the library and pushed back into place the bookshelf that had swung open to let him through. A gallery wrapped around the upper portion of the room on three sides. He tiptoed forward, crouched down, and looked through the ornamental gaps in the parapet.

Father sat before the chessboard and stared at the pieces. He was a handsome man, with black hair and green eyes that Leighton had inherited. Compared to Herb, he was quieter, more restrained, yet in some ways far more intense. Sometimes he made Leighton think of strings on a violin that had been pulled too taut. But he never snapped, though sometimes he disappeared into his study for days on end. Nobody had to walk on eggshells when he did that—there was no belligerence or brutality to Father—but the entire house would be so quiet, almost funereal, and every sound seemed to produce a distant echo.

Herb did not sit opposite Father, but paced. Prowled like a caged wolf.

All at once he stopped and spun around to face him.

Father did not look up from the chessboard. But underneath the table, where Herb could not see but Leighton could, Father's hands clenched and unclenched continuously.

Herb strode toward Father. Leighton bit his lower lip. They were such good friends; he didn't want them to be at odds.

Herb pushed the chess table out of the way. Pawns wobbled; two knights fell over and rolled onto the floor. Father gripped the armrests, his person pressed into the back of the chair.

Leighton half rose to his feet, a plea emerging.

Herb leaned forward, took hold of Father's face, and kissed him.

Leighton covered his own mouth, spun around, and crouched low. The inside of his head sounded like a battlefield, all exploding ordnance and hurtling shrapnel.

"You know we mustn't," Father said all of a sudden, his breathing labored. "My brother will find out."

Sir Curtis, Father's half brother by a different mother, was fifteen years older than Father. Father always became agitated before one of Sir Curtis's infrequent visits, as if he were a pupil who had to sit for an examination for which he had not prepared. Mother, too, behaved strangely when Sir Curtis was around, prattling on about her support for missionary work abroad and the fact that Leighton had read the Bible end to end, both the King James and the Latin Vulgate translations.

Was *this* why?

"There is no one here except you and me, Nigel," said Herb— incorrectly. "All your servants are abed, dreaming their own dreams."

"Still, we shouldn't," said Father, his voice anguished. "I made a solemn vow that I would never endanger your soul with our friendship."

Passages in the Bible that hadn't made particular sense before now leaped out at Leighton, heavy words avowing eternal damnation to men who consorted with other men. His fingers shook; he clamped them between his knees.

"You assume that my soul isn't already damned," said Herb. "And don't insult me. *Friendship?* I love you, Nigel, and you love me. But I can only go on for so long waiting for you to come to your senses."

"Herb, please don't say things like that."

"What am I supposed to say, Nigel? It's been years. *Years.* Maybe you are meant for platonic love, but I am not. If you fear your brother more than you love me, let me know and I—I—" Herb exhaled, a heavy sound that reverberated in the silence of the night. "Then I shan't come around to bother you anymore."

Leighton dropped onto his knees, his hands braced against the carpet. Still he felt dizzy, as if he had spun around for a solid five minutes and then come to an abrupt stop. They were not friends, Herb and Father. At least, not just friends, but men who desired to be more to each other—Father wanting it no less than Herb, only that he did not dare.

This was why it had grown tense, Father wishing things would continue as before, and Herb no longer content with that arrangement.

"It is not my brother I fear," Father pleaded, "but God."

The desperation in his words made Leighton's throat close. He did not know everything about the facts of life, but he knew enough to understand that in such matters there could be no compromise. Either Father must hold completely to his position, or he must abandon it just as completely.

"Listen to yourself, Nigel." Herb sounded as if he were holding back tears. "You don't fear God. If you did, would you allow your wife to visit her lover with your blessing? You would be on your knees begging her to think of her eternal soul. But not only do you let her go, you let her take Marland to see his natural father."

Leighton clamped a hand over his heart. Marland wasn't Father's son?

Father's reply was barely audible. "It's only fair, since I can't be the husband Anne deserves."

"But you can be everything to me, Nigel. We can make this arrangement work for all of us."

"I can't. If Curtis found out, he would make it unbearable for everyone involved—you, me, Anne, *and* the boys. He would put me into an institution and take our children away from Anne. He would punish you too, Herb, in ways I dare not even imagine."

"Why do you let him? You are not financially or legally dependent on him. You are your own man."

"I am not." Father's voice quavered, close to cracking. "Before Curtis I will always be a coward. He is the monster of my nightmares, the wrath of an unforgiving God. He is...he is what I deserve for being who I am."

Leighton had never liked Sir Curtis, but for the first time he became afraid of the man. Father's fear was as heavy as a London fog, seeping into Leighton's pores, making him shiver.

There came a long silence. "I am the same as you are," Herb said, his tone oddly flat. "Do you mean to tell me then that I may never expect any measure of happiness in this life?"

"That wasn't what I meant at all, Herb. There is nothing I wish more fervently for than your happiness."

"But you won't lift a finger for it. You want me to exist in a state of desperate chastity so that you may have your cake and your eternal soul too."

"Herb—"

"Please say no more," said Herb. He took several deep breaths. "I'm sorry for being so overwrought. I'm sorry for asking more. You told me from the very beginning that this was how it would be; it was my fault for thinking I could change you.

"I can't live like this, but I'm sure someday you will find someone who can, someone with a soul far loftier than mine. Convey my regards to Leighton and tell him—" Herb's voice turned hoarse. "Tell him I will miss him with every fiber of my being."

Leighton squeezed his eyes shut. No. *No.* Herb could not simply walk out of their lives.

The door of the library opened and closed.

Soft sounds came from below—Father, sobbing.

A long time passed before Leighton realized that he too had tears rolling down his face.

HERB HAD FIRST VISITED STARLING Manor almost three years ago, on a miserable day for Leighton: Mother had left on yet another trip without him.

She had explained, with a catch in her voice, that the cousin she was visiting was elderly, that they would spend all their time drinking tea and chatting about long-dead relatives, that the only reason Marland was going was because he was too young to be without her.

But Leighton did not find old people boring, a rail journey by itself would be interesting, and she hadn't considered Marland too young to be without her when she'd gone for three days to a great-aunt's funeral.

She had not taken Leighton because, in the end, she had not wanted to. And that knowledge had weighed like a millstone upon his chest.

Then Herb had appeared, as if by magic. His first question to Leighton had been, "So, my young friend, what does one do around here for fun?"

And though Herb had been a stranger to Sussex, he had found more fun things to do than Leighton had known existed under the sun. They explored Arundel Castle, almost as old as the Norman conquest of Britain, hunted for fossilized shark teeth at Bracklesham Bay, and sailed a sloop out of Chichester Harbor into the Solent.

Even without venturing afield, Herb made his stays the stuff memories were made of. A game of bowling on the lawn, a ride in the surrounding countryside, a rainy evening spent inside, taking turns reading *Pride and Prejudice* out loud to Father.

Herb's joie de vivre had infected Father and Leighton. And in a way enfolded them, almost as if in a cocoon, and made it possible for Leighton to ignore certain cold, hard truths about life at Starling Manor.

But now that protection was withdrawn. Now there was nothing between Leighton and everything that frightened him.

Nothing but what a boy two weeks short of eleven could do for himself.

THE COTTAGE, WITH ITS SMALL sitting room and even smaller bedroom, had been the home of the groundskeeper until a larger place had been built for the man. When Herb began visiting Starling Manor regularly, he had asked for the use of the cottage to stow the portable darkroom he'd lugged down from London, to take photographs of Leighton and Father around the estate.

The pungent odor of silver nitrate hung in the air. There were several developed plates in trays of fixers, the images imprinted on the transparent surfaces just visible. Leighton had taken two photographs of Father and Herb—he had become quite adept at the entire process, from the preparation of the glass plate to the final exposure of the albumen paper—and Herb had taken one of Father and Leighton.

Leighton waited in a corner of the cottage's sitting room, a lit taper on the table beside him, alternately dozing and starting awake as the mantel clock chimed every half hour.

"Leighton. What are you doing here?"

He opened his eyes. Herb, valise in hand, was crouched before him. Leighton glanced toward the clock: quarter past five.

"I thought you might come here before you go."

"How do you know that—"

Herb stopped.

An uneasy silence grew between them.

Leighton got up from his chair, went to the linen closet in the bedroom, and brought back a box. In the box was a book of pressed flowers and two geodes, one with a tiny cave of amethyst at its center, another a walnut-size opal of a blue at once milky and shimmery. "I found the geodes in the attic—I think someone brought them back from

Australia ages ago. And Mother said we could give the pressed flowers to Miss Cromwell."

Miss Cromwell was the daughter of Herb's solicitor. She'd lost her twin sister almost two years ago and had been inconsolable. Herb had decided that the best way to cheer the girl up was to send her a monthly box of interesting gifts. Leighton had loved being involved in the process, collecting all kinds of fun miscellany and then, together with Herb, making the final selections for that particular month's package.

But there would be no more of that in this future he could not bring himself to think about.

"Do you want me to help you pack up the portable darkroom?" he asked.

Herb shook his head. "No, I'm leaving everything for you—you are already quite the accomplished photographer. Just thought I'd check on the plates before I left, to make sure they were coming along properly."

Another uneasy silence descended. It seemed to have an outward pressure of its own, pushing Herb and Leighton apart.

"I'll walk to the railway station with you," Leighton said.

Herb hesitated. He opened his valise, stowed the geodes and the book of pressed flowers carefully inside, and pulled out one of his daycoats. "Put this on then. It will be chilly outside."

It *was* chilly outside—frosty, almost. It was the middle of May, but nothing about the morning felt like spring: the damp, raw wind, the shivering branches, the gray gloom that promised a murkiness even after sunrise—Leighton was glad for the sturdiness of his friend's daycoat. The wool held a hint of Herb's French shaving soap, a bar of which he had promised Leighton, as soon as it was needed.

The house was five miles from the nearest railway station. They walked silently, the only sounds their boots on the dirt path and the occasional lowing of a cow at early pasture.

The road became busier as they neared the village. After the second time they let a farmer's milk-laden cart pass, Herb said, "I was going to leave you a note in the cottage, but I take it you already know all is not well."

Leighton said nothing. He didn't want to acknowledge anything aloud.

"I—I will be in town for a while. If you'd like to write me, here's my address." He handed Leighton a calling card. "Would you allow me to send you a birthday present?"

He had never needed permission to send Leighton birthday presents before. It was as if he had suddenly become a stranger, as if they had never laughed over being caught in a downpour or discussed the possible secret lives of field mice.

Leighton swallowed a lump in his throat. "I will need to ask Father about the present. And about writing letters."

But they both knew he wouldn't. It would hurt Father too much.

"Of course. Of course." Herb smiled weakly—there were dark circles under his eyes. "Maybe I should go abroad for a while—visit India again or something."

The three of them were going to visit India together when Leighton came of age, to see all the places that Herb had loved, especially the mountains of Kashmir and the beautiful hill station of Darjeeling.

"I'm sure it will be a wonderful trip," Leighton somehow managed to say.

They fell quiet after that, a silence that lasted until Herb's train pulled away.

THE NEXT EVENING, LEIGHTON WAS back at the railway station to meet Mother's train.

When it became clear that Mother would never take Leighton on her trips, he stopped going to the station to meet her upon her return. But this had upset her, so he had resumed the old habit, parking himself on the platform every month, even on the most bitterly cold days of the year.

Mother's train puffed into the station. She disembarked promptly, in a traveling dress of burgundy velvet, the cut and the color both striking.

She wore somber colors at home: grays, browns, and dark, subdued blues. But for her trips she brought out warm, vibrant hues. The realization stole upon Leighton—it was as if she were only completely alive when she boarded the train to see her lover.

She smiled at Leighton with a gladness that was polluted with guilt and nudged Marland forward. "It's your big brother, darling."

Marland's hair was blond, almost Nordic, whereas Father's hair and Leighton's own were dark as pitch, and mother's a coffee brown without any hint of gold.

Marland, only a half brother.

But then Leighton lifted Marland, Marland wrapped his arms around Leighton's neck, and none of the grown-ups' complicated choices mattered. He pressed a kiss to Marland's forehead. "Welcome home, brother."

Outside the railway station two carriages awaited them: one for Mother, Marland, and Leighton, the other for Mother's maid and the luggage. They drove through the long twilight, Marland falling asleep with his head on Leighton's lap.

Leighton touched Marland's plump cheek—it was warm and just slightly sticky. On the opposite seat, Mother gazed at the two of them. She did not say anything.

It had been like this for a while, this silence filled with things they did not say to each other. Not that they didn't speak to each other frequently—Mother took great interest in his well-being and his studies—but the most important subjects were never addressed.

Sometimes Leighton had a feeling that he lived in a dollhouse—there was such an ostensible outward perfection to their lives: the handsome family in the beautiful country manor; kind, caring parents; good, obedient children. An enviable existence all around.

And yet. And yet.

That silence would only grow greater, now that he at last understood why she did not take him with her—why she believed it futile to even explain: No matter what, Leighton would never be a son to the man she visited every month.

She had carved out another family for herself, and that family did not include him.

"Are you well, Leighton?" she asked softly, almost hesitantly.

She was still his mother and he wanted to confide in her. *No, I am not well. And neither is Father. Perhaps we will never be well again.*

"I am very well, thank you," he said. "And you, ma'am?"

She bit her lower lip. "Very well, too. Thank you."

Three

Amah

A RATTLING OF HAND CLAPPERS, followed by a melodious half wail. Cold sour plum juice, no doubt about it. Ying-ying's mouth watered like that of a puppy with a pork bun thrown before it.

Her home, a spacious residence of three interconnecting courtyards, was located in a quiet corner of the Chinese City, the half of Peking that was south of, and separated from by a wall twenty feet high, the Tartar City, where only Manchus were allowed to live.

But the quietness was relative: They might be far from the major thoroughfares and the markets, but roaming street vendors, selling everything from toys to a shave and an ear cleaning, did not neglect the tucked-away alleys of her neighborhood. Most of the time Ying-ying was oblivious to the muted clamor. Yet her ears perked up whenever some delicacies came by, be those candied haws on a skewer or bowls of wonton in a steaming broth, kept hot by an ingenious little stove.

Standing in her way, of course, were Amah's strictures. Amah didn't trust the hygienic practice of itinerant food sellers, and she was especially suspicious of those peddling beverages. "How do you know they boiled their water properly? Your hair could all fall out from drinking that filth," was her usual objection.

But today, luckily for Ying-ying, was the sixteenth. On the sixth, the sixteenth, and the twenty-sixth of every month, Da-ren visited. And for some reason, Amah was more vulnerable to prolonged whining in the hours before his arrival.

One last batch of cough potion for Mother simmered on the stove in Amah's storeroom. Amah herself was seated on the *kang*, stitching a pair of black trousers.

"The sour plum juice vendor is outside," Ying-ying began. "It's so hot today, and I'm so thirsty. Can I have one, please, please, good Amah?"

She settled in to await Amah's usual objections. Even on a sixteenth, Amah could be counted on to hold out for a few minutes. But today the coins were instantly forthcoming. "Don't drink too fast. The chill wouldn't be good for your stomach," was all the advice Amah gave.

It was odd, but Ying-ying was not about to question her good fortune. She slipped out of the red front gate and bargained with the vendor as if she knew what she was doing. When the vendor finished expressing his dismay at this too-clever girl who surely meant to cheat him out of his livelihood, he lifted a large narrow-mouthed jar and poured her a full bowl of his purple-black concoction.

She sat down on the doorstep. With every sip she smacked her lips and wiggled her tongue at the supreme tartness of the drink. In between—now that the negotiation was finished and the relationship between them most amicable—she chatted up the vendor and asked for news.

The outside world fascinated her. It was permitted to her only in the smallest doses. Two nights a year, on the occasions of the Lantern Festival and the Mid-Autumn Festival, she was allowed to venture as far as the nearest thoroughfare, accompanied by Amah, to admire the multitude of brightly lit lanterns. In spring, Mother took her on a three-day pilgrimage to Taoist temples in the hills outside the city. The rest of the time Ying-ying lived within the confines of the courtyards, rarely permitted out the front gate, and never beyond the end of the alley.

Merchants who came to call were her greatest source of news, their younger apprentices the only people she knew of her own age. But she did not speak to those boys. Confucius's rules forbade fraternization between the sexes once beyond age seven. Not to mention that her embroidered silk blouse and expensive jade bangles acted as an additional barrier, keeping the apprentice boys in blue cotton tunics an awed distance away.

The sun angled lower in the sky. The alley, bordered on either side by courtyard walls, sat almost entirely in the shade. She was still extracting outrageous rumors the vendor had heard of intrigues in the Forbidden Palace when the sound of horse hooves reached her ears.

Da-ren was arriving.

She was strictly to be out of sight when he came. Hastily she poured the remainder of the juice down her throat and ran back. Once inside her own rooms, she closed the door and only then opened her window a crack to peek out.

Her row of rooms was in the same courtyard as Mother's. Da-ren's and his servant's horses would be brought into the first courtyard.

While the servant tended to the mounts, Da-ren would cross the second courtyard and enter the third, where Little Plum waited to take his hat.

Ying-ying kept hoping he'd show up in full court dress, with the kind of intricate embroidery that ruined the eyesight of ten men to complete. He never did. He wore everyday clothes—in silks and brocades, but everyday clothes nevertheless. And his black skullcap, with a rectangle of jade over the forehead, was no fancier than Boss Wu's.

But he radiated an aura of authority. Little Plum, who was saucy and pert with the merchants, never spoke an inappropriate word while he was in residence. He wasn't a particularly handsome man, yet Mother, who now appeared at the door of her suite, looked upon him as if she'd never seen a finer sight.

More than ever Ying-ying wished he had fathered her. It was no dishonor to be the child of such a powerful man via his acknowledged concubine.

Unlike being the child of a despised foreign devil.

IN THE EVENING AMAH BROUGHT Ying-ying's dinner: rice, a stir-fry of eggs and new tomatoes, a dish of tofu cooked with black mushrooms, and an enormous bowl of steaming peppery broth. She made sure Ying-ying drank all the soup. "It's to counter the chill from the sour plum juice."

The sky had not fully darkened when Amah put her to bed—it wasn't as if Ying-ying were allowed to do anything else this evening. She kicked the silken sheet Amah had put over her, until her feet and calves were exposed. "Does the emperor have many uncles?"

"Some, but not as many as you might imagine," Amah answered. "K'ang-hsi Emperor and Chien-lung Emperor had dozens and dozens of sons, but lately the emperors have not been prolific. It's a sign of the times."

So Da-ren wasn't one of a swarm of uncles, but one of a few. The Han Chinese emperors never permitted their male siblings any political power. From her readings of history, Ying-ying knew that often the latter had to go out of their way to establish their disinclination toward the affairs of state. But the Manchus were less strict about it. Their princes were allowed as advisers in court.

She sat up. "Is Da-ren the emperor's favorite uncle?"

Amah pushed her down gently. "I don't know that. But the dowager empress seems to like him well enough."

"Do you think he'll have us live with him if his wife dies?" Da-ren's wife was a spoiled woman who did not allow her husband to keep concubines at home. Not that most men paid attention to the opinion of their wives, but when that wife was a favored cousin of the dowager empress—one she loved as a sister—it was quite a different matter.

"No." Amah firmly negated her fantasy. "He is Manchu; we are Han. Even if his wife passes away—and don't talk like that—he'd still only take into his household Manchu concubines."

But Ying-ying kept on thinking of Da-ren, hoping he'd like her better as she grew older. He commanded so much respect, honor, and prestige. If only a little of it would rub off on her. If only...

UNFORTUNATELY, EVEN WHEN SHE DID fall asleep, it was no peaceful slumber. All the sour plum juice and all the soup in her stomach kept waking her up to use the chamber pot.

The first two times she practically sleepwalked, finding the pot by sheer force of habit, stumbling back to bed to immediately start dreaming again. But after the third time she stayed awake.

This nocturnal wakefulness happened to her from time to time. She hated lying alert in the middle of the night. Time advanced as if it had minuscule bound feet like Mother's and could only totter along laboriously. She fiddled with the straw mat that covered her *kang* in summer. She adjusted a pillow and squeezed her eyes shut tight. She even tried to cover her head with her silk sheet, but that only suffocated her.

She sat up. A thin, pale light came through the windows, casting latticework shadows on the floor. But it was the kind of light that only emphasized the impenetrable darkness of the further recesses of the room, and illuminated objects just enough to make them murky and sinister. Her washstand looked a half-size, skeletal monster, the washbasin atop it a bulbous, poisonous head. A breeze blew, the willow tree in the courtyard swayed; shadows of its limp branches crawled across the floor like the tentacles of some strange, lurking beast.

She shrank and called out for Amah, who slept in the adjacent room, but no one answered. She called again, still no answer. Strange—Amah was a light sleeper who usually came to check on her at the least noise.

Disgruntled, Ying-ying swung her legs over the side of the *kang* and went to wake her.

But there was no one on Amah's *kang*, no one beneath the neatly laid out blanket.

She gasped, beginning to feel afraid. Then she remembered that on a different night a few months ago, when she had gotten up to use the chamber pot, she had looked out the window and seen Amah, fully dressed, returning from the next courtyard. Amah had told her that she had felt a gnawing hunger and had gone to the kitchen to eat something.

Perhaps Amah was in the kitchen again. Too afraid to stay in her rooms alone, Ying-ying decided to go look for her. She put a blouse over her kerchief-front chemise and padded out to the courtyard.

The moon was still full, shining bright and clear in a cloudless sky, its cool light silvering the stones in the courtyard and the gray tiles of the roof. The willow danced, pliant and yielding, a pretty yet ghostly sight.

She curled her toes. The walkway beneath the long eave was cold on her feet. Amah did not like her walking barefoot.

The sounds of drums beating rose in the distance. No, not drums—the night watchman's clappers. At first she thought they were marking the passage of the hours. But the *tock-tocks* were urgent and without rhythm.

It must be a criminal pursuit. A night thief, perhaps even a flying thief, one of those martial arts-trained criminals who could bound three men high and leap across rooftops.

Her pulse accelerated as she realized the sounds were moving closer to her. Perhaps it wasn't so bad to be awake in the small hours after all. If she could catch a glimpse of the thief, it would mark the most exciting event in her nine years of life.

A door in the row opposite hers opened. Out stepped Da-ren's servant Bao-shun, a curved broadsword by his side. He cocked his head and listened carefully. Then he saw her and blinked in surprise.

He marched across the courtyard. "Bai Gu-niang, it's chilly at this hour. You should be abed."

"I can't sleep," she replied. "Can you tell me what is that sound? It's coming this way."

Bao-shun was taken aback. "You can already hear it? Bai Gu-niang has sharp ears. It's probably nothing. The law chasing night robbers."

"Can we go out to the alley and look?" she asked hopefully.

He immediately shook his head. "No, no, no. Fu-ren would have my head if she knew I let you out in the middle of the night with a criminal on the loose."

There were times when she hated being a girl. She pushed her lips out into a prominent pout, the kind on which one could hang a bottle of oil, as Amah would say.

"Bai Gu-niang must not become cross with me—Da-ren would punish me if I upset you." But for all his kind cajoling, Bao-shun did not back down. "Now please go back to your room. I'll go have a look to make sure nothing's wrong."

The banging sounds rose appreciably. Between the beats, men shouted. Ying-ying pretended to acquiesce, retreating into her room. But as soon as Bao-shun entered the next courtyard, she came out and silently followed him.

Bao-shun walked about the middle courtyard, looking all around. Satisfied, he went into the front courtyard. She tiptoed into the middle courtyard, staying close to the wall-hugging rooms, on the walkways in the shadow of the extended eaves.

In the front courtyard, Bao-shun must have finished his inspection, for she heard him lift the bar on the front gate. She inched closer to the moon gate, a round opening in the wall between the middle and front courtyards, and was about to slip through when a movement at the periphery of her vision made her look back.

A black-clad figure was crouched on the roof, barely a stone's throw from where she stood. She froze. For all her eagerness to witness a real, live outlaw on the run, she hadn't imagined that he'd come this close to her. To her horror, he took a great, lithe bound, an abrupt yet graceful motion like that of a lizard, and landed *in* the middle courtyard, his feet silent as a cat's.

He was on her side of the courtyard now, little more than the length of a *kang* away. She heard a whimper. It came from her own throat. The outlaw's head turned. He was masked, but his eyes burned directly into hers.

All the stories she had ever heard about bandits and robbers scuttled amok in her head. He'd capture her and sell her into slavery somewhere so far away that nobody would ever find her again. Worse, he'd sell her to mountain bandits who loved the taste of children, especially a pampered child like her, with extra-tender flesh from having never done a day of work in her life.

Bao-shun was her only hope. She must alert him. He'd come and rescue her.

She opened her mouth to scream. But the only sound she made was a muffled "Hmmm" against a hand that was suddenly clamped over her face.

"Be quiet!" the outlaw whispered.

Her eyes bulged. The outlaw spoke with the voice of *Amah*.

She had no time to react. Amah pulled her forcefully along the fifteen paces or so to the storeroom. The next thing Ying-ying knew, they were inside the storeroom and Amah had collapsed.

The aura of power and danger that radiated from her was gone. She lay in a heap, her breaths alternating between quick gasps and gurgling, painful-sounding wheezes. Ying-ying stood petrified, her mind empty except for an ever-expanding shock.

"Shut the door, you stupid girl."

Her feet felt like two clumps of mud, but Ying-ying made herself move. Outlaw or not, the woman was still her amah, the person who had brushed her hair and laid out her clothes every day of her life.

She had enough wits to close the door as quietly as she could, peeking into the courtyard as she did so. Bao-shun had not yet returned from the alley, and no one else was astir.

"Get me on the *kang*," Amah ordered.

Ying-ying would never have believed Amah, who wasn't much taller than her, could be this heavy. She thought her back would break. Amah's teeth ground with pain as Ying-ying, unable to lift her fully, half dragged her along the floor. At the edge of the *kang*, Amah grasped onto its side, and Ying-ying used her shoulders and back to push the older woman up. At last they had half of Amah's body on the *kang*; Ying-ying strained and flopped her over.

Amah sucked in a breath. Ying-ying tried to put a pillow under her head.

"Don't waste time," Amah panted harshly. "Make a fire in the stove."

Then she vomited a stream of blood onto her own chest.

That set Ying-ying running. Despite the darkness inside the room, she was able to find the basket of scrap paper and wood chips without any difficulty. Making a fire with shaking hands, however, was much harder: It took her five tries to get one going.

"Boil water."

Amah kept a wide-mouthed, knee-high crock of water near the door. Ying-ying lifted the woven reed lid and filled an empty clay pot. She fed a few bigger pieces of wood to the fire.

While the water heated, Amah rasped more instructions. Ying-ying located some dried flower buds on the bottom shelf. Tossed into the water, the buds gave out a clean, fresh scent, almost enough to mask the smell of regurgitated blood.

She was then directed to climb onto a chair and bring down a cloth bundle that had been concealed above the lintel. Inside were round balls the size of quail's eggs wrapped individually in squares of silk, and a small porcelain jar. She unwrapped two balls, plopped them into the clay pot, and took the jar to Amah.

Amah struggled to pull her shirt up. A small package fell onto the *kang*. She ignored it and snatched Ying-ying's palm to rest against her rib cage, below her left breast. "This is where you apply the salve."

Ying-ying gasped—what she touched was cold as ice. She yanked back her hand, opened the jar of salve, and dug out a dollop.

"Warm it first," Amah warned hoarsely.

Ying-ying kept the salve between her palms until it smelled faintly of leaves and bark. It began to sting her hands, making her palms prickle hotly. She smeared salve where Amah's skin was unnaturally cold and kept her palm over Amah's strange injury until Amah called for the brew.

When Ying-ying brought the bubbling potion, Amah drank it directly from the clay pot, stopping only to cool her tongue and gasp for air. When she had finished with the potion, she told Ying-ying to pull her shirt down and place the still-hot clay pot over where she had applied the salve.

"And put another pot on the stove. I must keep continuous heat over this."

Ying-ying scampered around the tiny room, heating pots, ladling water to keep them from cracking, pouring water from one pot to the next, holding the hot pot on the right spot on Amah. She did this for what seemed like hours while Amah lay in a half faint, saying only, "Again," and, "More."

At last she said, "That's enough. I'll live."

Ying-ying shuddered. She had been blindly, unthinkingly following directions, too busy and confused to consider that Amah might have been in mortal peril. She set aside the clay pot she had been holding, stretched her cramping arm, and let herself pant for a while.

The night outside was peacefully silent. The pursuit must have been called off—or taken to a different quarter of the city. Bao-shun was returning to his room, the bells on his sword tassel jingling faintly as he crossed the middle courtyard.

Amah snored lightly. Ying-ying stared at her curled-up form on the *kang*. How had Amah become injured? Where had she learned to leap off rooftops without breaking her ankles? And why was she the one being chased by the law, as if she were a dangerous criminal who needed to be apprehended?

Ying-ying pulled a bedspread over Amah. As she tucked in it around Amah's person, her fingers came into contact with the package that had fallen from Amah's shirt.

She took it to the stove where the fire still burned and lifted the stove lid for a bit more light. Inside the cloth was a small, thin panel of white jade, decorated with the image of a dancing goddess, the ribbons on her flowing robe floating all about her as if lifted by a gentle breath.

To the goddess's left, the words, *Emptiness is no other than form; form is no other than emptiness.* And to her right, *Form is exactly emptiness; emptiness exactly form.* The famous Buddhist tenet, so well-known that even Ying-ying, who had never visited a monastery or studied a sutra, had heard of it.

A nice piece, the jade tablet, but to Ying-ying's thinking not quite worth the trouble. It was too small and insubstantial, for one thing. And as pretty as white jade was, the material was not nearly as beautiful or valuable as kingfisher jade from Burma, which was as green as bamboo leaves in the shade.

"Give it back," said Amah, startling her.

Ying-ying wrapped up the jade tablet again before placing it in Amah's outstretched hand. "I thought you were asleep."

"Maybe I was. But what do I keep telling you about digging into other people's things?"

And the jade tablet, did you *have to dig into other people's things to get it?*

But Ying-ying did not say it.

"Go back to bed," Amah went on. "But before you leave, kneel and kowtow to me three times."

"What?" Ying-ying couldn't believe her ears. "Why?"

Amah's demand was preposterous. Ying-ying liked Amah. She adored Amah. But Amah was a servant. One did not kowtow to servants. Three times? She kowtowed to Mother only three times a *year*, on New Year's Day, Mother's birthday, and her own birthday. Was Amah out of her mind? If anything, Ying-ying should be the one expecting a show of gratitude for all she had done to save Amah's life. Why, her feet were completely chilled.

"To acknowledge me as your master."

Ying-ying would have laughed out loud if she hadn't been so stunned. "My master in what?"

"Your master in the Order of the Shadowless Goddesses."

"What's that?"

Amah sighed, a sound somewhere between bitterness and irony. "Three hundred years ago every child south of the Yangtze River knew of it. But now it will be just you and me."

"I don't want to join," Ying-ying protested. "I don't want a master to order me around."

She was old enough to know that the word "master" was not bandied about lightly. She'd be bound to obey and serve Amah. The thought did not appeal to her at all. Their current arrangement, where she listened only when she wished, suited her much better.

Amah's voice turned unforgiving. "You know my secret. Join or die."

It was not a tone Ying-ying was used to from the woman who daily cajoled her to eat her vegetables and wash her face, who never had a harsher word for her than empty threats to inform her mother of some particular mischief.

"You can't kill me!" she responded indignantly.

"No?" Amah chuckled softly.

Before Ying-ying knew what happened, she felt an icy stab in her chest. A rising scream never made it past her throat as Amah's finger, like a snake rearing from the grass, jabbed her twice along her jawline.

Her mouth became soldered shut. She could not get her chin to drop nor her lips to part. Trembling, she looked down. A tiny, straight-bladed knife glinted dully in the nether light, its tip straining against her thin blouse.

She swallowed. There was no arguing with *that*.

Sensing her victory, Amah retracted her knife. It disappeared up her sleeve. She jabbed again at Ying-ying's face and unlocked her jaw.

Unhappily, Ying-ying performed the three kowtows, but she did them most sloppily.

Amah only sighed. "Go now. I need to rest."

Ying-ying got up without a word. As she stopped at the door to peer outside, Amah's voice came again. "And if you must skulk about at night getting yourself into trouble, at least put on your slippers."

Four

The Upending

GROUSE SEASON HAD BEGUN, AND every self-respecting gentleman must ready his firearms. Leighton sat before a large table, reassembling the components of his fowling piece that he had taken apart to clean and oil.

The house had actual antique guns: flintlock blunderbusses, Long Land Pattern muskets, carbines that had seen service during the French Revolutionary War. Compared to those, the fowling piece was quite new, commissioned for Father when he had been a boy.

Outside, leaves rustled and birds chirped. The breeze that came in from the window was warm—and sweet with the scent of grass and honeysuckle. The sky was a lovely blue, the color of Marland's eyes.

Mother had taken Marland away again—Leighton missed him with a painful ferocity. Leighton's tutor, Mr. Hamilton, was also away on holiday. The hours never passed. They were fat with heavy, immobile minutes, with seconds that emptied as slowly as an old lady's glass of sherry.

He and Father took a turn on the downs every day, but without Herb's easy camaraderie, those walks were largely silent, just a man with too much on his mind walking beside a boy he still considered too young for the truly troubling matters of life.

The shotgun reassembled, Leighton set its stock against the pocket of his shoulder and pointed the barrel out the open window. He hoped words would come more easily when they were shooting grouse—Father was an excellent shot and took pride in Leighton's marksmanship.

He pointed the muzzle up, and then slowly swept his aim lower. A man stood on the gravel drive at almost point-blank range.

"Is this how you greet an old friend, my dear boy?"

Herb! In the three months since Leighton had last seen him, he must have lost at least a stone in weight—his Adam's apple protruded and there were hollows under his cheekbones—but his smile was as wide and brilliant as ever.

And then that smile wobbled and faded. "Will you not say hullo, Leighton?"

Leighton realized he was staring. He put down the shotgun, climbed over the window ledge, and leaped ten feet to the ground below. Herb had him in a tight embrace almost before he'd straightened from the landing.

"My dear boy," Herb murmured. "My dear, dear boy."

"You didn't go off to India!" Leighton blurted out.

"Not without you, my dear boy. And not without your father."

Leighton stood in his embrace for a little longer—all was right with the world again. Then he took Herb by the arm and they ran toward the front door. "Why didn't you cable? We had no idea you were coming."

They almost collided with Father, sprinting out of the house. There was a sheen of tears in Father's eyes. When he shook Herb's hand, he grasped the latter's forearm too.

"I hoped you would come." Father's voice quavered with gratitude.

"You knew I would," said Herb, "the second you sent word."

They gazed at each other. It was only for a moment, but Leighton suddenly felt as if he ought to be elsewhere.

"Father, may I go do some shooting by myself?" he asked.

"Of course." Father beamed. "Make sure you are back in time for dinner. Tonight we shall feast."

Leighton strode away from the house—no one would notice that he didn't have his firearm with him. And he didn't want to shoot anything; he only wanted walk and run and savor this burst of brightness in his heart.

Which was followed by a gnawing fear: Did Father and Herb truly risk eternal condemnation?

He walked for a long time before the cloud in his heart dissipated: He knew nothing about eternity, but he was certain that if they could *not* be together, then they were condemned for this life.

He was glad that Father had asked Herb to return. He was glad that Herb would remain in their lives. And he would never be anything but glad and grateful that they were now a family again.

LEIGHTON COCKED THE AIR RIFLE, aimed, exhaled, and pulled the trigger.

"Excellent," came Herb's voice behind him. "Bull's-eye."

"It's all right," said Leighton, though he was quite pleased with the shot. He was using an archery target that he had found in one of the outbuildings on the estate, and his pellet had struck dead center.

"No shooting today?"

"Doesn't seem fair to disturb the grouse day after day."

"You are as kind as your father," said Herb, his eyes shining.

To grouse, maybe. To people, Leighton wasn't so sure. He didn't have Herb's easy embrace of others, nor Father's ready compassion.

"And you must have grown two inches since I last saw you," Herb went on.

"Only three-quarters of an inch."

His increase in height had been much remarked upon the past few weeks, especially on Sundays, after church. Usually the comments embarrassed him and made him feel like a puppy that had sprouted a second tail. But Herb's observation was friendly and matter-of-fact, reminding Leighton that he did rather relish becoming taller.

They began walking in the direction of the house—it was almost tea time.

"Do you know what I did this summer?" asked Herb. "I gave my jade tablet for appraisal."

Decades ago, Herb's father had brought back two nearly identical tablets from China—two out of the three clues to the location of the treasure, if one believed the legend. Herb had given one to Father and kept the other for himself.

"Were you going to sell it?" Leighton's voice was more alarmed than he had meant for it to be.

"No, absolutely not! Before they were...Well, they were once my father's engagement present to my mother. I was thinking of the British Museum."

Leighton exhaled. "Oh, that's all right, then."

"That's what I said to myself: It's quite all right if it ended up in a temple of art and history, admired by millions. But before I could do that, I needed to make sure that it really was a valuable antique, and not just on my father's say-so."

"What did the appraiser say?"

"Ah, the appraiser. I'm sure I proved quite a trying client—he had to write me three times before I returned to speak to him. Two weeks ago I called on him at last, and he told me that he would put the tablet at about a thousand years old, dating from the middle of the ninth century."

A true antique, then.

"And remember the legend about the treasure?" Herb went on.

"Did the appraiser know about it?"

"No, he didn't. But when I mentioned it, he was able to provide some historical context. The persecution the Buddhist monks feared actually came to pass. After a tremendous flourishing of the religion earlier in the Tang Dynasty, there came an emperor who both hated foreign influences and needed his treasury replenished after a costly border war. Almost all the monasteries in China—nearly five thousand in number—were destroyed, their wealth seized, and hundreds of thousands of monks and nuns forced to return to lay life."

Leighton stumbled a step—he wasn't looking where he was going, but at Herb. "Are you sure?"

"I am faithfully repeating what the appraiser told me. According to him, the persecution didn't last terribly long—the emperor was on the throne for only five or six years—but the damage was quite thorough. Buddhism in China never quite regained its former glory."

And the legend, which Leighton had thought endlessly glamorous, was actually nothing of the kind, but a story of heartache, desperation, and unimaginable tyranny—the despotism of one man destroying the hopes and dreams of so many.

"Quite something, eh?" said Herb, looking at him.

"Yes, quite something," answered Leighton, almost mechanically.

The monks of a millennium ago had been apprehensive. They might even have been afraid. But the wholesale annihilation of their entire way of life must have exceeded even their worst fears.

It could happen, the upending of life as one knew it.

It could happen anytime.

LEIGHTON, HOWEVER, DID NOT EXPECT the upending of their lives to take place only three days later.

They had gone for an excursion to the coast and camped overnight on a stretch of cliffs overhanging the sea. And in the morning they had risen early and picked their way down to the beach below to watch the sunrise.

"The world is such a beautiful place," Herb said, his voice full of joy. "How fortunate we are to be here together."

Leighton wanted the moment never to end, standing barefoot on the beach with his father's hand on his shoulder, the murmur of the sea in his ears, and the majestic curvature of the sun breaching a horizon that was all scarlet and gold.

In the first light of this wonderful day, they rebuilt the fire from the previous night and roasted sausages for breakfast. Afterward they held a footrace on the beach, swam, and dug rather incompetently for clams. They returned to Starling Manor in time for a slightly late luncheon, after which Father and Herb both pleaded fatigue and retired to their rooms for an afternoon nap.

Leighton, not given to naps, climbed up the big oak on the far side of the trout stream. Where the main trunk divided into a dozen branches, there was a depression that made for a decent seat. On warm summer days he liked to read there, under the shade of the boughs.

The book he brought was *Voyage au Centre de la Terre*—an English translation was available, but Leighton wanted to read in the original French, and Herb had obliged. Leighton did not entirely believe the book's premise—a vast ocean many miles under the surface of the earth? Hadn't he read somewhere that it became hotter and hotter as one descended? That subterranean ocean would boil the ichthyosaurus and plesiosaurus that supposedly swam in its waters. All the same, the story was fast-moving and enjoyable, and he stopped reading only when he realized he had forgotten to bring a canteen and had become quite thirsty.

As he approached the house, he saw a fair-haired woman handed into a waiting carriage by a man. The man nodded as the carriage drove off.

Recognition came like a kick in the kidney. The man was *Sir Curtis*.

Leighton sprinted for the service entrance. Mr. Mims the butler would put Sir Curtis in the drawing room and serve him tea and biscuits. And while Sir Curtis waited, Leighton could run up unseen from the service stairs and warn Father and Herb.

But when he reached Father's apartment the door was wide-open. Father's bed was all smooth counterpane and perfectly fluffed pillows. No one had napped in it—no one had even put a hand on the bedspread.

And then Leighton saw the fireplace, one end of which was now a foot and a half from the wall. He didn't know about this particular hidden passage, except to instinctively grasp that the last person who had passed through could not have been Father, who would not leave such a secret out for everyone to see.

That was when he remembered that both Father and his estate had been under Sir Curtis's guardianship for some years. Sir Curtis could very well know the house as well as anyone did—and the idea filled Leighton with anxiety.

He was halfway to Herb's room when he heard the sound of something like a sack of flour being thrown against a wall.

He stopped. He was too late. Sir Curtis had come upon Father and Herb.

The door opened, and out spilled Herb's words. "Please, sir, you must not punish Nigel. He has been the very example of goodness and rectitude. I am the one responsible. I am the one at fault."

"Of course you are the one at fault," said Sir Curtis, one foot in the corridor, his face turned back toward the inside of the room, his voice thin but perfectly clear. "It is too bad Nigel's previous institutional stay did not cure him. This time I will spare no expense—and no treatment—and he will emerge from the sanitarium a new man, no matter how long it takes. You, Mr. Gordon, on the other hand, are going to jail for your rampant homosexuality. And I will see to it that you stay there a very long time. I daresay society would heave a sigh of relief were you to die there. Indeed, if you should do me the courtesy of returning home and firing a bullet into your head, I would be much obliged."

The ease and maliciousness with which Sir Curtis suggested that Herb *take his own life*—Leighton felt as if he had been trampled under a stampede.

And Father…That "previous institutional stay" that Sir Curtis had mentioned so cavalierly—no wonder Father was so afraid of Sir Curtis. He must have locked Father up and subjected him to…treatments, treatments that made people lower their voices when such words as "Bedlam" and "asylum" were mentioned.

Sir Curtis emerged fully into the corridor looking energetic, purposeful, and not particularly disturbed, as if he weren't about to send Father to one kind of prison and Herb to another, but had only scolded a pair of footmen for their lack of punctuality.

His glance fell on Leighton as he passed, but he said nothing. Only as he reached the stair landing did he turn around and admonish casually, "See that you do not become like them."

INSIDE THE ROOM, HERB SPOKE. Leighton didn't need to make out the words to feel the anguish in every syllable. He stared at the closed door, thinking for no reason at all of the sunrise from that very morning.

It seemed aeons ago, when actual dinosaurs still roamed the Earth.

Herb at last fell silent. The silence twisted and smothered; Leighton bit the inside of his cheek until he tasted blood. He knocked, thinking that Father must have left via the secret passage. "It's Leighton."

The door opened. Herb was wrapped in a dressing gown, his face puffy, the rims of his eyes red. Behind him sat Father on the floor, in only his trousers and an untucked shirt, his feet bare, his back against the wall, his head in his hands.

Instead of letting Leighton in, Herb came out of the room and shut the door. "Don't worry. It's all right," he said bravely.

"I know what happened," Leighton said.

Herb rubbed his hand over his face. "Your father, he hasn't spoken a word. Not a single word."

"He doesn't want to go back to an asylum."

Herb jerked. "What asylum?"

"Sir Curtis mentioned that Father had been committed once. Did you not hear?"

"Jesus! Forgive my language—I meant to say I didn't hear anything your uncle said. It was as if someone plugged my ears. I saw his lips move, but all I could hear was this thunder inside my own head."

At least then he hadn't heard Sir Curtis's malevolent words toward *him*.

Herb pinched the bridge of his nose. "Are you sure, my dear boy, that he mentioned an asylum?"

"He said that Father's previous stay did not cure him, so he would commit Father this time for however long it takes."

"Goddamn it—sorry, please excuse me." Herb thrust his fingers into his hair. "But Nigel has never mentioned such a thing, not in all the years we've known each other."

Leighton rather thought he wouldn't mention it either if he had been locked up and treated as if he were mentally disturbed. And Father would have been young, since by age twenty he was already married, and Leighton had been born shortly after his twenty-first birthday.

Herb, pacing in the corridor, stopped abruptly. "I'm sorry. I am still not hearing things properly. Did you say Sir Curtis threatened to send your father to another asylum?"

Leighton nodded.

"Can he? Nigel is a grown man with all his faculties intact, a good landlord and a devoted father. Surely it cannot be such a simple matter to put him away against his will."

Leighton did not answer. All he could see was Sir Curtis's cool, self-satisfied expression. The man did not anticipate any difficulties.

"What should we do?" Herb let out a trembling breath. "What should we do?"

None of this felt real. Was this how the monks of ancient China had felt when their monastery was leveled before their eyes, as if the tragedy were happening elsewhere, elsewhen, to people no one knew?

"I'll go get Father's whisky." It was the only useful thing Leighton could think of to do.

"Yes, good idea," said Herb gratefully. "Thank you."

After Leighton went downstairs, however, he did not immediately go to the library, where Father's kept his decanter, but first sought out the butler.

"Mr. Mims, has Sir Curtis left?"

"Yes, Master Leighton. When he sent Miss Saithwaite away, he asked that a carriage be prepared for him. I believe he departed more than an hour ago."

"Who is Miss Saithwaite?"

"I believe she might be Lady Fitzmaurice's niece."

Lady Fitzmaurice was an old woman who lived about ten miles away from Starling Manor.

"But more to the point," added Mr. Mims, "I believe she must be Sir Curtis's fiancée, or Sir Curtis would not have brought her here, the two of them alone."

Sir Curtis was engaged? Leighton had believed he would remain a widower his entire life. Now Sir Curtis's sudden appearance made more sense. He had accompanied his new fiancée to visit her aunt—or perhaps it was at her aunt's place that he proposed. Then he—or Miss Saithwaite—had decided that the good news should be shared with his family too.

They would have been waiting in the drawing room. Mr. Mims, after a fruitless search, would have returned to deliver the news that the master was not in his room taking a nap, nor in the library, nor the billiard room. He would have asked whether Sir Curtis and Miss Saithwaite cared for another cup of tea.

Was that when Sir Curtis had asked about Mother's whereabouts, or whether there were other guests at the estate? It didn't matter. The point was, Miss Saithwaite had no clue what was going on, but Sir Curtis did. That was why he'd sent her away before he made his presence known to Father and Herb.

Herb was still in the passage, leaning against a wall, when Leighton returned upstairs with the whisky and two glasses. "Bless you, my dear boy," he said, the corners of his lips trembling as he tried to smile.

He opened the door. "We brought fortification, Nigel. Have some. It'll take your mind off..."

His voice trailed off. Father was no longer inside—he must have returned to his own rooms via the secret passage.

Herb sighed. "Can't blame him for wanting a bit of peace. I talked too much, and said such silly things too—I had no idea that his fear of ending up in an asylum had a perfectly rational basis. I kept telling him that nothing terrible would come of it, nothing worse than mere unpleasantness."

He took the decanter and the glasses from Leighton and set them down. "I'll get dressed. Let's go for a walk—the inside of my head still rings a bit. And then after dinner we'll talk to your father again."

Herb was dismayed, but not afraid yet. "You should be careful too," said Leighton. "When Sir Curtis said he would send Father to an institution, he also said he would send you to prison."

Herb started. "He can't do that." And then, in a smaller voice, "Can he? That would be downright barbarous."

But Sir Curtis *was* barbarous. That was why Father feared him. That was why, when he came to visit, Mother tried to pass herself off as a simple woman with nothing on her mind but her children and her charities.

"I think you should take Father and leave the country," said Leighton.

Herb stilled, a glass of whisky raised halfway to his lips. "What?"

"He is too afraid of Sir Curtis to protect himself, so we must protect him—by making sure Sir Curtis cannot get to him. People go overseas for their health all the time, don't they?"

Herb hesitated. "I will if that would help matters. Would he come?"

"I think he'll do anything to not go back to an asylum."

Herb bit his lower lip, then nodded slowly. "You might be—"

A shot ran out, cutting Herb off—a shot that sounded as if it came from the direction of Father's rooms. Herb turned to Leighton, his face pale. "Was that...was that a firearm going off?"

Leighton couldn't speak—it *had* been a firearm going off. He could only stare at Herb. *Don't! Don't even think such thoughts. Father wouldn't. He couldn't do such a thing.*

"Why don't you stay here?" Herb said, his voice shaking. "Stay right here."

But Leighton couldn't. He followed two steps behind Herb, who shuffled, as if sleepwalking, toward Father's rooms.

Already Mr. Mims and a footman were racing up the stairs. Mechanically Leighton held out a hand. They stopped on the steps, regarding him uncertainly.

"Is everything all right, Master Leighton?" asked Mr. Mims.

Leighton did not answer.

Up ahead, Herb had his hand on the knob of Father's door. His lips were moving. It looked as if he were calling Father by name, but no sound emerged.

Or was it because Leighton could not hear anything over the upheaval in his own head? He was almost at Herb's side when Herb, with a grimace, at last pushed the door open.

Immediately Herb recoiled. A fraction of a second later his hand came over Leighton's eyes. Leighton pushed it away.

Just beyond the door was the sitting room of Father's apartment, where he was slumped over the writing desk. Leighton knew a moment of intense relief—Father was tired, that was all.

Then he saw the blood on the wall behind, the blood that pooled beneath Father's head, the blood that fell, drop by drop, onto the floor beneath the desk.

Someone tried to restrain Leighton. He struggled, shoving his elbow into that person's side, only faintly registering the pained cry as Herb's as he freed himself and ran to Father.

Father's eyes were open, an almost surprised expression on his face. In his hand was an ivory-handled dueling pistol that had been in the family at least a hundred years. It still smoked faintly at the muzzle, the tang of gunpowder as overwhelming as the scent of blood.

A note sat on top of a stack of books, the ink not quite dried yet. *I am sorry. I am so sorry. But I cannot go back to an asylum. I cannot. I am sorry.*

Leighton thought it was Herb whimpering in anguish. But it was him, making half-strangled noises in his throat, not wanting to understand what happened, but unable to keep a rising horror from swamping him.

He stumbled backward until he was stopped by a wall. And from there he sank to the floor, his hand clamped over his mouth.

He was wrong. *This* was what the monks must have felt when their monasteries had been torn down: despair and utter futility, before a pitiless darkness that would swallow the entire world.

Five

The Truth

YING-YING WAS NOT GRACIOUS IN defeat. She sulked when she lost games of chess or *go*, and refused to let anyone tell her answers to riddles she couldn't solve herself.

What Amah did to her was unforgivable, forcing her to kowtow at knifepoint. Never had she been so insulted in her whole life, and by a servant, a nobody! She feigned illness for a day, and afterward, to Mother's surprise, spent her days in Mother's study, poring over volumes of poetry and history, practicing calligraphy with a vengeance, even willingly plucking away at the Chinese zither, a difficult instrument that rebuffed her every attempt at making music.

Amah, for all that she had seemed at death's door, was abed for only one day before going about her duties as usual. To continue her snubbing, what hours Ying-ying had away from Mother's rooms she spent in the kitchen, where she'd never be caught alone. Cook didn't mind her presence, and often Ying-ying had gossip to listen to when Little Plum came in to lend a hand.

One afternoon, when Amah was out buying herbs at the apothecary shop, she came up as a topic.

"I don't know how she does it," said Little Plum, as she helped Cook shuck a pile of pea pods. "If I never went out anywhere for myself I'd be like an ant on a hot pot lid."

The servants had few sanctioned holidays, but they each had their own ways of slipping out. Little Plum visited her sweetheart during Mother's summer afternoon naps. Cook extended the length of her market trips for her own business. Judging from the frequent appearances in the kitchen of servants on social calls from other households, it seemed a universal practice.

With the exception of Amah.

Amah, as far as anyone knew, had no family, no romantic entanglements, and, despite her popularity, no close friends. But even lonesome servants stole out to buy some nibbles they craved, a jar of hair ointment, or to go down to the teahouse-theater to catch a performance of their favorite actors. Not Amah.

"I told you my cousin Old Luo once saw her in that gambling place," Cook said placidly.

"Old Luo couldn't see his fingers if he stuck his arm out." Little Plum shook her head. "If he were any more blind he'd be a fortune-teller."

"That's true enough," Cook concurred. "He's gone into the wrong courtyard several times because he couldn't tell which one was his own front door."

The words were on the tip of Ying-ying's tongue to inform them of Amah's nocturnal jaunts, something sensational that neither Cook nor Little Plum knew: Amah not only going out, but going out—gasp—in the middle of the night to unspeakably dangerous places.

But the memory of Amah's knife at her chest silenced her—just as it had whenever she thought of telling Mother. She ate another candied plum instead.

ON THE TWENTY-SIXTH, AFTER DA-REN'S arrival, Ying-ying could no longer avoid Amah. Mother was pitilessly strict on this: Ying-ying had to stay in her rooms, out of sight, while Da-ren was in residence.

And this night Da-ren, when she spied upon him from her window, seemed to be in a grim mood, his gait without its usual energy.

At dinnertime Amah entered Ying-ying's suite of rooms. She brought a cucumber salad, a stir-fry of chicken with cashews, and an egg-drop soup with dried scallops and slices of ham. Ying-ying filled her bowl with rice and began eating without saying anything. Amah sat down on the opposite side of the square table and did the same.

Amah didn't speak until she was finished eating. "Still angry with me?" she asked, setting down her chopsticks. She didn't sound irate, but neither did she sound apologetic.

Ying-ying refused to answer. She wasn't as fast an eater as Amah, so she buried her face in her bowl and pretended not to have heard anything.

It didn't seem to matter to Amah. "I have been thinking of making you my apprentice since you turned five," she said, her tone matter-of-fact. "You are now a month short of nine and I still haven't. Because I knew you'd be a trying student."

Ying-ying's head snapped up. She stared at Amah indignantly.

"The order, by tradition, admits only orphaned girls, or those who have been sold off by their families. For good reason—they are beyond grateful and they work hard. But you, clever and agile as you may be, are spoiled, lazy, and too willful for your own good."

"I am not!" Ying-ying shot back. "You are—"

The slender, glittering knife was in Amah's hand. She set it gently down on the table, the blade pointed at Ying-ying. What Ying-ying was about to say froze in the back of her throat.

"I have been too lenient with you." Amah didn't raise her voice; she had no need to. "But the graver fault lies with Fu-ren. She has raised you as if you were somebody, when in fact you are nobody."

Ying-ying gasped in outrage. She was not a nobody. She lived in this splendid courtyard with pomegranate trees and goldfish big as her hand swimming in huge urns. Her clothes were made of the finest silk from Hangzhou. The pins in her hair were adorned with real pearls. And though she wasn't a flawless beauty like Mother, she was a very pretty girl. Everyone always commented on her large, lovely eyes, her perfect double eyelids, and—the envy of all—her long, long eyelashes.

"You are talking rubbish!"

"Am I?" Amah asked. "Who's your father, then, if you are somebody?"

Ying-ying opened her mouth, but nothing would come out. She thought back to the photograph, the foreign devil with the aggressive stare.

"You dug up that picture," Amah said, as if reading her mind. "Didn't you wonder who he was?"

Ying-ying shook her head so hard her vision swam.

"He was your father, an Englishman, though you never saw him, nor he you."

"You are lying!"

It became Amah's turn to act as if she hadn't heard. "Your mother came from a scholar's household. But her father tried opium and liked it too much. He drained the family purse feeding his habit. Then his son fell sick. There was no money for a doctor or medicine. So he sold your mother. After all, she was only the offspring of a concubine, and only a daughter. The slaver took her to Shanghai and sold her to a fancy brothel."

Ying-ying wanted to stick her fingers in her ears. She couldn't. The story was dreadful, but dreadful in such a way that she must go on listening.

"She was beautiful and learned, so she didn't suffer the fate of common prostitutes. They billed her as the loveliest girl in Shanghai. Your father came to see her out of curiosity. He liked what he saw, so he bought her from the brothel. But after two years, the big crash came. He lost everything. One night he got drunk with his friends and never came home. Three days later they fished him out of the Huang-pu River."

Ying-ying stared down at the table, at a refinished spot where she had tried to carve her name into the wood.

"I found your mother tottering on a chair, trying to put her head through a noose. He had left her with nothing but a big belly. But she was too young to die, only nineteen."

That would make Mother twenty-eight now. Ying-ying never knew her age.

Amah sighed. "I still remember the day you were born. I had a big basin of water to drown you if you turned out to be a girl. A son could advance in the world, and repay the suffering of his mother. What good was a girl but another mouth to feed?"

Ying-ying gaped at her in disbelief. Drown her? Of course, she knew that lots of people, particularly in the south, killed infants, most often girls, that they couldn't afford. But those were illiterate, ignorant people. How could anyone as cultured as Mother even think of such a thing? Drown her? *Her?*

"After you came, I sent the midwife away and told your mother to pull the bedcover over her head. She was crying. I had forgotten to tell the midwife not to give you to her. She had seen you and held you." Amah's voice was losing its steeliness. "Newborns are usually wrinkled and bloody. But you were a sweet-looking baby, all pink and clean, eyes wide open. My hands shook and shook when I tried to lower you to the water. And I've killed grown men in my time without so much as a backward glance."

Ying-ying's teeth hurt. She looked down and realized she had been biting on the rim of her bowl. She stuffed her knuckles in her mouth instead. Obviously she had survived, but she was frightened nevertheless.

"I held you by the neck, my thumb against your cheek. Just when the back of your head touched water, you turned your face and started sucking on my thumb. And I couldn't bear to put you in any further. That was when your mother bolted up in bed and screamed, 'Don't do it! Don't do it! Give her back to me.' I did. Then the two of us huddled over you and cried until we had no more tears left." Amah fell silent for a long time. "That was the last time I cried."

Ying-ying felt a hot wetness on her face. She didn't know whether she was weeping for her own lucky escape or for the despair of the two women who couldn't manage to kill her.

"So she kept you and went back to the brothel." Amah picked up where she had left off, her voice once again steady. "The next year Da-ren met her on a visit to Shanghai, when she was engaged to appear at a feast put on for him. And within three months we were all in Peking."

Ying-ying's throat burned, yet her fingers were cold. "Does...does anyone else know I'm a foreign devil bastard?"

"Besides Fu-ren and me?" Amah shook her head. "No one, except perhaps Da-ren. I don't know whether he knows."

Did Da-ren and Mother ever speak of her past? On his visits they often talked deep into the night—sometimes Ying-ying could see their silhouettes upon the window of Mother's room, their heads bent toward each other. Once she had asked Amah what they talked about, and Amah, instead of telling her to mind her own business, as she so often did, had said that they might be discussing past precedents of great reforms, as they were both well-versed in history.

The next day Ying-ying had started to read the history books in Mother's study.

No, she thought, she could not imagine Mother ever wanting to bring up the past. Not just the sordidness of it, the anguish and fear of being all alone in the world, but the betrayal of her own family, a wound that would never heal. Was this why sometimes she gazed out the window and looked haunted, despite what Ying-ying considered the absolute perfection of her life?

"Do you understand why I have told you everything?" asked Amah. "Your mother has raised you to be like her—she probably still has hope of a respectable marriage for you. But your birth and parentage are too irregular. No one who is anyone will allow their son to marry you as a first wife. Even if Da-ren himself intercedes, he might at best place you as third concubine to some official he's trying to influence."

Ying-ying drew her hand from her mouth and gazed, unseeing, at the red teeth marks around her knuckles. Boss Peng, who owned several grain shops in the district, had acquired a young third concubine not long ago, age sixteen or seventeen. He was sixty years old and had a granddaughter who was older than his new concubine.

Was this what awaited Ying-ying beyond the confines of her childhood, beyond the walls of these beautiful courtyards?

She couldn't breathe.

"Can't...can't Mother just keep me with her? I'll look after her in her old age."

Amah looked at her. Was that a trace of pity in her eyes?

In her mind Ying-ying saw Mother turning to one side, coughing into her bright scarlet handkerchief that would not show any flecks of blood. Was this Amah's way of hinting that there would be no ripe old age for Mother? That life as Ying-ying knew it might be upended any moment?

She realized that part of the reason she desperately wished to be a daughter to Da-ren was because she wanted Mother to stop worrying about her. She hadn't needed the entirety of the truth to be ashamed — she had always known, deep down, that there was something unspeakable about her origins. That Mother's small frowns and almost inaudible sighs over her imperfect brushstrokes and much worse zither playing were not just about music and calligraphy, but about her future.

About what would happen to a girl raised in the lap of luxury who yet did not belong anywhere.

But if Da-ren valued her then she would always belong, and Mother needed never fear again, at least not on her behalf.

Da-ren certainly valued Bao-shun, who was handy with a broadsword. Was there a possibility that he would find Ying-ying worthy if she were to become a tremendously skilled martial artist?

Or would he instead be horrified? Mother no doubt would be, if she knew what Amah intended. If she knew that the woman she trusted to look after her daughter not only wielded deadly blades, but was a fugitive from the law.

Ying-ying pressed her hands to either side of her head, but she could bring no order to the chaos inside. "Suppose I had your martial skills. What do I do with them?"

Besides getting into trouble in the middle of the night.

"Suppose a marriage has been arranged for you to a man thirty years your senior, whom you've never laid eyes on before. What would you do?"

Ying-ying grimaced, shutting her eyes tight.

"I know you. You'd want to run away. But how will you survive beyond the walls, soft, pampered girl that you are? Do you think you will even last a day before you are robbed—or worse?"

"So I learn how to crush skulls and the bad people leave me alone. But then what? Do I go and become a servant like you? What good are those skills to *you*?"

Amah's face turned hard. Ying-ying shrank a little, afraid she'd gone too far. But Amah only rose and piled the dishes back into the bamboo steamer. "Well, if you prefer to warm an old man's bed—it's more comfortable that way."

Ying-ying felt as if a giant hand had clutched around her lungs. "Is—is this the only choice I have?"

"It's more choice than Fu-ren ever had," Amah answered quietly.

Ying-ying watched her bowl—and her unfinished meal—being taken away. Reluctantly, but of her own volition, she bowed her head. "I understand now, Master."

Six

The Guardian

THE MORNING AFTER FATHER'S PASSING, Mother returned home looking pale and tense. She descended from the carriage alone. When she was in the drawing room with Sir Curtis, a dogcart pulled up and let out Marland and her maid.

Leighton, from the window of his room, noticed this precaution on her part. Looking back, he realized that Marland had never been presented to Sir Curtis. On the latter's infrequent visits, Marland had always been excused as having a cold, a tummy ache, or some other troublesome but not particularly dangerous ailment.

Only Leighton, who looked very much like Father, who was quiet and self-contained, and who could quote the scripture in both English and Latin, was ever put forward for Sir Curtis's inspection.

Leighton had always considered himself grown-up, someone who dealt calmly and competently with everything that came his way. Now he realized how little he actually knew of life, that the "everything" he had felt himself so capable of handling was actually the most privileged, most sheltered existence imaginable. The adults around him conducted their own lives with sacrifice and secrecy so that he could have this peaceful, even-keeled childhood.

So that he could go about his days largely free of the fear that they endured. So that he would not see that everyone around him was a prisoner of some sort: Father, whose freedom depended upon his "good" conduct; Mother, who could experience happiness only a few days at a time; even Herb, weighed down by the heaviness inherent in the Atwoods' lives, the heaviness inherent in any kind of incarceration of the spirit.

It was probably always going to fail, this precarious protection. But now it had fallen apart and exposed the inner workings of their household to Sir Curtis's all-too-sharp gaze. How long would it be before he learned that Mother hadn't been visiting some elderly relative? That Mother and Father had been quietly permitting, perhaps even encouraging, each other to embark on the kind of conduct that suggested Sodom and Gomorrah to Sir Curtis?

Leighton had once thought Father's fears exaggerated. No more. The kind of cruelty that could drive a grown man to take his own life...Did Mother understand her peril?

Did any of them understand their peril?

Leighton took the jade tablet from his nightstand drawer and smoothed his finger over a line of raised characters. As soon as he had left the scene of Father's death the day before, he had gone to the library and taken the jade tablet from the display case. What Herb never said aloud but Leighton now understood was that it had been a present to mark Father and Herb's love for each other, much as it—together with the tablet still in Herb's hands—once celebrated Herb's parents' desire to spend their lives together.

If Sir Curtis knew, he would confiscate the jade tablet, perhaps even destroy it.

Leighton could see Father's face so clearly, the first time he had shown the tablet to Leighton. The corners of his eyes had crinkled as he smiled at Herb. *Do you want to tell Leighton the legend?*

Leighton had loved those rare, glowing smiles. He had loved the long walks with Father to the railway station to meet Herb's train, five miles of eager anticipation. And more than anything else, he had loved the sensation of closing the library door behind himself after he had said his good-nights, the safe, replete feeling of knowing that Herb would still be there in the morning and Father would still be happy.

Two drops of liquid splashed onto the jade tablet. Leighton wiped them away with his fingers. Two more drops came. And two more.

He tilted his face up to the coffered ceiling, the blue-and-white pattern a complete blur. Father was dead. He didn't know where Herb was. Nor could he extract Mother from her unpleasant interview with Sir Curtis.

He wrapped the jade tablet in a silk cloth, hid it more carefully, washed his face, then went to the nursery.

"It's a nice day," he said to Marland's nursemaid. "If it's all right with you, I'd like to take my brother to the trout stream."

They could not keep Marland out of Sir Curtis's sight forever. But they could for another day.

Marland ran to Leighton and wrapped his arms around Leighton's legs.

Leighton lifted him up. "Come, Master Marland. Let's go skip some rocks."

THE FACT THAT FATHER HAD died by his own hand was hushed up. The inquest returned a verdict of accidental death due to the unanticipated discharge of an antique firearm while being cleaned.

The tale, as trumped up as it was, did not encounter much resistance—it was still less unlikely than suicide on the part of a man who seemed to have everything to live for, and who had appeared, in the days immediately preceding his untimely demise, to have been in the finest of both health and spirits.

His funeral was thickly attended and many extravagant words were spoken about his kindness, his generosity, his devotion to his duties and his family. Leighton had been afraid he would cry, but he remained dry-eyed through the eulogies, as if they sang the praises of a complete stranger.

When Leighton had been little, Father would secretly pass him a morsel of sweets on Sunday mornings, which would be Leighton's to enjoy during the sermon, as long as he kept his enjoyment still and silent. The Sunday after he turned seven he'd declined the bribe, feeling himself quite capable of suffering through the sermon like a man. Father had ruffled his hair. *Seven going on twenty-seven, aren't you?*

Perhaps he was in danger of weeping, after all.

He blinked back the tears. Several mourners away, someone leaned forward slightly to look at him: Sir Curtis's fiancée, Miss Saithwaite.

Before the funeral he had met Miss Saithwaite for the first time. She was almost eye-wateringly beautiful, blond and ethereal. But more than her beauty, he had been struck by her age: She could not be more than nineteen. And Sir Curtis, despite his slim figure and unlined face, was nearly fifty.

Her gaze was quite impersonal, almost Sphinx-like. And swift—a second later her attention had already turned back to the eulogist. Briefly Leighton wondered what kind of woman would marry Sir Curtis. If he'd been told, sight unseen, that Sir Curtis's bride-to-be was nearly thirty years his junior, he would have guessed that she had been compelled by her parents to accept his suit.

But this girl, with her cool pride that verged on arrogance, was not the kind to allow herself to be compelled by anyone. She was marrying Sir Curtis because she wished to.

It was terrifying, the idea that there existed a kindred spirit for Sir Curtis.

WORDS OF SYMPATHY FLOWED LEIGHTON and Mother's way as they made their way out of the church. Many a hand came to rest on Leighton's shoulder—he only wished that he could draw actual strength from the crowd of mourners. Or that they could form a true barrier between Sir Curtis and the rest of the family.

A man stood at the very back of the sanctuary, looking as if he hadn't eaten or slept in a week. Herb! The backs of Leighton's eyes stung. He wished he could run to Herb; he wished they could be alone. With him there would be no shame giving in to the tumult inside. They could weep, scream, or destroy an entire room at the needlessness and injustice of Father's death.

But Leighton only dared give a tiny nod as he filed out behind Mother.

"Mr. Gordon is here," he said to her, when they were out of earshot of Sir Curtis and his fiancée.

"Yes, I expect he has been asked by the solicitors to come and hear the will."

She sounded nervous, yet half hopeful, as if she expected the reading of the will to be an emancipation.

Leighton should have thought of the question sooner, but he hadn't. "Do you know whom Father appointed as our guardian, ma'am?"

Mother briefly laid her hand on his arm. "Not Sir Curtis. You can be sure of that."

Father was buried at the family's private cemetery, which gave out to a wide vista of rolling hills and green fields. They had often stopped here on their long hikes through the surrounding countryside. Leighton could still see Father as he was the last time, his coat on the grass, his sleeves rolled up, dividing a large sandwich into three, making sure that Leighton and Herb had the bigger pieces.

Herb, too, was at the interment, but he stood halfway down the slope, gazing up at the sight of his beloved being lowered into the ground. He wiped at his eyes.

Leighton was the last person to drop a handful of soil onto Father's casket. Inside the casket, lying upon Father's no longer beating heart, was an envelope that contained a copy of Leighton's favorite photograph of the three of them together, on the bank of the trout stream before a canoe, each with an oar in hand.

On the back of the photograph, he had written, *Rest in peace, Father. I will look after everyone you loved.*

IN THE NURSERY, MARLAND, WHO hadn't attended the funeral because he was judged too young, was knocking over column after column of blocks. The moment he saw Leighton, he came running and grabbed Leighton's hand. "Did they bury Father?"

Father had loved Marland, albeit with an anxiety that Leighton had not understood completely until he'd learned that Marland was not Father's natural son: It had been the apprehension of a good man who had the charge of another man's child. He must have worried about doing everything right by Marland, and perhaps he had been especially concerned that Marland should never feel he was treated differently from Leighton.

"Yes, they buried Father."

"Will he be lonely?"

Leighton crouched down so he was at eye level with Marland. "We can visit him often, to keep him company."

Tears rolled down Marland's face. "Can we visit him now?"

The door of the nursery opened and in the doorway stood Sir Curtis. Marland stared at him. "Who are you?"

Sir Curtis did not answer. He looked from Marland to Leighton and back again, something like a pleased smile on his face. Without a word, he closed the door and left.

"Who was that?" Marland asked Leighton.

"Sir Curtis," said Leighton.

The answer was good enough for Marland. "Can we go visit Father?"

The satisfaction Sir Curtis had derived from seeing Marland, however, chilled Leighton. He caressed Marland's hair, so blond that it was almost white. "We can, but not now."

LEIGHTON SLIPPED INTO THE LIBRARY from the secret entrance up in the gallery and listened to the reading of Father's will, which the solicitor finished in only a few minutes.

Father had left handsome gifts to the seniormost servants. To Mother and Marland he gave a substantial settlement each. Starling

Manor would come to Leighton when he reached majority, along with tracts of land in London, Manchester, and Birmingham. To Leighton himself he left the jade tablet. To Herb, his collection of stamps.

To Sir Curtis, absolutely nothing, which gave Leighton a savage pleasure.

Father also named Mother and Mr. Henry Knightly, Mother's cousin, as Leighton and Herb's guardians. Again, a deliberate repudiation of Sir Curtis. Leighton was almost giddy—until he remembered Sir Curtis's smugness, looking into the nursery.

But what could Sir Curtis do? He did not hold their purse strings and he had not been appointed guardian.

Sir Curtis, however, did not seem the least bit upset by the reading of the will. After the servants and the solicitor had vacated the library, he strolled to the ivory-inlay console table where Father's decanter was kept and tapped a finger on the crystal topper.

"Any fortification for you, Mrs. Atwood? And you, Mr. Gordon?"

They both shook their heads, Mother uncomfortable but stoic, Herb stone-faced but unafraid. Like Leighton, they had been bolstered by the contents of Father's will.

"Well, then, we will start with you, Mrs. Atwood—ladies first." Sir Curtis gave a thin-lipped smile. "You are an utterly useless woman."

Mother flinched. Leighton gritted his teeth.

"Get out," said Herb. "You will not insult a lady in her own home. And there is nothing more for you to do here."

"So speaks the man who might as well have pulled the trigger on my brother," said Sir Curtis coldly.

Herb swallowed.

Sir Curtis turned back to Mother. "It is the role of the wife to uphold the vows of marriage and the sanctity of the family. But you, Mrs. Atwood, you had no strength and no conviction. You chose to seek your own pleasures and left your husband vulnerable to temptation. A better woman would have guarded him and kept him safe for as long as she and he both lived. But you, full of weakness and selfishness, abandoned your duties long ago."

Each of his words seemed to strike a blow upon Mother, who shrank and shrank.

Leighton saw now that he had been blind, that Father's death had left Mother badly shaken. Had she been blaming herself the way he blamed himself? Had she been wondering whether things would have been different if only she hadn't been so far away from home when Sir Curtis unexpectedly arrived?

"Do you actually think I will let an unrepentant adulteress be guardian to my nephew? Don't act so surprised. When he died did you think I did not notice you were not at home? Did you think I did not find out that one week out of every month you took that other child of yours and left on some supposed trip to visit elderly relations? And from then on, did you think it was all that difficult to find out about the tall, blond Californian?"

Mother spoke, her voice almost choked, but defiant. "It doesn't matter. There is nothing you can do."

"To the contrary, there is a great deal that I can do. No doubt my brother believed your cousin Mr. Knightly to possess not only robust health, but a sterling character. I suppose you neglected to inform him that Mr. Knightly had been sent down from university for forging cheques?"

"That was more than twenty years ago, and for all of five pounds!" cried Mother. "It was only a youthful prank—Henry just wanted to see whether it could be done."

"But how can we be sure such deceit has been eradicated from his character? Not to mention that Mr. Knightly is wretchedly poor for a man with a demanding wife and four daughters who will need London seasons very soon. Would the Court of Chancery look kindly upon his fraudulent past? I do not think so. Not when there are substantial rents that come in every month from lands that belong to my nephew, and every opportunity for embezzlement.

"And when I have removed him from this guardianship, I will, of course, ask that I myself be made a coguardian of the boys. You blanch, Mrs. Atwood. Does the thought not please you? You are afraid I will take them from you, are you not? You are wise to fear, for that is exactly what I will do. Nigel did not see fit to punish you for your adultery, but I will."

Mother emitted a strangled sound.

"You cannot do this!" Herb said heatedly. "No one wants your interference. Nigel has seen to the protection and welfare of his widow and children. He intentionally left you out of his will. Why can't you respect that?"

Sir Curtis turned to Herb. "Tell me this. Did Nigel beg you not to lead him into temptation? Did he plead for his soul? Did he resist, with what little courage and fortitude he had, the lures of the flesh that you dangled before him?"

Herb fell silent.

"He did, didn't he? And you overrode his good sense. You overrode his love of God. You brought him to his doom and now you want a say in the welfare of his children?"

"That is not—"

"Shut up, you sodomite wretch. I will deal with you later. Now, where were we, Mrs. Atwood? Ah, yes, your unfitness as wife and mother."

They had all three been standing. But now Sir Curtis sat down on Father's favorite padded chair, his hands on the armrests, one ankle over the other knee—completely at ease, every inch the master of the manor.

"I am not inclined to be lenient—leniency serves no purpose except to encourage the delinquent. But I must consider my wife-to-be, who will not wish for a scandal to mar her wedding. So I will offer you a choice, Mrs. Atwood. We can publicly reveal your adulterous conduct and strip you of your guardianship via sworn statements in the Court of Chancery, or we can resolve this privately. You take your bastard child and leave the country altogether. Invent some excuses. Say that his health is frail and must need the sunshine and mildness of California. Once you are far away, you may marry your paramour or continue to consort with him in sin. It will no longer be my concern."

"But Leighton—"

"My nephew, who is very much my concern, will come under my guidance."

"No!"

"Think carefully. You have acted foolishly and arrogantly and you are about to pay the price. Now the question is only, Will you pay with one of your children, or both? Remember, the other boy is not my flesh and blood. Now leave us and consider your choices. Go."

THE DOOR CLOSED BEHIND MOTHER.

Leighton shook.

He had met Cousin Knightly a few times, a short, bald fellow full of glee and laughter. His daughters adored him, though he could not buy them new dresses or fashionable hats. His wife complained loudly of their poverty, but even she, Leighton thought, was in truth quite fond of her husband.

And now Leighton would lose a good-natured guardian for a five-pound forged cheque from before he was born.

"So," said Sir Curtis, "you have not ended your miserable existence yet."

Herb started—Leighton had not passed on Sir Curtis's command for him to kill himself. "I have no intention of ever taking my own life."

"Hmm. Let me tell you about your other choice then. There is a grieving mother whose son died of an overdose of chloral. She blames his death on the fact that he had recently been spurned. By another man. The homosexuality of the liaison does not bother her—one of those stupid women who can never find a single fault with her own child—but she is out for blood against that man.

"Only she does not know his identity. I, however, have decided that you are that man, Mr. Gordon. It will be quite easy for me to convince her of that, as you and her son do frequent similar circles. And then it will be only a minor step to have her go to the police and report you for the deviant you are."

"But others will be able to testify that I do not know her son."

"In the end it would not matter. It will be about whether you have committed the kind of perverted acts that the law condemns. And it really is too bad that you will receive only a prison sentence, and not a trip to the gallows."

"You can't do that," said Herb, but he sounded impotent.

"I can and I will," answered Sir Curtis, anticipation in every syllable. "And I will enjoy your downfall, Mr. Gordon. So it is up to you: a quick, private end or months of public humiliation followed by years of misery.

"This just came back from the inquest. It would be poetic justice, wouldn't it?" He opened a case on the library desk, which contained a pair of antique dueling pistols. Leighton recoiled—Father had used one of the pistols to take his own life. "Hell now or hell on earth. Make your choice, Mr. Gordon."

Sir Curtis left. Slowly, as if sleepwalking, Herb approached the desk and picked up the pistol that was still marred by bloodstains.

"No!" Leighton cried.

Herb, startled, looked up.

Leighton ran down the circular stairs. "Please don't even think about it."

Herb gently set down the pistol. "I wasn't. I promise I wasn't—not seriously, in any case. I was thinking more of your father. How desperate he must have felt, how terrified, to resort to such a measure."

Anguish weighed down his words.

"It isn't your fault," Leighton told him. "Father—he loved every moment he had with you."

Moisture glistened in Herb's eyes. "And I him. And I loved coming here. I loved spending time together, all three of us."

He settled his hands on Leighton's shoulders. "Please don't ever think he meant to abandon you—or anyone else he loved. Sometimes it's hard to think clearly when you are in a panic. I wish he'd drunk himself to a stupor instead, or smashed up a room—anything but this."

Leighton was shocked. It had never occurred to him that something as grave and irreversible as suicide could have been a moment's impulse.

"Believe me, I've had friends who have jumped from bridges and then never did anything to endanger their own lives again. If only...There are so many if-onlys, aren't there? The important thing to remember is that he never meant to leave you unprotected. He loved you very much, and he was infinitely proud of you."

"He loved you too. He wouldn't want you to listen to anything Sir Curtis says."

Herb glanced at the pistol on the desk. "I'm afraid that man isn't bluffing."

Sir Curtis would probably consider it an affront to his honor and capability to bluff. No, he was a man of action. The right hand of God. "But he doesn't have infinite reach. You can leave the country. You haven't committed any kind of crime that would make the law chase you over international borders."

Herb exhaled. "Where would I go?"

"Anywhere. As long as you will be safe."

"Then come with me. We'll run away together. We'll travel all the way to China and search for the monks' treasure."

And what a wonderful adventure that would have been, under different circumstances. Leighton felt a hot prickle in his eyes. "How much do you think a Buddha statue made of pure gold would weigh?"

"Anything bigger than the size of a bust and the two of us might not be able to lift it."

"We'll have to get stronger fast," said Leighton.

They laughed, a sound Leighton hadn't heard in ages.

Tears fell down Herb's face. All at once he looked crumpled, a man with everything taken out of him. "I don't know what I'm going to do. It *was* largely my fault—I couldn't leave well enough alone and had to have everything. How can I live with myself, knowing the calamity I had caused?"

Leighton could not stop his own tears. "It *wasn't* your fault, and please don't ever think so again. If you believed that, Father would never be able to rest in peace."

Herb gripped Leighton's arms. "Come with me. Your father would have wanted me to look after you."

Leighton wanted that more than anything else. "That *would* set Sir Curtis and the law after you, for the abduction of a minor."

Herb laughed bitterly. "There is that, isn't there? I can't seem to do anything right these days."

"Just look after yourself for me. I need to know that you are safe—and well. Can you do that for me, please?"

More tears fell down Herb's face. "I will, my dear boy. I will do anything you ask."

MOTHER WAS IN THE SOLARIUM, standing before the window, a handkerchief crumpled between her fingers. She turned around at the sound of Leighton's entrance. Her face was pale against the black crape of her mourning gown, the rim of her eyes red.

"Leighton, my dear," she said softly.

They used to walk together in the gardens, Mother and Father. In the evenings they took turns reading books aloud to each other. And from time to time Leighton would catch Mother looking at Father wistfully, as if remembering him—or herself—from a different time.

Father had loved her too, a gentle, respectful love tinged with traces of regret.

And Leighton would take care of her—by removing her and Marland from Sir Curtis's sphere of influence. Except he didn't quite know how to go about it. From time to time Mother could be stubborn. If she was determined to stay and protect Leighton...

"I heard what Sir Curtis said to you after the reading of the will," he told her. "I heard him tell you to take Marland and go."

She squared her shoulders. "I will not. I will not leave you alone with that monster."

His hand closed around the door handle. He could try to reason with her about how the monster would terrorize Marland, but he didn't think she would hear him.

"So you do not dispute anything that was said?" he said, making his voice cold.

She swallowed. "No, I do not dispute it. Please understand, Leighton, that—"

"So that's what you had been doing all these years—neglecting Father, neglecting me, and neglecting everything else to sin with your illicit lover."

She flinched as if he had slapped her.

He forced himself to continue, speaking as if he were Sir Curtis himself. "And no wonder Marland has such anemic looks. He isn't even an Atwood. How do you live with yourself? The forty thousand pounds Father settled on him should have been mine. That is money you—and he—stole directly from me."

"That has never been my intention in the slightest!"

"And yet you plan to continue living in my home, on my income, and to go on saddling me with the expenses of raising a parasite."

Her hand came up to her throat. Her fingers shook. "I thought you loved Marland. I thought you loved—"

I thought you loved me. Except she couldn't bring herself to say it.

Herb was wrong. Leighton was not kind—he was capable of all kinds of atrocities.

"Do we...do we really disgust you so much?" Mother's voice had become barely above a whisper.

"You have no idea how ashamed I am to be related to you and that child of yours."

Her hand closed into a fist. He fully expected her to hit him.

"If you really feel so," she said, her voice hoarse, defeated, "if you really feel so, then perhaps Marland and I ought to go."

Why did she not realize that no trespass on her part could ever equal the cruelty he displayed now? Why did she let him ride roughshod over her with his trumped-up moral outrage, when she ought to strike him for his utter want of propriety and respect?

Why did the good people of the world so meekly allow themselves to be ill treated and trampled over?

"Yes," he said, "I feel so. Very strongly. Very, very strongly."

MOTHER AND MARLAND LEFT THE next morning. Marland cried and struggled. It took both Mother and his nursemaid to force him into his carriage.

Leighton did not wave good-bye. He gazed somewhere above his brother's red, bawling face. They had gone to Father's grave at the crack of dawn and made a honeysuckle wreath together. He would remember that instead, and Marland's plump little hands gently patting the mound of earth on which they had placed the wreath.

Sleep tight, Marland had said to Father. *Sleep tight.*

Deep in the big trunk that held many of Mother's books, Leighton had hidden a package that contained everything he could not bear for Sir Curtis to get his hands on: hundreds of photographs, just as many letters from Herb, and, of course, the beautiful jade tablet that had been wretchedly difficult for him to let go of.

He had tried to write a letter, to explain and to apologize. In the end he had burned all his drafts. Better for Mother to believe that he was as monstrous and callous as Sir Curtis. She would be safer that way, and Marland too.

The carriage clattered along the drive, becoming smaller and smaller. Then it was gone.

And he was all alone.

Seven

The Apprentice

MOTHER STUDIED THE FINELY TEXTURED *shuen* paper spread on her desk. She had finished the background of a new ink painting, a mountain with ridges sharp as swords.

Ying-ying had been grinding ink for her. Now she picked up the massage roller made of polished agate and applied it to just beneath Mother's shoulders.

Mother glanced back, astonished. "When did you become such an example of filial piety?"

Ying-ying didn't say anything. When she looked upon Mother now, the sensation in her heart was very nearly one of pain. Several times alone in her room she'd broken down in tears as she imagined what Mother must have gone through in those darkest days of her life.

She was at once beyond happy for her—that she had found peace, quiet, and security at last—and beyond frightened that it wouldn't last.

"Does Da-ren like paintings?" she asked.

She had always been curious about Da-ren, but she could not remember the last time she'd posed a question about him directly to Mother.

Mother picked up a smaller brush and dipped it in the ink Ying-ying had freshly made. "I suppose he would, if he had time for such things."

Ying-ying set down the roller and returned to her station beside the ink stone. "Why is he so busy?"

"Well, he is an important adviser at court. And he has many ideas for…reforms." Her tone turned slightly grim as she uttered the last word.

"Are reforms not good?"

Mother looked out the window at the caged songbirds that hung beneath the eaves—and the blue sky beyond. "The dowager empress was in favor of sweeping changes when the emperor first ascended the throne. But her appetite for reform has grown less and less, while Da-ren aims for more and more. He wants to make Western sciences part of the civil-service examination and reduce the importance of the classics, and that is...that is not..."

She rested the brush against the side of the ink stone and turned to face Ying-ying, the jade beads that dangled from her hairpins clinking softly. "You don't worry about such things," she said gently. "You be a good girl and I will ask Da-ren to find you a kind husband."

She probably still has hope of a respectable marriage for you.

Ying-ying felt a stab of guilt. Mother would be thunderstruck if she knew of Ying-ying's training behind her back—certainly not the kind of training undertaken by "good" girls.

"Yes, Mother."

Mother smiled at her. "Now go find Little Plum—she'll know how to put everything back. I had better lie down for a bit."

Ying-ying gazed at her as she walked toward her bedchamber, this frail woman who somehow made her difficult progress elegant—and who had carved out a corner of beauty and serenity for herself and her child in an otherwise bleak world.

"No, no, no," Amah snapped, her patience waning. "Quieter, slower, softer."

Ying-ying gritted her teeth. Breathing, which she had performed successfully since birth, had lately become an impossible feat. No matter how diligently she worked at it, she couldn't get it right. According to Amah she was always breathing too hard, too fast, too loud. To make things worse, her legs screamed from sitting cross-legged for the duration of a whole incense stick, her back ached because she had to hold her spine rod-straight all the while, and her neck sorely resented the weight of her head.

"I can't do it."

Whack came the rap against her shoulder blade. It stung. Amah the master, unlike Amah the nanny, possessed no tender heart. "You can't do it because you are not trying hard enough. Such things take years of practice. Stop whining."

Normally a rap would make Ying-ying hold her tongue for a little while. But today, against all the other pains she was suffering, the smack hardly registered. "Why don't you teach me something useful instead?" she retorted. "Like how to thrash robbers—or leap walls?"

Or just to jump down from a high place without hurting herself, as Amah had the night she'd returned home injured. And then maybe she could ask Amah where exactly she had gone, what had she been doing, who had been the martial-arts expert powerful enough to injure her—and maybe even who were the men she had killed years ago without a backward glance.

Questions that Ying-ying didn't dare ask without a really good opening.

Amah looked down at Ying-ying in disbelief. "And how do you expect to thrash robbers or leap walls without first learning to control your breathing?"

"I can already control my breathing," Ying-ying said. "I know when I'm inhaling and when I'm exhaling, and I can hold my breath too."

"I am not talking about things any imbecile can do, so don't you play stupid with me," Amah replied, handing Ying-ying another knock on her shoulder. "I've already explained to you: The goal of merging your consciousness with your breath is to access your chi. Without mastery over your chi, you won't jump higher than a pig, and you, a girl, will be no match for the strength of a man."

Ying-ying rolled her eyes. She had heard all this before. She knew what chi was. It was what doctors droned on and on about when anyone fell ill: The chi was weak; the chi was too diffuse; the chi was pooling in wrong places. To her, chi was like blood, just there in the body everywhere. She could no more control it than circulate blood backward.

"I see you don't believe me," Amah said. She looked Ying-ying up and down. "You think you walk softly, right?"

Ying-ying nodded.

"And you think you breathe softly too?"

Ying-ying nodded again. She had been breathing so softly she not only could not hear herself, she could barely feel any flutter of air in her nostrils.

"Fine. Where is that handkerchief your mother gave you last Spring Festival?"

"In my top trunk."

"Get up and go get it."

When Ying-ying returned with the large square of embroidered green silk, Amah had seated herself on the cushion on the floor. "Blindfold me, and bring me that bowl of fried soybeans from the table."

Ying-ying did as she was told.

"Now go somewhere in the room. Go quietly."

It was a hot, windy day. The leaves of the willow tree rustled. Some distance away, the stove of an itinerant rice popper emitted an explosive bang as the grains fluffed up. Ying-ying made her move in the wake of the noise.

No sooner had she approached the washstand than she yowled in pain. Something small and hard had hit her squarely in the temple. A fried soybean fell to the floor beside her. She looked at it in disbelief, then looked back at Amah, who sat tranquilly, the handkerchief completely covering the upper half of her face, her fingers rolling the next soybean.

"I told you to be quiet," she said.

Ying-ying tried again, this time holding her breath and walking on the very tips of her toes.

The fried soybean found her at the back of her neck.

After four more hits, two on her cheeks, one on her forehead, and one between her shoulder blades, she was told to exchange places with Amah.

"You don't need to hit me. Just tell me where I am."

Ying-ying strained her ears. She could hear all the cicadas on the pomegranate trees, the scratching of Cook's iron spatula against her wok in the next courtyard, the lilting, melodious notes of Mother playing on the zither in her rooms, but nothing of Amah's movement, nothing at all. Yet when she was finally directed to loosen her blindfold, the first thing she saw was a perfect circle of fried soybeans placed right around the cushion on which she sat.

She was speechless.

"No, it's not witchcraft," Amah said. "It's nearly thirty years of diligent practice. You are gifted, but your sinews are lax and your mind is undisciplined. You have a long way to go."

Ying-ying bit her lip. She crossed her legs and laced her fingers together before her abdomen. "Give me the directions one more time, Master. Please."

Eight

Rose Priory

LEIGHTON HAD NEVER BEEN TO Sir Curtis's house on Dartmoor. He expected something dark and sinister, with gargoyles and bats that emerged from the belfry like a dark cloud at the close of the day. But Rose Priory itself was completely charming.

The house, situated atop a small incline, was built of a light gray, dense-grained stone, which was barely visible beneath the luxuriant ivy that climbed nearly to the roof. The land surrounding the house had been terraced into several levels of gardens, with pebble paths that crunched underfoot and the last of the summer flowers still in bloom. And beyond a wall that came up only to his waist stretched the moors, green, mysterious, and beautiful.

The interior of the house was decorated with a great many Japanese motifs: wallpapers with patterns of stylized waves, cherry blossom screens, and dinner and tea services painted with misty mountains and slender pagodas. The room given to Leighton was plain but clean and serviceable, and from its window he could see the winding progress of a sparkling stream, the banks of which were studded with many small boulders.

There was no governess or tutor at Rose Priory. Furthermore, most of the staff were away in London, at Sir Curtis's town house: Sir Curtis, who held the charge of all the prisons under the purview of the Home Office, did not personally escort Leighton to Dartmoor. And his absence was like the slightly misty air of the moors, every breath a sharp, sweet reprieve.

Leighton walked for hours every day, exploring the countryside in all directions. In the evenings he read. Rose Priory's collection of books was not as large or as interesting as that at Starling Manor— more than half were sermons or missionary reports. But there were a good many histories, and he started on the first volume of Gibbon's *The Decline and Fall of the Roman Empire*.

Once a week he wrote to Mother at her temporary address in London, reporting truthfully that all was well at Rose Priory, that he had the run of the house and all the freedom anyone could desire. She, in her replies, assured him that she was well, Marland was well, and that preparations for their departure to America proceeded apace.

Very civil letters—no one would guess that he had accused her of gross immorality and that she had believed him. He always felt like crying after reading one of her letters, and sometimes he did.

There were no letters from Herb. Leighton hoped this meant he had already left the country and was now far from Sir Curtis's reach. He had brought all the books Herb had given to him, but only once did he tried to reread one. The moment he opened the book, it was as if he were back where he had last read it, on the bank of the trout stream at Starling Manor, sitting next to Father, both happily anticipating Herb's arrival the next afternoon.

He even remembered what they'd had for lunch that day: sandwiches made with braised slices of ham and a robust mustard studded with tiny brown-and-black mustard seeds. And over that picnic lunch, Father, a quiet man by nature, had talked about his first time on a railway journey, going to the seaside.

Leighton had closed the book immediately. But he could not stop the emptiness in his chest from furiously expanding. He missed Father desperately. He missed Herb desperately. He wished...

He calculated the exact number of days that remained until he reached his twenty-first birthday, when he would be a man in full in the eyes of the law. When he would be free from Sir Curtis at last.

Too many days, thousands and thousands, but one fewer with each sunrise. And when he turned thirteen, he would be sent off to school and not have to return to Rose Priory except during holidays.

He could live with that.

He could wait.

For now.

DESPITE SIR CURTIS'S ABSENCE, THERE was a subtle undertow of unhappiness at Rose Priory. At first Leighton thought it was his own loneliness coloring his perception. Then he realized that he was actually reacting to the servants: The staff at Starling Manor was unobtrusive, but the servants at Rose Priory seemed not so much quiet as subdued.

Oppressed, even.

Some of them started at loud noises. Others muttered to themselves as they worked in the gardens. The man in charge of the stable never quite said no to Leighton's request for a horse to ride, but there had been such dismay in his face, something close to outright fear, that Leighton had not inquired again.

The man in charge of this skeletal staff was named Twombley. Leighton didn't think he had ever come across anyone so high-strung and twitchy. Twombley was completely fixated on every little detail of the running of the house. A single speck of dust on the windowsill or one lonely weed poking its head out of the ground in the gardens would somehow summon him from wherever he was to hold a whispered yet vehement conversation with the servant responsible for this dereliction of duty.

It was as if a state of perfect housekeeping at Rose Priory were the only thing that kept the sky from collapsing.

The next time Leighton was at the village, he asked Mr. Brown, the clerk at the post office, whether he knew anything about the servants at Rose Priory.

"So you noticed something odd about them, eh?" Mr. Brown glanced about to make sure that no one else was near. "They are ex-convicts—or at least that's what I hear."

"Are they?"

"Your uncle is a brave and noble man, he is," said Mr. Brown. "I would be afraid of having my throat cut in my sleep in a house full of criminals. But Sir Curtis, they say he believes in modern methods, not punishment but rehabilitation. He's a godly man, so the good Lord must be looking after him and keeping him safe."

Leighton's heart thudded unpleasantly. "I see. Thank you."

"Haven't made you afraid, have I?" asked the clerk.

"I'm all right," said Leighton.

But he wasn't. Not because he lived in a house with ex-convicts, but because they were broken ex-convicts. Sir Curtis held something over each of them, Leighton was sure, just as he'd held something over Father. Father, who'd had a wealthy mother and an income larger than Sir Curtis's, had been able to escape to Starling Manor. But to the end of his days, there had been something damaged inside him, something fearful and anguished that even Herb's love could not cure.

How long would it be before the monster turned his gaze to Leighton?

SIR CURTIS MARRIED MISS SAITHWAITE at the end of September. Three weeks later they arrived together at Rose Priory, both looking supremely pleased with life and each other.

Along with them came a Mr. Jonathan Colmes, Leighton's new tutor, a slightly stooped man in his early forties. As Sir Curtis made the introductions, Leighton was almost startled to realize that despite Mr. Colmes's somewhat nervous manner, he was not a shattered man barely held together by an animal instinct for self-preservation.

"I have heard excellent things about Mr. Colmes—he was the result of a diligent search," said Sir Curtis.

The very timber of his voice made Leighton's skin crawl. But there was something else too: a trace of malicious mischief. Leighton glanced warily toward Mr. Colmes, wondering whether the latter was going to be an instrument of Sir Curtis's ill will. But in Mr. Colmes he could sense nothing worse than an awkward desire to please. He didn't know what to make of it.

Sir Curtis dismissed Mr. Colmes and sat down behind the desk of the study. Leighton felt the hairs on the back of his neck rise—he had never before been alone with the man.

"And how are you, my dear nephew?" asked Sir Curtis softly.

"Very well, sir. Thank you."

"Do you miss your mother?"

"Sometimes."

"It must be difficult to be left behind. Does she write of her new life? Lady Atwood ran into her once in London and said she seemed to be enjoying herself enormously."

It was meant to hurt and it did. Leighton wanted Mother to get on well. He wanted her to be happy. But always there was the fear that she would forget him altogether—that he didn't matter at all.

Sir Curtis was a connoisseur of fear, a man who knew how to extract and refine it, how to forge it until he could wield it like a blade, every word leaving a gash upon the heart.

"She writes that she is busy getting ready to leave," answered Leighton.

Sir Curtis tented his fingertips and cocked his head to one side. He reminded Leighton of a bird of prey, with coldly intelligent eyes. "You resemble my brother a great deal, young Master Leighton. But I see you are made of sterner stuff."

It occurred to Leighton that until this moment, Sir Curtis had not paid any particular mind to him: He had separated Leighton from his family to punish Mother—and as an exercise of his own power; what manner of boy his nephew was mattered not at all. But now he perceived something in Leighton, something he had not expected.

A strength of will. More than that: a strength of will that could turn into cruelty. He saw a boy who was capable of turning on his mother.

Leighton said nothing.

Sir Curtis took a sip from the cup of tea sitting before him. "The day before my wedding, I received a letter from Mr. Herbert Gordon, asking for the album of stamps that had been bequeathed to him in your father's will."

This was the first time Leighton had heard Herb's name in months. He barely stopped himself from scooting forward in eagerness.

"Quite an insolent demand," continued Sir Curtis, "given that he was directly responsible for your father's death. I sent him the pistol with which Nigel killed himself."

Leighton felt as if someone stepped on his throat. Herb wouldn't, would he?

"Quite a coward, Mr. Gordon. I heard he left the country instead."

Leighton did his best to not exhale too obviously. Herb was safe—for now.

Sir Curtis leaned back in his chair. "I am quite sorry that you had to grow up amid such nefarious influences."

Leighton remained silent.

"Are *you*?" asked Sir Curtis.

A chill ran down Leighton's back—this was a question he could not bypass.

He should lie. Sir Curtis would believe him—Sir Curtis who believed that strength must always detest frailty. And hadn't Leighton lied brilliantly before Mother, convincing her that he was as self-righteous as Sir Curtis?

"No, sir," he said.

Sir Curtis raised a brow. "No?"

"No."

He could never be sorry to have been born to Nigel and Anne Atwood. He could never be sorry to have Marland for a brother. And he would always, always be glad to have had Herb's friendship.

For Mother and Marland, he was willing to undertake the Big Lie. But he would not denounce everyone he loved just so that he might have an easier time at Rose Priory.

Sir Curtis shook his head slightly. But he only said, "I'm sure Mr. Colmes is waiting to begin your lessons. You may go."

LEIGHTON HAD HALF EXPECTED MR. COLMES to be incompetent, but the man was quite good at his profession, and two hours passed quickly under his tutelage. As the clock struck four, Mr. Colmes put away his chalk and closed his book. "That will do for the day. Come now, Master Leighton, let's go for a walk in the gardens."

It had turned cold in the past few days. Rain pelted the windows of the house. A fog floated on the moors; one could not even see down to the low wall that surrounded the lowest level of the garden, let alone beyond.

Leighton wouldn't have guessed Mr. Colmes to harbor a fondness for the outdoors. But as he himself was game for venturing outside in any kind of weather, he fetched his coat, hat, and mackintosh, and walked out beside his tutor.

They had walked for no more than a few minutes before Mr. Colmes exclaimed that it was chillier than he had thought and he would need a heavier coat. He returned to the house to change. Leighton continued to follow the garden path—and ran into Lady Atwood, coming from the opposite direction.

He bowed. She nodded.

He thought they would walk past each other, but she stopped, looked at him a moment, and said, "You are an odd one—quite wary for a little boy."

He was hardly little—already he stood taller than some grown women. But he did not argue with her characterization of him.

She studied him more closely. "You don't like me."

"I don't know you enough to not like you," he said carefully.

"That is not true. You dislike me strongly. Why?"

She didn't seem at all affected by the distaste she had perceived in him, her curiosity wholly impersonal.

"I don't know you at all," he repeated himself.

"You are at least correct about that. So if you have no reason to dislike me personally, then..." Her eyes narrowed. "What do you have against my husband?"

He said nothing.

"If nothing else, you should admire him," Lady Atwood admonished. "He is a godly man who donates his time to the service of his nation, a generous friend, and a devoted husband. And when he retires in a few years, we are going to Africa to save souls."

Leighton almost laughed aloud. Herb would have made a better hangman than Sir Curtis would a missionary.

Lady Atwood's countenance darkened. "You think there is something funny about God's purpose for me?"

So she was the one who wanted to be a missionary. "Was that your condition before you would marry him? That in a few years you will be able to go?"

"That was his promise to me."

"Good luck with it."

"You dare doubt his integrity?"

"Send me a photograph when he is under the African sun, preaching to the unconverted."

Mr. Colmes happened to return just then. He paid his respects to Lady Atwood and they spoke of their impressions of Dartmoor. Leighton walked two steps behind them, Lady Atwood's exalted opinion of her husband echoing in his head.

He could never see Sir Curtis as anything but a monster. But he hoped for her sake that she was right about her husband's integrity, that when the time came he would honor his promise and allow her to fulfill her dream.

By the time they had walked one round in the garden, his thoughts had drifted away from Lady Atwood's future to Herb's present. Was Herb on a train now, or a steamer? Was he headed east or west? Or had he already settled down someplace in Paris or Milan?

What Leighton wouldn't give for a ten-page letter full of details.

He came to a stop.

What if Herb *had* written?

LEIGHTON MADE SURE HE DIDN'T leave the grounds of Rose Priory during the ten days of Sir Curtis and Lady Atwood's stay—he didn't want Sir Curtis to know that he liked walking in the countryside.

After they left for London, however, with his morning lesson done, he immediately set out. But as he was about to open the picket gate in the garden wall, a gardener of about fifty came running.

"Master Leighton! Master Leighton!"

"Yes, Adler?"

"We didn't know before, but Sir Curtis told us that your health is no good, Master Leighton," Adler said urgently. "That anytime you catch a cold you might develop pneumonia."

Leighton blinked. He had never been sick a day in his life.

"Please go back into the house, Master Leighton," Adler beseeched.

"And what if I don't?"

Adler swallowed. "Then Mr. Twombley will write to Sir Curtis."

Mr. Twombley was in charge of the staff at Rose Priory. "And?"

"Mary—Mary Pye in the town house. She is my sweetheart, you see, and she was just made upper maid. Her knees are in bad shape. If she has to go back to the heavier work of a lower maid...Please, Master Leighton. It's nice and warm inside the house."

Leighton did not need to be nice and warm. He wanted to go into the village to speak to Mr. Brown. But as he looked at Adler's weather-beaten face, he could not make himself refuse the man's entreaty—not if it would lead to pain and suffering on the part of the woman Adler loved.

In refusing to condemn his parents and Herb before Sir Curtis, he had not only shown defiance, but his character. And unfortunately for him, Sir Curtis had read him all too clearly and now understood exactly how to fetter Leighton with his own scruples.

"Very well," he said, his voice raspy.

The house, for the first time, felt small and stuffy.

A FEW DAYS LATER, LEIGHTON climbed out of the house as the clock struck midnight. It was eerie to be out on the moors in the dark, the light of a half-moon the only source of illumination, a faint scattering of silver gleam that only seemed to make the shadows impenetrable. And the silence was so profound that he, who had always lived in the country, found it unnerving.

He almost screamed as he came unexpectedly upon a pair of Dartmoor ponies. A few minutes later he stumbled into a stream that he had easily leaped across many times. The water was icy cold and he dared not remain abroad for longer than necessary with his trousers and boots soaking wet.

The return journey was teeth-chatteringly cold, but he made it to his room without further incident, built up the fire in the grate, and spread his wet clothes on the seat and the back of a chair to dry. Then he cleaned his boots as best he could with a towel and stuffed more towels inside to pull out any additional moisture—he had seen Father's valet do this one time when Father and Leighton had both fallen off their rowboat and returned with squelching wet shoes. He set his alarm clock at quarter past six, shortly before the time the maid would come in to sweep the grate and relight the fire, to put away the dried clothes and take the towels out of the boots, so that nothing would appear abnormal.

The next night he managed to get past the stream without getting wet, but had to turn back when he noticed that the stars were disappearing behind clouds. He barely managed to find the house as a dense fog rolled in.

The third night he at last reached his original goal: a tor about two miles from the Rose Priory. He added a rock to the tor and wished he could set down his nocturnal adventures in his letters to Mother.

The next afternoon he returned to his room after his lessons to find that an iron grille had been installed on his window. And a locksmith was working on the door, putting into place a bolt that could be opened only from the outside.

"I hear you are a sleepwalker, young master," said the man from the village who had come to do the work.

Leighton could not understand. How? How had he been found out? He had not seen nor heard any movements in the house when he left nor came back at night. His door had been locked from inside. And there had been no habit on the part of the servants to come and check on him after his bedtime.

He realized his error only when he took his walk in the garden with Mr. Colmes: He had failed to take enough care with the ivy outside his window. It looked trampled, the leaves broken, the vines bruised. He swore under his breath. But it was no use.

He was now a prisoner in Sir Curtis's house.

Nine

The Prisoner

AS AUTUMN DEEPENED INTO WINTER, things did not improve for Leighton.

First, out of concern for his "health," he was dissuaded from walking even in the gardens, since the days were cold and wet. Then his curriculum, hitherto that of a classical education, narrowed to only the study of the Greek Bible. A few days later the locksmith was back in the house, and when he was gone, the library and its two hundred-some volumes of history that Leighton had counted on to last him until his departure to a public school were no longer accessible.

All the changes he accepted numbly, almost meekly—defying Sir Curtis had its cost, and he had known that there would be repercussions. But when Twombley came and took away the books Leighton had brought with him from Starling Manor, many of which had been gifts from Herb, a slow-burning anger at last ignited inside him.

With it arrived the realization that there would be no public school education for him: With its hundreds of potential playmates, a proper curriculum, and a plethora of sports, a school could prove to be far too pleasurable an experience. And Sir Curtis, who had made it plain that there was no such thing as a cruelty too small, would probably cut off his own nose before seeing Leighton enjoy himself.

In a way, it was a relief to at last understand his situation. Now he no longer needed to dread what else would be taken from him. Now he understood the answer to be "everything." Now he could plan his countermeasures.

He would run away—there was no other choice. Either he must break free or he would be slowly crushed under the weight of his shackles.

But how did he break free? Just as important, how did he remain free? He did not have access to his inheritance—nor any other significant sources of money. And even if he could somehow scrape together enough funds, he was a child—a child from a prominent family, no less. There would be a search. And if he were found and brought back, Sir Curtis would make sure that he never escaped again.

In December, Sir Curtis and Lady Atwood returned, as devoted to each other as ever. During their previous stay, Leighton had seen little of either. But Yuletide called for greater family proximity, and on several different occasions he and Mr. Colmes were summoned to keep the master and the mistress company, as the latter admired the newly trimmed tree, dispensed gifts to the servants, and posed for photographs. Sir Curtis even had Leighton sit for a solo portrait, declaring that his mother would treasure such a photograph.

On Christmas day, after the goose had been properly demolished, the company retired to the drawing room to open presents. Leighton received one Bible each from Sir Curtis and Lady Atwood, one in Parsi, one in Arabic.

"And, of course, Mr. Colmes will see to the purchase of the necessary dictionaries and grammar books to help you study the scripture in those languages," said Sir Curtis magnanimously.

Lady Atwood's smile was quite frosty.

Leighton made sure that he seemed barely able to keep his disappointment in check. But in fact he was thrilled. He adored learning new languages, and what better way to do so than with text the meaning of which he already knew?

After the presents had been opened and put away, Lady Atwood asked Mr. Colmes to read aloud from a magazine while she bent over her embroidery frame. Leighton sat in his chair in a corner of the drawing room, waiting for the moment of his dismissal.

But Sir Curtis beckoned him instead. "My dear Master Leighton, will you bring out the chess game?"

When Leighton had, he was instructed to sit down opposite Sir Curtis at the card table and set up the chess pieces.

"Do you know how to play, young man?"

"A little, sir," Leighton answered cautiously.

"Excellent. Let us have a match."

Leighton, playing white, opened with his king pawn. Sir Curtis countered with his own king pawn. Leighton advanced his king bishop pawn. Across the drawing room, Mr. Colmes's voice lovingly described the architecture of the Taj Mahal.

"How are you, my dear nephew?" asked Sir Curtis, as he contemplated his next move.

Leighton tensed. Their previous conversation had begun much the same way—and had not ended well. "Very well, sir. Thank you."

"Enjoying your life at Rose Priory?"

"Yes, sir."

"You are very fortunate, Master Leighton. You are young, you are healthy, and you have a certain restraint in your character that should serve you well."

The compliment only made Leighton warier. "Thank you, sir."

"Not everyone is so lucky. Take Mr. Colmes, for example. Mr. Colmes has never married, but he has a daughter."

An illegitimate child, in other words.

"To compound that mistake," Sir Curtis went on, "he failed to provide the kind of strict, morally uplifting upbringing particularly necessary to children born in sin. The girl ran away from her foster parents and fell in with undesirable company. She began to offer her...time, shall we say, to men. And when she stole from one such man, she was arrested, convicted, and sent to prison."

Leighton wished he could plug his ears—these were things Mr. Colmes would not want anyone to know—but he was forced to listen.

"She was not there for very long, just long enough for her to reflect upon her choices in life. When she was released, she decided that she wished for a respectable life after all. With some help from Mr. Colmes, who probably provided a forged letter of character, she managed to become a companion to a Miss Mulberry in Yorkshire, far from her former haunts in London.

"Her employer is very pleased with her. And after the squalidness of her misspent years, Miss Colmes has quite taken to the wholesomeness of life in a quiet, close-knit village. She sings in the church choir and does the flower arrangements for the altar. I hear there is even a widowed yeoman farmer who is shyly courting her.

"Mr. Colmes, needless to say, is thrilled. He believes that the mistakes of her youth are well and truly behind her, and hopes that her future will be secure. But mistakes of a certain kind never lose their destructive power, do they? Miss Colmes's new life is fragile. The least whisper of her past and it will all come tumbling down."

The relish in Sir Curtis's voice turned Leighton's stomach. How could anyone not wish Miss Colmes well? How could anyone not want her to succeed in her new life? But he knew now that the Sir Curtises of the world only ever saw the mistakes. Miss Colmes would only ever be a prostitute in need of punishment, and any happiness on her part was abhorrent and therefore intolerable.

Sir Curtis took out Leighton's king bishop pawn. Leighton stared at the board, barely able to think. "What will happen to Miss Colmes?"

"Nothing, of course," said Sir Curtis smoothly. "I want Mr. Colmes to focus on his task of educating you."

A lexicon could educate Leighton, since his lessons now derived solely from the Greek testaments.

"As long as he shows himself competent and has you well in hand," Sir Curtis went on, "I will have every incentive to keep him content."

It wasn't until Leighton had moved his knight that Sir Curtis's meaning struck him: If Leighton attempted to run away, Sir Curtis would see to it that Miss Colmes's new life was destroyed. So that even if Leighton managed to escape, he would always carry with him the heavy burden of knowing that his freedom came at the happiness of another.

The chess match ended in a massive loss for Leighton.

SIR CURTIS AND LADY ATWOOD departed for London in the first week of January. A few days later, as Leighton and Mr. Colmes took their afternoon tea, Leighton asked, "Do you have children, sir?"

Mr. Colmes, who had just reached out for a slice of buttered toast, stilled. "I do," he said after a moment, "a daughter who lives in Yorkshire."

Leighton spread clotted cream over his scone, gathering enough gall for his next question. If he was to give up his freedom, he had to make sure it wasn't merely a hoax on Sir Curtis's part, that there indeed was a young woman whose reputation and livelihood were at stake.

He felt sick as he forced himself to ask, "And has Miss Colmes ever been incarcerated?"

Mr. Colmes's chair scraped as he scrambled to his feet. "How...What..." His face turned red; his hands shook visibly. He took a deep breath. "Did one of the servants say something to you?"

"Sir Curtis told me."

"Sir Curtis? But I've never mentioned my daughter to him."

"He knows these things."

"But why? And why does he still employ me if he knows about my daughter's disgrace?" Mr. Colmes made a sound half between a laugh and a moan. "It isn't as if I am so exceptional a scholar that such things can be overlooked."

Mr. Colmes's utter lack of suspicion made Leighton feel almost as vicious as Sir Curtis. "Do you really think my health is so frail that I cannot be allowed outside at all? And do you really believe that I have locks on my door and bars on my window because I am a sleepwalker?"

Mr. Colmes stared at Leighton. "I still don't understand."

"I am here against my will. Against the will of my family. But Sir Curtis knows their Achilles' heel just as he knows yours, and they could not prevent him from taking me away."

"I'm...I'm so sorry." Mr. Colmes sank heavily back into his chair.

"He knows that I don't want to spend the rest of my minority here— and that someday I might succeed in escaping. So he tells me about Miss Colmes to let me know that such action on my part will have consequences."

Mr. Colmes shot out of his chair again, owl-eyed with incredulity— and the beginning of horror. "He is threatening my daughter?"

"Yes."

Mr. Colmes stumbled over to the window and rested his forehead against a pane of glass. Outside snow fell, the moors white and silent. Mr. Colmes had his eyes tightly shut.

"You don't need to worry," said Leighton, his voice seeming to come from somewhere far away. "I won't do anything to jeopardize Miss Colmes's position."

"Thank you, Master Leighton," said Mr. Colmes, his voice muffled, his hands now covering his face. "Thank you."

I know how you feel, Leighton wanted to say. *I know what it is like to not be able to protect those you love. To go through life wishing that you had been able to prevent that one terrible thing from happening.*

But he didn't know Mr. Colmes—or his circumstances—well enough to be so familiar in his manners. And he was only a child, after all.

He ate his scone in silence, fairly certain he would never wish to taste clotted cream again.

A LETHARGY SETTLED OVER LEIGHTON.

He ate very little, slept far more than he ever did, and paid scant attention during his lessons—languages were his natural strong suit, and the Greek Bible posed few difficulties. He read aloud when asked to and answered questions correctly but tersely. Mr. Colmes, possibly even more preoccupied than Leighton, did not challenge him to any greater feats of scholarship.

He even lost interest in Mother's letters. She was still in London, only two hundred miles away, but she might as well be on the rings of Saturn. Besides, she wrote very little that was new—she was fine; Marland was fine; she was waiting for this to finish and that to come through. Her letters had become infrequent. But that was his fault: He hadn't written in a while, unable to muster the energy to present a coherent account of an idyllic life in the country.

From time to time he opened his wardrobe and looked at the place where the books he'd brought from home had once been stacked. And from time to time he stood before the barred window and looked out to the moors, to the open acreage he used to explore at will. At such moments he would feel a faint flicker of something, like the sparks that flew when one disturbed coal that was almost but not quite spent.

Then numbness would reign again, smothering the embers of frustration and longing.

Months passed. He now felt tired as soon as he opened his eyes in the morning. His stomach grew intolerant of anything with actual taste or texture; he subsisted on porridge, broth, and an occasional boiled pudding, from which he discarded all the raisins and candied orange peels.

He stopped paying attention to his lessons altogether. The Parsi Bible lay on his desk, opened to the same chapter of Genesis as it had been for weeks. Beside it sat the latest letter from his mother, already ten days old and still in its sealed envelope.

"Master Leighton," said Mr. Colmes.

They were at their afternoon tea again, with Leighton staring into a cup the contents of which he had been stirring aimlessly. "Yes, Mr. Colmes?"

"Master Leighton, you cannot go on like this."

He had to go on like this; didn't Mr. Colmes see? Spending his days swaddled in apathy was the only way to pass through the years—the only way to keep from being eaten alive by the utter atrocity of it all.

"No, indeed, sir," he said.

Now, why couldn't he have spoken so docilely when Sir Curtis had asked him whether he was sorry about having been surrounded, growing up, by those imperfect people he loved so much? Why did he have to be so proud? Had he been more careful, more calculating, today he might still have the run of the moors. And what wouldn't he give to walk miles and miles without seeing a single soul. What wouldn't he give to fall face-first into an ice-cold stream in the middle of the night!

Anger stirred, a beast with burning claws. It wanted to burst out of his chest. It wanted to grab the fireplace poker and smash everything in the room. And it wanted to take the train to London and use that same poker on Sir Curtis's skull, again and again and again.

Hastily he derailed his train of thought. *Stir the tea. Just breathe—and stir the tea.*

"You mustn't lose hope," said Mr. Colmes.

Leighton almost laughed. He didn't—he was afraid he might cry instead. If only he could go to sleep and wake up to find himself twenty-one years of age, this long, long nightmare behind him.

He stirred his tea.

Mr. Colmes rose, sat down again, and cleared his throat. "After what you told me about Sir Curtis, Master Leighton, I was terrified. Unbearably ashamed, too, about all the mistakes I'd made, which not only led to a trying life for my daughter, but also indirectly to your current difficulties. But mainly I was frightened. So much had gone wrong with Cordelia's life. To see her thrive as she has been of late—I cannot tell you how glad I was. The idea that it could all be taken from her…I was in a state of torment. If Sir Curtis is truly a man as you've described, then she isn't safe, even if you remain meek as a lamb under his thumb.

"Finally I decided to go see her. If there are dark days ahead, I thought she should know—and not be caught unawares. So that was what I did two weeks ago."

Leighton had the vague impression that Mr. Colmes had indeed been gone for a few days this month.

"I arrived on her half day and we went for a long walk. At first her reaction was much the same as mine—perhaps even more extreme. I believe at one point she screamed. At another point she wept. And then, amazingly enough, she shrugged. She said that she had been saving her money, that she always thought it was too good to last, that she had inquired into emigration to Australia on the few occasions when she went to York."

Leighton blinked, feeling as if the light in the room had suddenly become too bright. "She will actually leave the country?"

"She isn't ready to do so yet: There is the matter of funds—and also her promise to her employer that she will stay with her until the end. She asked me to apologize to you for any inconvenience her timetable might cause. I told her I didn't think you were quite ready to run off just yet. Are you, Master Leighton?"

Leighton shook his head, half dazed by the news.

Mr. Colmes continued. "On my way back, I visited Starling Manor."

Leighton jerked. It had been so long since he'd heard that name, the house might as well be on the rings of Saturn, along with Mother and Marland.

"How…how was it?" he heard himself ask, his voice a croak.

"Lovely place. It has been let to an industrialist from the north. The family wasn't in residence at the time of my visit, so the housekeeper conducted me on a tour."

"Mrs. Everly?"

"Yes, the very same. She also gave me permission to wander the grounds. I took the liberty of visiting your father's grave—I thought you'd have wanted me to do that."

Leighton's vision grew blurry. The last thing he had done before leaving Starling Manor was walk to the family cemetery at the first light of dawn—and kiss Father's gravestone.

"And looking down from the cemetery, I saw whole fields of red poppies—an absolutely astounding sight."

Leighton blinked again. The poppies, *blooming*? "It's…it's spring?"

"Not everywhere yet—it was bone-chillingly cold in Yorkshire, but spring has most certainly arrived on the Sussex downs."

A year ago Father, Herb, and Leighton had picnicked on the slope just beneath the cemetery, with that wide vista of brilliant poppies before them. And when Marland had come back from his trip with Mother, Leighton had taken him to play in the poppy fields, the two of them running through the sea of flowers, leaping and laughing.

Tears fell down his cheeks.

"I asked Mrs. Everly about your father," Mr. Colmes went on. "She told me it had been a tragic accident—that his pistol had accidentally gone off while he was cleaning it. But if you will forgive me, that is the excuse one usually gives for a suicide involving a firearm, is it not?"

Leighton nodded.

"Please don't despair as your father did. Please don't throw away your life. You are young, spring is here, and Sir Curtis, for his seeming omniscience, has not counted on my daughter's courage. There is hope yet."

There is hope yet.

At the beginning of their conversation Mr. Colmes had said something similar, but then those had been mere words, trite sounds that had no meaning whatsoever. Now, however, each syllable struck Leighton with the force of sunlight and blue skies.

There is hope yet.

He looked at Mr. Colmes, at this seemingly unremarkable man who had proved to be anything but the timid, useless scholar Sir Curtis had judged him to be.

"Thank you," he said, his voice shaking only a little. "I believe you."

MOTHER'S LETTER, THE ONE THAT had been languishing on Leighton's desk, turned out to also contain significant news.

My dear son,

I write to you from the great city of New York. Yes, we have made the voyage at last.

The passage was not easy for me, but Marland loved every minute we spent at sea. I am glad that our eventual destination is San Francisco, where he will always be within view of the ocean—or so I am told.

Mr. Delany has proposed and I have accepted. But we will make no announcements with regard to our engagement, and we will wait the full two years of my mourning. You may not believe me, but I have the greatest esteem for your father and would never bring whispers of impropriety upon his name—or yours.

I hear Marland. He has returned from Central Park Zoo and no doubt will have tales to tell. He asks about you a great deal. I hope you will write soon. He is always anxious for your news—as am I.

Love,
Mother

P.S. We depart for San Francisco next week, a trip that will take us by rail across the entire continent. Address your letters to the Grand Hotel in San Francisco and they should reach me.

P.P.S. I hope quite fervently that with the passage of time and the increase in distance you will have come to think more kindly of us.

Tears welled up again in Leighton's eyes. They were in America. They were at the beginning of a new life. But more than that, she was reaching out to him. Despite all the cruel things he had said, she wanted him to know that they still considered him very much a part of the family.

There is hope yet.

He read her letter several more times. Then he walked to his window and yanked open the curtains. Spring had arrived here too, the moors a heart-stopping green, the stream in the distance a slender, glittering ribbon under the sun.

The bars were still on the window, but he was no longer a prisoner.

Now he had hope again.

Ten

Chi

EVERY SPRING, ACCOMPANIED BY MOTHER, Da-ren traveled to the hills one hundred and fifty *li* northwest of Peking and ascended the Great Wall. They made a leisurely trip of it, taking as many as six or seven days, so that it would not be too demanding on Mother's health.

Amah had been looking forward to the outing for months. Not that she and Ying-ying ever joined the sightseeing, but because the courtyards would empty completely during that time: Little Plum always went with Mother, and Cook always took the opportunity for an extended visit to her family.

Amah had been teaching Ying-ying hand-to-hand combat stances inside their suite of rooms. As they were limited in both space and privacy, she couldn't train Ying-ying as rigorously as she wanted to. But with everyone else away they could at last practice in the middle courtyard, where there was ample area for maneuvers without having to worry about knocking over furniture or kicking a hole in the window.

The stances were a series of postures that flowed one into the next. Ying-ying had been practicing them in a set sequence. But, as Amah now explained, once mastered, the individual elements would become hers to use as she saw fit, like musical notes on a scale.

The process fascinated Ying-ying: Motions that she had considered choreographed and immutable were suddenly broken down into versatile components. Amah had Ying-ying attempt to hit her with fists, palms, elbows, knees, and sweeping kicks. Then for each of Ying-ying's attacks, she demonstrated a defensive move culled from the same stances, sometimes exactly as it had been taught, sometimes with variations in footwork.

"First you learn how not to get hit," Amah said.

"When am I going to learn how to hit others?" Ying-ying asked, launching another fist.

Amah sidestepped it easily. "Shame, shame. What kind of nice girl wants to hit others?"

Ying-ying couldn't help giggling. "My kind of nice girl."

Amah too, cracked a rare smile. "No wonder we don't have matchmakers lined up to see you."

"Ha!" Ying-ying retorted. "I'm going to be so good at this that my husband will never dare look at another woman."

Amah's smile vanished. Her forearm met Ying-ying's in a strong parry. "You don't know men. The pain of death never stopped any man from sniffing roadside blossoms."

Ying-ying turned on her side and rammed an elbow toward Amah's solar plexus. "Then I will kill him in truth."

Amah formed a saddle with her palms and shoved Ying-ying's elbow out of the way. Ying-ying stumbled back several steps. When she righted herself, she was surprised to see Amah glowering at her.

"Do not speak so lightly of killing."

The corners of Ying-ying's lips bent downward. There was no pleasing Amah these days. "Fine," she mumbled.

Amah didn't comment on the tone of Ying-ying's answer. She shifted her weight onto her back leg, lifted her front foot up on the toes, and beckoned Ying-ying to attack her again. "This time, think of your chi. Starting at the center of your lower abdomen, let it rise through your chest, into your arms."

Since the previous August, on several different occasions Ying-ying had become aware of tantalizing flutterings of heat along various chi paths in her body. But the sensations had been fleeting, small bursts of warmth that afterward she could not be sure had not been her imagination.

So she took a deep breath and imagined—since she couldn't reliably feel her chi—a current of energy sparking out of her midsection like reverse lightning. Front knee bent, back leg straight and low, she threw herself at Amah, thrusting her right fist forward.

And felt the flow in her arm—not a torrent, but much more than a trickle, a steady, forceful stream that coursed along her veins directly into her fingertips. When her fist struck Amah's palm, it was no longer the same contact of flesh and bones, but something both more elemental and more buffered.

"Good!" Amah yelled. "Again!"

Ying-ying needed no encouragement. She swung her fist one more time, and felt again the exhilarating vigor of her chi rushing to her aid. But the same sensation was not there for her left fist. As for her kicks, the situation was reversed, with her chi pulsing smoothly through her left leg but not in her right.

Ying-ying quickly became disgusted with herself. But Amah's excitement spilled over. She had Ying-ying sit down—even went and fetched the cushion herself—and told her she was about to begin a new series of breathing exercises. "When I first started, it took me two years to get to this point. Now concentrate."

Ying-ying sat still, eyes closed, one hand on each knee, palms up, thumbs and middle fingers lightly pressed together. But Amah's instructions did not come. She opened her eyes to find Amah frowning, listening to something with her head tilted.

It was another moment before Ying-ying heard the shouts and the running feet rushing in their direction, a ruckus exactly like that on the occasion of Amah's injury, except without the night watchmen's clappers.

Ying-ying's heart skidded. Had the law come back for Amah? "Leave, Master," she whispered urgently. "If they come to the door, I'll say you went to visit your brother in...in..."

She searched for the name of some faraway province.

"Nonsense," Amah said, and headed for the front gate.

Ying-ying stared after her. And then amid the noises of the men's pounding feet, she heard Little Plum's voice, gasping and panicky. "Don't jostle her, big brothers. Go smoothly, won't you, please?"

Ying-ying started running. She had nearly reached the opening of their blind alley when she had to flatten herself against the wall as a four-man litter, now carried by eight, careened past her.

The men set the litter down before the gate. Ying-ying ran back. Little Plum flapped aside the front curtain of the litter. Inside slumped Mother, her breath coming thin as a thread, her face entirely colorless but for two splotches of bright red on her cheeks.

Amah came out of the courtyard. Little Plum spoke to her. Snatches of their conversation drifted to Ying-ying. *Vomited blood...fainted...had to come back...court doctor on his way*. The two women hoisted a limp Mother to her room, Ying-ying scampering uselessly in their wake.

They settled Mother in her bed, covering her thickly. Little Plum set to work stoking the braziers. Amah rushed off to cook a potion that would help clear the lungs. Ying-ying lingered before Mother's bed, not knowing what to do but loath to leave. She had never seen her mother so helpless, twisting, moaning, shivering, strands of her black hair smeared on the pillow.

Little Plum wiped Mother's face and throat with a warm, damp towel. Then she drew the bed curtains and placed two stools before the bed for the doctor's arrival, one for his esteemed behind, one with a small cushion for mother's wrist, so he could study her pulse.

She shooed Ying-ying out. Ying-ying slunk into the store room, where a clay pot already simmered, with Amah staring at it.

"Will she die?" The question left her lips before she could think better of it.

"Don't ask such things," Amah answered impatiently. Then more softly, "She is still young."

Ying-ying crept out to her own room and sat down on her *kang*.

She wanted Mother to have the time for a hundred more landscape paintings and a thousand more conversations with Da-ren. She wanted to see her change from a beautiful young woman to a beautiful old woman. She wanted her to live long enough in happiness and security that she would never again be haunted by the past.

But she could not give any of those things to Mother. She could only draw her knees to her chest, put her head down, and weep.

Eleven

China

THROUGHOUT SPRING AND SUMMER, LEIGHTON gradually recovered. He was not impatient about it: He had only just turned twelve and he could not realistically go on the run until he at least *looked* old enough to cross borders on his own.

When he was eating properly again and no longer feeling lethargic or dizzy, he began to exercise. Rose Priory was not very big, about a third the size of Starling Manor. But even small distances added up. He walked all the corridors and all the rooms still open to him, and climbed up and down the staircases, putting in about three miles a day.

Inside his room he did calisthenics exercises that Mr. Hamilton, his old tutor, had shown him. He wanted to be strong, but nimble and fast. Not that he thought he would be literally running away—what were steam-powered transports for, after all?—but he needed to be able to sprint, leap, and pivot if he were to elude a grown man chasing after him.

He started again on the Parsi and Arabic Bibles, taking to Parsi much more easily—he simply seemed to have a greater affinity for its structure and vocabulary. He also resumed his church attendance. The village church was where he hoped to speak to Mr. Brown, the post office clerk, before or after the service. But he had to be careful not to appear to single the man out, not while Mr. Twombley was nearby.

It was the middle of autumn before he exchanged more than a nod with the clerk. Another month passed before he learned that Brown was the lead caroler of the village. He promptly invited the carolers to come to Rose Priory, especially since Sir Curtis and Lady Atwood would be spending their Christmas in Italy.

The carolers arrived at Yuletide, the day after the photographer hired by Sir Curtis came to take Leighton's portrait. Mr. Twombley, who had been informed ahead of time, was ready with hot punch, cake, and a donation for the church on behalf of the absent master and mistress. Leighton and Mr. Colmes mingled with the carolers. Leighton spoke to several other church elders before he wended his way to Mr. Brown and complimented him on his singing.

"I'm glad to see you looking so well, young Master Leighton," answered Mr. Brown. "For a while it was said your health suffered."

"I'm glad to be feeling well."

"I'm sure the good people who write you faithfully from abroad must be relieved too."

Interesting—he brought up the topic before Leighton could. "They are," said Leighton.

"I've been admiring the stamps on those letters. The American ones are nice—they are. But the ones that come from farther afield are so much more interesting. How I coveted the stamps issued by the colonial office in Shanghai!"

Shanghai, good gracious. Herb had reached *China*.

Leighton was right: All this time, Herb's letters had been kept from him.

"And the ones from Shanghai aren't even regular British stamps overprinted with local currency, but their very own stamps!" Mr. Brown went on. "You don't suppose, young Master Leighton, that if you were to get duplicates, you might consider trading one of them with me? I've a fairly substantial philatelic collection, some of them quite novel and rare too."

Leighton thought quickly. "I would. Unfortunately, I don't have a collection of my own. But Lady Atwood does, and she has asked Mr. Twombley to send all the stamps to her in London. And you know how Mr. Twombley is—hard to get him to deviate from his duties."

"Oh, I know that, all right."

"But you know what you could do?" Leighton leaned in a little closer and lowered his voice. "You could take the next letter, cut out the stamps, and just give me the rest."

Mr. Brown nearly dropped his glass of hot punch. "But that's a crime, tampering with the Royal Mail."

"Not if you have the recipient's permission. We just don't want Mr. Twombley to know about it. That's all."

Mr. Brown took out a handkerchief and wiped his forehead—it was warm in the drawing room, with the roaring fire and the press of bodies. "Let me...Let me think about it."

Leighton nodded and left him to see to the other carolers, praying that it would be only a matter of time.

BY THE FOLLOWING MARCH, LEIGHTON had reached the New Testaments in the Parsi Bible, the Book of Proverbs in the Arabic Bible, and the end of Leviticus in the Sanskrit Old Testament, which had arrived by post, a Christmas present from Sir Curtis, who had yet to realize that he actually did Leighton a favor with such gifts.

The second Sunday of that month was a miserable day, full of high winds and lashing rain. Leighton and Mr. Colmes took a carriage to church, instead of walking as they almost always did. Still they arrived in the sanctuary with their trousers wet to the knees.

Mr. Brown sauntered up to Leighton and handed him a new hymn book. "A thank-you present for Sir Curtis from the vicar," he said, "for his donation at Christmas."

Any sense of discomfort Leighton felt was immediately forgotten as he saw the small space between the pages—there was something inside, near the very back.

"Thank you, Mr. Brown." He managed to sound normal, even as his heart slammed.

When Mr. Colmes turned around to speak to a yeoman farmer's wife, Leighton slid out what was between the pages—an envelope missing its stamps, with Herb's familiar handwriting—and hid it in his pocket. For the rest of the service he sat with his hand hovering near the pocket, touching it every minute or so to make sure that the letter was still there.

Herb. After all this time.

Sunday dinner, served at Rose Priory after church, had never been so long. Leighton wolfed down everything and waited, barely able to stop himself from tapping his fingers on the table, for Mr. Colmes to finish each course—Mr. Colmes was not a good liar, so they had decided a while ago that it was safer for both of them for him to know as little as possible of Leighton's actual plans.

When they finally rose from the table, Leighton excused himself, climbed to his room, and leaned his back against the door that could not be locked from inside. With shaky fingers, he extricated the letter and unfolded the pages.

My dear boy,

I am still in Shanghai, but not for much longer.

This week I agreed to travel to Peking, to see about teaching English to the sons of an important Mandarin. The Mandarin, whose exact identity I have not been told, had engaged someone from Oxford University. But that gentleman apparently changed his mind and an urgent search had to be mounted for a replacement. There are other qualified men in Shanghai, but they already have their ambitions, professions, and families. I, on the other hand, am unattached, and have no demands on my time.

It would be good for me to remain in one place for some time. I do not want to travel anymore, but I still cannot see myself putting down roots anywhere. My heart belongs always to the Sussex downs. To Starling Manor, where I spent the happiest hours of my life.

Every time I open the world map I carry with me, I wish the Earth were flat and could be folded up like a map. So that wherever I find myself, I would be but one quick crease from touching England again. Would that not be marvelous?

Do please write. I long for your news. When I passed through India I gathered up my courage and wrote to your mother. Thanks to reliable consular mail service, her reply found me in Shanghai a fortnight ago. She informed me that you are well. That you write beautifully of your new home on the moors, of your long walks and little adventures with wild Dartmoor ponies. But I dearly wish to hear directly from you, to know all the details of your new life.

You can write to me care of the British Legation in Peking. Even if in the end I choose not to take the tutoring post, I will most likely stay and explore awhile in that ancient imperial city before I head elsewhere. And of course I will always leave a forwarding address for you.

Your faithful friend,
Herb Gordon

P.S. As thrilled as I was to receive your news from Mrs. Atwood, I was also greatly saddened. For some reason, I had come to believe that perhaps Sir Curtis had instituted a wholesale embargo of mail where you were concerned. But as that was not the case...Have you become angry with me at last for my part in the great disaster? I should be too ashamed to beg for your forgiveness, but I do. Not an hour passes that I do not think of how my recklessness has damaged your life. How it has damaged the lives of so many. I can never make it up to you, but please let me try.

P.P.S. As much as I hate the thought of a deliberate cold shoulder on your part, I still prefer it to the idea that Sir Curtis is somehow responsible for your silence. For years I had blithely dismissed your father's warnings. Now I do not dare put anything past him. Nor can I truly believe, as much as I want to, that the man who had tormented your father so would grant you this easy, picturesque childhood. Has he somehow managed to deceive Mrs. Atwood as to your happiness and well-being? Are you in need of help? If so, please, please let me know.

P.P.P.S. I have drafted and redrafted this letter so many times that my wastebasket overflows with crumpled pieces of paper. Somehow I can never write at any length without all my fears and suspicions leaping onto the page. Please forgive me. I miss you immeasurably.

P.P.P.P.S. Last night I dreamed of the poppy fields just beyond the boundaries of Starling Manor. Do you remember them? Do you remember our picnic there May before last? I woke up with tears on my face.

P.P.P.P.P.S. I feel silly for telling you the following again—I've mentioned it in every one of my letters. You must be quite sick of the repetition by now. But here it goes. When your uncle sent me the pistol, I sat shaking for hours with anguish for Nigel, shame and loathing for myself, and above all fear for you, that you will be under his heel for far too many years, with no buffer between you and his cruelty. For that reason, before I departed England, I left you something. Think of Mr. Cromwell. And remember that I worry that this letter may not reach you. Or at least may not reach you unread.

P.P.P.P.P.P.S. Be well, my dear boy. And please don't think your old Herb is in a constant state of dejection. I am all right. And when I think of you, when I think of how strong and kind you are, it gives me hope. It gives me every hope.

If indeed the world were foldable like a map, Leighton would be in China this very minute to reassure Herb that one of his fears could not be farther from the truth: There was no force in the world strong enough to tear apart the bonds of their friendship.

Upon rereading the letter, something niggled at the back of his mind. He realized after a minute that his mother, in her letters, had never once mentioned any communication from Herb. It was possible that she had withheld that information, but it was much, much more likely that some of her letters had also been intercepted.

He read the letter another few times. Why had Herb mentioned his solicitor? Did he mean that he had left something with Mr. Cromwell in London for Leighton to retrieve? Probably not, giving his warning that he knew this letter might not reach Leighton unread.

It didn't matter too much for the moment. What mattered was that in the midst of his own grief and fear—not to mention the chaos of uprooting his entire existence—Herb had remembered Leighton and planned for what Leighton might need for the future.

Leighton allowed himself to shed a few tears—for sorrow, for hope, and for all the gratitude in his heart.

Twelve

The Bounty Hunter

"BE GOOD," MOTHER SAID TO YING-YING.

She'd become frightfully weak. In the lamplight her face seemed all hollows and shadows. Her hair lay loose on the pillow, the dark strands making her appear even more gaunt.

"Yes," Ying-ying said, holding her eyes as wide open as she could, afraid that if she blinked, her tears would come falling down.

It would not do to cry before those who were desperately ill. She must appear cheerful and optimistic, even if they both knew that those would probably be Mother's last words to her.

As Amah led her out of Mother's rooms, Da-ren strode in. It was the first time that Ying-ying had ever been in his path. She and Amah hastily stepped aside and curtsied. He did not acknowledge them as he hastened to the deathbed of his beloved.

That night Ying-ying did not sleep. Toward dawn Little Plum came, her eyes red, and said that Fu-ren was no more. Da-ren did not leave until past noon. When he came out of Mother's rooms, he had to brace a hand on the doorjamb.

He stood under the overhanging eaves, looking wan, exhausted, and—Ying-ying realized to her shock—infinitely lonely.

She remembered Mother's tone when she'd mentioned the reforms he wanted. She'd been afraid for him, afraid of what might happen if he was thought to be causing too much trouble at court.

He had probably been losing supporters for his cause. And now he had lost his greatest solace in the world.

Da-ren wiped eyes with his sleeve and marched out, calling for Bao-shun as he went.

Ying-ying wept again, this time for him.

MOTHER'S FUNERAL WAS A GRAND MONSTROSITY. Though she had never crossed Da-ren's threshold, she was accorded all the pomp and circumstances of a favorite concubine of a man of his station: twenty Buddhist monks and ten Taoist priests chanting sutras and prayers, a gaggle of hired mourners tossing paper coins high in the air along the route of the procession, and a catafalque so enormous that it took sixty men to carry.

And there was Ying-ying, one lone small relation, swaddled in mourning white, with Amah by her side, Cook and Little Plum a few steps behind, walking the long way from home to the cemetery amid the dolorous music the monks made, the hired mourners' expert bawling, and the grunting and shuffling of the pallbearers.

They burned a small mountain of paper money—special underworld currency—by the fresh mound of her grave. Before they left, they placed bowls of rice before Mother's tombstone, so that she would not go hungry in the afterlife.

"Why does the money need to be burned for her to use but not the rice?" Ying-ying asked Amah on their way back.

Amah said nothing.

A MONTH LATER LITTLE PLUM brought home the man she had been secretly seeing, a jade polisher, and asked Amah for her freedom to leave and marry. She had been in Mother's service for eight years, from the day her family had sold her into domestic work at age twelve. Amah, now the de facto mistress of the household, granted her wish.

Little Plum left on the day of her wedding, all dressed in red, a red veil over her head, in a fancy red sedan chair hired especially for the occasion. Ying-ying cried. Little Plum had been part of the household for as long as she could remember.

Cook, too, departed soon thereafter. Her son's business had prospered. He would not have her toil anymore. She was to go live with him, and be served by her daughter-in-law.

Now, in a compound that could easily accommodate a family of ten plus a multitude of servants, Ying-ying and Amah were the only ones left.

Amah turned out to be not much of a cook. Ying-ying picked at the dishes at dinner and ate mostly plain rice.

"You can try cooking, if you don't like what I make," Amah said one evening.

"Why don't we just hire another cook, and buy another girl to clean?" Ying-ying had been given all the sweeping and dusting. Amah had told her it was good for her sinews to be more active. But still, it was menial work. She didn't care for it.

Amah laid down her chopsticks. "Come with me."

She led Ying-ying to Mother's old bedchamber, opened a locked chest, and took out a yellow cloth bundle. Inside the bundle was a pile of silver ingots, shiny and pretty. Ying-ying sucked in a breath. She had never seen so much money at once.

"This is how much Fu-ren used to receive from Da-ren's treasury every month," Amah said. She took out less than one-sixth of the silver ingots. "This is how much we get now."

Ying-ying bit the inside of her cheek. "Where did you get the silver for Little Plum's dowry then?"

It had been a handsome parting gift.

"Fu-ren was always careful with money. She knew in her heart she'd never see old age. She had some silver set aside for you—for your dowry, in case your luck turned out much better than hers."

"Let's use that money then. Didn't you tell me no one who's anyone would have me for a first wife?"

"Stupid girl. This is for you to live on when you leave here. Or do you really want to live in the wild?"

Ying-ying stared at Amah. What did she mean? Leave? Where? This was her home.

"You don't own these courtyards," Amah said. "Da-ren does. And when he gets himself another concubine or three, he will have need of this place."

Ying-ying was chilled to her toes. "He wouldn't turn me out, would he?"

"He may not—this is a big place. But can you stay on when the new concubines have taken over the best rooms? Can you stand sleeping in the kitchen, and fetching tea and rouge for them all day long?"

She could not imagine it. Mother had meant so much to Da-ren—how could he ever install anyone else in her place? But Ying-ying was coming to realize that things she could not imagine had a way of happening.

"You are right: We should be spare with the silver," she said. "I'll try cooking."

AFTER SOME DAYS OF TRIAL and error, Amah became pleasantly surprised at Ying-ying's culinary output. Her diced vegetables weren't perfect cubes, her sliced meat nowhere near as paper-thin as that prepared by Cook, but she proved herself competent in the kitchen, with a deft sense for combining sauces and spices to create dishes that were robust without being heavy.

"Good," Amah said. "If you can feed yourself, that's one less worry for me."

There were no more lessons in calligraphy, literature, painting, or music, though Ying-ying sometimes plucked at the zither and tried to duplicate the beautiful, clear notes Mother had so effortlessly created.

Amah intensified her training. Before dawn Ying-ying rose for her breathing exercises, circulating her chi throughout her torso and limbs. Hand-to-hand combat came after breakfast. Soon Amah introduced weaponry: poles, steel-spined fans, and then swords, which hitherto had all been hidden in the spaces under her *kang*.

The swords were long, slender, and surprisingly heavy, their cold, deadly beauty at once frightening and fascinating.

"Don't use swords," Amah admonished, "unless you plan to draw blood."

The pole was a good weapon for a beginner, its length offering a defensive advantage. The fan could be used to conveniently incapacitate one's opponent, its even head, when closed, perfectly suited to deliver blows to acupuncture points, which existed along longitudinal and latitudinal paths. Nerves intersected at these nodes; chi pooled. Just as needles could be inserted there to cure diseases and ease internal blockings, force correctly applied served many purposes, from stopping one's own bleeding to utterly disabling an enemy. One could kill a man outright with a hard strike at the Jade Door Point behind the skull, or make him cry like a baby by a subtle but persistent pressure to the Tear Points on the sides of the nose.

Soon Ying-ying was covered with bruises: The pole packed a tremendous wallop; the steel spines of the fans were most unforgiving.

Not to mention that Amah made her practice scaling walls. However, Ying-ying would not be leaping from the ground straight to the rooftop, as she had imagined. Amah scoffed at that idea. Perhaps some venerable lady of the order had been able to accomplish that feat in years far beyond count. But she couldn't. Nor had her own master. Or her master's master.

Instead, Ying-ying was to take a running start, harnessing her chi as far up her person as possible, make for a corner in the walls, and run up half of it, so as to get high enough to hoist herself up the rest of the way.

Her behind quickly became black and blue from falling down splat. Amah drove her pitilessly. "I learned it this way. You will too."

This time, however, there was no inspiring demonstration. Ying-ying wondered whether Amah had completely recovered from her injury, and whether she'd ever be able to run up a wall again.

"Is this how we climb really high walls also?" She wanted to scale the sky-high city walls one day, if only for the adventure of it. She didn't like the thought of running halfway up *that* and crashing back down to earth.

"No, for those we use grapple hooks," Amah answered.

The next night she took Ying-ying outside the city. In the shadow of the looming wall—eight men tall and as many wingspans thick—she showed Ying-ying how that was done.

When spring came at last and the ponds and lakes thawed, Ying-ying practiced skipping rocks. Amah watched and made occasional adjustments to her technique. She didn't want a toss but a flick. She was interested in the flexibility and strength of Ying-ying's wrists. After Ying-ying could make every pebble skip five or six times across the surface of the water, the exercise changed to hitting targets at ten paces, mostly other rocks, then circles Amah drew on walls and tree trunks, then individual leaves in trees. When she could hit designated leaves with some accuracy, her target turned to living things.

Amah took her into the hills and fields of the countryside. There Ying-ying did her best to strike at crickets, lizards, moths. Amah also made her chase after hares, groundhogs, porcupines, any creatures that came across their path. "Remember your breath! Gird your chi! Circulate it high!"

But mostly Ying-ying remained within the confines of home. And whenever she went anywhere, Amah was always careful to give the outing legitimacy by claiming that she was taking Ying-ying to visit Mother's grave or Mother's favorite temple to pray for her in the underworld.

For it was important to keep Da-ren satisfied that Ying-ying was being brought up in a correct manner. The property belonged to him, and by extension, so did Ying-ying.

He visited once a month, on the seventh, to sit by himself in Mother's old rooms, which Amah kept spotlessly clean and exactly as they had been when Mother had been alive. Before he left each time, he'd summon Ying-ying and Amah to him and inquire briefly into

Ying-ying's doings. Amah responded artfully and mostly truthfully and said Ying-ying had been learning household management, culinary arts, and needlework (firing clusters of golden needles from between her fingers, an intricate and daunting task).

The interviews unnerved Ying-ying. For as long as she could remember, he had been at the center of her life. And part of her felt that she knew him as well as any daughter could know a father: She shared his grief and she understood how lonely and embattled he must feel, with the political climate turning against his ideas.

But he, severe and aloof, always spoke to her as if she were a complete stranger.

Sometimes, after he left, she would remain in Mother's room with a stick of Mother's favorite incense slowly turning to ashes, and wonder why those who should be each other's closest companions remained as if on two shores of a deep, wide sea.

ONE SPRING NIGHT, SIX MONTHS after Mother's passing, Ying-ying shuddered awake from a dream of Mother, in her morbidly exquisite funeral clothes, gurgling up spurt after spurt of blood, splattering splotches and streaks of red all over herself.

With a shaking hand she wiped away the damp perspiration from her neck and her chest. Had the dream been a message from Mother's ghost? Did ghosts get sick? If so, how could she and Amah get some medicine to her? Should they burn the herbs along with a prescription for how to prepare the potion, or should they prepare the potion and then pour it over Mother's grave?

Ying-ying couldn't go back to sleep. The least sound, even that of her movement on the straw mat, made her heart pound. She was ashamed to be afraid of her own mother's ghost—Mother had never harmed a living creature when she had been alive. But Ying-ying was frightened nonetheless.

She got up and put on her slippers. She would go sleep with Amah. Amah now slept in the same room Bao-shun had used. The *kang* there was big enough for both of them.

But Amah was not there. Ying-ying stared at the empty bed. The door slammed. She jumped and screamed, looking around for a weapon while furiously praying it wasn't a ghost, as the weapons of mortals didn't work on ghosts, and she knew nothing of necromancy.

But it was only a gust of wind. She stood panting, momentarily relieved, but no less afraid. Where was Amah? Surely she had not gone out again. Didn't she remember what had happened to her?

Ying-ying lit a candle. Shielding the flame with her cupped hand, she went from room to room, her heart thumping, mumbling whatever incantations she could remember, calling for protection on the Jade Emperor, the Supreme Old Lord, the merciful and compassionate bodhisattva Kuanyin.

No ghost seized her. No signs of Amah. Where was she? Had she been injured again? Ying-ying didn't even know where to look for her if she were lying somewhere in a pool of her blood. She paced around the courtyard until the chill of the night forced her back into her own room. She blew out the candle, crawled under the covers, and waited.

It seemed that she spent hours sitting up at every noise. But the next thing she knew, Amah was at her side, waking her and telling her to dress and begin her breathing exercises. Ying-ying stared at her. Amah looked little different from other mornings, except for darker circles under her eyes. Her hair was neatly oiled and pulled back, her clothes fresh and unwrinkled. And if she noticed Ying-ying's strange look, or the candle that had burned down to a puddle of wax on the table, she said nothing.

For the next month and half, as far as Ying-ying could tell, Amah stuck to the courtyards at night. Then she again stole out by herself. Then she was gone two nights in a row the next month.

The next morning, as Ying-ying stood in the kitchen, chopping vegetables, she recalled something Cook had said long ago.

Cook had told Little Plum that her cousin Old Luo had seen Amah once at a gambling den. Little Plum had scoffed at the reliability of the witness: Old Luo was notorious for his bad eyesight. But not only that, Amah was well-known to be dead set against gambling. She had repeatedly warned Ying-ying that it was a slippery slope leading straight to crime and penury. The claim had been promptly dropped as being too ridiculous even for a rumor.

Now Ying-ying wasn't so sure. Old Luo's eyes were faulty, but he wasn't blind. If he saw Amah up close, there was no reason for him not to recognize her, nor to mistake her for anyone else. After all, the few times he had come to the kitchen, he had never mistaken Ying-ying for one of Boss Wu's apprentice boys.

A horribly disloyal thought erupted in her head. If Amah did gamble, was she gambling with their monthly stipend from Da-ren, or worse, Ying-ying's inheritance?

The key to the chest was in the bottom of Mother's big trunk. When she lifted the lid of the chest, the taels of silver and the ropes of coins were exactly where they were, in cloth bundles and a silk-lined redwood box. The silver certificates, from several of the most reputable clearinghouses, lay safe and crisp in a volume of *Analects*.

She returned to the kitchen, somewhat reassured. The idea was stupid. When Da-ren came every month, he must check on their store of currency to gauge whether they had been thrifty or profligate. Amah wasn't dumb enough to touch that money.

She was reading too much into it. It might not be gambling at all. Perhaps Amah enjoyed midnight strolls. Perhaps she had a man she liked somewhere. Perhaps there was some interesting and dangerous technique she could practice only out in the wild.

The front gate creaked. Amah had come back from the morning market with fresh pork for lunch. She entered the kitchen. Ying-ying went over to her to relieve her of her market basket.

She tripped on a low stool that she had forgotten to put away. Her arms flung out. One of her hands grabbed Amah's right arm to hold herself upright. Amah cried out in pain and dropped her market basket. Ying-ying hastily pulled her hand back.

"Are you all right, Master?"

Amah's face had gone white. "I'm fine. It's nothing."

How could she have caused so much pain to Amah with a simple grip? Ying-ying glanced down at her hand. She gasped. There was a faint smearing of red on her palm and fingers. Blood. She looked at Amah's sleeve. It was a dark brown that showed nothing.

"Why are you bleeding?"

"I cut myself during practice. The blood might have soaked through the bandage," Amah said brusquely. "Have you finished cutting all the vegetables yet?"

A novice such as Ying-ying might cut herself with her own sword. But Amah? "No, not quite."

"Wash your hands. Hurry up and finish."

They were both silent during lunch, with Ying-ying peering at Amah's arm. Amah had changed her clothes, and presumably her bandage, as no bloodstain seeped through her gray blouse-tunic.

What was she up to? And what would Ying-ying do if one morning she woke up to find that Amah had not come back? She had no one else.

"I haven't been sleeping very well lately," she said. "I don't know why. Is Master sleeping well?"

Amah's face was inscrutable. "I sleep very well. If you have trouble sleeping, I'll make you a potion."

"No, no, Master mustn't trouble herself. It's not that bad."

They did not speak again for the remainder of the day.

ON THE ANNIVERSARY OF MOTHER'S passing, Da-ren came and summoned Ying-ying and Amah before him.

"She is not a child anymore." As usual, Da-ren addressed Amah, as if Ying-ying weren't there. "Two females living alone—it is not a safe or desirable arrangement for the long term."

Ying-ying raised her head in surprise. The arrangement had lasted a year, long-term enough in her view. And he had never before said anything about its suitability or lack thereof. Unless...

His wife had died two months ago. The dowager empress's favorite cousin had been a demanding and jealous woman. But now that she was gone...

Da-ren lifted the lid of his teacup and took a sip. "It's time you came to live with me."

Ying-ying was stunned. Was he acknowledging her existence at last? The bond they shared via their love for Mother?

Amah curtsied. "Da-ren's kindness is boundless. We hardly know how to express our gratitude. But I fear it would inconvenience you too much. And we are lowly, uncouth beings, hardly suitable for the exalted life in your esteemed residence."

"No more uncouth than some who have lived under my roof," Da-ren replied. "I will not compel you. But I believe you will see the wisdom of my preference."

In other words, they would be complying with his wishes in short order.

They bowed and curtsied him off, Ying-ying all afluster.

Amah caught her in her bedroom, flinging clothes into a big trunk. "What are you doing?" Amah asked coldly.

"Packing." Ying-ying almost danced as she tossed in another handkerchief.

"We are not going anywhere."

Ying-ying stared at Amah. Amah *had* to politely decline Da-ren's offer. That was how one spoke during social discourse. An invitation must be extended again and again before it was gratefully accepted. But surely Amah could not refuse in the end. "Da-ren wants us to go."

"You won't like living in his household. There will be many rules. You will chafe, untrammeled creature that you are."

Ying-ying didn't like that characterization at all. She preferred to think of herself as her mother's daughter, graceful and beautifully comported. "There have always been rules in this house too, and I've done just fine."

"We won't be able to practice freely."

"Then we'll be more careful."

"I hear Da-ren has bratty sons, spoiled by their late mother. They will pester you."

"Only if they can catch me." Ying-ying scooped up an armful of blouses.

The look Amah gave her was full of both pity and alarm. "Well, in that case, you may go. But I shan't be going with you."

That brought Ying-ying to a complete standstill. "What?"

"You heard me," Amah said. "I won't be going with you."

"Of course you have to come with me."

"No," Amah's said resolutely. "I will not go into Da-ren's household. If you want to remain with me, you remain with me. If you want to live with him, you live with him. You cannot have both."

Ying-ying's voice rose. "Why? What's wrong with Da-ren's household?"

"I have no need to explain it to you."

Ying-ying set down the stack of blouses in her hands, struck by a stray thought. "Does this have anything to do with your disappearances at night?"

Amah's expression changed. "Don't ask such questions."

"I didn't—for two years I've kept my mouth shut. But if you are going to force me to choose between you and Da-ren, then I must know why."

Amah shook her head. She often shook her head at Ying-ying—more when Ying-ying had been younger—but this time it didn't feel like exasperation or resignation on her part. Rather, Amah seemed simply...unhappy.

"One of these days I am going to find out. So you had better tell me now," said Ying-ying.

Amah was not the only one who could be implacable.

Amah exhaled. "Fine. I will tell you. But you will not repeat what is said here. Do you understand?"

All at once, Ying-ying felt sick to her stomach. Did she really want to know, after all? *Dig long enough and you'll always find things you wish you hadn't,* Amah had once told her. Was she about learn something that she would wish to unlearn as soon as she'd heard it?

She nodded slowly, making her promise of silence.

"It was at Da-ren's residence that I was injured," said Amah.

Ying-ying gaped at her, remembering the jade tablet that had fallen from her shirt all those years ago. "What were you doing there?"

"It doesn't matter. The point is that I fought someone inside Da-ren's residence, someone who most likely lived there."

Da-ren had martial-arts instructors for his sons, just as he had Confucian masters for them. It wasn't so surprising that someone who lived there had the skill to fight—and injure—Amah.

It was only dismaying to wonder what she must have been up to. Ying-ying would not deny it: She considered herself a bit above the rules. After all, they weren't exactly ordinary women leading ordinary lives. But then, neither were they engaged in criminal activities.

Or so she had believed.

Hoped.

"It was too dark for me to see him, and he couldn't have seen my face," continued Amah. "But we battled once. If we were to clash again, within three exchanges we would recognize each other."

"But why would you want to fight him again?" Ying-ying's voice came out thin and shrill.

"I don't. But you don't suppose I was the only one injured that night, do you? I dealt him a heavy blow too. If he realized who I was, do you think he would stand by and do nothing? " Amah sighed. "You see now why I can't go there?

"You are not a small child anymore. By your age, many girls are already married and living under their in-laws' roofs, with no one to care for them except themselves. Move to Da-ren's, if you want. In the long term, he is the better choice. Even if he falls out of favor at court, he is still a prince of the blood, still a man who commands respect wherever he goes. Whereas I..."

Amah trailed off. After a moment she said, "What are you still doing here? Dinner doesn't cook itself."

THAT NIGHT YING-YING COULDN'T SLEEP.

She wanted so much to be useful to Da-ren. Were she in his household, she could become the daughter he never had: listening to him after he'd had a long, trying day, playing games of chess with him to help him relax, and accompanying him when he went to sweep Mother's grave.

But could she really go without Amah?

She wanted to think of herself as capable and grown-up, but she'd never been a day without Amah's protection. And the thought of being alone, of facing the entire world by herself, made her quake inside.

She was at last dozing when she heard the sound of running feet on distant roof tiles. More than one set of feet. She jerked awake. Either there were two night thieves in the neighborhood at the same time or...

Someone skilled in the art of lightness was successfully following Amah home.

She crept to the window and opened it a crack—the small, thin mother-of-pearl squares set into the window frame let in light during the day, but weren't exactly transparent. A masked person leaped down from the roof into the courtyard, rolled to a standing position, and immediately ran under the nearest walkway. Amah. She crouched down in the darkness and waited. An instant later, another black-clad, masked person jumped into the courtyard. A man this time, by the looks of it.

Ying-ying leaped back from the window. Wildly she looked about the room. But there were no real weapons. The swords, the steel fans, and even the poles were always put back in their secret places under the storeroom *kang*. She grabbed a handful of copper coins that she had been using to practice extinguishing candles at ten paces.

In the courtyard, Amah fired a burst of needles, barely visible in the light of the half-moon, at the man. He cartwheeled to the left. Amah flung a second cluster, forcing him right, while she launched a third stream to catch him in the middle. He leaped high in the air, somersaulted, and landed without a scratch.

"Is this all you can do, mending my shirt?" He laughed coldly.

The next moment he unsheathed a cruel-looking broadsword only a little shorter than Ying-ying and bounded headlong onto the shadowy walkway where Amah had hidden herself. Ying-ying squinted and saw two flashes—Amah had pulled out her twin swords.

The weapons chinked, clanged, and sometimes braced in silence while the two contested their strength. One moment Amah would jump onto the low balustrade to attack her opponent from a greater height; the next they were circling a pillar. It was obvious Amah hoped to stay under the walkways—she had the advantage of knowing the courtyard better in the dark. But it was equally obvious that her enemy was cunning. He continually framed his thrusts and hacks to force her out in the open, where it was brighter, and where, other than the willow tree, there was nothing for her to hide behind.

Amah's quickness astonished Ying-ying. Her swords slashed and wheeled like the wings of an iron eagle. The man, however, was as agile and skillful as she.

And stronger.

Ying-ying shook. She wanted to help, but she didn't know whether she would make matters worse.

They were now in the courtyard. The man wielded his broadsword freely, no more worries about it being stuck in a window frame or a pillar. Every opportunity he had, he swung against Amah's left side, her weaker side. The crush of metal on metal jarred Ying-ying's eardrums. The coins in her hands jangled.

The coins.

His next downward stroke sent Amah's left-hand sword flying.

Silently, Ying-ying came out her door.

Amah saw her. She fought with renewed vigor, leading with her footwork so that the man had his back to Ying-ying.

Ying-ying closed her eyes tight for a moment. Then she opened them wide and flicked her first coin. It caught the man squarely on the shoulder of his sword arm, right on the spot. His arm sagged, the broadsword falling from his hand. Without waiting, Ying-ying launched two more, hitting him on either side of his lower back, partially disabling his legs.

Amah kicked him in the abdomen. He staggered back. Ying-ying struck him along points on his thighs and calves. He fell with a loud thump. Ying-ying sank to her own knees, breathing heavily, trying to remember in which room they kept the ropes.

But to her horror, Amah advanced on the man and drove her sword through his heart. The man groaned and jerked, his right foot twisting and shaking as if possessed. After what seemed to be an eternity, Amah pulled her sword out and wiped the darkly stained blade on the man's tunic.

Ying-ying's mouth open and closed uselessly. When she finally found her voice, her scream came out as no more than a vehement whisper. "Why did you kill him? I thought you taught me not to kill."

"I taught you not to kill lightly," Amah answered coldly, even though her breaths, too, came in short bursts. "He is a bounty hunter. If I didn't kill him, he'd have turned me in."

A bounty hunter? Ying-ying's head spun. "There is a bounty on you? Why is there a bounty on you? Are you a..."

Amah waited, as if daring her to complete her sentence.

"You *are* a gambler, aren't you?" Ying-ying's voice rose with her anger. She had heard talk of what inveterate gamblers did. They'd sell their wives and children. They'd even sell their mothers. What was a little thievery then? "You steal things so you can gamble. And you got caught tonight."

Amah exhaled heavily. "I always said you were a clever girl."

"Not clever enough to know not to take up with you!" Ying-ying shot back.

Amah laughed bitterly. "Of course I'm a fool for gambling. I don't need you to tell me that. But stealing? I forgot to tell you. It's what we do, those of us who belong to the Order of the Shadowless Goddesses. We are women who have no family, no husbands, no children. We don't farm and we don't embroider. How do you think we survive?"

Ying-ying was speechless for a second. "You never told me I was joining a band of common thieves."

Amah stopped laughing. She let go of her sword. It fell to the paving stone with a clang. For a moment she stood motionless. Then she came toward Ying-ying. Ying-ying cringed a little, expecting to be hit. But Amah only knelt down and made to cup Ying-ying's face in her blood-spattered hands. Ying-ying recoiled.

Amah pulled back. Suddenly she looked much older. "You didn't. I may have become a common thief, but that's my own fault."

She slumped to her haunches. For a long time silence reigned. And when Amah spoke again, her voice was as Ying-ying had never heard it before, soft, almost dreamy. "You've never seen our secret abode in Mount Hua in the south. Such a beautiful place. Clouds floating in valleys, green-and-black peaks, waterfalls thin as threads that disappear into the mist. The locals built a shrine to us halfway up the mountain. Because when we sold what we stole—and we stole only rare and beautiful things worthy of our skills—we kept a small portion for ourselves and gave all the rest to those in need on the plains and the foothills, especially the women. They really believed we were benevolent goddesses."

"Is it still there? The abode?" Even though she'd prefer to keep a stony silence, Ying-ying couldn't help asking. Amah had never before told her anything about her own past.

"It probably is, but it was falling into disrepair even when I was growing up. When a house is five hundred years old and inhabited by people who didn't like to fix roofs and walls, well, it'd go to pieces like that."

"Is anyone still living there?"

Amah shook her head. "I was the youngest, the only disciple of my generation—the order had been in decline for generations. The others were already old women before I left. They must be dead by now."

"Why did you leave?"

Amah closed her eyes. "I didn't leave. I was expelled."

Ying-ying thought nothing else could surprise her. But this did. If Amah had been expelled from the order, then Ying-ying was not a legitimate member either. "Why?"

"Because I took up with a man, and that was forbidden." She wiped her hands on her tunic and glanced at Ying-ying. "You want to ask me where this man is now."

Ying-ying remained silent, the paving stones of the courtyard icy under her knees.

"He was the first man I killed. I gave up my entire life for him. He loved me for six months, hooked me on gambling, and took up with another woman." Amah paused, her hands balling into fists. "After that I fled to Shanghai, because no one knew anyone in Shanghai. I found work in a foreign devil's house, your father's, and that was how I came to know your mother."

Though Ying-ying had joked with Amah about hitting others and killing unfaithful lovers, she had only ever considered her study of martial arts as a matter of self-defense, so she could avoid a fate like Mother's, of being passed around like chattel with no say in the matter. But now she saw that it was a double-edged sword. If Amah didn't possess the skills she did, would she have undertaken all her dangerous and criminal deeds? And would Ying-ying become similarly careless when she grew up, trusting that she would be able to extricate herself from any peril, until she couldn't?

"Get up now," Amah said. The moment of sentiment had passed; she had returned to her old, unemotional self. "We have to be rid of the man."

"Where?" Ying-ying demanded. They couldn't throw him down a neighborhood well and curse the water for the surrounding folk. Nor could they simply leave the body before the door of some courtyard or shop; that would be considered devastatingly bad luck for those within.

"Doesn't matter. First we get him out of here."

They fashioned a crude body bag from the burlap sacks that had held their supply of cabbages the previous winter. The man was heavy as a nightmare and turned corners most unwillingly. At every bump in the road, his skull made hideous noises against the cobblestones. Ying-ying jumped at every thud, convinced that all the night watchmen within a three-*li* radius must have heard.

It was nearly dawn when they returned home. The courtyard itself had to be scrubbed clean of blood. Then Amah fed her clothes to the kitchen fire while Ying-ying crouched to the side, vomiting into a slop bucket.

Amah handed Ying-ying a warm towel when Ying-ying had at last emptied the contents of her stomach.

Ying-ying wiped her mouth. "That jade tablet—you stole it from Da-ren?"

Amah said nothing. Was that why at one point she had been distracted before Da-ren's visits? How many times had she gone to Da-ren's residence before she found the jade tablet?

"Would the bounty hunter have been so hard for you to handle if you hadn't been injured over that theft?"

Amah glared at her. "What are you going to say next? That I risked so much for something that hardly seems spectacular? You know nothing, girl. The jade tablet holds clues to the location of a great treasure—I heard Da-ren speak to your mother about it."

And that treasure would last Amah how long? Half a year of gambling?

Amah had been the bulwark between Ying-ying and the more awful fates that could so easy befall an orphan girl, someone she could turn to even if Da-ren should abandon her altogether someday. But no more, now that she had shown the other side of herself, a gambling addict who would do anything to feed her habit, who could not be counted on to control herself even after she had sustained a life-threatening injury.

Ying-ying got up slowly. Her legs were stiff and heavy; her heart seemed to weigh as much as the dead man they had left at a crossroads. "I've made up my mind. I'm going to Da-ren's as soon as possible."

Amah passed a hand over her face. "I'll go with you. I'm not safe here anymore."

"What?!" cried Ying-ying. "Are you going to bring bounty hunters to his place too? And what would happen when he finds out that you stole his prized possession? You'll ruin everything for me. I won't have you—"

The slap came so hard that for a moment she could see nothing.

"Shut up," Amah said hoarsely. "I will ruin nothing for you. You will hate living at Da-ren's residence. Mark my word. You will hate it."

Thirteen

The Foreign Devil

"IT'S...IT'S...IT'S SUCH DIMINUTIVE EXQUISITENESS," Ying-ying made herself say.

The courtyard Da-ren had assigned to them was small, but hardly exquisite: four plain walls, a patch of packed earth, and a few unprepossessing rooms. It had nothing of the spaciousness and charm of her old home—no trees, no flowers, no gossamer-finned goldfish. A few chunks of rock, rejects from some artificial hill, squatted forlornly in one corner.

"My amah is an expert gardener," Ying-ying said to the majordomo, as Amah stood by silently. "She can put in some chrysanthemums now and in spring some peony bushes and maybe even a few cherry saplings. That is, if you will be so kind, Master Keeper Ju."

"I will see what the gardeners can spare," the majordomo said coolly. "Now come with me to present yourselves to Da-ren."

Da-ren's compound was large, and the enclosed courtyard set aside for Ying-ying was but one of a number inside. Some of the other courtyards looked as disused as hers, but a few were neat and pretty, dotted with dozens of potted plants, with round painted silk fans scattered on chairs, games of chess and *go* spread on tables under the eaves, and birdcages swaying gently from the latticework bracings of the walkway.

Da-ren had no daughters, so those courtyards must be where his new concubines lived. She felt an ache for Mother. Had she been replaced in his heart? Did he love someone else now?

They came to a garden near the northwestern corner of the compound. A fine-boned pavilion, set against a steep artificial hill slightly taller than it, perched at the edge of a lotus pond. Leading away from the pavilion was a miniature marble bridge that arched over the pond. Gold and silver koi glided lazily between lotus stalks. Long-legged cranes ambled beneath plum trees.

The last of the water lilies had already bloomed. Only a few faded heads remained, their once pink-and-white petals brown and withered about the stems. Mother would have found this view a perfect tableau for a black-ink painting, *A Scene in October*.

To complement the autumnal ambiance, a man sat in the pavilion, turning pages of a volume of poetry, a flagon of spirits on the round stone table before him, his face invisible behind a pillar.

He must be a household scholar. All grand households hosted a number of them. They served as advisers to the master, tutors to his children, and general sycophants. Ying-ying would not have given him a second look had his shoes not caught her eye. They were made of shiny leather and had horribly stiff-looking soles, like those on the feet of the foreign devil in Mother's photograph.

She wanted a better look at the household scholar's face. But now her view of him was entirely obstructed by the rock hill. As she progressed around the pond, following in the majordomo's wake, gradually he became visible again. First his shoes, then his long, plain blue tunic, and at last his head.

She stopped dead in her tracks. A real live foreign devil, with hair the color of straw! To say he looked like the man in the photograph was to say that she looked like Amah. But he looked more like that man than anyone else she had ever seen.

She stared, unable to help herself. He glanced up and caught her gawking at him. She would have glared had she caught anyone staring so baldly at *her*. But he seemed to find nothing egregious or even noteworthy in her rabid attention. He nodded and turned his gaze back to his book, as if he could comprehend Chinese.

Amah pulled on her. Ying-ying shook free and started walking again. But her eyes remained glued to the foreign devil, until she had gone through a moon gate into a different courtyard and an intervening wall once again obscured him from her sight.

It became Amah's turn to stand still. She scanned the courtyard, her face tense. But there was no one there and the courtyard, with its prolific jade-green bamboos and a meandering stream, appeared perfectly peaceful and contemplative, just the sort of environs one would expect for a gentleman's study.

Ying-ying was about to tug on Amah's sleeve when understanding dawned. Was this where Amah had met the other martial-arts expert and became injured?

Amah took a deep breath and resumed walking. Together they caught up to the majordomo.

Da-ren's study faced south, to take advantage of the light and warmth of the sun's natural progress in the sky. The furnishings were spare and elegant: a writing desk, a few chairs, and Mother's zither, which he had sent a pair of servants to fetch the day before Ying-ying and Amah's move. On the north wall hung a large black-ink landscape, beside it two calligraphy scrolls bearing words that praised duty and love of country—Mother's artworks, each of which bore the vermilion imprints of several of her personal seals.

An intense relief came over Ying-ying: Da-ren might have new concubines, but Mother remained the love of his life. A moment later, a searing pain in her heart: He would always grieve for the one he had lost too soon.

More than ever she wished she could comfort him.

Along the east and west walls were intricately latticed shelves displaying rare and beautiful objects of jade, porcelain, and bronze. Each set of shelves was divided into four quadrants around a central niche. Notably, the central niche on the west wall was empty, as if Da-ren hadn't quite found the item to cap his collection.

Or perhaps he had. Perhaps that was the place the jade tablet Amah had stolen had once occupied.

Da-ren sat beneath a calligraphy scroll, reading a dispatch. He did not look up when they came in, and set aside the dispatch only after the majordomo approached him and, bent from the waist, informed him of their obvious presence.

Ying-ying's stomach tightened. When he looked at her, did he ever see her resemblance to Mother? Their faces were the exact same shape—and she had Mother's brows and lips.

She moved a step toward him and curtsied low. "This lowly maid has come to offer her humble greetings and deep gratitude to Da-ren."

"Rise," he bade her.

She obeyed, her head still lowered. Mother had drilled into her that women should be, or at least appear, meek and sweet-tempered. "Thank you, Da-ren."

Da-ren said nothing more for a while, until her neck was beginning to feel strained. From the corner of her eye she spied the majordomo leaving. Only when the man had gone beyond earshot did Da-ren speak again. "The great debt you owe your mother, you do realize?"

"Yes, Da-ren."

"You are alive only because she was too soft of heart."

117

She quailed. He had to be referring to her brush with death as an infant, something that still made her shiver whenever she thought of it.

"I cannot fault her for her kindness," Da-ren went on, his tone severe. "But you were a constant burden to her."

Ying-ying's ears rang. She had always wished Da-ren would speak directly to her, but she had not thought that when he finally did, it would be only to remind her that everyone's life would be less complicated had she never been born, the bastard girl with no prospects other than becoming someone's third concubine, and one whose temperament seemed certain to make a disaster even of that.

"Da-ren is right, of course." She forced the words past her lips, though what she felt was not humility, only humiliation. "I will keep Mother's magnanimity and Da-ren's generosity always foremost in mind."

"Good." But there was little approval in his tone. "Reflect often on what you owe your mother's memory. Squander not your time in frivolities. Become as your mother would have wished."

"Yes, Da-ren."

"Look after her strictly," he spoke to Amah. "Be not spare with discipline."

"Yes, Da-ren." Amah curtsied. "Thank you for your sage instructions, sir."

"You may leave," he said. "And you need not come every day to offer your greetings."

In other words, unless summoned again, they were not to disturb him for their own purposes.

Silently they made their way out. When they passed the garden, the pavilion was empty, the foreign devil gone. The faded lotus heads shivered in a sudden gust of cold wind.

Winter was in the air.

"He had to speak like that," said Amah. "Now that he has taken you into his home, you will remain his responsibility until the day you marry—or until the day one of you is no more. Heavy words now are better than heavy words too late. And for a girl like you, only words as heavy as mountains have a hope of holding you in place."

Ying-ying said nothing. She could find no solace in Amah's explanation. And with every step she took, she crushed a few more of her own hopes underfoot.

THE BOUNTY HUNTER LAY ON the ground, gasping his last breaths, his foot twitching maniacally. But instead of looking on from the side, Ying-ying was now the one holding the sword, drops of gleaming, black-red blood trickling from its tip. As she glanced up, still shaking with the fright and relief of the kill, none other than Da-ren materialized beyond the dying man. His gaze horrified her. The sword fell from her grip. She dropped to her knees, bowed her head to the ground, and tried incoherently to explain. But when she looked up, he was already gone.

She jerked awake and slowly sat up, relieved that the dream was over, but dreading the long hours of the day.

Nothing had gone right since Amah killed the bounty hunter. Nothing.

Each night, a manservant came to lock the gate to their courtyard—from the outside. Not until the arrival of breakfast would it be unlocked. Amah pointed out that it was how things were done in all lordly homes. That did not make it less offensive to Ying-ying, this assumption that unless she was locked up, she would be indulging in wildly inappropriate behaviors.

She had thought her movements restricted and her person carefully watched since birth, a fish in a small pond. But a fish in a pond had greater freedom than a fish in a bowl—what she had become now.

Worse, she was no longer the daughter of the house, but a nobody. Amah had predicted as much. But nothing could have prepared Ying-ying for how much of a nobody she had become.

"May I go for a walk today?" she asked, giving a listless stir to her breakfast porridge. The food was not bad, but she hadn't the appetite.

The same request she had made daily since their arrival a fortnight ago. Amah had always denied it. She thought it a bad idea for Ying-ying to be prancing around when she ought to impress everyone as timid and uncurious. So she kept Ying-ying inside and tried to teach her about medicinal herbs, which bored Ying-ying to no end.

"May I?" Ying-ying pleaded, but without much energy. She had no real hope. She was imprisoned between these walls until the day Da-ren informed her that he was gifting her to a crony. And then she would have to escape to the wilds, to be plagued by outlaws, mountain cats, and head lice, never to sleep in a proper bed again.

"I won't trouble anybody. I won't let Da-ren's sons see me. And I most certainly won't let anyone guess I've been studying the martial arts," she droned.

"Fine, then," Amah answered almost nonchalantly, her chopsticks stretched out toward a dish of pickled radish. "But you can't go until you've eaten properly."

Ying-ying goggled at her, astonished. Then she grabbed a steamed bun and began shoving it into her mouth, afraid that if she didn't eat and slip out fast enough, Amah would change her mind.

THE VOICES WERE SOFT, THE laughter playful. Ying-ying stopped. No woman she knew had ever laughed that way, at least not within her earshot.

Keeping to her promise to Amah, Ying-ying had stayed away from the more populated areas of the compound. She was now near the southwestern corner, in a narrow alley that led from a row of storerooms to what she thought might be the stables.

She crept to where the alley intersected an equally narrow path that was likewise walled on both sides. A quick glance revealed a man and a woman standing close together, their backs to her, less than a stone's throw away.

Ying-ying flattened herself against the wall behind her. She was old enough to know that she had stumbled upon a situation that did not welcome intruders. But her curiosity outweighed her sense of propriety. She perked her ears.

"Good sister," the man wheedled, "let me have a kiss."

Ying-ying twisted her lips. This was too coarse. She'd hoped for something slightly more refined. An exchange of small presents, perhaps. Or an elegant lament for what could not be—if this thing had any hope in marriage, it would not be a boy and a girl meeting clandestinely in back alleys, but their families and matchmakers conferring openly in front halls.

But apparently "good sister" had not expected anything different. "You kiss me here," she answered saucily, "then return to your chamber to kiss Little Orchid."

The name Little Orchid rang a bell. Ying-ying, in Amah's company, had done the requisite visits to the womenfolk of the compound: Da-ren's concubines and a few elderly female servants who by their sheer seniority had more authority than the new mistresses.

Mrs. Mu-he, an old woman who had once been Da-ren's wet nurse, had mentioned a Little Orchid. There was talk that the maid would be given over to Da-ren's elder son for his bedchamber uses once he turned sixteen. It would be an elevation of sorts, but not enough that Ying-ying should bother to go around and pay her respects, Mrs. Mu-he had decreed.

The boy must be Shao-ye, then, the lordling. The spoiled one. For it wasn't true that Da-ren had two bratty sons. His younger son, a boy about Ying-ying's age, was considered a studious, obedient child, though not too clever, from what Ying-ying gathered.

Ying-ying risked another peek. Shao-ye, who was fifteen years old, had Da-ren's features, but none of the power and—dared she say it— ruthlessness that made Da-ren riveting to the eye. His long black robe stood in sharp contrast to the maid's pink tunic and trousers.

"So jealous already?" He laughed. "Do I need to avow my love?"

"Vows are just words," the maid said.

"What's your favorite dish? I'll have the kitchen make it today."

"And what good does that do?" The maid pouted. "By the time a chicken gets to the likes of us, it's all bones."

"I'll have it sent especially to you," promised Shao-ye. "A kiss?"

Ying-ying had heard enough. The more she knew about men, the less dreadful a life in the wilderness was beginning to seem.

She retraced her steps until she came to another pathway that would take her deeper into the compound, to the garden she had passed her first day here. She didn't like to admit it, but she wanted another look at the foreign devil. None of the women she visited had mentioned him, and she had not thought it a good idea to ask.

A girl with not-black eyes should not appear too interested in foreign devils.

SHE HAD NOT EXPECTED HIM to be there, but he was, seated at the same stone table in a long gray tunic, the kind worn by scholars, *Chinese* scholars. She hesitated, and then entered the garden. She would walk about as if enjoying the scenery, and study him when he was not looking.

He didn't notice her. He was staring into the distance as if his mind were far away, well beyond the boundaries of China. Was he thinking of his own country? Of the people he had left behind?

He ran a hand through his short hair. It was the pale yellow of leaves in autumn. His beard, however, was more of a light brown. She inched closer and pretended to be inspecting the fish in the pond. He had changed footgear. Instead of the shoes, he had on short boots in brown leather. They shone brighter than a bald man's pate.

She looked up to find him studying her. What should she do? How did one comport oneself before a foreign devil? They were said to possess no understanding of the proper rules of conduct.

He rose, set aside his book, and came to the ornate railing. There he greeted her, right palm over left fist, both raised to chest height. "What is Gu-niang's esteemed family name?" he asked—in *Mandarin*.

She had heard Mother's parakeet speak better Mandarin, and she had heard Amah speak worse—Amah having never lost her thick southern accent. The foreign devil's Mandarin, while far from perfect, was both correct and intelligible.

The next thing she knew, she was walking out of the garden as fast as she could without breaking into an outright run, the inside of her head as messy as a sheet of paper with too much ink spilled onto it.

She was halfway across the residence when she stopped. Why had she fled? Was she afraid of the foreign devil? Or was she afraid someone would see her speaking to him?

A middle-aged manservant carrying a bamboo steamer turned onto the path. He greeted her cursorily and went on his way.

"Is this the sweet walnut soup for my mistress?" a female voice asked. Ying-ying turned around and recognized the speaker as a maid to one of Da-ren's new concubines.

"Yes. It's piping hot. Gu-niang take care not to burn your fingers," the man answered with much bowing and scraping as he handed over the steamer.

The maid thanked him and left. The manservant started back. Ying-ying called him as he passed her. "Master Keeper, there is sweet walnut soup in the kitchen today?"

He did not look happy to be asked that question. "A little, not much."

"Will you have some sent to my rooms?" Amah greatly enjoyed the delicacy. It would be a treat for her.

He sighed. "That might be a bit difficult, Bai Gu-niang. We have Da-ren, the mistresses, the two young lords—I'm afraid there will be none left over."

Ying-ying did her best not to flinch openly. "That's that, then. It's anyway too cloying for my taste."

The man bowed a little and hurried away. Ying-ying stood in place with a strange burning in her chest, a sense of rabid futility. She was at the bottom of the hierarchy; she already knew that. But would it have been too much to spare a mouthful of the dessert? Must even the kitchen treat her with such scorn?

The outcome of their exchange would have been different had Ying-ying been able to grease the servant's palm as she made her request. But they'd had to hand over the silver certificates and the taels of silver into the majordomo's keeping when they moved in and now must be spare with their coins.

Only the foreign devil seemed to display the slightest interest in her. She took a deep breath, spat on the spot where the manservant had stood, and headed back to the garden. Let the servants see her with the foreign devil. They could not be more contemptuous of her than they already were.

She stormed back into the garden. The foreigner looked up in surprise.

"My family name is Bai," she said, as if a quarter stick of an incense's time hadn't passed since he asked her the question.

He stood up again. "To meet Bai Gu-niang is the good fortune of three lifetimes."

Not only did he speak decent Mandarin, he spoke it like a courtier. But the strange thing was, he seemed to mean it, as if he truly was glad that she had not stayed away, but had come back.

An even stranger sensation settled over her: a desolation that was almost like despair. She never realized it before, but until now she had no idea what it felt like when someone was glad to see her. Mother's gaze had always been worried, Amah's critical, and Da-ren's severe. None of them had ever been glad that she had come into the world: From the very beginning she had been a problem that they did their best to prevent from becoming a bigger problem.

She curtsied, her hands together at her right hip. "What is your esteemed family name, sir?"

"Here my family name is Kuo-tung."

"It is a privilege to be received in your presence, Master Kuo-tung."

He didn't look like he ate babies. In fact, he looked harmless, not at all beefy like the mental picture she carried of foreign devils. He was tall, but slender to the point of thinness. In single combat, she'd take him down in the time it took to blink an eye.

"Is Bai Gu-niang a guest of Da-ren's?" he asked.

A very nice way of putting it. "Da-ren has been so kind as to host me."

"A guest of Da-ren's is a guest of mine," he said gallantly. "Would Bai Gu-niang care for a cup of tea?"

She never thought she would be having tea with a foreign devil. But then, she never thought she would hate living in Da-ren's residence. "Master Kuo-tung is too generous. But I fear to impose."

"I will be honored. I only worry that my fare is too poor for Bai Gu-niang's exquisite palate."

They went back and forth a few times, as dictated by good manners, before Ying-ying finally accepted. He came out of the pavilion and crossed the bridge to where she stood to properly welcome her. "Bai Gu-niang, please."

And so it was she found herself across the round stone table from this man with light blue eyes and a sharply ridged nose. Up close his skin was not white, but pink, and remarkably unwrinkled. She had thought him in his forties, judging by the thickness of his beard. Now she could see that he was much, much younger: no more than thirty, if that.

"Little Dragon," he called, clearing some crumpled papers from the table.

A boy of about sixteen appeared instantly, startling Ying-ying. He must have been nearby if he answered the summons so quickly, but she had not been aware of him at all. The rather illicit excitement of making Master Kuo-tung's acquaintance must have rendered her oblivious to everything else.

"I have some jasmine tea. I hope Bai Gu-niang does not think it too humble," said Master Kuo-tung.

"Only if it isn't too much trouble," she answered, casting another look at the boy. He was almost as tall as Master Kuo-tung, fair of complexion and good-looking. But he did not have the correct demeanor for a servant: He stood with his back and neck straight, no nodding head, no obsequious smile.

Master Kuo-tung related instructions to Little Dragon in a foreign tongue. To Ying-ying's astonishment, Little Dragon answered in the same language.

"He has been learning French from me," said Master Kuo-tung after Little Dragon's departure, in reply to the question she had yet to ask.

"Does Master Kuo-tung hail from France then?" Ying-ying felt a flicker of disappointment. For some reason she had thought him an Englishman, like her fa— like the man in Mother's photograph.

"No, I came from England," he said, nudging a tray of snacks toward her.

So he *was* an Englishman. She felt a quiver of nerves.

"But in my country, many educated men speak French," he continued. "I teach both the young masters English and French, but most of their time is spent studying the Chinese classics."

There were schools that taught foreign languages, but only those who aspired to be no more than lackeys attended, since the merit tests that determined a young man's future in officialdom still relied exclusively on Confucian learning. Ying-ying had no idea Da-ren was this progressive in his thinking, having his own children learn foreign languages.

"Did Da-ren also instruct Master Kuo-tung to teach Little Dragon?"

"Little Dragon assists me when I hold classes for the young masters. Most of what he has learned he picked up on his own—he seems to have a particular affinity for French."

"So he is not a student of Master Kuo-tung's?"

The question puzzled the Englishman. Then he laughed. "I keep forgetting the concept of 'student' is very different in China. If you are asking whether he has kowtowed to me and whether I have formally accepted the grave responsibility for his tutelage, then no, he is not my student."

She had not noticed the sadness in his eyes until his laughter dissipated. Now she wondered how she hadn't seen it from the very beginning. It wasn't obvious, not the hollow-eyed grief in her mirror following Mother's death. More a sorrow that had become less acute with time—but there nevertheless.

For some odd reason, he reminded her of Mother. She, too, had a habit of sitting with a book open before her, looking off to some distant time and place.

"Is it lonely for Master Kuo-tung to be far from home, far from family and friends?"

The moment the question left her lips, she regretted it. His eyes widened, as if he were taken aback—she hoped he didn't think her a very nosy girl, though that was probably exactly what she was.

And then he smiled. "Yes, sometimes it is."

There was relief in his voice, as if he not only didn't mind, but was glad that someone had asked that question.

She exhaled. She couldn't remember ever meeting anyone who was so easy to talk to—except Bao-shun, maybe. But Bao-shun, though good-natured and willing to indulge in a bit of silliness from time to time, always treated her as a child. This foreigner, however, spoke to her as if she were his equal.

"Has it been long since Master Kuo-tung left England?"

"Two years."

"Master Kuo-tung has been traveling for that long?" She could very well believe it.

He smiled again and shook his head. "No, I arrived in Peking at the beginning of the year—and that's after stopping at quite a few places along the way. I could probably go around the entire world in six months, if I wanted to."

Now this was shocking. "Six months? The whole world?"

There were places under the control of the imperial court that would take six months to reach.

"If I took steamers and trains as much as possible."

"So Master Kuo-tung could be back in England in..." She wasn't sure exactly how far England was from China.

"Three months, more or less." He sighed. "But I can't go back yet—and maybe not for some years to come."

"Why not?"

Once again she regretted her question. He had been very, very kind to indulge her curiosity, but now she had truly overstepped the bounds of propriety.

"I have offended a very powerful man," he answered quietly.

"Oh," she said, at once thankful that he had replied and saddened on his behalf. "That happens a great deal here in China. Has Master Kuo-tung ever heard of Jiayu Pass?"

"No, I have not."

"It's the westernmost gate of the Great Wall. And those who offend the court are exiled beyond, where there is nothing but wasteland and desolation. They weep and lament by the gate, but they are not allowed back inside."

Master Kuo-tung rolled his pen under his fingers. "In that case, I must count myself fortunate. In my exile I am allowed to sit in this beautiful garden, study Chinese poetry, and make friends."

It was odd for him to call her a friend—he was a generation above her; were he Chinese, she would be addressing him as Uncle. But the solace he took in her company felt so genuine that she scarcely knew what to do with herself. She selected a piece of candied kumquat from the tray of snacks on the table so she could go for a bit without talking.

Little Dragon arrived with the tea service. Adroitly he poured boiling-hot water into the red-sand clay teapot, whirling it around to warm the interior.

"I know I offered Bai Gu-niang jasmine tea," said Master Kuo-tung. "But I also have tea from Darjeeling, which is much beloved by the English. Would Bai Gu-niang be interested in sampling a cup?"

She had no idea the English drank tea; nor had she ever heard the name Darjeeling. "I will be delighted to try."

"I don't think I have come across another young person so courteous since..." He shook his head slightly and turned to address Little Dragon in French.

Little Dragon gave her a stony look, as if it were her fault that he was being asked to fetch a different kind of tea. He left and returned a minute later, set the tea to brew, and withdrew.

The fragrance that wafted from the teapot was a darker, deeper scent than what she was accustomed to. "Oh, it is red tea."

"Yes. In English we call it 'black tea.' This particular variety is grown in the foothills of the Himalayas."

The Himalayas formed the southern boundary of Tibet, and she could not remotely imagine the climate in Tibet as suitable for the cultivation of tea. Then she realized he must mean foothills on the *other* side of the great mountain range.

"This tea is from India?" she marveled. She knew nothing of India, other than that it was hot and the birthplace of the Buddha.

"Yes, indeed. I drank a great deal of this tea in England. Now, not so much—it makes me long for home."

At the end of his words, he bit his lower lip, as if embarrassed.

His homesickness echoed in her. "I miss my home too," she confessed. "My home is only few *li* away, but I don't think I will ever see it again."

This was something she could not have told anyone else in Da-ren's residence. Gossip would spread and people would think her ungrateful. But she felt completely safe speaking to this outcast foreigner, with his young face and melancholy eyes.

He poured tea for both of them. "Will you tell me something of your home?"

She did. As she sipped his fragrant brew, she described the pomegranate trees with flowers like flames, the goldfish that glittered under the sun, and even Mother's parakeet that spoke better Mandarin than he did, which made him laugh, the corners of his eyes crinkling.

He, in turn, told her about a house in the south of England, situated amid rolling green hills, that he had loved to visit. There he would ride, paddle rowboats, and sometimes hike for great distances with his friends.

"I have visited in winter, of course, when it was cold and rainy—we used to stay inside, drink Darjeeling tea, and talk all day long. But for some reason, whenever I think of my friend's house, it is always warm, always summer."

She didn't know why, but his words brought tears to her eyes. "I remember my home in all seasons, but I think I understand what you mean."

She no longer recalled Mother's sighs and frowns. Instead she remembered the time Mother taught her how to play dominoes. The time Mother had given her a full-fledged compliment for coming up with the second half of a couplet. And the time Mother, in a particularly good mood, had sat Ying-ying down to brush out her hair and recoif it into a more sophisticated arrangement.

Ying-ying had worn her hair in the same style ever since.

Before Master Kuo-tung could answer, Little Dragon arrived at his side and spoke to him. Master Kuo-tung turned to Ying-ying, an expression of surprise on his face. "I am told that my lunch has been delivered—I did not realize it was so late. Would Bai Gu-niang care to join me?"

Ying-ying leaped up. It was already lunchtime? She had better rush back, or Amah might never let her out again. Hastily she thanked

Master Kuo-tung for his hospitality. He in turn invited her to return for tea anytime.

"My lessons with the young masters are in the afternoon. My mornings are quite free. And it would be my good fortune and privilege to have Bai Gu-niang's company again."

She dared not promise anything, but all the way back to her own courtyard she could not help skipping. And she need not have worried about lunch: It had not been delivered yet, given that their courtyard probably ranked last in importance in the entire compound.

Amah was in the midst of a set of breathing exercises, seated cross-legged on her bed. She opened her eyes when Ying-ying poked her head in the door.

"I didn't run into Shao-ye," Ying-ying told her.

Amah nodded, closed her eyes again, and went on with her practice.

FOUR DAYS LATER, WHEN AMAH allowed Ying-ying out again, she headed directly for the garden at the northwestern corner of the residence.

Master Kuo-tung, as he'd promised, was in the exact same spot. He rose as he saw her, a wide smile on his face.

Fourteen

Catherine Blade

YING-YING TOOK THE PIECE OF paper out of the redwood box, the one that contained all the mementoes from Mother's days with her English protector. She was fairly certain the writing on the paper was English, which Master Kuo-tung would be able to read.

And then he would be able to tell her what it said.

She put the piece of paper back again. Maybe it was better for her not to know.

A few moments later she had the piece of paper in her hand again. And then again it was back in the box.

"If you aren't going for your walk, you can come and stir this potion for Master Keeper Ju," Amah said from the next room.

Three months after their move to Da-ren's residence, Amah had already gained a measure of renown among the senior servants for her medicinal skills. Every few days she would be concocting a brew for someone. Four days ago she cooked up something for Mrs. Mu-he's arthritis, before that for a household scholar's weak liver, and now a special preparation for the majordomo's headaches.

"I might spit in it, if I did," Ying-ying answered.

She had not forgiven the majordomo for how he had received them.

"As highly placed as he is, he is still a servant, and takes his cues from his master," came Amah's rebuttal.

And that was the crux of the matter, wasn't it? Da-ren didn't value her, and therefore no one else did.

Except for Master Kuo-tung. With him she never felt that she was lesser, or out of place.

She opened the redwood box, took out the piece of paper, put it up her sleeve. Then she shrugged into Mother's cape.

As she adjusted the fasteners under her chin, Amah came into the room. Lately things had become less tense between them. The credit, to Ying-ying's thinking, lay largely with Master Kuo-tung. Amah let her out only once every four or five days, but that meant the rest of the time she had her next visit with Master Kuo-tung to anticipate, which made an astonishing difference. Even lessons on medicinal herbs had become easier to tolerate.

"You should make some potions for yourself," she told Amah. "Your color doesn't look too good."

She had become thinner and her skin now had a gray undertone.

Amah waved a dismissive hand. "I'll drink medicine when I need to, and not before."

She came forward and set the last two fasteners in place on the cape. Then she stepped back and inspected Ying-ying. "You are growing up. It isn't advisable for you to spend so much time with the foreigner."

Ying-ying had never mentioned Master Kuo-tung to Amah. Did Amah hear about it from the other servants or had she followed Ying-ying without her knowledge? The latter, she decided. Amah would have said something if Ying-ying had become a topic of gossip.

And of course it wasn't advisable—or she wouldn't have run away the first time Master Kuo-tung greeted her. But she didn't want to get into an argument with Amah about him, so she said, "I will remember that, Master. And since Master has been out and about, has she discovered the identity of the martial-arts expert yet?"

If Amah noticed that she had changed the subject, she did not remark on it. "All I know is that it can't be the man who teaches self-defense to Da-ren's sons—he has no lightness skills at all. Bao-shun is the only other person said to be good at martial arts, but he was at our courtyard that night, and not here."

"Maybe that man is no longer here."

"Maybe, if I'm so lucky."

But Amah did not sound convinced.

YING-YING RAN INTO LITTLE DRAGON on the way. He carried a carafe of spirits and a small cup on a tray. She looked at him quizzically— what business did he have in this part of the residence?

"Bai Gu-niang," he greeted her coldly as they passed each other.

She gave a small nod.

Then, behind her, she heard him say softly, "The wind is strong today. Would Master Keeper Chang care for some heated spirits?"

She looked over her shoulder. He was speaking to a middle-aged manservant, rail-thin and stooped, who was sweeping the snow that had fallen onto the walking path.

She would never have pegged Little Dragon as the kind-hearted type, but he treated the older servant as if the latter were his father.

The garden where she had first seen Master Kuo-tung was empty; she kept walking. When weather turned cold he had invited her to his rooms, where they could be nice and warm inside. That was when she learned that he lived in the Court of the Contemplative Bamboo, which also housed Da-ren's study, in a row of east-facing rooms.

It is so his sons would take their lessons with me seriously, Master Kuo-tung had explained as to why he had been given such a place of honor.

Do they? she had asked.

He had smiled and shaken his head slightly. *The younger one takes everything seriously. The older one, well, I'm afraid the older one doesn't take anything seriously—or at least not his studies.*

Which had not surprised Ying-ying at all.

She stopped just outside the moon gate to peer into the Court of the Contemplative Bamboo—she didn't want to run into Da-ren and then have to explain what she was doing there. Once she was sure she was safe from that possibility, she skirted around the bamboo grove and slipped past Master Kuo-tung's door—he had told her there was no need for her to knock, and she had immediately taken him up on his offer, happy to not make any noises that might attract Da-ren's attention.

If Da-ren was home, that was. He was still a busy man and left the residence almost daily for business at court and elsewhere.

The arrangements of Master Kuo-tung's rooms was a familiar sequence to her: the first room for receiving and dining, the second as a study, and then an inner bedchamber—Mother's rooms had been laid out exactly that way.

He was not in the receiving room. She called him and received no response. She poked her head into his study—and nearly stumbled a step backward: He had in his hands the jade tablet Amah had stolen from Da-ren!

She must have made some noise. He glanced up and smiled. "Ah, Bai Gu-niang, when did you come in? I didn't hear you at all."

Her mouth opened and closed several times before she could ask, "If you don't mind my curiosity, Master Kuo-tung, how did you come by your artifact?"

"This? From my father. He purchased two such tablets in Nanking many years ago, after the First Opium War."

He made it sound so ordinary. Perhaps Da-ren—and consequently Amah—had been wrong about the value of the tablet. Perhaps it was one of those oft-copied pieces that had no particular significance at all.

"When I was growing up," Master Kuo-tung continued, "one of the tablets was always on my father's nightstand, and the other always on my mother's. After they passed away, I inherited the jade tablets. Then..."

His voice trailed off. He gazed down at the small tablet as if he could see through it to another place, another time. "Remember the house I told you about, the beautiful house where it is always summer in my memories? I gave one jade tablet to the master of that house, and this one I kept for myself."

For a moment Ying-ying forgot her alarm: There was only the intensity of his longing and the sweetness of the past forever torn from him. "It must have made for a beautiful present."

He smiled faintly. "It was very kindly received and very much cherished." He held out the tablet toward her. "Would you like to see it more closely?"

She almost took it in her hand before she remembered. "Master Kuo-tung, I must tell you something: You should hide this tablet and never let anyone see you with it. Da-ren had one just like it and he treasured it, but it was stolen several years ago."

"Oh," said Master Kuo-tung, looking astounded. "Exactly like this one? You have seen it?"

She hesitated. "No, I have not seen it myself, only heard it described. And the theft happened before you came to China, of course. But you understand what I mean, do you not, Master Kuo-tung?"

It would not look good if Da-ren were to come to know. What were the chances that a foreigner would have in his possession a nearly identical object as that which had been taken from him?"

"Yes, I understand. And don't worry," he reassured her. "This is the first time I have taken it out to look at since I arrived in Peking. No one else knows I have such an item."

"You should put it away right now."

He looked down at the tablet a long moment. "I believe someday I will donate this to the British Museum. Perhaps I had better do it sooner, rather than later."

He excused himself to go into the inner room; she shrugged out of her cape. When he came back, he offered her a cup of Darjeeling tea, the scent and taste of which she had come to love, and they spent a few minutes talking about what a museum was, a concept entirely novel to her.

It wasn't until he was refilling her cup that she remembered the piece of paper she had brought. She waffled again, wondering whether she ought to say nothing of it.

"Bai Gu-niang."

"Yes?"

He smiled. "Bai Gu-niang hasn't heard anything I said. Is there something on her mind?"

She bit the inside of her cheek, extracted the piece of paper from where it was stowed up her sleeve, and handed it to him. "I was hoping Master Kuo-tung might be able to read this for me."

"Certainly."

He scanned the lines of text. His brows rose. Then he looked back at her. "This letter was addressed to an unmarried lady who has the same family name as Bai Gu-niang. But it dates from a while ago—1864."

"And what year is that?" She was unfamiliar with the Western calendar.

"I apologize. I mean the third year of Tung-chih Emperor's reign."

Her pulse quickened. "That's the year I was born."

"And I remember reading something about a crash in Shanghai that year having to do with a huge influx of refugees that was expected but never materialized." He read the letter again. "How did this come to you?"

"I found it among my mother's things. So it was addressed to her?"

Master Kuo-tung glanced at her again. "It seems that way. It is a letter of condolence concerning the death of a man named Blade."

"Buh...lay...de," she repeated slowly.

"Mr. Blade perished in an accident. It would seem that the recipient of the letter was then with child—Mr. Blade's child. And the writer informed her that Mr. Blade had been looking forward to the birth of the baby and that he would have named it Charles, if it turned out to be a boy. And if a girl, Catherine."

The foreign devil in Mother's photograph had a name—a surname, at least. And Ying-ying, unbeknownst to herself, had always had an English name.

"It is a beautiful name, Catherine—a queenly name," said Master Kuo-tung, as he handed the letter back to her.

She didn't know what to say. She wondered whether the letter made it clear that she was illegitimate.

"The moment I met Bai Gu-niang, I wondered whether she wasn't of mixed heritage," Master Kuo-tung said quietly. "And when I saw Bai Gu-niang's eyes up close, I became fairly certain."

She lowered her face, ashamed of her eyes, which so easily gave away her secret to one who knew what to look for.

"Has Bai Gu-niang ever thought of visiting England and perhaps meeting members of her father's family?"

The suggestion flabbergasted her. "Did the letter mention any such family? And the English, they do not mind children born outside of wedlock?"

He looked pained. "No, the letter didn't mention any family. And I'm afraid the English do mind—very much."

She shook her head. She could just imagine the horror on the part of her father's family, to have this wild seed arrive on their doorstep from the far ends of the earth. She would not put herself through such humiliation—and rejection.

"But you should still visit England someday," said Master Kuo-tung. "The English countryside is beyond compare. And of course there is London, one of the greatest cities in the entire world. There are magnificent parks and tremendous museums. There is the Thames River, flowing through the middle of the city. And from April to July, there are endless, endless fun things to do for a young lady."

He grew more enthused. "You see, the English gentlewoman isn't quite as restricted as her Chinese counterpart. Here the ladies never seem to step outside their front door. But in England, going out and about is an essential part of life. Young ladies walk in public parks with their friends, attend garden parties and dinners, and then they dance all night long at grand balls."

The life of an Englishwoman sounded completely uninhibited. Almost debauched. "When you say they dance, you mean they perform?"

"No, no, ladies don't perform. They dance for their own pleasure—and to mingle with young men." He left his seat and a moment later came back with a book, opened to an illustration of a man and a woman standing close together, practically in an embrace. "This is one of the most popular dances."

Ying-ying's jaw fell—it *was* debauched: The woman was practically naked on top. "This is allowed?"

He smiled. "I suppose people would think it shocking here. But I assure you, at home it is considered perfectly respectable. Besides, how else would young men and women find someone to marry if they do not mingle together?"

Another shock. Young people picked their own spouses? And their parents let them?

She shook her head again. She could not imagine herself wearing that kind of foreign clothes or taking part in any of those very foreign diversions. And she just might break the fingers of any man who dared to touch her.

He closed the book and set it aside. "That's quite all right. You don't ever need to do anything you do not wish to. But think of all the places you would discover if you were to journey to England. You could stop in India and visit Darjeeling, for example, and see entire hillsides covered in rows upon rows of tea bushes. Stand upon the bank of the Ganges, the holy river. Visit the Taj Mahal, which is an astonishingly beautiful white marble edifice built by a king in memory of the one woman he loved above all others. And if at all possible, you should include a tour of Kashmir—the mountains will take your breath away."

His words invoked a fierce yearning inside her for the entire world outside the walls of Da-ren's residence. "Do you really think I could?"

"Of course," he said, his eyes shining with sincerity. "Perhaps not now—you are still very young. But yes, someday. I can see you traveling the whole world and experience it with great zest and pleasure."

No one had ever spoken like this to her. No one had ever looked at her and seen wonderful things to come. "Thank you," she said, her voice thick with gratitude.

She didn't know whether she dared believe him, but she would always treasure this moment: when she heard the strength of his hope— and the echo of all the possibilities she could never have imagined for herself.

He smiled at her, a smile of great affection and infinite goodwill. "I have been meaning to ask you, Bai Gu-niang, would you like to learn

English? Even if you never visit England itself, it is still quite a useful language to know."

She had been wondering the same thing herself. She didn't know whether she wished to visit England—or whether she could even venture as far as India. But she could not help but respond to the enthusiasm in his voice. Could not help but feel some of his optimism.

The future, which had always loomed like a wall to be crashed into, a wall as tall and thick as that surrounding the Tartar city, now revealed itself to have gates. Gates that were tightly locked for the moment, but gates nevertheless. And who knew? Perhaps in studying English, she might manage to give herself the key to one of those gates.

She smiled back at him. "If Master Kuo-tung does not consider me too poor material to instruct, I would be honored beyond words."

Fifteen

Vows of Marriage

IN AUTUMN OF 1875, MOTHER married Mr. Delany in San Francisco. Two months later, her wedding photograph reached Leighton. She looked beautiful—and quite young still: She had been only eighteen when Leighton was born. Mr. Delany, though it was the first time Leighton had ever come across his image, looked instantly familiar; Marland had the same eyes and same cheekbones.

Leighton gazed a long time at the photograph. He had very nearly forgotten how it felt to carry Marland, the little boy's head on his shoulder, his fine, soft hair tickling Leighton just under the ear.

Except Marland wasn't so little anymore. He was six going on seven. Did he still remember his big brother?

He certainly wouldn't know Leighton as a writer of interesting letters. Despite his suspicion that not all his letters made it through, Leighton wrote once a week, faithfully. But his dispatches might as well have been hectograph copies of the first letter he wrote after he emerged from what he now thought of as his comatose period: How much could there be to report when he left the house once a week for Sunday service, met no new people, and spent much of his time at activities he did not want Sir Curtis to get wind of?

Mother had probably sent photographs of Marland to Leighton. Marland might have even written on his own, a few lines in a child's ungainly handwriting. But no such mementos had ever reached Leighton, who had only his memories.

And his hopes.

LEIGHTON CONTINUED TO STUDY PARSI, Arabic, and Sanskrit. As part of Sir Curtis's "magnanimity," Mr. Colmes was allowed to purchase anything either written in or dealing with these languages. In addition to the Bibles, Leighton read the Quran in Arabic, the poetic works of Rumi in Parsi, and in Sanskrit the *Mahabharata* and, in honor of the Buddhist origins of the jade tablets, the Tripitaka.

Before he had packed Father's jade tablet among Mother's books to be sent to America, he had made a rubbing of it. From time to time he took out the rubbing to study the intricate details that had been captured. He could almost hear Herb's voice recounting the legend behind the tablets' creation.

That piece of paper he kept inside his Bible, the book least likely to be taken away from him. Inside the Bible there was another piece of paper, a note that had accompanied a birthday present from Herb when Leighton had turned ten.

My dear boy, I do not say this enough: It is a joy and a privilege to be your friend. Thank you for having welcomed me into your life with such grace and kindness. I treasure every minute in your company and look forward to many more years of fond companionship. Your ever devoted friend, H.

Sometimes he opened the note and read it. Most of the time he only passed his fingers over the paper.

He knew what it said.

He knew what had been lost.

IN THE SPACE OF SIX months Leighton outgrew all his clothes and shoes. When he was much younger, he had taught himself to walk on his hands. After the growth spurt he had to relearn that skill almost from scratch, as his shape and weight had changed so much.

His voice dropped. Just before he turned fourteen, the beginning of a mustache appeared above his upper lip, and not a faint, barely-there sprinkling of hair, but quite dark and noticeable.

Now when he attended church, much was made of his height and physical maturity. The teasing from the ladies embarrassed him. But he did not think less of those who showered him with this unwanted attention—it was all kindly meant. And after having experienced true malice, he would never again quibble with any good-natured and completely harmless gestures, even if they might prove somewhat vexing.

He remained on friendly terms with Mr. Brown, the post office clerk, but they did not steal any more letters: Mr. Brown never asked for more stamps—the one time for the Shanghai colonial stamp was probably all the rule breaking he could bring himself to do. And it was fine with Leighton: He already knew where to go. And even if he should find Herb no longer in Peking, he would have a forwarding address from the British Legation.

In his studies, he had long ago reached the end of the Greek Bible. And since he'd already read the Latin Vulgate Bible before he'd come to Rose Priory, Mr. Colmes wrote Sir Curtis for permission and they started on the German Bible. On his own, Leighton had made his way through the Parsi Bible twice and finished with the Sanskrit Old Testament. Arabic, on the other hand, was proving to be an unusually difficult language to master. He longed to have better instruction than two dictionaries and a book of grammar, both of which were written in a manner that hindered understanding more than they aided it.

When he wasn't studying or exercising, he read every word of the daily editions of the *Times* and the *Manchester Guardian*, to which Mr. Colmes had subscriptions.

Mr. Colmes visited his daughter every two months, taking the Scotch Special Express from London to York. When he returned, he always made sure to put his copies of *Bradshaw's Guide*—he had one for Britain and one for the Continent—in the top drawer of his desk. When Leighton was alone in the schoolroom, he would study the rail and steamer timetables, calculating the cost of his escape according to the listed fares.

Father used to give him few pennies now and then so that when Leighton walked to the village nearest Starling Manor, he could buy himself a glass of ginger beer and a nice big scone. Sometimes Father even handed over a whole shilling. For birthdays Leighton would receive a bright, shiny gold sovereign. The pennies he sometimes spent, but the shillings and the sovereigns he had always kept safe in a secret drawer of his nightstand.

When he came to Rose Priory, he brought his savings—plus a few pounds he had pilfered from Mother's petty cashbox during the chaos of her abrupt departure. That money he hid in the room opposite his, inside a pillar candle that was never lit, eleven pounds, four shillings, and seven pennies in all.

It wasn't an inconsiderable amount of money—a scullery paid at Rose Priory was probably paid only a pound or two more per year. But third-class passage to Shanghai, according to Bradshaw's guide to continental travels, would cost him at least thirty-three pounds. And that was from Marseille, where there were ships with third-class fares. Unlike the Atlantic route, heavily used by emigrants, the eastbound steamers didn't necessarily cater to those watching their every last farthing; in second class, thirty-three pounds wouldn't even get him from London to Bombay.

He could only hope that Herb left him enough money for a passage to India, at least.

He also studied Mr. Colmes's tattered map of London, memorizing the layout of the streets between Paddington Station and Waterloo Station, which he needed to reach to take a southbound train to Sussex.

By mutual consent they never spoke of Leighton's plans—the less Mr. Colmes knew, the better for both of them. But sometimes Mr. Colmes would talk about his daughter, and about the health of her employer, whose condition had been deteriorating for the past year.

Leighton, who understood that Miss Colmes would depart for Australia after her employer had passed on, listened carefully to these updates.

In physical appearance he could now pass for a boy of seventeen or eighteen. In temperament he was calm and self-possessed. But he had very little experience outside English country houses. When he actually ran away, would it be very much like the first time he tried to walk on the moors in the middle of the night, falling splat into a frigid stream even though he proceeded cautiously, with his eyes wide-open?

That was something for which he could not practice or prepare. He could only wait, plan, and hope that no one would trouble or give a second look to a respectable-looking young traveler. And that he would cover ten thousand miles unharmed and undetected.

MUCH TO LEIGHTON'S SURPRISE, IN June of 1876, not long after he turned fourteen, Lady Atwood came to Rose Priory by herself—all her earlier visits had been in the company of her husband. She was still stupendously beautiful—the menservants grew tongue-tied around her. But to Leighton she felt different. Lesser.

There had been a hauteur to her, the utter confidence of someone who had never been denied anything. She still conducted herself with great condescension, but now there seemed to be a just perceptible brittleness beneath her air of superiority.

Beyond the initial welcome on his and Mr. Colmes's part, he saw little of her. She walked on the moors; he traipsed about the house. She took her meals in the dining room; he sat with Mr. Colmes in the classroom, as was their custom. Only at Sunday dinner, after church service, did they all break bread together. Mr. Colmes and Lady Atwood conversed sedately; Leighton, still considered a child, followed the rule that he should be seen but not heard.

One afternoon he heard her come back into the house. She was earlier than usual and he had not finished his rounds yet. He kept on going. So what if she were to see him and report him to Sir Curtis? He still had to get in his daily quota of exercise.

A quarter of an hour later her voice came from behind him. "Why are you going into and out of all the rooms? Why don't you go outside instead?"

He turned around and gave a half bow. "I am not permitted to go outside, ma'am, on account of my deplorable health."

"Your health looks fine to me."

"Yes, it is quite amazing, ma'am, that I am never sick despite being so frail."

She gave him a hard stare and walked away. He resumed going into and coming out of all the rooms.

THAT EVENING HE OVERHEARD HER address Mr. Twombley. "The library is locked. Unlock it so that I may go in and choose a book."

"I'm sorry, Lady Atwood, but I am not permitted to unlock the library unless the master is here."

"I am the mistress. Is my wish not enough?"

"I apologize, ma'am. But my orders were very specific: Only when the master himself is at Rose Priory."

Silence.

Her footsteps, when she walked away, were very quiet, almost inaudible.

THE NEXT AFTERNOON SHE FOUND him in the schoolroom. He had finished with his walking and was reading the day's papers.

"I suppose you don't really sleepwalk either?" she said from the door.

He rose from his seat. "No, ma'am."

"What will you tell me next, that your father wasn't a homosexual?"

"My father loved a man—it was true," he answered coldly. "But no one minded. At Starling Manor he was much beloved."

"Too bad he was so ashamed of himself that he put a bullet to his head."

"Perhaps he was ashamed of himself. But he pulled the trigger not from shame, but because he could not bear the thought of being sent to an asylum again, as Sir Curtis had done when he was younger."

"It was for his own good."

"Remember that when Sir Curtis reneges on his promise of a missionary life in Africa because you have not produced any children. He will tell you it's for your own good."

The servants gossiped; Leighton listened. In the last few days he had learned that Sir Curtis and Lady Atwood's childlessness had been a source of consternation in their household.

Sharp color rose in her cheeks. Her hands clenched at her sides. "How dare you!"

"I see. It has already happened, hasn't it?" He was silent for a moment. "I'm sorry."

"Are you gloating?"

"No." He could never like her, this woman who had found so much to enjoy in Sir Curtis for so long. But he could not help but sympathize with her disillusion.

She moved into the room and sank down onto the nearest chair. She didn't speak. He didn't know what to do, so he rang for tea. And when the tea tray arrived he poured and set a cup before her, along with a plate of cake.

"He courted me since I was sixteen. I made sure to take matters very slowly, because marriage is such an irreversible commitment. I thought I'd taken every precaution. I thought my happiness would be invulnerable."

"I'm sorry," Leighton said again.

"He said that I have pledged to obey him, and that covenant supersedes any words he might have spoken to secure my hand in the first place. Do you believe that vows of marriage override all prior promises?"

"No."

"Neither do I. And he is mistaken if he believes I will allow such a breach of honor—such a betrayal."

Leighton could almost taste her vehemence, an acrid sensation on his tongue. "What will you do?"

"I will give him a few chances to see the light."

"And then?"

She lifted her teacup, suddenly all serenity and condescension again. "And then we shall see what I *won't* do, in the name of justice and fairness."

Sixteen

Escape

MID-AUGUST, LADY ATWOOD CAME back to Rose Priory in her husband's company—it was grouse season, and every self-respecting man of property must retire to the country for sport. She was as frosty toward Leighton as she had ever been, giving no hint of having confided her private anguish in him two months before.

She also appeared as devoted to her husband as before, though Leighton felt her smiles now carried a flinty edge. Did Sir Curtis realize that his wife had turned against him, or was he so secure in his power over her that he required only her obeisance, not her love?

On the third day after their arrival, during their morning lesson, Mr. Colmes kept standing up and sitting down, clearly agitated. Finally, near the end of the lesson, he pulled a letter from his pocket and set it down in the middle of his desk.

"You go on reading," he told Leighton. "I'll go and speak to Cook about luncheon—yesterday's salmon patty gave me quite an attack of indigestion."

When Mr. Colmes had closed the door behind himself, Leighton rose. With only the slightest hesitation he picked up the letter. It was from Miss Colmes, and the envelope had already been opened.

Dear Father,

A quick word to let you know that Miss Mulberry's cold has unfortunately turned into pneumonia. She is quite brave about it, but the doctor has told me to cable her great-nephew. He doesn't expect her to outlast the week.

I am glad that my own plans are all in place, which allows me to direct all my attention to ensuring Miss Mulberry's ease and comfort in what will likely be her final hours on this earth.

Love,
Cordelia

Leighton felt a little dizzy. This was Mr. Colmes informing Leighton that Miss Colmes was ready to leave—and move beyond Sir Curtis's reach. Leighton, too, must not miss this window of opportunity: Wait any length of time and Sir Curtis would devise some other infernal scheme to hold him a prisoner at Rose Priory.

But was he ready?

Yes.

He put the letter back in the envelope and put the envelope back on the desk. Then he opened the drawer. Immediately the smell of glue assaulted his nostrils. The railway timetable, when he picked it up, felt heavier—and jangled slightly. He opened it to find the last few pages of advertisements glued together and still somewhat damp at the edges. Inside this hastily formed envelope were coins—their shape unmistakable even through the paper.

He didn't imagine Mr. Colmes was paid extravagantly—or Miss Colmes. They probably had to pool their resources together for her new life in Australia. If only Leighton didn't need funds so desperately—it would take more than a pound for the rail journey to London, in third class—he would have returned the gift to Mr. Colmes.

As it was, he would simply have to pay Mr. Colmes back after he gained control of his inheritance.

As usual, Leighton and Mr. Colmes ate their lunch in the schoolroom. Over roast beef sandwiches, Leighton brought up Mr. Knightly, Mother's cousin whom Father had appointed as Leighton and Marland's guardian—until Sir Curtis decided to remove him from said guardianship. "He lives in Derbyshire and I've always wanted to visit him."

Mr. Colmes looked quizzical, until he understood that Mr. Knightly had been thrown out as a red herring. "Derbyshire, eh? I was there once, almost thirty years ago. Was pickpocketed at Euston Station on my way."

This was one of Leighton's biggest fears: that what little money he had would be stolen.

"After that I learned to carry only small change in my pockets. Anything of value I sew into the lining of my waistcoat."

Which was what Leighton spent his afternoon doing, after pilfering Mr. Colmes's sewing kit: digging the coins out of the candle, then cutting open the lining of his waistcoat and carefully stitching around each coin so that it would stay put and not jangle even when the waistcoat was violently shaken. Having never done any needlework in his life, he kept pricking his fingers. But he barely noticed, his mind churning around the precise steps—and timing—of his escape.

That had always been the problem. If he left during the day, it would be easier to catch a train on the Moretonhampstead line to Newton Abbot. But that would leave Mr. Colmes with the burden of covering for his absence—otherwise Mr. Twombley would immediately come after Leighton—and he didn't want any of the blame for his disappearance to fall on Mr. Colmes.

If he left at night, after Mr. Twombley locked him in, by the time he walked to the nearest railway station he would have missed the last train out. Not to mention that his absence would be discovered by six thirty the next morning, when Mr. Twombley came to unlock his door—and the first train of the day didn't reach the platform until a good forty-five minutes later.

Sir Curtis's presence at Rose Priory further complicated matters: The house was more crowded, more people could potentially see Leighton as he left, and, worst of all, the moment he was discovered missing Sir Curtis would know, reducing the already narrow window of time during which Leighton must reach London and disappear.

But the silver lining was that the servants also had more duties to perform. And with a dinner the master and mistress were giving on the morrow, they would be busier yet.

With luck, Leighton could buy some time for himself.

With a lot of luck, that was.

LEIGHTON COMPLAINED OF MUSCLE CRAMPS and stomach pain as soon as he awakened the next morning. Lady Atwood had been suffering from similar symptoms; he hoped he could get away with claiming the same.

And just in case Lady Atwood's discomfort was brought on by feminine problems—not something he could co-opt for his own purposes—he also achieved a feverish and flushed appearance by asking for a fire to be laid in his room, then wrapping himself under several blankets until he was perspiring profusely.

Mr. Twombley muttered darkly of the possibility of a bout of summer influenza. "You had better stay in your room today, Master Leighton. Wouldn't want Lady Atwood to develop a fever too."

"But...but," Leighton protested weakly.

"No, no, young master. You stay here and ring if you want anything."

Leighton took him up on his offer. Every fifteen minutes he rang—for milk, tea, biscuits, toast—and a different jam for his toast, please. He asked for the newspaper, a fresh bottle of ink, another pad of blotting paper, a better nib for his pen, his Sanskrit dictionary from the schoolroom—all before ten o'clock in the morning.

In between pulling the cord on the quarter hour, he checked and double-checked everything he planned to take with him. And did sit-ups and push-ups to settle his nerves.

In the middle of the afternoon Mr. Colmes poked his head in. "Are you quite all right, Master Leighton?"

"I will be, in time," he answered. And then. "Thank you. Thank you for everything."

It was good-bye and farewell—or so he hoped.

Mr. Colmes seemed as if he might say something, but in the end he only nodded and closed the door quietly.

Leighton sat for a few minutes with his eyes closed, praying for the best for Mr. Colmes and his daughter. Then he yanked on the bell cord again.

AN HOUR AFTER HE ASKED for his afternoon tea, Leighton requested an early supper. "Only soup and sandwiches, please. I can't handle anything heavier."

He drank the soup and packed away the sandwiches. When the maid he rang for arrived to take the plate away, he asked her to bring Mr. Twombley. The latter, no doubt deep in preparation for dinner guests who were arriving in ninety minutes, was not happy to have been disturbed—and he was no doubt aware that this entire day Leighton had put his staff to myriad frivolous uses.

"I'm all worn-out, Mr. Twombley. Why don't you lock the door now? I want to go to sleep—without having to wake up to answer you if you were to come at ten o'clock."

Mr. Twombley always knocked and waited for an acknowledgment from Leighton before he locked the door at night, to make sure Leighton was actually inside. He did not need to be asked twice to grant Leighton's request.

When he was gone, Leighton listened to make sure that no one else was nearby. Then he took out his file, which he'd stolen from one of the servants in those days after he'd recovered his will to live but before he'd resumed church attendance, when he was left alone in the house on Sunday mornings with no one but a deaf groundskeeper on the property.

In a house full of former criminals, he'd been more or less certain he'd be able to find some useful items—and his intuition had proved correct.

Since then, on the staff's half days, when those with families nearby went off to visit and others whiled away the hours in pubs or at card games held away from Rose Priory, he had slowly filed away at the bars outside his window. He made sure he always did his filing on the side away from the window, so that the deterioration would not be visible from the inside—and with the ivy climbing around the window frame, it was also undetectable from below. Now he filed off the last bits and brought the grille inside.

He did not wait for dusk: If he didn't arrive at the nearest railway station, which was seven miles away, by quarter to nine, he wouldn't get on the last train out.

He climbed down from the window, closing it behind himself as best as he could. Near the house the landscape was largely treeless, but there were still small copses of ash and boxwood hedges. He slipped behind the first hedge, his heart pounding. No hue and cry came from Rose Priory. He ran, half hunched over, and almost tripped over a stone.

He sprinted from cover to cover until he was half a mile away from the house. He remained cautious afterward, skirting farmhouses where the residents might recognize him, and taking only footpaths that bypassed the village.

He huffed a little from the rise and dip of the land—walking inside a house, even if he climbed the staircase many times a day, was still no substitute for actual hiking. But the fatigue was nothing compared to the intoxication of freedom—or the fear of being found and brought back. He moved as fast as he could, praying with every step.

The sky darkened faster than he'd anticipated—a storm gathered on the western horizon. This was not good news. Mr. Twombley usually checked the house only on the inside before he retired for the night. But if he anticipated inclement weather, he was likely to make a round outside too. And if he should notice that the grille on Leighton's window had disappeared...

Leighton walked even faster. The seven miles he covered in an hour and forty minutes, according to Father's old watch. Night had fallen by the time he reached the railway station and bought his ticket. Instead of sitting on the platform to eat the sandwich he'd brought, he had his supper in the shadows outside the station, afraid of well-lit and sparsely populated places, afraid of running into someone he knew.

But he got on the train without encountering any acquaintances. The third-class compartment was austere but clean. He kept his hat pulled low on his head and his face turned toward the window—except when the train entered stations. Then he opened a local paper that had been left on the seat and hid himself behind the newsprint.

It seemed impossible that his escape could go off so smoothly. But he arrived at Paddington Station without any incident shortly after midnight. At a hotel several streets away he asked for a room. He had a story ready: He was an Eton student who had gone to visit a classmate during summer holiday and was now on his way home. But no one asked his age, and no one seemed to have the least inkling that he wasn't where he should be.

He barely slept that night, opening his eyes at the least noise. Before dawn he was already up and rechecking the items in his small bag. At first light he had left the hotel and walked along London's deserted streets, relying on the map that he saw clearly in his mind for directions to Victoria Station.

Before the sun had risen he was already headed south. At Brighton he changed for a branch line and got off at the village of Claymore. Little had changed here. The smell of the air, the green of the downs, and the sound of his soles on the country lane that led toward Starling Manor were all infinitely familiar. He didn't know whether he wanted to laugh or cry.

He bypassed the gate of the estate and entered via a hidden path. He had decided that the clue Herb had given, *Think of Mr. Cromwell,* was a reference not to the solicitor, but to the latter's daughter, for whom Herb and Leighton used to gather their assortment of presents every month. Any item that Leighton thought had potential he stowed in the small cottage where Herb kept his portable darkroom. And it was there that they would make the final selections for each month, which Herb would take with him when he departed for London, to send to Miss Cromwell via the post.

The groundskeeper had the key to the cottage. But there had been another one hidden under a loose brick near the door. It was this key that Leighton pulled out, a little rusted, but still in working order, and used to open the cottage.

Herb's portable darkroom was still there, in a corner of the parlor, though there were no longer any baths of fixers lying about, with photographic plates inside. Leighton walked into the tiny bedroom—the cottage was even smaller than he remembered—opened the door of the linen closet, and pulled out the storage box. The moment he lifted the lid, he saw the envelope with his name on it.

My dear boy,

I don't know when or under what circumstances you will come to this. But I trust that the Bank of England should still stand and that you will find some use for these banknotes.

H.

The note was dated October of 1873, and there were five crisp bills inside the envelope, one hundred pounds altogether. Leighton leaped in the air a few times and kissed the envelope, euphoric with gratitude.

He could smell it already, the salty tang of sea air. The scent of freedom itself.

He should leave the way he came, but he couldn't come so close without stopping by Father's grave. And then he succumbed to the desire to taking a look at Starling Manor itself.

But as he approached the main house, he noticed the two men in town clothes. They weren't gardeners or footmen; nor were they anyone from the village come to deliver bread and produce. They whispered to each other, pointing and signaling; then they spread out.

Leighton retreated deeper into the copse of trees he had been using for cover. His gladness evaporated, and in its place, a hard knot of fear. No thieves would come for the contents of a house at ten o'clock in the morning. These men were here for him.

Had Sir Curtis guessed, from all those letters of Herb's that he had confiscated, or from an understanding of simple human nature, that Leighton would wish to visit home before he ventured farther afield?

And would Leighton's attempt at escape end before twenty-four hours had even passed?

Seventeen

Lady Atwood

LEIGHTON TRIED TO THINK THROUGH HIS PANIC.

He knew every inch of the surrounding area. He could get back to the railway station unseen. But what if a third man patrolled the platform, waiting for him to turn up?

There was another railway station fifteen miles away. It was on a smaller branch line and the service was infrequent, but under the circumstances it was probably far safer. He looked at his watch and then consulted the *Bradshaw* he had taken from the schoolroom. If he could complete the fifteen miles in four hours, he might yet make the afternoon train to Brighton.

After a long, hot walk, he arrived at the tiny, nondescript railway station with a parched throat, blisters on his feet, and five minutes to spare. He didn't dare ride the train all the way into the main Brighton station, afraid that there might be someone examining the arrivals. Instead he got off at a smaller station east of Brighton and hired a hansom cab to take him to the station in the town of Hove, immediately to the west of the larger city.

His ploy paid off. He was able to reach Southampton without anyone on his tail—at least none he could see. It was evening. Ticket agents were closed. He found lodging for the night, took off his shoes, grimacing, and collapsed on the bed.

The next morning he woke up starving. He had already eaten all the food he had brought with him from Rose Priory, so he bathed, dressed, reluctantly put his shoes back on, and walked down gingerly to breakfast.

In the dining room there were a pair of ladies. One was rather round, perhaps in her mid-forties, the other quite thin and about ten years older—but judging by the likeness of their features, they were quite obviously sisters. Leighton bowed slightly. The round lady returned a formal nod; the thin lady gave him a smile.

Leighton demolished his plate of hot breakfast. He was systematically polishing off the slices of toast that had been provided when a man in an elaborate turban and a white flowing robe entered the dining room and sat down.

The serving girl approached him rather warily. "The full breakfast, sir?"

She was met with a burst of foreign syllables.

"I beg your pardon?"

Another barrage of foreign syllables.

The serving girl looked around, as if hoping someone might be able to help her.

"You don't suppose he's speaking Arabic, do you?" ask the thin lady of her sister.

The turbaned man repeated himself one more time, pointing at the two ladies' table and Leighton's table by turn. Suddenly the sounds of his language coalesced into meaning.

"He is asking whether the breakfast contains pork," Leighton said to the serving girl.

The language wasn't Arabic, but Parsi, except it sounded harsher and more guttural

than Leighton had imagined.

"Oh, thank you, sir. Can you tell him that we'll be happy to serve him kippers and potted chicken instead of bacon and sausage?"

Leighton had no idea how to say either "kippers" or "chicken," so he turned to the Persian and told him in Parsi that the hotel would provide him fish and fowl in place of pork. He was certain he sounded absolutely horrendous—probably incomprehensible. But the man gave a half bow and replied in the same language, "That would be acceptable. Thank you, young man. Peace be upon you."

"Peace be upon you," Leighton returned the greeting.

Five minutes later, finished with his tea and the last piece of his toast, Leighton rose from the table, only to see the thin lady beckoning him. He approached their table. "May I help you, ma'am?"

"Yes, I am Miss McHenry. This is my sister, Miss Violet McHenry. And we are off to see the world."

"That sounds excellent."

Miss McHenry beamed. "Indeed it is. Allow me to tell you a little about the peculiarity of our family: We run to girls. There were seven of us at one point, four still surviving. But of my four sisters who married, there resulted only three boys, as opposed to eleven girls, who successfully reached adulthood. One of the boys, unfortunately, is good for nothing. Another is a practicing lawyer and very busy. The last, our great hope, after much dithering, decided that finishing university—"

"And courting his professor's daughter," added Miss Violet rather grumpily.

"And that, of course. He decided that together they constituted a better use of his time than accompanying his spinster aunts into the great unknown. Naturally we were quite disappointed. Any venture that involves more than two hundred pounds of luggage ought to have a stronger back than ours, don't you agree, Mister..."

Miss McHenry waited.

"Ashburton," he said. It was Mother's maiden name.

"Now you, Mr. Ashburton, seem to be a very helpful young man. And strong of back. And fluent in Arabic."

"Parsi—the gentleman is Persian," he said. "And I can speak only very little of it."

Though he had become quite literate in that language.

"And modest too. I like that. Therefore I would like to propose that you come into our employ and be our..."

"General dogsbody?" he supplied.

Miss McHenry chortled. "Oh, goodness, I was going to say our valued assistant. Unfortunately we can't pay you very much—it takes money to see the world. But we can provide for your food, lodging, and transport—everything decent, of course. And you will have fifteen pounds a year, in quarterly installments, for three years running—that's how long we expect to be traveling. Don't you think it is a tremendous opportunity? To be compensated for seeing the world?"

He couldn't disagree. "I do very much think so, ma'am. Unfortunately I am traveling myself and have a tight timetable to keep."

Miss McHenry's face fell, a disappointment that felt genuine—and greater than what he would have expected on her part, for what must be an impulsive offer to a random stranger. Her sister, on the other hand, seemed to be breathing a sigh of relief.

"Are you sure we cannot tempt you?" said Miss McHenry rather urgently. "Eighteen pounds a year? Introductions to the lovely daughters of our friends in Cairo and Bombay?"

"It's most kind of you, but I must regretfully decline."

"Oh, well." Miss McHenry's shoulders sagged a little. "We don't sail until day after tomorrow. You can always ask the reception to give us a message, if you change your mind."

"I will remember that. Thank you for your generous offer, Miss McHenry." He offered her his hand to shake. "And I hope you have a wonderful journey."

LEIGHTON DEBATED WITH HIMSELF.

He could take a P&O liner on the eastern route via the Suez Canal. But the Royal Mail Steam Packet Company had a steamer leaving in two days that would deposit him at Colón, Panama, where he would take a train across the isthmus and then get on another steamer on the Pacific side. And that particular steamer would call upon San Francisco.

Did he dare visit Mother and Marland before setting sail across the Pacific?

Hobbling a little—his feet hurt with every step—he visited the ticket agent for the P&O line. Then, spying a chemist's shop, he bought some bandaging and sticking plasters and dressed his feet so that they wouldn't chafe so badly. Feet somewhat better and more than a little bold, he called on the ticket agent for the Royal Mail Steam Packet Company for more details concerning its passage to Shanghai via Panama and San Francisco, of which only the most skeletal information had been given in the *Bradshaw*.

As he was about to walk into the ticket agent's office, a meaty hand took hold of him by the arm. "There you are, young Master Leighton. If you would come with us nice and easy, we will take you back to your uncle."

For a moment his entire vision turned black; his head roared as if a tornado hurtled through. He turned to see a beefy man with a red face.

"Kindly unhand me," he said. "You have the wrong person. My uncle is dead and I don't see how you can possibly reunite me with someone six feet underground."

"Cool as a cucumber, ain't he?" said the beefy man to a smaller man next to him.

Leighton took an instant dislike to the other man, who had cold, calculating eyes. Compared to him, the beefy man looked almost jolly.

"My name is James Ashburton and I suggest you take your hand off me this instant."

The beefy man chuckled. "Or what, young master? You are going to knock old John Boxer on his back?" He turned to the other man. "Show me the picture again, Jenkins."

Jenkins brought out a framed photograph, an excellent likeness of Leighton, from Christmas last. Leighton had always thought Sir Curtis's promise to send the pictures to Mother too much kindness. Now he knew he was right: Sir Curtis wanted his image captured only so that Leighton would be more easily found, should he choose to run away.

"See? That's you. I'll wager my last farthing," said Boxer. "So why don't you come with us, young sir? If we are wrong, then no harm done."

"Of course there could be harm done! You could make me miss my steamer's sailing."

"Then I'll have you booked for the next passage," Boxer answered cheerfully.

There was no malice to his words—he was but going about the task he had been assigned, retrieving a wayward child and returning him to the bosom of his family. But there was also no room for bargaining: He clearly considered Leighton a minor who could not be relied upon to make his own choices.

And now he propelled Leighton firmly forward, toward a waiting carriage.

LEIGHTON BRACED HIMSELF TO FACE Sir Curtis, but the carriage was quite empty. Boxer and Jenkins sat down on either side of him, wedging him in tightly. At the railway station they each held one of his arms. On the train they again sat closely together, packed like matches in a box.

Leighton veered between panic and misery. He considered somehow breaking the window of the train and throwing himself outside. He considered screaming kidnap. But the former would probably give him broken limbs, and the latter would only bring him to the attention of the law. And the law, unfortunately, was squarely on Sir Curtis's side.

He felt faint as they approached London, even fainter as they piled into a hansom cab. But he persisted in his protest. "You've got the wrong man, I tell you one last time. Aren't you going to be embarrassed when whoever this uncle fellow is has to apologize? And make no mistake, I am going to report this to the police."

"Then why haven't you?" said Jenkins, his voice reedy and unpleasant.

"Because you would have made a scene. And I have been taught to never make scenes," said Leighton, with as much certainty and scorn as he could muster. "Now, where are we going? Where are you taking me?"

"I already told you, to your uncle's house in Mayfair," answered Boxer.

How tightly secured was Sir Curtis's house? Would he be able to effect another escape? And if he couldn't, would he be able to tolerate the next almost seven years before he came of age?

Sir Curtis's house was situated in the middle of a row of town houses, with redbrick facing, a wrought-iron railing, and a green park opposite. To Leighton's surprise—and a sudden burst of hope—when his captors rang the bell, no one answered.

"Didn't you wire ahead to say we were coming?" Boxer asked Jenkins.

"I did. Maybe we traveled faster than the cable did?"

"No, we can't have, you blockhead," said Boxer casually.

Jenkins gritted his teeth. "I don't mean we traveled faster than the electrical currents. I meant the post office still needs to write out the message and then send it for delivery."

"Still, it's been at least two hours since we left Southampton. Ring again."

Jenkins did, his jaw tight.

This time the door opened. The two men both drew in a breath at the sight of Lady Atwood.

She looked at each of them in turn, Leighton included, in that haughty way of hers. "Who are you and why are you calling at this residence?"

Leighton almost gasped in astonishment. "I am James Ashburton," he said immediately, willing his voice not to shake. "I have no idea who they are, but they keep insisting I am someone I am not."

Boxer lifted his hat. "We are men acting on Sir Curtis's behalf. We've brought back his nephew from Southampton."

"I am Lady Atwood, and I can tell you I have never seen this boy. He is not my nephew."

Leighton hoped no one could hear his heart pounding—to him it was as loud as explosions.

"Are you sure, your ladyship?" Boxer asked uncertainly.

"Are you telling me I don't know what my own nephew looks like?"

Her hauteur was daunting. Boxer shrank a little. "No, no, of course not. But you will agree that he bears a remarkable resemblance to the photograph we've been given."

He gestured at Jenkins, who produced the photograph and extended it toward Lady Atwood. But Boxer snatched the picture from him and handed it to her himself.

Jenkins's jaw worked.

"That isn't my nephew," Lady Atwood said coldly. "You had better come inside."

They followed her to a dark parlor, its curtains drawn. She reached for a large silver-framed photograph on the mantel and showed it to the men. "*This* is my nephew. See the family resemblance?"

This was a boy of about seventeen, who looked very much like Lady Atwood. One of her brothers, probably.

"What have I been telling you all this time?" Leighton said. "I told you and told you and told you that you made a mistake. One of my mother's cousins is a judge. How would you like to be sentenced for kidnapping?"

Boxer blanched.

"Now, now, young man," said Lady Atwood, as impersonal as ever, "there is no need for unnecessary threats. My father was a judge, and I can tell you that in such circumstances, when an honest mistake has been made, it is quite unlikely for anyone to be prosecuted. But you have my apology, and these gentlemen will kindly escort you to Victoria Station and buy you a ticket for wherever you need to go."

"That's it? That's all the recompense I am to receive?" said Leighton, since it seemed a reasonable thing to demand, if he had truly been kidnapped by mistake.

"Very well then." She left the room for a moment and returned with a reticule. Reaching inside, she took out a few sovereigns and dropped them into Leighton's hand. "Enough recompense for you?"

She was extraordinarily convincing, almost as if she'd had time to— Of course. If Sir Curtis was out arranging for Leighton's capture, she would have been the one to receive the cable—and she would have had a bit of time to prepare.

Leighton was beyond grateful. He would like to thank her profusely, but doing so would jeopardize his newly regranted freedom. So he only nodded. "Very decent of you, ma'am."

"Then off with all of you."

"What about the photograph, ma'am?" asked Jenkins.

Lady Atwood turned an arctic gaze his way. "You no longer require the photograph, as you no longer work for Sir Curtis. I've had to dip into my own funds to buy off this young man. Do you think he would tolerate that sort of incompetence? When he comes, I will tell him that you have found better employment elsewhere."

BOXER LOOKED BOTH DEFEATED AND apologetic, Jenkins just as tight-faced as before. Leighton hoped he appeared vindicated and appropriately scornful, rather than boneless with relief.

In silence they arrived at Victoria Station. From his own pocket, Boxer paid for a second-class ticket to Southampton for Leighton. "Sorry about all that, Mr. Ashburton."

Leighton took the ticket from him. "I hope never to see either of you again. Good day, gentlemen."

The two men left. Leighton breathed for what seemed like the first time this day. He climbed into his rail carriage, sat down, and bowed his head in prayers of thanksgiving.

A hand gripped his arm. He started.

Jenkins.

"What do you want *now*?"

"I want you to get off this train nice and quiet and come with me. Boxer is a fool, but I can always tell when a woman is lying. You are the one we're looking for, all right. And this time I'm going to take you straight to Sir Curtis himself."

Leighton felt as shattered a glass hurtled across the room. Was there to be no escape after all? Was he doomed?

"What is it to you? Why do you care so much?"

"There is a nice reward for your return, don't you know?"

"How much?"

"Fifty pounds."

"Let's make a deal," he said, his voice strangely calm, even as his head throbbed and his palms perspired. "If you walk out of this train, I will give you sixty pounds."

Forty pounds would still get him as far as Bombay. He would worry about the rest later.

"You don't have that kind of money."

Leighton removed his right shoe with a wince and pulled out the three twenty-pound banknotes he'd put in there in the morning. "I do have that kind of money."

Jenkins's eyes narrowed. He was not a particularly unsightly man, but to Leighton he was all ugliness. "Take off your other shoe."

"What?"

"You heard me. Take off your other shoe."

Thirty seconds later, Jenkins had the other forty pounds from Herb.

Leighton was beginning to tremble. What would he do with less than ten pounds and half the circumference of the Earth to cover?

"Now your waistcoat."

Leighton couldn't even exclaim in dismay—a giant fist seemed to have closed around his throat.

"That's right. Don't think I haven't felt the coins in the lining. Now hand it over."

Leighton felt as if his entire person had turned to wood. He could almost hear his arm creaking like a rusted door hinge as he struggled out of the waistcoat. What was he going to do with no money whatsoever?

"And now the money the woman gave you."

Leighton had forgotten the four sovereigns Lady Atwood had dropped into his palm. With that memory came a sudden infusion of angry resolve. Slowly he turned to Jenkins. "No."

Jenkins was taken aback. "No?"

"No," Leighton repeated, his voice low. He felt the weight of the syllable as it left his lips, a thing of substance, as cold and hard as an artillery shell.

Jenkins's expression turned nasty. "Then how would you like to come with me after all? Another fifty pounds for me on top of everything else."

Leighton realized that it had been Jenkins's plan all along to bilk everything he could from Leighton, and then turn him over to Sir Curtis for the reward.

Strangely enough, he felt himself smile. "Guess what I will tell Sir Curtis when I see him? I will tell him that you took two hundred fifty pounds from me. And guess whom he will believe?"

Jenkins blinked.

"Have you any idea the lengths he would go to?" Leighton went on, his voice soft but vehement. "And you don't look like a particularly law-abiding sort to me. Within a week he will find something on you that will have you arrested, if you can't pay him back double what you took from me. You have five hundred pounds to spare?"

Jenkins recoiled, as if Leighton had suddenly developed a highly contagious disease.

"If I were you I'd go right now, before I decide that I want to punish you more than I want to get away from him."

Jenkins's left eye twitched. He looked at Leighton long and hard, then rose and left without another word.

A minute later, the train departed the station.

Leighton set his face in his hands and shook the entire length of the journey.

IT WAS ONLY TEA TIME when he walked back into his hotel in Southampton. He could not believe it—he could barely remember the hope that had luxuriated in his heart when he woke this morning. Now he was free by the skin of his teeth, but all his plans of a swift reunion with Herb—and with Mother and Marland—had gone the way of soap bubbles under the sun.

Four pounds, and perhaps a stray penny or two in addition—that was still enough money to get to France, but just barely. Was it better to find employment here and save up some money first—or safer to at least put the English Channel between himself and Sir Curtis?

His head pounded, and he was weak with hunger—Boxer had offered him a sandwich en route, but the thought of food had turned his stomach. He dragged himself into the dining room. He really should not be eating here, now that his circumstances had been drastically reduced. But he was tired and afraid. And his feet, to which he'd paid scant attention since his capture, were once again hurting badly.

"Oh, look, Violet," said a thin, elderly woman in a hat trimmed with a stuffed finch. "It's Mr. Ashburton."

The rather well-upholstered woman next to her nodded regally.

Leighton stared at them dumbly. He had a vague memory of having spoken to them at some point, aeons ago, when the world had been an entirely different place.

Recollection jolted through him. He stared at them some more. Then he was next to their table, hunger and blisters forgotten. "Miss McHenry, Miss Violet, good afternoon. You wouldn't happen to be still in need of a general dogsbody, would you?"

Eighteen

The Tea Set

From Southampton, Leighton and the misses McHenry sailed to Madeira.

Given his employers' age and ready confession that they were no sportswomen, Leighton had expected a gentle itinerary. But the misses McHenry wanted Adventure.

Each morning they rose at dawn and set out on horseback up narrow roads so steep that Leighton feared someone in the party would tumble backward. Then they would dismount, send the horses back, consume a hearty breakfast, and proceed on foot for the hike proper.

The landscape of Madeira was like nothing Leighton had ever experienced before, all sheer cliffs and precipitous gorges, unbearably breathtaking, and almost unbearably arduous for the uninitiated.

His first three days were sheer agony. Not his feet, thankfully—his blisters had healed during the steamer passage, and the misses McHenry had bought him a pair of laced-up boots made of soft, pliable leather, well suited to the demands of the terrain. But his muscles, entirely unaccustomed to the sustained exertion required for the almost vertical climbs and the equally steep and even more treacherous descents, screamed constantly in protest.

The bread, cake, and tins of corned beef that he carried on his back would feel like bricks by midmorning—and like iron ingots by the time they finally stopped for lunch. His thighs would be burning, his breaths coming in gasps, and his arms trembling visibly from holding on to his alpenstock.

And his employers, far from demanding that he look after them, would hasten to pat his cheeks with handkerchiefs that had been dipped in water. Then they would hand him a cup of coffee they had made on the Etna stove, to which a drop of cognac had been added to better revive him.

"How do you manage it?" he asked on the fourth day, fanning himself with his hat.

This day they walked along miles of narrow aqueducts, called *levada*, that carried water from the western part of the island to the east. There had been sections of the *levada* that passed through easy countryside, and other sections that required pith helmets, torches, and very sure footing for one to not slide off into the deep ravines the *levada* skirted.

It was also the first day on which he felt remotely helpful, assisting the ladies across some of the more vertiginous stretches of their path.

"Well, we are half Scotch, for one thing," said Miss McHenry, "though of course I must admit that we've spent most of our lives south of the border."

"It's from having been cooped up all our lives," said Miss Violet. "We are afraid that if we don't climb every mountain and sail every sea now, we won't have the time for it later."

"Our mother passed away before she was our age, you see," explained Miss McHenry. "Several of our sisters are also no more. And Miss Violet here had a rough winter herself."

"You had it worse, having to look after both Father and me," answered Miss Violet. She turned to Leighton. "Our father was never an easy man. He believed his children ought to conduct their lives exactly as he directed: boys doing manly things and girls settling down in marriage. But my sister and I never wanted to go down the path of matrimony, and for that we were considered failures. And the older he—and we—became, the more he considered our lives utterly wasted."

The more Leighton knew of life, the more he perceived the strictures that ladies must endure. Not just in the paucity of choices in terms of what they could do with their lives, but in the pervasive pressure placed on them to not *desire* anything else.

"We could have left to live on our own," said Miss McHenry, a trace of regret in her voice. "We had a sister who married well. Her husband had left her a considerable dower, and when she passed away she provided amply for all her siblings. But our father was vehemently opposed to the idea, even though we were both well past thirty at that point. We acquiesced—we had grown accustomed to yielding to him."

"We also thought he wouldn't live much longer," added Miss Violet.

In the beginning it had seemed that Miss McHenry was the more open of the two; but as it turned out, Miss Violet was far more likely to speak the blunt truth.

"Well, there was that," admitted Miss McHenry. "But he had the constitution of an ox, and at one point we feared he was going to outlast us all."

"And it was terrible to think that we had wasted our entire lives as a spiteful old man's marionettes," said Miss Violet.

Leighton had not realized it before: He never had to wrestle with any attachment to his captor—it had always been revulsion, pure and simple. But for the ladies it would have been a long and painful struggle, disillusionment alternating with hope that perhaps their father could still change.

"But you outlasted him instead," he said.

"By the skin of our teeth. At one point Violet was in a bad way. And I thought to myself, if the influenza spared him, but took her..." Miss McHenry drew a deep breath.

Miss Violet patted her hand. "We promised each other that if I recovered, we would leave him and finally start our own lives, whether he survived or not. In the end we didn't need to test our resolve, but trust me, we would be here today even if he were still fuming daily over his afternoon tea about how nothing is as it was or as it should be."

Miss McHenry smiled at Leighton. "And now you know how we do it. We are driven by this insatiable desire to see and experience everything. I love every mile of ocean I have crossed and every step I have taken on Madeira, even if I sometimes feel as if my skeleton is about to rattle apart."

Their guide came and said something to Leighton in Portuguese. Leighton had never studied Portuguese before, but it was similar enough to Italian that during their steamer journey, he had picked up quite a bit from the Portuguese sailors.

He thanked the guide and turned to the misses McHenry. "Senhor Lima says that three miles ahead there is a very nice waterfall."

"Then let's not dawdle anymore," Miss Violet rose. "I do believe we set out from England with the express purpose of seeing every waterfall in the whole wide world."

THE TEA SET WAS QUITE beautiful, the silver teapot at once heavy yet delicate, the silver filigree pattern on the tea glass holders as intricate as the finest lace. Miss McHenry and Miss Violet whispered to each other, debating whether they really ought to acquire anything that was both expensive and liable to break during their travels.

Miss McHenry pointed out that the bottle of Madeira that they had acquired on the island itself had arrived in Tangier—via the Canary Islands, three cities on the coast of Maghreb, an excursion into the Sahara Desert and one to the Atlas Mountains, no less—without any mishap. Miss Violet ceded that particular victory but reminded her just how much trouble it was to lug said bottle of Madeira around for the pleasure of two small sips every evening.

Leighton listened to their exchange with half an ear. All about them, merchants haggled with potential customers and laughed with one another. Grains and spices were weighed and wrapped, yards of wool and silk draped around shoulders to show off their color and texture.

He paid attention because he found everything fascinating. And because ever since his capture in Southampton he couldn't help but be acutely aware of his surroundings, sometimes excruciatingly so in crowded places.

Miss McHenry was about to capitulate to Miss Violet's argument in favor of practicality when Leighton saw the shabbily dressed boy slinking through the bazaar. As the misses McHenry moved on from stall to stall, the boy came closer and closer.

A poor boy who appeared unlikely to afford the wares wasn't necessarily a criminal. But this boy had lingered too long to be an apprentice on an errand for his master, or a houseboy sent by the cook to buy a handful of prunes for the evening's tagine.

Leighton caught the pickpocket by the wrist as the latter reached toward Miss Violet's reticule. The boy jerked, stilled, and stared at Leighton, his eyes huge with fear. He was Leighton's age, but almost half a foot shorter, with chapped lips and hollow cheeks, a boy who probably didn't eat every meal—or even every day.

Still holding on to the boy's hand, Leighton dug into a hidden pocket in his waistcoat with his free hand and extracted two three-falus copper pieces.

The boy only looked more afraid when the coins dropped in his palm.

Leighton let go of his wrist. *"Salaam."*

The boy gaped at him another moment. Before he could get away, their guide clasped a hand on his shoulder. "Is this lowlife bothering you, sir?"

The misses McHenry always introduced Leighton as their nephew, and he was thus treated as a patron, rather than a fellow servant.

"No, not at all," he said.

"Are you sure, sir?"

"Yes, I'm quite sure. Let him go. He is harmless."

The guide glared at the boy before releasing him.

Leighton exhaled. In his most desperate hour, had Miss McHenry not smiled up at him and said, *Of course we are still in need of a young man like you*, he too might now be a petty criminal, existing at the edge of hunger.

There but for the grace of God go I.

Leaving his employers for a moment, he returned to the merchant who had the gleaming silver-and-glass tea set for sale. After some negotiation, they settled on a price. Later that day he returned with sufficient coins and purchased the entire set.

He wanted to give his present to Miss McHenry after dinner. But he felt too shy. The same the next evening. At the end of their stay in Tangier, he packed away the tea set in his luggage.

He would say nothing of it to Miss McHenry until it was time for him to leave their employment.

From Tangier they sailed to Gibraltar, and from there to the isle of Capri, where the ladies took a house for the winter, a white-walled, red-roofed villa perched over a steep cliff that dropped several hundred feet to the cobalt waters of the Tyrrhenian Sea below.

Leighton made himself useful, going to the town of Capri for provisions, making tea and sandwiches, and delivering calling cards and invitations from the ladies to members of the tiny English community on the island.

But a more leisurely pace of life, one that did not have him constantly on the move, gave him too much time to think. Before he left Southampton he had sent a letter to San Francisco. Not to Mother, but to the shipping firm run by Mr. Delany's family, addressed to Mr. Delany himself, in the hope that it would escape the attention of Sir Curtis's agents, in case there had been any hired locally to keep an eye out for Leighton's arrival.

It was a short note, asking his stepfather to tell Mother that he was safe, that he might not be able to write for a while, and that everything he'd said, the last time he had spoken to her, had been bilge and drivel, the farthest thing from his true sentiments.

He had no way of knowing whether his letter had reached its intended recipient. Nor did he dare write any more letters, for fear that should they end up in Sir Curtis's hands, the postmarks would set Sir Curtis on his trail.

What if Mother never received his note? Would she worry? Would she believe that the lack of communication from him meant that he had stopped caring altogether?

And Mr. Colmes—was he able to escape Sir Curtis's wrath? And what about Lady Atwood? If ever Sir Curtis were to find out what she had done...

Such thoughts made the heavy sack he carried, full of flour, fish, olive oil, and hothouse tomatoes, feel even heavier. He lugged his load up the final few steps into the villa and handed it into the care of the housekeeper, an elderly woman who was thrilled to not be ferrying the groceries herself up the steep path to the house.

"I make you nice pasta tonight, *signor*," she said to Leighton in Italian.

"*Grazie*, Signora Mulino," Leighton answered. He enjoyed her brightly flavored pastas.

The ladies were not home; they must have gone for a visit with some of the British expatriates. Leighton made himself some coffee and went out to the balcony with half a *pan brioche dolce* for his midmorning snack.

He heard Miss Violet's return well before the latter reached the villa: She sometimes enjoyed scratching the tip of a stick along the garden walls of the other houses she passed. The front door opened and closed. After a few minutes she came out to the balcony and sat down next to him.

Wordlessly he offered her the *pan brioche dolce*, which he hadn't touched yet. She pulled off a piece and popped it into her mouth, and then another.

When she had eaten enough, he asked, "Did Miss McHenry not come back with you, Miss Violet?"

"No, she has agreed to sit for a portrait. I'm somewhat doubtful of the artist's skills, but she is always willing to give everyone a chance."

Leighton nodded. He went and fetched a cup of coffee and handed it to Miss Violet. She accepted with a nod and they sat for a while in companionable silence, watching sunlight ripple on the bright sea.

"You've been with us six months now and we haven't celebrated a birthday for you yet. Have we missed it, by any chance?"

Her question pulled Leighton out of his imagined reunion with Herb. "No, ma'am. We've a few months to go until my next birthday."

"And how old will you be by then?"

Leighton's coffee cup paused on its way to his lips. They had asked him his age earlier and he had said that he was eighteen. Was it merely a case of forgetfulness on Miss Violet's part? "Nineteen."

Miss Violet gave him a baleful look. "Why don't you tell me the truth instead, Mr. Ashburton? And that isn't your name, is it?"

Carefully Leighton set his coffee cup aside. "Why the questions, Miss Violet?"

Had she run into someone in town? Was it possible that Sir Curtis had sent an agent to a place as unlikely as Capri? If so, he—or they—most likely would have arrived at the Marina Grande on the northern shore. Could Leighton slip away from the little marina, the Marina Piccola? Would there be a fisherman willing to ferry him directly to the—

"I believe you know that Hazel and I are two of seven daughters born to our parents," said Miss Violet.

Leighton blinked, not sure what that had to do with anything. "Yes, I do."

"Well, there were actually eight of us, seven sisters and a brother. His name was Robert, and he ran away from home when he was fifteen—he simply couldn't take one more day under our father's thumb. Three years later we found him in the slums of London, suffering from an advanced stage of consumption. He died within the month.

"You look a bit like him. He had dark hair and green eyes and was tall for his age. I don't remember him that well—he was seven years older than me—but he and Hazel were close. As soon as you walked into that hotel in Southampton, Hazel noticed you."

He hadn't noticed anyone. But then, he had been dead tired, his feet full of blisters, and all he'd wanted was a place to take off his shoes, lie down, and close his eyes.

"She listened to you speak to the clerk. When you'd taken the key and left, she turned to me and said, 'But he's a child. What is he doing in Southampton by himself?'

"I admit that I did my best to dissuade her. But my sister, as sweet as she is, does not change her mind easily once it has been made up. She saw something of Robert in you and she was determined that no one else should lose a beloved brother the way we had.

"That was why she called you over and asked you about yourself. That was why she offered you a position even though we hadn't the remotest plan of having anyone else travel with us. That was why she overrode all my objections, despite my certainty she was inviting trouble and we'd be at best robbed blind and in the worst case stabbed in our sleep."

Leighton's jaw dropped. "I didn't realize I gave the impression of a cutthroat."

Miss Violet chuckled. "No, you gave the impression of tremendous dignity and reserve. But I always prefer to suspect villainy everywhere and in everyone—it saves the trouble of being disappointed later."

She took a sip of her coffee. "You must be wondering why I am telling you all this now."

He did—with a sense of foreboding. Truths were like icebergs, capable of causing unlimited wreckage. He was afraid of the truth Miss Violet was about to reveal.

"We hadn't planned on staying so long anywhere, for winter or not," she went on. "Our original plan was to continue to the Levant, Egypt, and then India. But Hazel hasn't been feeling well of late."

"Oh," said Leighton, his stomach sinking. "I thought she just needed to recover from all the traveling."

"That's what she had told me at first. But now I think it's far worse than she lets on. And I don't believe she's gone to have her portrait painted. For something like that she doesn't need to persuade me to go home—I'd have gladly stayed to keep her company. I think she just wanted me gone so she could visit a physician without my knowledge."

Miss Violet clasped her hands together. "I don't know what is going to happen. We might have to go to Naples for her treatment. And if her condition worsens beyond a certain point, we might have to return to England. One has to go home for certain things."

If Miss McHenry were found to be dying, she meant.

Leighton's throat tightened—he had become even fonder of the sisters than he'd realized. "Is she really in such a serious condition?"

"Well, keep in mind that I'm a pessimist. But yes, she could be. Should the worst happen, I want to know how I could do right by you. But I can't do that if I know nothing of your background—we both thought you'd have opened up to us by now, but you are quite the tight-lipped young man."

"It's not that I don't trust you and Miss McHenry. I do. It's just that I've become used to not saying anything to those I care about—the less they know, the less trouble I would cause them."

"But you did run away from home?"

Leighton carefully considered how to answer Miss Violet's question while giving away the minimum amount of information. But then he opened his mouth and out poured all the words he had kept inside since Father's passing. He told her about Starling Manor, about the two men who loved each other and adored him, about those long idyllic summer days that he still dared not think too much or too often about, the memories so bright and sharp they were like daggers in his chest.

Of Father's death and its aftermath he gave a spare account, and he elided over most of Sir Curtis's cruelties, ending with, "And then I left—and met you and Miss McHenry. The rest you know."

Miss Violet leaned forward and took his hands. "I'm so sorry about everything that's happened to you."

He squeezed her hands, feeling the heat of tears in his eyes. "My father's death would never not be a tragedy, but I have been unbelievably fortunate. When I most needed it, always someone has stepped in and saved me."

"And that is as it should be," said Miss Violet firmly. "I'm glad Hazel asked you to come, I'm glad you agreed, and I'm glad that I was wrong about everything."

She smiled at him. He smiled back.

For a moment there was nothing but sunshine in his heart, but anxiety returned all too soon. "What about Miss McHenry? I want to help you look after her, but I don't think I dare go back to England."

Miss Violet took a deep breath. "If that day comes, I will take care of Hazel—goodness knows she has taken enough care of me through the years. You, young man, you will keep going east, toward your friend and your family. Toward everything that has kept your hope alive all these years."

LEIGHTON UNEARTHED THE MOROCCAN TEA set from his luggage and polished it until the silver glowed. That afternoon he served tea to the ladies from the exquisite set.

Miss McHenry gasped. "Violet, didn't we see a set exactly like this in Tangier? What a coincidence that they should have it in this house, more than a thousand miles away."

Miss Violet raised a brow at Leighton.

He swallowed, still feeling shy. "It isn't a coincidence. I bought the set that day in the bazaar...for you."

"Oh, you shouldn't have!" exclaimed Miss McHenry. Then she grinned mischievously. "But I'm so glad you did—after we left Morocco I used to think about this tea set and wish I'd gone ahead with the purchase, the devil with practical concerns."

Leighton lifted the gleaming teapot to pour into glasses set in the silver-filigree holders. "Well, now it's all yours."

Puzzlement came into Miss McHenry's eyes. "But if you've had it all this time, why are you giving it to me today, instead of, say, last Christmas?"

For Christmas he had given Miss Violet a bottle of limoncello and Miss McHenry a small oil painting of her favorite vista on Capri, purchased from a local artist.

"Because—a gift not given is like a book not opened."

Miss McHenry gave him a quizzical look, but did not press him for a more clear-cut answer. "Very profound, my dear. Now do let us raise these very, very pretty glasses and have a toast."

"What shall we toast?" Miss Violet asked.

Miss McHenry grinned from ear to ear. "That an old woman's burgeoning hypochondria turned out to be just that, a whole lot of well-stirred nonsense."

Miss Violet blinked. "Do you mean—"

"Yes!" cried Miss McHenry exuberantly. "I know you've been worried about my health. And I've been scaring myself with thoughts of tumors and whatnot. But today I saw the finest internist in Naples—"

"You went to *Naples*?"

Miss McHenry chortled. "Well, actually I paid for him to come to Capri, to the house of our artist friend—and he declared me in fine health, except for the ulcers that I've developed in the course of our travels. Now I shall have to eat much more carefully. No more indulging in strong coffee or spicy food—alas that I discovered both so late. But if I coddle my stomach with porridge and plain broth, he sees no reason why I shouldn't live to be ninety."

Leighton laughed out of sheer relief. "Thank goodness. Miss Violet had me convinced your health was rapidly deteriorating."

"Well, I did tell you I was a pessimist." Miss Violet smiled sheepishly. "Perhaps in the future I should say that I am a raging pessimist."

"You did some good," said Miss McHenry to her sister. "Because you convinced our young fellow here that I had one foot in the grave, I finally got my tea set."

They all laughed at that. Then Miss McHenry lifted her glass again. "Let's drink to the pleasure of being alive, boring dinners or not."

Miss Violet did likewise. "To the best sister in the world."

Leighton clinked his glass with them both. "To friends. May they ever flourish."

Nineteen

Shao-ye

YING-YING STOOD IN THE MIDDLE of the room, blindfolded, listening.

Amah was moving about the room. Her footsteps were completely soundless, her breaths likewise. But sometimes the edge of her blouse-tunic brushed against a corner of a table and gave Ying-ying an idea of where she was.

Which was helpful if the objective of the exercise was for her to hit Amah—and occasionally it was—but today's goal was something else.

In the next courtyard a songbird chittered. Running feet on a walking path to the west—a lackey was delivering something in a hurry. A shrill yet wobbly musical note, followed by a burst of laughter—one of Da-ren's concubines was learning to play the flute, though she really shouldn't.

In Ying-ying's rooms, silence.

Then, sound: a barely perceptible disturbance of the air.

Ying-ying lifted the painted silk fan in her hand and blocked the incoming object a handspan from her face. She spun around and knocked another one that was coming for her shoulder. Then another, aimed at her knees.

The tiny missiles kept coming; she kept deflecting them, her mind blank, her concentration absolute.

At last they stopped. She did not let her guard down. Amah sometimes waited a long time, just until Ying-ying began to relax, before attacking again.

But today she said, "That's enough."

Ying-ying pulled off her blindfold and fetched the broom: There were mung beans all over the floor that needed to be swept up. Since direct hand-to-hand combat was unwise even inside their rooms—sounds still traveled—Amah had become quite inventive in Ying-ying's training. And though most of the maneuvers she devised did not involve any real weapons, they still pushed Ying-ying to her limits. Today's exercise, for example, required Ying-ying to infuse the fabric of the fan with her own chi; otherwise a mung bean sent from Amah's fingers would easily put a hole in the silk.

When she had cleared away the evidence of their training, she made a cup of tea and brought it to Amah. "Master looks tired."

It had been a while since she appeared in the pink of health. From time to time Ying-ying ventured to suggest medicinal potions to feed the spleen or nourish the gallbladder, but Amah always waved them aside.

"I'm all right," Amah said.

Ying-ying wasn't entirely sure about that. Sometimes she wondered whether their lack of freedom wasn't affecting Amah, especially since, as far as Ying-ying could tell, she hadn't gone out on one of her nocturnal forays since their arrival in Da-ren's residence nearly three years ago.

Did a woman addicted to gambling sicken if she couldn't have any illicit excitement with cup and dice?

"Maybe we should ask the kitchen to—"

Amah cut her off. "Don't be so long-winded. I already said I'm fine."

Ying-ying turned her face aside and rolled her eyes. Lately there was no pleasing the woman. "In that case I'll get ready to go to my English teacher."

Ying-ying had thought her lessons with Master Gordon—that was his real name—would be a secret between the two of them. To her shock, he had applied directly to Da-ren for permission—and received it. She had been both profoundly relieved and more than a little disconcerted. Too much education for girls was frowned upon. Had Da-ren allowed it because he admired learning—as in Mother's case—or because Ying-ying might as well, since she was a bastard with foreign blood?

But whatever Da-ren's reasons, with his sanctioning, Ying-ying could proceed openly to Master Gordon's rooms every other morning—she wouldn't have minded daily lessons, but Amah had put her foot down and Ying-ying had acquiesced.

She gathered up a stack of English newspapers to return to Master Gordon—he received them by post and thought they provided not only good material for a learner, but a glimpse or two into how the English lived their lives. The book he loaned her, *Pride and Prejudice*, was more difficult for her to understand—and not just due to the language barrier. As she made her way through the chapters, frequently checking the English-Chinese dictionary he had gifted her, her mouth was almost always open from astonishment.

Such unfettered lives they led. The men of China—and maybe most of the women too—would be aghast. But having women who enjoyed a great many liberties didn't seem to have hurt the English any. They were strong, powerful, and constantly advancing, while China lumbered and lurched, taking two steps backward for every step forward.

She tucked the newspapers under her arm and grabbed an umbrella. The day promised rain, for which she was glad—it had been quite hot in the past few days. Out into the courtyard there were still no fish and no songbirds, but otherwise Amah had transformed the formerly barren space into a pleasant garden. A row of young pomegranate trees lined an entire wall; along the opposite wall, tree peonies that in spring bloomed a lovely, creamy pink. And in big glazed pots there were China roses, cockscombs, and ornamental peppers.

Her headache medicine must have worked wonders for the majordomo.

The rain started when Ying-ying was halfway across the residence and came down quite heavily by the time she reached the garden outside the Court of Contemplative Bamboo. Inside the garden, Little Dragon was unloading a cart full of big rocks, the hem of his robe tied around his waist. And in the pavilion, out of the rain, sat a thin man drinking a cup of tea, looking permanently hunched over.

She recognize him as the same lackey to whom Little Dragon had delivered a flagon of heated spirits one winter day: Chang, a man of very little importance in Da-ren's household, someone sent out to do the work no one else wanted. It puzzled her how this man managed to have someone as proud as Little Dragon treat him with such consideration.

Little Dragon greeted her with his usual frostiness. "Bai Gu-niang."

She returned an equally aloof nod.

MASTER GORDON WAS OPENING HIS windows as she walked in. He had told her that compared to London, it hardly rained in Peking. And when it did, the rhythm was exactly the opposite, with summer being the rainiest season, and the rest of the year almost bone-dry.

"Enjoying the sound of rain?" she asked, knowing that he did—through the ache of nostalgia, that was.

"Ah, yes—and the memories of my carefree youth."

He poured tea for her. Sometimes they drank jasmine tea, sometimes green tea, and once in a while a spectacularly expensive white tea from Fukien; but when it rained the tea was always from Darjeeling.

The scent of which always recalled their first meeting. How fortunate she was to have met him. What her life would have been like otherwise, she dared not even think.

"I know an exquisite poem about listening to the rain," she told him.

While he taught her English, she also helped him with his Chinese. Mother would have considered her understanding of poetry completely woeful, but it was more than adequate for explaining the intricacies of the language to a foreigner.

"Will you write it out for me?" he asked, excited.

She still regarded her own handwriting with disdain, but he loved to watch her wield a brush, with the kind of admiration that must have been shining on her own face when she'd watched Mother at her calligraphy practice. She smiled at him. "Of course."

He went inside his study to retrieve his set of Chinese writing implements: They always used the front room, to show that they had nothing to hide—Da-ren's permission not withstanding, Ying-ying still needed to be mindful about how her conduct would be perceived.

As soon as he left, Little Dragon entered. She didn't know how, since he had been doing heavy work just a short time ago, but his clothes looked completely spotless, with barely even a speck of rain on his shoulders.

He set down a pile of newspapers, magazines, and letters on a side table. "These were delivered from the British Legation. Bai Gu-niang, please see to it that Master Kuo-tung has them in hand."

The expression of distaste on his face...She could not understand him. Other servants disdained her because she was nobody, but he wasn't the sycophantic sort. What cause did he have to despise her, she who had never asked him to do any extra work or treated him disrespectfully?

"I will," she said.

He withdrew. Master Gordon came back with a brocade-wrapped box that contained the "four treasures of the study"—ink stone, ink stick, writing brush, and writing paper. He ladled a small amount of water on the ink stone and ground the ink stick in a gentle circular motion, as she had shown him.

"Master Gordon, why do you suppose Little Dragon thinks ill of me?" she heard herself ask.

His hand stilled for a moment, before he resumed the grinding. "I do not believe it is anything against you, per se. It's more..."

He glanced at her. "Do you not see the similarities between the two of you?"

His question made no sense. She could see nothing in common at all between herself and Little Dragon.

"Would it help you if I tell you he was born the year after the French ransacked the Old Summer Palace?"

She did not comprehend immediately. Then her hand moved on its own to cover her mouth. Was he implying that Little Dragon was also of mixed blood? "He *told* you?"

"He didn't need to. He does not have eyes like yours, but he has unusual height for a Chinese. His skin is several shades fairer than the most housebound Chinese women. It would also explain his interest in learning French and not any of the other languages I speak," answered Master Gordon.

She was still flabbergasted. "If you are right—if we are indeed both of European paternity—then why does he treat me as he does? Wouldn't he want to be friends instead?"

"But look at the difference in your stations in life. You may think you are a nobody, my dear, but you are still a guest of a prince of the blood. You have a courtyard of your own, an amah to look after you, and even an Englishman to give you lessons.

"His life has probably been immeasurably more difficult. Once he asked me whether he could give some spirits that Da-ren had gifted me to this servant, Chang. I asked who Chang was and Little Dragon said he was the man who had saved him from a life begging on the streets of Tientsin."

So he detested her because she was no better than he was, yet had enjoyed a life of ease and plenty.

She shook her head.

"I know it isn't fair," said Master Gordon gently, "to be judged for circumstances beyond your control. But his opinion diminishes him, not you."

She blew out a breath of air and dipped a fine-tipped brush into the ink he had produced. "Well, at least now I know. And by the way, a delivery came for you from the British Legation."

MASTER GORDON HAD RECEIVED LETTERS and packages before, when Ying-ying was with him. Always he had set everything aside and continued with their lesson. But today he leaped up from his seat, his face flushed with something that was half excitement and half dread.

"Would Bai Gu-niang mind if I took a moment to read this letter?"

They now conversed largely in English, but at her insistence he still called her Bai Gu-niang, instead of Miss Blade.

"Of course not."

She wrote out the poem while he stood in a corner of the room and read his letter. He was practically shaking when he came back to his seat.

"I hope it's good news," she said, setting down her brush. She couldn't tell one way or the other.

"I—I think so. I hope so. My goodness, I hope so."

"What happened?"

"Do you remember the house in the south of England? I gave one of the jade tablets my father had brought back to England to the master of the house."

"Yes, of course. He was your dearest friend."

"Well, he passed away five years ago. The letter is from his widow. She tells me that there is a possibility that his son might be on his way to visit me."

"But that's wonderful!"

"Yes, it is. But it would not be an easy journey for him. I am beside myself, imagining all the worst-case scenarios." He shook his head as if to clear it. "Forgive me—I'm a little overcome."

"It's quite all right," she reassured him, feeling rather overcome herself—she wanted so much for him to be happy.

He poured the remainder of his tea down his throat and made a valiant effort to start the day's lesson. But she excused herself after some time, knowing he probably wished to read the letter again and again and do whatever it was that people did when they had news that was both exhilarating and unsettling.

"Just remember," she said as she rose. "Don't do that."

They both knew what she was talking about: the jade tablet. She had come upon him at the beginning of the previous year looking at it with fierce concentration, oblivious to her presence—and had admonished him for not heeding her warnings about never having the tablet in the open again.

"Not a chance," he replied, smiling.

At the door she turned back. "I hope he comes."

"I hardly dare hope," said Master Gordon, his voice cracking just a little. "But yes, I hope so with every fiber of my being."

WHAT IF MASTER GORDON'S FRIEND'S son did come? There was certainly space in Master Gordon's rooms for him to stay. But would Da-ren allow it, or would the thought of two foreigners under his roof be too much even for him?

All those thoughts and more careened inside Ying-ying's head. She scarcely knew whether she was on her way home or charging headlong into Da-ren's study.

"...can't leave yet. Wait a little longer, please, I beg you."

She blinked—the voice belonged to Little Dragon. She was in the garden outside the Court of Contemplative Bamboo, and he was speaking from the other side of the artificial hill. Amah had always instructed her to walk heavily: a noiseless progress was the surest sign of a martial-arts expert. But distracted by Master Gordon's news, she must have forgotten—and Little Dragon and whomever he was speaking to had no idea that she was within hearing range.

It was not a bad place to hold a private conversation for those who otherwise could not find any privacy. Most other servants didn't come to this part of the residence, as the majordomo frowned on anyone making unnecessary noises near Da-ren's study. And Little Dragon had no doubt counted on Ying-ying and Master Gordon being absorbed in their lesson.

"How much longer?" came a girl's voice. "You said we can go to Tientsin. You said you can find work with the foreigners. That was two years ago."

Her words were not plaintive, but anguished.

"I know it's my fault. I know we should have gone years ago. But he is scared to leave. He doesn't even dare visit his old mother—and he's desperate to see her."

"Every day Shao-ye calls me stupid. Useless. He says I can't even smile properly. He says he wished he'd asked for Little Lotus instead. He has no idea how much *I* wish he had asked for Little Lotus instead. Or maybe he does—maybe that's why he hates me so much."

It was all Ying-ying could do to not make any sounds. The girl was Little Orchid, the maid who had been given over for Shao-ye's bedchamber use. Little Dragon was playing with fire. Even if Shao-ye had wearied of Little Orchid, Ying-ying didn't think he would want her to rendezvous with another young man, especially one who was both taller and better-looking.

She didn't want—or dare—to listen anymore. If Little Dragon knew that she had learned his secret...She circulated her chi as high as it would go, and retreated silently back into the Court of Contemplative Bamboo, all the way back into Master Gordon's rooms.

He looked up in surprise at her reappearance, the letter open before him. She pointed at the umbrella she had left behind and took it in hand. And then she said loudly, "I'm leaving, Master Gordon. I had better get home before a thunderstorm comes."

She stomped out, making her footsteps almost heavy enough to crack the paving stones. This time, when she passed through the garden, it was silent as a tomb.

YING-YING COULD NOT STOP THINKING about Little Orchid. Little Dragon would do fine for himself someday—if he could manage to keep his pride in check. But the poor girl...her plight made Ying-ying's teeth hurt.

The path she was on ended at a wider path. She had to stop for a moment to reorient herself. The next courtyard was where Mrs. Mu-he lived, and usually Ying-ying avoided this part of the residence, because it was too close to where the lordlings' Confucian masters lived.

This particular path, however, did not take her past the Confucian masters' courtyard, and she had no reason to suppose Shao-ye would ever visit old Mrs. Mu-he. But as she passed by the front gate of Mrs. Mu-he's courtyard, a man came out.

Shao-ye. She immediately bent her neck and walked even faster.

"Halt," he ordered.

There was no one else on the path. She stopped.

"Come back here."

Slowly she complied, keeping her face down. What was he doing in Mrs. Mu-he's courtyard? Of course, she should have remembered: Mrs. Mu-he had a new maid, a plump, pretty girl.

"I wasn't here today. Do you understand?" he said softly. "You never saw me here."

Ying-ying understood. Shao-ye had been in considerable trouble last month. Apparently he had become enamored of a young concubine of one of Da-ren's friends. That was fine—nothing made a middle-aged man happier than to have a woman who inspired lust all around. But the lordling went several steps beyond. He sent her gifts. He proposed rendezvous. That had infuriated the Da-ren's friend and had put Da-ren into an unusual display of rage. Shao-ye was supposed to be on his best behavior now, not going around trysting with maids.

"Yes, Young Master."

"Good. Go." He waved an imperious hand.

She bent her knees slightly and left, exhaling in relief.

"Stop. Turn around," he commanded anew.

What now?

"Lift up your face."

"This humble maid does not dare."

"I grant you permission. Lift up your face."

Her jaw clenched tight, she raised her face but kept her eyes downcast. He sucked in a breath. "Lovely. Most lovely. Who are you? How have I never seen you here?"

She was a little short of fourteen, but very tall for her age. And since her monthly flow started the year before, her chest had begun to burgeon in an embarrassing fashion. She could easily be mistaken for someone two or three years older.

"I'm Bai Fu-ren's daughter."

Mother's name took a moment to register with him. "I'd heard she was the most beautiful woman. But her daughter rivals her."

"Young Master is too generous with his praise." What rotten luck. Why did he have to be here today? She had taken so much care to never cross his path.

"Not at all. You are far more exquisite than that Peony Petal Minister Chao is so proud of. Fairer, too."

Ying-ying cursed inwardly.

A young lackey came running. "Da-ren is looking for you, Young Master. You had better make haste."

He swore. But he didn't leave immediately. He stared at Ying-ying some more—and for good measure trailed a fingertip along her cheek. "Now that I know Bai Gu-niang lives here, and that her beauty shames the spring blossoms, I hope to see much more of her."

She broke into a run as soon as he turned away. She must wash her face immediately. "Where have you been?"

Da-ren. Ying-ying had already sprinted around the corner; now she froze—until she realized that Da-ren wasn't address her, but his son.

"Just…just out walking," stammered Shao-ye.

"And when did you develop that habit?" Da-ren snapped. "Whose courtyard is that?"

No one said anything for a long moment. Then the young lackey answered, his voice not quite even, "That would be the majordomo's."

The slap reverberated in the walled alley. "You dare lie to me? That's Mrs. Mu-he's or I'm a Han."

Another slap, even louder. Shao-ye moaned.

"Is this how you teach your lackeys? You are to give them moral guidance, not signal them to lie."

"He lied on his own. I didn't tell him to do it."

This time Da-ren slapped him twice. "Shut up. You, go in the courtyard and bring out everyone."

"Yes, Da-ren." The lackey's voice trembled. "Right away."

Ying-ying smiled grimly. This promised to be good. There was chaos in the courtyard: Mrs. Mu-he demanded to know what was happening, and why was everyone headed outside just when she was getting ready for her bath.

Distant knocks came. Someone was rapping on a courtyard gate, but not gaining admission. The knocks became louder and more impatient. "Anybody home?" a sullen voice shouted.

Was the lackey knocking on the door of *Ying-ying's* courtyard? If so, why hadn't Amah answered? Where was she?

Ying-ying ran again.

THE MANSERVANT HAD LET HIMSELF into the courtyard and now stood before the door of the reception room, shifting his weight from foot to foot.

He turned around as soon as he sensed Ying-ying's approach, the same servant who had refused her the sweet walnut soup years ago. "Bai Gu-niang? What's going on? Why is there no one to take this food? I can't stand here forever. My joints suffer enough without having to shiver in the cold."

Usually lunch never came so early to their courtyard—but she'd heard the majordomo's headaches had become much less frequent, thanks to Amah's ministrations. Perhaps this was another way of repaying her.

Ying-ying put on a conciliatory smile. "Master Keeper Po," she said sweetly. Only the majordomo was properly addressed as Master Keeper. But all the menservants, especially the older ones like Po, adored the elevation of their meager office. "Master Keeper, so sorry you had to wait out in the cold. My amah must have been called away—you know how everyone always needs her to brew a bowl of medicine."

She opened the door and quickly glanced inside. Amah wasn't in the reception room. "Here, I'll take it from you." She took the double steamer. "Please wait a moment."

She went to the next room and retrieved a small sealed urn of eau-de-vie from a bottom cabinet. Da-ren had kept a number of them with Mother. Now that they were without ready access to coins or silver ingots, the liquor had become their currency.

"Here, Master Keeper, this will keep your joints smooth." She pressed the spherical earthen urn into his hands. "Thank you for your trouble."

Po's grin made his eyes disappear. "Bai Gu-niang, I've always told everyone you are the nicest, most generous girl."

A whimper of pain, barely audible, came from the inner rooms. Ying-ying's stomach dropped. But she widened her smile. "Master Keeper leave well."

"Many thanks, Bai Gu-niang. I'll set aside some sweet walnut soup for you next time."

Amah was on the floor of the innermost room, her arms under her, her legs still half-stuck in the cross-legged position, as if she had simply toppled over from her bed in the middle of a set of chi exercises.

"Master!" Ying-ying cried.

She ran to Amah, turned her over, and gasped at the blood on her face, her clothes, and the floor. She wiped the blood off Amah's chin. "What happened? Who did this to you? How badly are you hurt?"

Amah's face twisted in pain. A long moment passed before she could answer. "Get me back up into the lotus position."

Ying-ying lifted her and put her on the bed. But Amah couldn't hold herself in lotus position. Ying-ying settled behind Amah and held her straight by the shoulders, her knees on either side of Amah's to keep her correctly aligned.

On a hunch, she took Amah's wrist and felt her pulse. She didn't know enough about to diagnose diseases, but Amah's wildly erratic pulse was clearly indicative of severe internal ills. "What's the matter? Has your chi gone all awry?"

Practitioners of exterior martial arts, like the lordlings' instructor, at most risked injury to skin and sinew. But those who delved into the interior arts, who sought to harness their chi, treaded a much more precarious path.

The more one manipulated and strengthened one's chi, the greater care one must take to keep it under control. The masters understood the challenge and were always diligent. But sometimes mishaps could not be avoided. A serious injury, such as the one Amah had sustained, could wreak havoc on chi: fragment the flow, damage the channels, and make it forever afterward difficult to control.

"Put your hand between my shoulder blades," Amah whispered hoarsely. "Guide my chi, if you can."

Amah had done it for Ying-ying before, when Ying-ying had minor troubles with circulating her chi fluidly. She had simply put her hand on Ying-ying back and, with a small infusion of her own chi, solved the problem.

Ying-ying bit her bottom lip. She put her hand where Amah told her to—and groaned. It was a catastrophe. No wonder Amah had spewed blood. Her chi rampaged like an angry beast. At the thought of having to tame *that*, Ying-ying's palms shook.

Gingerly she pushed a trickle of her chi into Amah's system, praying to all the gods and bodhisattvas that she knew what she was doing. She didn't. Not at all. This task was beyond her meager skills.

But she hadn't counted on Amah's expertise. As the new flow entered, Amah used it to calm and nudge her own chi into a more regular circulation.

"Don't stop until I tell you, or you might kill me."

Ying-ying perspired. The pressure of the situation made her eyes bulge and her teeth chatter. *Concentrate, concentrate*, she told herself. *Breathe. Pretend this is nothing more than a regular morning chi exercise. Keep your own internal flow fluent. Keep it up. Keep it up. Don't falter now. Don't kill her. Whatever you do, don't kill her.*

An aeon passed before Amah said, "Remove your hand."

Ying-ying felt as empty as if all her marrow had been sucked out of her. She staggered off the bed, peeled off Amah's bloody clothes, put her in something clean, laid her down, and drew a cover over her. Next she put a few of Amah's medicine balls in a clay pot. While the brew simmered, she washed the soiled clothes and scrubbed the floor.

When the medicine was ready, she brought it in a bowl to the bed. "Are you feeling better, Master?"

"I'll live," Amah rasped.

Ying-ying fed her a spoonful of the medicine. "What happened?"

Amah sighed. "I've been having trouble with my chi for a while—ever since that bounty hunter. I was in no shape to fight him. If only I'd been able to shake him loose…"

That was why Amah had looked sickly ever since. Ying-ying was ashamed that she had never guessed.

"Things were going badly today," Amah went on, "I could barely hang on. I wanted to bring my chi back to center and quit, but couldn't, so I had to keep battling with it. I had no idea how long it was taking—I was concentrating hard. And then that lackey came with lunch. My concentration broke when he began banging on the door."

Ying-ying bitterly regretted the quality liquor she had given Po. She should have kicked him instead.

She fed Amah some more of the medicine. "Will you recover?"

Amah sighed again. "I don't know. The only way to find out is to go on a long retreat."

"You should do it. You can do it right here. I'll stay home and make sure nobody disturbs you."

"It isn't possible here," Amah said. "I cannot simply disappear for three months. People will ask questions."

Three months! "Then you should go away for that much time," Ying-ying said with a bravery she did not feel.

"I can't do that either. Not immediately, anyway."

"But you just can't let your condition drag on."

Amah drank nearly the entire bowl of medicine before she pushed it away. "You don't worry. A fortune-teller once told me that if I can live past forty, I'll live to eighty."

That comforted Ying-ying more than she thought possible. "I'll make you some porridge."

It wasn't till later in the afternoon that she realized Amah hadn't turned forty yet—and wouldn't do so for another six months.

Twenty

Departure

"BAI GU-NIANG. BAI GU-NIANG. BAI Gu-niang is so hard to find."

Ying-ying hated that voice. It belonged to Big Treasure, Shao-ye's most loyal lackey. He leered at her.

Now, on days when she had her English lessons, Big Treasure and another lackey, Little Bull, waited for her to come out of Master Gordon's rooms. And sometimes they caught her.

"Why are Master Keepers looking for me?" She kept walking. They put themselves to either side of her.

"Always for the same reason, of course. Young Master misses you. He can't eat or sleep for the love of you."

"Master Keeper exaggerates. I hear Young Master hosted a feast in the Pavilion of Dainty Blossoms only three days ago." What better way for the young profligate to celebrate a night of freedom, with Da-ren away on court business, than to carouse and debauch in one of Peking's premier houses of pleasure?

Big Treasure didn't miss a beat. "It was for the sake of appearance. He sighed and pined for you all night. Didn't he, Little Bull?"

"He did. I felt really sorry for him," Little Bull came in right on cue.

"So won't you come with us to see him?" the elder lackey beseeched, his tone oily. "He'd be so happy if Bai Gu-niang only had a kind word for him."

"I'm afraid not. My amah is most strict, on Da-ren's instruction."

"Your amah wouldn't know."

"She has her eyes on the clock when it's time for me to arrive home."

Ying-ying turned a corner. Big Treasure kept on her, but Little Bull ran off in a different direction—no doubt to inform Shao-ye that they had caught her en route.

For some reason, Shao-ye was intimidated by Amah. After two attempts to see Ying-ying in her courtyard, he had stopped. And Amah had smiled, too, while denying him any privilege that would conflict with the proper upbringing of a young woman. If Ying-ying could make her way home, she was safe. She wished Amah would accompany her. But Amah, ever fearful of being discovered by the unknown martial artist who had injured her, was reluctant to venture far afield from their own courtyard.

"Bai Gu-niang really is so heartless?" Big Treasure's tone was losing its false obsequiousness.

Ying-ying said nothing. The abuses would come now. Big Treasure was nothing if not predictable.

"Bai Gu-niang can't be so obtuse, can she? Young Master's desire is a compliment to her. Who is he? He is a cousin to the Son of Heaven. The dowager empress herself is taken with him.

"And who are you? We don't even know. Your mother was once a whore—that everyone knows. What's the daughter of a whore got to be so proud about, I ask you?"

It would be so easy. One direct swipe across the face and he'd go down like a straw man. A few taps on strategic points in his body and he'd writhe as if tortured by the agents of hell. Amah was not unfamiliar with the darker side of martial arts, and neither was Ying-ying.

"If you serve Young Master well, he might ask Da-ren for you," Big Treasure went on, oblivious to his peril. "If you go on being so obstinate and ungrateful, Da-ren might just wash his hands of you and give you to the likes of us."

Then wouldn't you *have a nasty surprise coming.* But Ying-ying kept her lips tightly clamped. There was no point in saying anything back, none at all.

"Who feeds you? Who clothes you? Who gives you a roof over your head? Da-ren. And you refuse to be nice to his son. I've never seen such ingratitude. And from a whore's daughter."

And so the repetitions began. The walk was long enough that Big Treasure would repeat himself three or four times by the time Ying-ying slammed shut the gate of her courtyard in his face.

"Bai Gu-niang, please stay your step."

Shao-ye. Ying-ying balled her hands into fists. Da-ren's advisers kept a close eye on him these days. Most of the time, even when his lackeys could locate her, he couldn't get away from the advisers to come pester her himself.

She should have consulted the almanac this morning. Apparently she had chosen the wrong day to step out of her front door.

She turned around and curtsied. "Young Master."

He smiled and advanced. A wave of his hand sent Big Treasure scurrying some distance away.

"It has been too long, Bai Gu-niang. Has Bai Gu-niang been well?" He had smooth manners. Smooth manners and lascivious eyes that scanned her up and down.

"Thanks to Young Master's blessings, this humble maid has been well."

"Bai Gu-niang grows more beautiful with each passing day."

"Young Master overpraises, as always."

"Not at all, not at all." He walked in a circle about her, inspecting her. "Such loveliness should be clothed in the finest silks and draped in the roundest pearls. I will be most honored if Bai Gu-niang permits me to supply her such trifles."

"My fortune is thin, Young Master. I dare not aspire to such rich presents."

"Bai Gu-niang is much too modest." He was undeterred. "I plan to speak to my father very soon. I do not think he will refuse me this request."

Ying-ying almost looked up. Big Treasure never neglected to mention that if she pleased Shao-ye in bed, he might raise her to an official concubine. But she had always considered that line so much deception, meant to make her think she might get more than Shao-ye's dubious lovemaking.

"After all, he took you in, so he is responsible for you. I will convince him that once he gives you to me, I will reform my ways and devote myself to my studies. I don't see why the solution shouldn't appeal to him."

She was thunderstruck. There was a certain twisted logic to Shao-ye's reasoning. What if Da-ren indeed came to see the matter from this point of view?

"Bai Gu-niang is shy." He moved closer and whispered in her ear. "But I can see she is secretly pleased with this idea. If we are to be united sooner or later, why not come with me today and learn a few of the pleasures of the bedchamber?"

Her nails dug into her palms. "I dare not, Young Master. My amah would beat me if I were late home."

He lifted a braid of her hair. "Surely she will understand if I say I detained you."

"She has her orders directly from Da-ren himself to strictly watch my every step. I'm afraid she'll yield only when he commands differently."

The lordling tore off an embroidered amulet sachet he wore at his waist and hurled it against the nearest wall. "Da-ren! Da-ren! My whole life I've had to listen to him. Everything I want, he stands in my way."

Ying-ying took an involuntary step back. An old man came running—one of Da-ren's advisers. "Young Master, here you are. I've been looking for you everywhere. Please come back. Otherwise what will I say when Da-ren asks where you are?"

Shao-ye's face contorted in rage. "If he asks, tell him I'm in the shithouse. Or am I not even allowed that anymore?"

The old man did not even blanch. Presumably it was not the first time he had heard such language from Shao-ye. Shao-ye hurled another string of abuses, but in the end left with the older man: It would not be wise for him to further antagonize Da-ren.

Ying-ying exhaled. She hoped Shao-ye would get caught being absent. And then Da-ren would be in no mood to listen to him ask for Ying-ying.

On the other hand, he could point out that Ying-ying had become a dire distraction for him, and that actually having her in his bedroom would be the best way to help him concentrate on more important matters.

She pressed her fingers into her temples. No wonder grown-ups had headaches. Life itself was beginning to seem one unending headache.

AMAH WAS STANDING OUTSIDE THE gate of their courtyard, waiting for her. She took one look at Ying-ying and sighed softly. "Come in fast. Your lunch is getting cold."

Only after Ying-ying began eating did she ask, "Young Master's minions got hold of you today?"

Ying-ying shoveled a round of rice into her mouth, along with a piece of fish. She could taste nothing. "He was there himself. He said he would ask Da-ren for me."

Amah set down her bowl. "He did?"

"Would Da-ren agree?" Ying-ying stared into her rice.

"There is a chance," Amah said slowly. "The boy has grown into a wastrel. But I hear that when he was small, Da-ren had quite adored him. Even today, Da-ren must still hope that he'll reform. And if the boy swears up and down that he'd make good if only he has you, he just might get what he wants."

This was not want Ying-ying wanted to hear. "What should we do then, if Da-ren agrees?"

Amah stood up. "If Da-ren agrees, it would be too late."

"Then what can we do?" Tears of panic and frustration welled up in her eyes. Would they have to flee? How could Amah's health take the abuse of a life on the move?

Amah came around and laid a hand on her shoulder. "I will think of something. He will not have you."

YING-YING AND AMAH BROKE ALL the rules Amah had set for them.

It was no small feat to get a drugged Shao-ye out of Da-ren's residence and to the vicinity of Minister Chao's. They hid and waited. It wasn't that late in the year, but the night was chilly. Ying-ying shivered grimly.

Near morning, Amah judged that Shao-ye would shortly awaken. Now came the crucial part of their plan: She placed a red pill into Shao-ye's mouth and carefully manipulated his jaws so that the pill dissolved and slid down his throat: True Words pill, its effect similar to a night of hard drinking.

Taking advantage of the last darkness before dawn, they placed Shao-ye close to the front gate of Minister Chao's residence and hurried home. Amah went to bed. But Ying-ying was too nervous to even sit down. She paced back and forth until breakfast came.

Po was surprised and pleased to see her. "Bai Gu-niang is receiving the breakfast herself?"

"My amah is slightly unwell," she said. "Thank you, Master Keeper Po."

He bowed but didn't leave. Instead, he leaned a little closer. "Has Bai Gu-niang heard the news?"

Her stomach tightened. "What news? You are first person I've seen today, Master Keeper Po."

Po lowered his voice. "I don't know for sure myself. But I think Young Master is in big trouble."

"How so?" Ying-ying hoped the tremor in her voice did not call attention to itself.

"Old Tang at the front door said that he was delivered back this morning by Minister Chao's servants. They said that at the crack of dawn he was shrieking outside Minister Chao's walls, calling him nasty names that I can't even repeat to Bai Gu-niang."

"Is it true?" Ying-ying widened her eyes. "The same Minister Chao he had already offended earlier by being too attentive to the man's concubine?"

"The very one! Young Miao from Da-ren's courtyard said Da-ren beat Young Master for the duration of a meal with a walking stick. He said Da-ren even drew his sword at one point, threatening to end Young Master once and for all!"

Ying-ying gasped and covered her mouth. "What is going to happen to Young Master now?"

AN ANGRY BUT DIGNIFIED MINISTER Chao came to see Da-ren in person. As a result, Young Master was packed off to a maternal uncle, a general stationed in Canton, at nearly the other end of the country.

Three days after his departure, Amah made ready to set out, a small cloth bundle tied diagonally across her back.

Ying-ying knelt down and put her forehead to the ground. "May the road agree with you, Master."

Amah sighed. "Rise."

Ying-ying did. Amah looked at her for some time. Then, out of the blue, she embraced Ying-ying, a quick hug that was over before Ying-ying realized what had happened.

"Keep up your lessons with the Englishman," she said, tucking a loose strand of Ying-ying's hair behind her ear. "And stay out of trouble."

"Yes, Master."

They went out the gate of the courtyard together. For appearance' sake, in case anyone saw them, Amah curtsied to Ying-ying, which unnerved her. "Will I see you again?" she asked, unable to help herself.

"Stupid girl, don't say such inauspicious things," Amah answered. "Of course you will, when I come back in three months."

"Please look after yourself, Master."

Amah shook her head, sighed again, and left.

WHEN THREE MONTHS HAD PASSED, Amah did not return.

Twenty-one

The Brightest Hour

THE INTERNIST FROM NAPLES PROVED entirely correct. Once Miss McHenry had banished everything exciting from her diet, her old vigor returned. She, Miss Violet, and Leighton departed from Capri and visited the Levant, Egypt, Kenya, and a number of places in between.

They arrived in India near the beginning of 1878 and proceeded to the usual destinations for English tourists. Miss Violet like to say, dryly, *Never has anyone been so captivated by the usual.* And so the usual—the Taj Mahal, the mountains of Kashmir, the forts and palaces of Rajasthan—managed to easily enchant them.

Ten months later, on their way back to Bombay, they spoke seriously for the first time about their eventual parting of ways. Hong Kong emerged as their final port together. From there Leighton would travel to Peking, and the ladies to New Zealand, where one of their nieces lived.

Hong Kong was far away yet, but at the end of their conversation, Miss McHenry already shed a tear. Leighton was both saddened and exhilarated. It had been two years since he left England, five years since he last saw Herb, Mother, and Marland. He was ready to throw his arms around any and all of them.

Back in Bombay, they stayed at the same hotel as before, but now Leighton had picked up enough Marathi to speak to the native attendants in their own language.

One afternoon, he and the misses McHenry came back from buying some provisions. An attendant named Aadil helped them carry their bags back to their rooms. Leighton tipped and thanked him. But the man hovered.

"Yes?" Leighton asked.

Aadil cleared his throat nervously. "Beg the sahib's pardon, but does sahib speak Hindi?"

It was an odd question. "Why do you want to know?"

"A sahib came around a few months ago. He asked whether we have had a young guest with black hair and green eyes who spoke to us in Hindi."

Leighton was suddenly cold. "And?"

"We didn't, of course. But he told us that any time we had such a guest, to let him know. Then you came back and spoke to us in Marathi. My friend Komesh and I had a debate. He said the two languages are similar enough that if you spoke to us in Marathi, it was as good as if you spoke in Hindi. But I didn't think so. Hindi is Hindi and Marathi is Marathi—to my thinking."

The backs of Leighton's knees had turned weak. He knew which one was Komesh, a sharp-eyed, clever fellow. "And where is this friend of yours?"

"I think he went to see the sahib about an hour ago. He said there would be a reward." The attendant suddenly looked crestfallen. "You think I should have gone with him?"

"No, no, absolutely not." Leighton emitted a bark of laughter, even though all he felt was a painfully sharp fear. "Now why don't you come in here. Let's play a practical joke on your friend."

The misses McHenry looked up in surprise as he ushered Aadil into the sitting room of their suite.

"Have you heard, ladies," he said, smiling tightly, "that the P&O steamer is going to sail early?"

Their expressions changed. They understood that he had been found and must go on the run immediately.

Leighton turned back to the attendant. "Let me have your uniform."

"I beg your pardon, sahib?"

"It's all part of the practical joke."

"How, sahib?"

"You'll see. You let me borrow your uniform and Komesh will not get any rewards. But you will."

This was good enough for Aadil. Ten minutes later, Leighton walked out of the hotel in the attendant's uniform, a satchel in hand, Miss Violet next to him to make it seem as if he were carrying her luggage instead.

There were several Punjabi attendants on the staff who were just as tall as Leighton, so he aroused no particular attention as he made his exit, even though he himself was painfully aware that the uniform was too short.

196

They almost ran smack into Komesh and an Englishman, coming into the hotel. Leighton averted his face, his pulse hammering.

He was not recognized.

They found a place for him to change out of the uniform and back into his own clothes. Then it was to the railway station, as the next steamer headed for Calcutta would not depart for another thirty-six hours.

He bought a ticket for the first train out. On the platform he hugged Miss Violet. She kissed him on both his cheeks and wished him good luck.

"You will be fine," she said.

"Thank you." He gave her hand a squeeze. "Thank you for everything."

IN ALLAHABAD HE BOARDED ANOTHER train, headed for Calcutta. By the time he reached his destination, he was a German university student who spoke only a heavily accented English and no Indian languages at all. He left within the week on a mail steamer. After calling at Rangoon and Penang, he disembarked in Singapore to await the next fortnightly P&O liner to take him farther.

He stayed at an out-of-the-way hotel, kept to himself, and made absolutely no attempt to learn any local languages. A clever realization on Sir Curtis's part that he would take the opportunity to learn and practice local languages--it was too bad that Leighton hadn't had the foresight to burn all his notebooks before he'd left Rose Priory. The moment one opened those notebooks, full of exercises and translations he had undertaken himself, his love of languages would become all too evident.

It was more than half a month into 1879, and two rather frightful South China Sea storms later, when he at last sighted Hong Kong, a far more mountainous and verdant island than he had anticipated. But as his steamer pulled into port, his sense of alarm tingled. It wasn't long before he spotted two men in a sampan, scrutinizing his steamer with binoculars.

Fear very nearly throttled him. Was this it? Would he truly go no farther, when he was at last in the same country as Herb?

He grabbed the steamer's second mate, who happened to be passing by. "Sir, those two storms have put me behind. I need to be in Shanghai this minute. Are any of those ships leaving immediately?"

The second mate scanned the harbor and its myriad vessels, then pointed toward one. "Today is Friday. The *Kaitsung* should be leaving for Shanghai in about three quarters of an hour."

Leighton waited and waited, keeping out of the view of the men with binoculars. Then he took a deep breath and climbed down into a sampan. Almost immediately the men with binoculars began rowing in his direction. He instructed his boatman to head full-speed for the *Kaitsung*.

The *Kaitsung* pulled anchor almost as soon as he came aboard. The men chasing him in the sampan shouted, but their words were drowned by the *Kaitsung*'s engines and the general din of the harbor.

It was a sunny, mild day. Though a stiff wind blew from the sea, it was still beyond pleasant to stand on deck, watch Hong Kong recede, and savor another day of freedom.

THE PROBLEM WITH HAVING BOARDED the first steamer leaving port, however, was that Leighton hadn't bothered to inquire after its itinerary. The *Kaitsung* called at every port along China's eastern seaboard—or at least at Amoy, Foo-Choo, and Ningpo, while Leighton paced the decks, impatience and frustration rising in tandem.

Now he had lost the time he had hoped to gain.

On the day the *Kaitsung* was to reach Shanghai, he woke up with a fever. His joints ached. And when he got up from his bunk he swayed—not from the rolling of the sea, but from dizziness.

He stumbled about, disoriented: He was almost never sick, and he must have been a small child when he'd last run a fever. When he was dressed, he lay down again, his stomach pitching with a greater intensity than the winter sea outside.

When he got up again a couple of hours later to prepare for disembarkation, he felt even worse. He forced himself to check his belongings, making sure that he hadn't left anything behind. Then he mentally reviewed what he had learned from his fellow passengers: Steamers arriving from Tientsin would advertise their departure in the local paper for the next day, though it was not unusual for them to remain in port for two or three days. Also, he should expect a journey of up to seven days, with rough seas at Chefu, and the likelihood of being stuck on a sandbar near Tientsin.

He was close. So close, the journey of ten thousand miles almost at an end. He just had to be careful, to evade his pursuer for a little longer.

But as he disembarked, clutching at the rope ladder to get into a sampan that would take him the remainder of the distance to land, he could barely manage to keep his balance, let alone be alert and observant. His stomach heaved. His brain felt as if it had been turned into a pile of hemp rope, full of rough fibers that scraped his nerves with every step.

Onshore he allowed a porter from Astor House, which he'd heard mentioned as a respectable establishment on the Bund, to conduct him to the hotel, a quadrangle of one-story buildings around a central greensward—a Western-style establishment, like almost all the other places he had passed inside the International Settlement.

At the reception he asked for a room, declined the offer of food— the thought of which made him recoil—and took a newspaper with him as he was led away. In his room he opened the English-language paper. But his eyelids drooped heavily.

He fell into bed, the newspaper crunching underneath his weight. A lovely feeling, all the aches and pains and nausea fading away, anesthetized by the long slide into slumber.

He jerked as a knock came on the door.

"Mr. Atwood, open the door, please."

He swore under his breath, but as there was no question of running away in his current condition, he only said, "Go to hell."

And closed his eyes again.

HE WOKE UP FEELING MUCH BETTER. His fever was gone, his stomach was at peace, and his joints moved without any discomfort. The newspaper crinkled as he sat up, reminding him that he had yet to scan the advertisement section for ships departing to Tientsin in the near future.

The next moment his heart thudded most unpleasantly. *Mr. Atwood, open the door please.*

He had registered under a false name. Anyone who knew his real name would be someone who meant to send him back to England. To Sir Curtis.

Outside his window a man stood in the fading light of a winter afternoon. Not one of the men he had seen in Hong Kong—a local helper, then?

He thought for a moment, left his bed, changed into fresh clothes, and combed his hair. Then he opened the door—there was no point cowering in the room—and came face-to-face with the man who had been waving and shouting at him as the *Kaitsung* steamed out of port.

"Ah, Mr. Atwood. Good afternoon. Allow me to introduce myself—George Lafferty. I have been sent by—"

"I know who sent you," said Leighton. He should be afraid, but somehow he wasn't. He was no longer fourteen. He was ten thousand miles from England. And unless he was very much mistaken, Astor House was in the American Concession, where British laws did not apply. "I am not going anywhere with you. You may show yourself out—or find out how management treats those who bother the guests of this hotel."

Lafferty appeared completely taken aback. "I'm afraid there must be a misunderstanding of some sort. I do not require you to come with me anywhere, sir. I am only a messenger, so to speak."

His surprise seemed genuine. Leighton narrowed his eyes. "What does Sir Curtis wish me to know?"

Lafferty immediately shook his head. "Oh, no, indeed, sir. Sir Curtis is no more. I have been tasked by his widow to find you."

"What?" It *sounded* as if Lafferty said that Sir Curtis was dead. But Sir Curtis wasn't going to die; he was going to endure until there was nothing left of him but skin and spite. "What did you say?"

"Three weeks ago I was engaged by the governor's office—the governor of Hong Kong, that is—on Lady Atwood's behalf. In her cable she said that she was almost certain you would have to pass through Hong Kong, and soon. A few days after that a man came to me and delivered a photograph of you. He said he had been engaged by Sir Curtis to watch for your arrival in Hong Kong but had been recently relieved of that charge—I wasn't sure why Lady Atwood wanted a different man to wait for you but I wasn't about to complain. And that was how I recognized you at the harbor—with the help of the photograph. I had no idea you would go on the run. Fortunately you took the slow boat, and I was able to overtake you and wait for you in Shanghai instead."

"No, no." Leighton waved an impatient hand. "Tell me the part about Sir Curtis being—deceased."

"Yes, he passed away about a month ago—or perhaps a little less. I read about it in the papers."

A month ago Leighton had been crossing the Andaman Sea, not having access to any newspapers.

"You are sure?"

"Well, now I wish I had made a cutting of the obituary. The paper was more than a week old by the time I picked it up to flip through, and it had caught my attention because just that day I had been engaged to deliver the cable for Lady Atwood."

"What cable?"

"Yes, of course." Lafferty reached inside his coat and pulled out a rather crumbled envelope.

Leighton tore it open.

Dear Master Leighton,

Your uncle is dead. I have recalled the men he had engaged to track you down and will find someone of my own to deliver the news to you. May this greeting find you well.

Alexandra Atwood

"I can go write my report to Lady Atwood, now that I've delivered her message," said Lafferty. "Is there anything you'd like me to convey, sir?"

Leighton was still stunned. He scanned the telegram one more time. "You may convey my gratitude to Lady Atwood—and tell her that I remain always in her debt. And thank you for coming all this way. I'm sorry to have inconvenienced you by leaving Hong Kong so precipitously."

Lafferty touched the brim of his hat. "Not a problem."

He turned to leave.

"Wait, please," said Leighton.

He took a handful of Mexican dollars, which was much preferred by the people of the Far East for the purity and consistency of their silver content, and handed them to Lafferty. The man smiled broadly, thanked him, and departed with a rather jaunty gait.

When he was gone, Leighton slowly closed the door and sank into a chair. Sir Curtis, dead. No more men who hunted him. No more dreading being taken back to Rose Priory—or someplace far worse.

He was...he was free.

His shock was still too great for him to feel euphoria—or even relief. But he understood now that everything had changed.

He understood that it was a whole new world.

HE CABLED HIS MOTHER. He cabled the misses McHenrys' niece in New Zealand. He wrote a letter to Mr. Cromwell, Herb's solicitor, asking for his help in finding out the whereabouts of Mr. Colmes—so many boxes he and Herb had sent to Mr. Cromwell, he had the man's address memorized, whereas he had no idea how to reach his own family solicitor.

He did not try to contact Herb, because there was no telegraph service between Shanghai and Peking, and he would arrive in person sooner than a letter could.

The next day he was on a Jardine, Matheson, and Co. steamer, headed for Tientsin. His second day upon the choppy East China Sea, however, all the same awful symptoms came back. His head throbbed, his joints were stiff with pain, and his temperature was so high that his own breath scalded the skin beneath his nostrils.

The next day he was much better, the day after torturous. But the day after that, as he disembarked in Tientsin, he was again well enough that his main thought was the acquisition of a passport and the arrangement of transports.

He was in luck. The passport was speedily granted, and a Frenchman who had organized relay ponies along the route for a swift trip to the imperial capital could not start for another week. Leighton gladly took over this preexisting arrangement and set out with a guide, a Chinese Catholic who spoke fluent French.

It snowed the entire way, the landscape silent and white except for squares and strips of scarlet paper inked with Chinese characters and affixed to every door and pillar they passed. The words on the long strips were couplets expressing good wishes and blessings, the guide explained, and on the red paper squares was the character for good fortune—Chinese New Year was barely a fortnight ago and everyone was expressing their hopes for a year of peace and prosperity.

As they rode inland, the snow kept falling and the temperature kept dropping. Leighton had not been anywhere so cold in a very long time. The wind bit right through his coat. His fingers were quite frozen in his gloves, and he'd stopped feeling his nose and ears hours ago.

They pressed on, changing ponies every few hours. It was as the walls of the imperial city loomed ahead in the deep twilight that Leighton started to shiver uncontrollably. He was burning, his head pounded, and it was all he could do to hold on to the pony and keep going.

"Are you not well?" his guide asked in French.

"I may need a physician," he answered, grimacing.

Night had fallen. The city was dark—what street lamps there were seemed no more than candles in latticework boxes backed with paper, the light they emitted so faint as to be nearly useless. In the nearly unbroken shadows, his awareness reduced to only the sway of his horse, the painful numbness of his fingers, and relentless heat parching his throat from the inside.

They stopped. Vaguely Leighton perceived an impressive gate. The guide explained that they had arrived at the British Legation. He didn't know Peking very well, but he was sure Leighton should be able to find a qualified physician within.

Leighton slid off his horse. He barely managed to pay the guide the second half of his money before he dropped to his knees, too weak to remain standing anymore. Then he slumped sideways into a bank of snow.

Voices cried out in alarm. He felt himself lifted and carried. He drifted in and out of consciousness until he was violently shaken.

"Young man, have you been having periodic fevers that recur every other day or so?" asked a gray-haired, stern-looking man, peering down at him.

He nodded weakly.

"You've passed through or near the tropics recently?"

He nodded again.

"Lack of appetite, nausea, body ache?"

He dipped his chin an infinitesimal distance.

"Well, we had better get you started on quinine immediately. You have malaria."

The medicine was thrust at him. He swallowed obediently, even though it was extraordinarily bitter.

And when he was allowed to lie down again, he said to the doctor, "Please, sir, can you have someone send a note to Mr. Herbert Gordon? He said I can find him by asking at the British Legation and I have come a long, long way."

"You rest," the doctor said gruffly. "I will see what I can do."

QUININE WAS ALMOST WORSE THAN MALARIA.

Leighton vomited. A sharp pain skewered his abdomen. He couldn't lift his head without being overcome by waves of dizziness. And his ears rang: He was sure the room was quiet and the night still, yet from time to time, for stretches of a half hour or longer, he would be plagued with a noise inside his head like that of steam whistle, until he was sure he would go deaf from its needle-thin and relentless pitch.

But the doctor assured him that those were fairly common symptoms in reaction to quinine. "You are young and strong. The reactions will go away as soon as you finish your course of treatment."

Toward dawn Leighton fell into an exhausted sleep. For the first time in years, he dreamed of the day of Father's death. Except this time, as he entered the room, it was Sir Curtis slumped over the desk, a hole in his head.

He woke up with his ears ringing. Staying completely still, his eyes shut tight, he waited for the noise to cease, afraid that the least light or movement would cause it to prolong—or grow even louder.

At times he thought he heard the rustling of the pages of a book, the swish of fabric, and even the slight creaking of a chair as a sitter's weight shifted. There could be another person in the room, or the sounds could simply be further manifestations of his tinnitus.

Finally, after enough time had passed for the Deluge to have receded, the inside of his head quieted. Slowly he opened his eyes and looked up at a ceiling of green and gold tiles set in a delicate latticework. It was hard to judge exactly what time of the day it might be: The dim gray light of the room could be that of near dusk, or the middle of the day under a leaden sky.

The chair creaked again. Very carefully Leighton turned his face toward the sound, expecting to see the doctor or a nurse. But it was a bearded man in a dark blue-gray tunic in the Chinese style—though he was clearly a European, judging by his blond hair.

Herb! Leighton had only ever seen him clean shaven, but there could be no doubt about it.

"It's you," he croaked. "It's *you*."

Suddenly the room was as bright as his memories of Starling Manor, of poppy fields under a cloudless sky.

Herb came forward hesitantly, almost as if he were sleepwalking. Then he closed all the remaining distance, knelt by the bed, and took Leighton's hands in his. His hands shook just perceptibly.

"My dear boy. My dear, dear boy." Tears rolled down his face. "This morning, when the message from the legation came, I...You have no idea..."

Leighton squeezed his hands. "I have every idea. You came back to us once, remember?"

Herb wiped his eyes with the heel of one hand. "That was only three months."

"That was forever—or so I believed. This was always just a matter of time. You knew I would come and find you as soon as I could."

Herb's face shone. "Yes, I did. I always did."

"So, what does one do around here for fun?"

Herb laughed, even as more tears splashed onto his cheeks—those were the first words he had ever spoken to Leighton. "Well, it goes without saying that you must visit the Great Wall, the Ming Tombs, and the Temple of Heaven. You should experience a teahouse-theater. And you must try candied haws—this is the season for them, and they are sold on skewers on every street corner.

"I might be able obtain permission for you to call on my employer's residence; then you can see where I live, a very elegant little courtyard with a bamboo grove inside. And if I arrange it really carefully, I might even be able to present you to one of my pupils—more a friend, actually—a beautiful young lady of mixed blood who has been studying English with me and teaching me Chinese."

What a fortunate girl, to have had Herb's company all these years.

Fear returned to Herb's eyes. He gripped Leighton's hands tighter. "But are you sure you are safe here? What if—"

He forgot he had yet to tell Herb the news. "Sir Curtis is dead."

Herb shot to his feet. "My God. My *God*."

"I know. You can go home now. We can go home together."

Herb's lips moved. "I—I can't make sense of it. Both my rational understanding and my imagination fail me." He looked back at Leighton, his face full of wonder. "Do you think this is how a seed feels when it finally breaks through to the world above? That nothing will ever be the same again?"

"Yes," Leighton answered. "It's a whole new world."

A knock came at the door and the same physician from the night before stuck in his head. "Mr. Gordon, I'm afraid I must ask you to leave very soon. It's time for Mr. Atwood's next dose of quinine, and he should not be disturbed afterward."

"I promise you, Dr. Ross, I will be no trouble at all," Herb pleaded his case. "I will sit and read my book and not speak a single word to my young friend here."

"I am sure you are a man of your word, Mr. Gordon. But my assistant and I will both be in here at various times, and it's too small a room for all of us to be cramped together," said Dr. Ross firmly. "Besides, your young friend here is going to be good as new in a few days. Then you will be able to catch up without any deuced interference from dour old Scottish doctors."

This made both Leighton and Herb smile.

"All right, then. I'll make myself scarce," said Herb. He set a hand on Leighton's shoulder. "Have I told you yet how very extraordinarily glad I am to see you, my dear boy?"

Leighton didn't know why, but the tears that he had been able to hold back until now were spilling unchecked down his face. "Yes, you have. You have from the very beginning."

Herb wiped once more at his eyes, bent down, and kissed Leighton on the forehead. "I will be back tomorrow."

"Yes, tomorrow," said Leighton.

What a wonderful word, tomorrow. And now they had all the tomorrows in the world.

LEIGHTON REACTED NO BETTER TO quinine this time. Afterward, he was so weak he could barely lift an eyelid. But Dr. Ross's assistant, a young man named Miller, told Leighton that Herb had left behind some things for him—"A letter and a small package." So now, with a mighty effort, he lifted his hand to feel for them on the nightstand.

He came across the letter first. It was from Mother.

My dearest son,

I fervently hope this letter finds you, and finds you well.

Mr. Gordon and I had exchanged letters early on in his exile. But my subsequent letters were returned, citing that they could not be forwarded. So it was quite remarkable that his somehow found me here in San Francisco, more than a year after it had been posted.

I replied to him right away, and I will include this letter with my reply, in the hope that should you find yourself in Peking before you find yourself in San Francisco, you will come across it.

And now I clutch my head, unsure how to proceed. So let me go back to the day I discovered the package you had secreted away in one of the trunks that I had brought from England. Until I married Mr. Delany and moved into his house with Marland, I opened that particular trunk only once, to retrieve a few of my favorite books. And your secret was buried a foot and half farther down.

There I was, supervising the moving and arrangement of several hundred books, when a maid came to me with a carefully wrapped bundle and asked what ought to be done with it. When I saw everything inside, I was overwhelmed. Your father was my first love, and I never felt anything but the greatest respect and affection for him, even after I realized he could never love me the way I loved him.

That afternoon I spent poring over the photographs, because it was the part of his life that I never saw—the part of your *life that I never saw.*

I wept and wept, partly because I thought you had shoved everything in my trunk in order to scrub Starling Manor of any reminders of your father and Mr. Gordon. That you had repudiated them as thoroughly as you had repudiated me. I am ashamed to tell you this, but not only did I believe every word of censure you spoke, I believed it more than I believed anything else in my whole life.

Your uncle played a part, of course. After what he had said to me, I had felt so unclean, so degenerate, that I quite despised myself—it was therefore not too difficult to imagine that everyone else must despise me too, if they only knew. But the other part—the far greater part, I must add—had been my own gross stupidity.

How could I, who had only ever known kindness and acceptance on your part, come to give credence to the idea that you were in fact a boy of unrelentingly harsh views? I do not know, and I will never forgive myself.

But there I was, sobbing away, when I came across a crumpled piece of paper: an unfinished letter from you. Most likely you never intended to include it, but it somehow found its way inside. In the letter you begged for my forgiveness, because you felt you had to do whatever was necessary to keep Marland and me safe.

I sat stunned at how wrong I had been—how unbearably foolish. The next morning I was on a train to the East Coast. I didn't care what I had to do; if I had to hire thugs to abduct you, then so be it.

But when I arrived at my hotel in New York City, there was a telegram waiting for me from Mr. Delany. He had received a letter from you and wanted me to know that he believed you had run away—and very possibly left England, given that the letter was sent from Southampton.

We spent a fortune cabling back and forth, debating what to do. I decided to proceed to England anyway, in case your attempt had failed.

While in England, via various channels, I ascertained that you had not yet been located. I didn't know whether it would help or hinder to send men out to find you, so I did the inverse. I hired men to keep an eye on Sir Curtis instead, as that would let me know with virtual certainty if and when you became recaptured.

(Knock on wood that would never be the case.)

Please, my son, stay safe. I pray constantly that you meet with only the kindest fellow travelers. That you will ever be in plentiful funds and abundant health. And that you will cable me at the first opportunity to let me know that you are well—or whether you are in need of assistance of any kind. Any kind at all.

Marland has stopped asking me when you will come to visit—I burst into tears when I hear that question. But I often catch him with a photograph of the two of you in his hand. He misses you as much as I do.

Come home to us. Until then we pray and we wait.

I love you more than I can say,
Mother

P.S. It is I who must beg for your forgiveness. Stay safe, my son, stay well, and stay free.

Leighton wiped at the corners of his eyes. She would have received his cable by now and learned that he was both well and free. And he would never need to lie or be cruel to her again—they were all safe now.

He read the letter two more times before he put it back into its envelope. As soon as he picked up the other item, the package, he knew what it was: the jade tablet in Herb's possession.

Herb had left him a note. *My dear boy, your mother wrote that you had sent your father's jade tablet with her to America for safekeeping. Which must mean that you have not seen it for years upon years. I thought you might like to see this one, for old times' sake. Love, H.*

Leighton didn't need to see it; just holding it through the layers of wrapping and already he was back in Starling Manor. It was summer, always summer. Father and Herb were always smiling. And his heart always brimmed over with hope.

He unwrapped it anyway, and held the tablet in his hands until the cool jade had become as warm as his skin.

Twenty-two

Lantern Festival

BANG. BANG. BANG. THE FIRECRACKERS detonated in rapid succession a second after they left Ying-ying's hand. Red confetti swirled in the air, then dispersed in a blast of fierce northerly wind.

She lit another firecracker with her incense stick and held it until the fuse had disappeared into the shell. She flung it. It burst almost before it left her fingertips. She felt the sting of hot black powder exploding bare inches from her skin. Like needle pricks. An acute sensation that fell just short of pain.

She took a deep breath. The air, after more than twenty days of Spring Festival celebrations, had that particular metallic tang Ying-ying always thought of as the New Year smell, a whiff of residual heat and warmth in the bitter January chill. Outside in the city, the streets and alleys would be covered with festive red bits and pieces, remnants of paper firecracker shells. And children would gather them into piles and make small bonfires.

She and Amah had once done just that, long, long ago. She remembered laughing and clapping around that little flame on the ground.

It had been five months. Amah still had not returned. In the beginning she had sent two letters every month. Her father's condition, which Ying-ying took to mean Amah's own, was improving, but not yet satisfactory. But after three months the letters abruptly stopped. This could mean a number of things: Something could have gone catastrophically wrong; she might be dead; or she could have fallen prey to her old gambling habits. Some people spent their entire lives in gambling dens, emerging only to forage for more funds.

There were days when Ying-ying was near frantic, imagining Amah lying in agony, with no one about to help her. Other days she was beside herself with anger. How could Amah so wantonly let go of her self-control? If she'd started gambling again, who knew what follies she'd commit to feed her habit?

She heard Master Gordon's footsteps as she let fly another firecracker. It burst in midair with a head-clearing bang.

"Too reckless, Bai Gu-niang!" came Master Gordon's voice. "You shouldn't hold on to the firecracker that long!"

She turned around. "You are back."

When she went to his rooms earlier, she had found a hastily scrawled note waiting for her, telling her that he had to be at the British Legation today.

"Yes. Do you remember the letter I received a while ago, about my dear friend's son? He arrived in Peking last night." His face was full of wonder. "He actually came."

She studied him. "I knew you would be happy—thrilled. But I didn't expect to see you..." She searched for a word. "Humbled."

"I am. I am overwhelmed by gratitude."

"I am not sure I understand. If you, a member of the older generation, traveled ten thousand miles to see him, then he should be overwhelmed by gratitude. But he, a member of the younger generation, taking some trouble to come to see you is as it should be."

Master Gordon expelled a long breath. "Well, you see, I hold myself partially responsible for his father's death. So the fact that he would see me at all, let alone come this far..."

His eyes reddened.

Ying-ying was staggered. Was there some sort of blood feud that Master Gordon had never told her about? Did it have something to do with his exile? And how could his friend's son still think affectionately of him, if he had been in some way responsible for the death of a father? "I'm not sure I understand."

"It's complicated, but I think I can at last talk about it, now that I know all is well—except I don't know where to start. Or even if I should explain the whole thing to you—you are still so young."

Yet old enough to be someone's concubine. And sometimes in her heart, already a thousand years old. "Did you do something terrible?"

"I want to say no, but I can never know it for certain."

She waited. He borrowed a few firecrackers from her, set them on the ground, and lit them with her incense stick, a blistering sequence of explosions.

"You know I have told you that you are a beautiful girl."

"Yes?" What did this have to do with her?

"And you are. Very beautiful. But what if...what if I told you that no matter how beautiful you are, and even after you grow up, I would never look at you the way a man looks at a woman?"

She certainly hoped not. It would dismay her to no end if one day he were suddenly to leer at her as Shao-ye had. "That would be fine by me," she said.

He shook his head. "Let me put it another way, then. What if I look at another man the way a man usually looks at a woman?"

He looked away from her, his face red with embarrassment.

She was puzzled. "Then you go with that man."

His eyes widened with astonishment. "What did you say?"

She repeated her answer word for word.

"I don't understand," he murmured. "How do you take it so lightly?"

"How should I take it, then?"

"I...I don't know. In my country, people like me can be put into jail."

"Because you like other men?"

"If I act on it."

What a strange place England was. Women were allowed to show their bosoms to the world but not wear trousers. And men were not only restricted to one wife, but also forbidden to go into the bedchamber with other men. "Why?"

He shrugged, the gesture he sometimes used when an adequate explanation was beyond him. "Because we are thought to be deviants. An abomination in the eyes of God, and a fair target for anyone high-minded enough to hate us."

"Why?"

He shrugged again. "It's always been so. Are you sure it's not just you who's particularly open-minded?"

She didn't think so. There had been emperors who liked handsome young men in addition to their hundreds of concubines. As long as a man sired sons to carry on the family name, no one cared that he might prefer his valet to his wife. "The majordomo—you know him?"

"Master Keeper Ju? Yes."

"He sponsors an opera singer. And when I still lived in my own home, the merchant who supplied my mother with her silks, Boss Wu, he was also very friendly with an opera singer."

"In England rich men also have opera singers and ballet dancers as mistresses," he said.

"No, no, not mistresses," she corrected him. "Our opera singers are all men, even those who sing the female roles."

"Oh, how did I forget." A moment later, Master Gordon turned to her, agape. "*Master Keeper Ju?* Does Da-ren know it?"

"Everyone knows it." His isolation saddened her. She had learned within weeks of coming into the compound. Not that people didn't snicker behind the majordomo's back, but before him they dared not show the least disrespect.

"And the merchant also? Everyone knew?"

"Yes."

For a long time he said nothing, only stared at the sinuous whiff of smoke rising from the incense stick in his hand. "My friend killed himself over it. We were caught. He thought it was the end of the world. He thought he was destroyed. So he took a pistol and put it to his head. His brother later sent me the firearm, with his dried blood still on it."

For some reason, Amah's voice rose in her head. *I gave up my entire life for him. He loved me for six months, hooked me to gambling, and took up with another woman.* How cold Ying-ying had been that night. How unforgiving. And how she regretted it now.

Lightly she touched her hand to his sleeve. "Your friend's brother is a heartless man," she said. "You are not responsible for someone else's cruelty."

"Was," he said. "My friend's brother *was* a heartless man. He is no more. He was the reason I couldn't return to England. But now I can."

He sounded so thrilled. She was happy for him, but dismayed for herself. Amah was nowhere to be found, and if Master Gordon also left... "Are you—already making plans?"

"Nothing concrete yet. Although come to think of it, even before Shao-ye was sent to Canton, he hadn't taken lessons from me in almost a year—not very intent on his studies, that one. His brother is also taking only three lessons a week—his Confucian masters have requested that he devote more time to his study of the classics. So I won't feel as if I'll be abandoning any pupils midstudy..."

"Except me," she said, trying to sound lighthearted. "I am also your pupil."

"And I have not forgotten that in the slightest. Ever since my young friend told me that now I am free to return to England, I have been thinking about you. Remember how we have talked about going to see the world together? Would you like to come with me?" he asked with great seriousness. "We will wait until your amah is back and can properly chaperone you."

She stared at him. It was one thing to imagine the impossible—and take a great deal of pleasure in doing so—but quite another to make an actual attempt upon a stronghold of impossibility. Amah's chaperonage or not, Da-ren would never permit her going abroad with two men who weren't remotely related to her.

She would not defy Da-ren on this matter, because she did not want to forever alienate him. It was too late for him to love her like a daughter, but he could still come to value her.

And then Mother could finally stop worrying in the afterlife.

"You don't like this idea?" said Master Gordon, a little crestfallen.

"I adore the idea," she assured him. It was a wonderful day for him; she would cast no shadows upon his happiness.

Besides, she did adore the idea. She was immensely touched that he wished to include her in his homeward journey. That she could always count on his esteem and affection. That he made her life sweeter simply by being who he was.

"Then we will make it happen," he said as he briefly touched her elbow, his voice at once warm and solemn. "You will see."

THAT NIGHT WAS THE LANTERN Festival, the fifteenth day following the New Year, and the last celebration before life returned to normal. Beneath the eaves of the Middle Hall, glowing lanterns swayed against one another, a vigilant front of redness and fire, enough to repel a battalion of evil spirits.

Inside the hall, the lanterns were of greater variety. They hung from every hook, and on cords especially strung for the occasion between the pillars. Red was no longer the sole color, nor round the only shape. Some cylindrical ones turned by themselves, tassels, beads, and lucky knots trailing in gentle swirls; others featured riddles, with promised prizes for those who could guess the answers.

The musicians who accompanied the opera singers were already in place, tuning their instruments at the side of the temporary stage that had been erected at the western end of the hall. In the middle of the hall congregated the servants, given the night off to enjoy the performances.

A large dais occupied the eastern end. Front and center were Da-ren and his concubines, both pregnant. But there was yet another pregnant woman present, Little Orchid, who was probably seven or eight months along and sat with Da-ren's younger son and several visiting cousins at an adjacent table. She was a pretty girl, but even when she smiled, she looked worried.

Little Dragon was not present, but Master Gordon was, seated near the other household scholars somewhere behind Da-ren, though at a table by himself.

Face lowered, Ying-ying walked behind Mrs. Mu-he, who had appointed herself Ying-ying's chaperone during Amah's absence. But she dozed so much during the day, Ying-ying practically had the run of the residence. The two of them made their obeisances to everyone in the front row, then took their seats at the very back of the dais, along with some other senior servants.

A servant brought them tea and small plates of appetizers—nothing like the fancy spread on the front tables, where cold plates had been arranged to look like open-tailed peacocks or goldfish frolicking amid lotus blossoms. Another servant brought a tiny ceramic jug of fiery grain liquor and a brazier, for the hall was cold, even with the heavy blankets that hung over all the entries. Yet another servant handed them a written list of the troupe's repertoire. Ying-ying read it aloud to Mrs. Mu-he. She herself was of too little consequence to pick anything. But Mrs. Mu-he, by her age, her long association with the family, and the fact that she had once suckled Da-ren, was entitled.

A great cheer rose from the milling servants as they were rewarded with two large urns of spirits to divide among themselves for the evening. To a one they bowed down and thanked Da-ren, the mistresses, and the majordomo. After they had settled, large bowls of liquor in hand and slurping happily, the master of the opera troupe appeared and did his speech to wish the family a multitude of good fortune and prosperity.

The performances opened with a raucous act from the *Westward Journey*. Actors pretending to be monkeys scrambled around, scratching themselves, scratching one another. The menservants responded with guffaws and much thigh slapping. Ying-ying glanced Mr. Gordon. He too was laughing, very much enjoying himself.

More sedate pieces followed, while dish after dish appeared on the tables. Ying-ying didn't much care for Peking opera. And she was already full after six dishes. She wished Amah were back so she could enjoy the delicacies and the entertainment. She wished Amah had never left. She wanted to give her a tremendous scolding. She would never get cross with her again if only she would come back.

She felt someone's eyes on her. To her left, Chang, the man who had once rescued Little Dragon from a life on the streets, stood just to the inside of an entrance, largely hidden from view behind a thick pillar. He beckoned her with his hand.

This was odd. What could he want with her? Besides his insistent gestures, he seemed also to be mouthing something at her, something along the lines of, "Gu-niang, please come."

She looked around her to make sure he wasn't communicating with someone else. No, everyone had their eyes on the stage. Chang had his eyes on her.

"I need to use the changing room," she murmured to Mrs. Mu-he, who was raptly absorbed in an act called "The Drunken Concubine."

"Master Keeper Chang, what's the matter?" she asked when she had made her way to him.

"It's your amah, Bai Gu-niang," he answered.

"My amah?" Ying-ying couldn't help her voice from rising. "She's *back*?"

Chang motioned her to keep her voice down. "I had to, uh, go to the outhouses just now. On my way back, I saw your amah. She wasn't feeling so well, so I told her to get inside, that I'd let you know she has returned."

She wasn't feeling so well. Amah should have recovered completely by the end of her retreat. So something *had* gone terribly wrong.

She didn't have money on her person to tip him, so she pulled a small gold pin from her hair. "Thank you, Master Keeper Chang."

"I'll come with you, Bai Gu-niang," he offered. "It isn't safe in the dark for a girl to walk alone."

She didn't want a bodyguard. But if she refused, it might appear odd. Most girls her age probably would not turn down such help. "Many thanks, Master Keeper Chang. Your heart is too kind."

"Not at all," he answered modestly. "If anything were to happen to Bai Gu-niang, how could I live with myself?"

Her courtyard was dark, but the gate was open. Her heart wrenched. Amah was back.

"Please don't let me keep you from the performances, Master Keeper Chang," she said politely. "You have my gratitude."

"I'll wait just a minute to make sure your amah is all right," he said. "She might need a doctor fetched."

A faint glimmering of moonlight entered the house with her, illuminating the outline of one of Mother's ink paintings that hung in the reception room. Ying-ying hurried deeper inside.

At the doorway of her bedchamber, she stopped. Someone was on her bed, lying just beyond a beam of moonlight. And this person breathed loudly—a vigorous noise, full lunged and easy.

Not an injured Amah.

"Who are you?" she demanded.

The person swung to a sitting position. "Bai Gu-niang has such good hearing. How do you know I'm not your amah?"

Shao-ye! How did he come back—and when? She had not heard anything of it. Nobody had.

She brushed aside her stupefaction. What did it matter how and when he came back? He was in her rooms and had sent for her to be lured here. Had she approached the bed, he would have dragged her in and attempted to physically overwhelm her.

He came toward her. She took a step back.

"Bai Gu-niang, don't be shy," he cooed. "Think how far I've trekked to be with you."

"Young Master should first pay his respects to Da-ren," she said coldly.

"I shall." He laughed. "After tonight. After raw grains of rice become cooked."

After raw grains of rice become cooked, a reference to things that could not be undone.

He lunged for her. To her surprise he was using a martial-arts stance, the Eagle Attack, his fingers hooked like talons, swooping down the way a bird of prey would seize a hapless barnyard hen.

For a split second she vacillated. What sweet satisfaction she'd derive from ramming an elbow into his kidney, or smashing a heel into his groin. Instead she ducked low, slid past him, and spun around. The exit was now behind him. Her only good option was to outrun him and return to the relative safety of the middle hall.

"Bai Gu-niang is agile," he said, sneering. "I like that. Imagine how she'll wriggle in bed."

He came at her again, in a Winter Bear stance. She swerved left, then right. Once past him she did not look back, but she did not leave the way unimpeded for his pursuit: She upended a table and two chairs and emptied a large writing brush holder. Some twenty writing brushes clacked to the floor, then rolled about in every direction.

Behind her, Shao-ye bumped into something and tripped. He cursed loudly. Her heart pounding, her feet barely touching the ground, she sprinted out of the courtyard—only to be stopped by Chang.

"Bai Gu-niang is out so soon?" he asked, his voice full of apparent concern.

She would have run by him without a word. But something about him jarred her, and made her stop short.

He was a good two hand widths taller! What happened to his pronounced stoop?

"Young Master has just made his way back from Canton, thousands of *li* over a treacherous winter sea," he said smoothly. "The first person he wishes to see is Bai Gu-niang. Isn't Bai Gu-niang the least bit touched?"

For the first time she took a good look at him. He stood in a stream of moonlight, his face clearly lit. He was younger than she had supposed, in his early forties as opposed to his fifties. His gaze was sword-keen. And his breaths...

Cold fear inundated her. He was an arm's length away, and she could not hear him breathe. He had not been some random servant bribed to trick her. He had been chosen for a reason. If anything, he had taught Shao-ye those stances of martial arts, but the young wastrel had been too dissolute to learn them properly.

Crash! Shao-ye must have fallen down again. Her mind churned madly. Time was short. How could she extricate herself now?

"I am humbled by Young Master's affection," she said, pretending to be shy, "but Da-ren would not be pleased if I pledged myself without his prior permission."

"What Young Master wants, Da-ren will eventually want for him," Chang said calmly, pitilessly. "Gu-niang might as well bow before the inevitable."

Ying-ying took a deep breath. Inside, Shao-ye had almost reached the door. It was now or never. "Without a matchmaker? Without even the proper rituals— Da-ren!"

She stared into the far end of the walled alley. Startled, Chang turned to look. Ying-ying sprinted in the opposite direction, toward the middle hall.

He cursed and came after her.

Ying-ying had thought herself light soled. But she could barely hear anything over her thunderous footfalls. It was only the cold sweat between her shoulder blades, the sense of absolute menace, that told her he was catching up to her.

She let fly Mother's fur-lined cape and hoped that it would land on him and slow him down. It did, but only for a second. Up ahead, a new wall loomed. The path was about to end in a perpendicular alley. She cut to the left. Another left and then a right turn, and she would be within view of the middle hall.

With a sound like a flag lashing in the wind, Chang catapulted past her in the air, landed, and blocked the left turn she was going to take. She didn't think. She took the right turn and kept on running.

"Why, Bai Gu-niang? Why make it so difficult on yourself?"

Her heart sank. She wasn't winded yet. But if she opened her mouth she'd slow down for sure. Yet his smoothly delivered words had no impact on his speed. Instead he was gaining on her again. Worse, there was a good chance he was toying with her.

Once again he launched himself into the air, landing ten paces ahead of her to barricade the way. If she stopped, she was doomed. She was no match for him.

She barreled toward him. That caught him by surprise. When he realized at last that she meant to crash into him, he stuck out a foot, angling for the acupuncture points on her leg.

She pretended to trip and aimed her fall squarely on his shin. He yelled in pain and fell backward. They went down together. She sprang up and kept on running.

The alley went on forever before another turn presented itself. She angled into it. Almost too late she heard the sounds of small objects hurtling at her. She slowed down just enough to avoid most them, but one hit her solidly in the upper thigh.

It hurt, the metallic ball. Luckily it just missed a major acupuncture point—had it hit a finger's width higher, it would have rendered her leg useless for hours. But the pain was searing enough that she would be able to only shuffle along, an injured hare easy for the fox to snare: The ball must have barbs.

She dropped to the ground facedown. Let him think that he had temporarily paralyzed her. She'd use this lull to remove the barbed ball, then circulate her chi to relieve pain and restore her strength.

"I didn't wish to hurt you, Bai Gu-niang, but you gave me no choice," Chang said, standing over her.

She made little whimpers of agony. She didn't have to pretend: The barbed ball had hurt like a ghost's teeth when she'd yanked it out. "My legs...my legs..."

"Best let them stay that way until I get you back to Young Master," he said.

He bent down to pick her up. With all her might she kicked him in the face. He jerked back, but she still caught him on the neck. He made a grab for her foot, but had to jump out of the way as she threw at him the barbed ball she had dug out.

She leaped to her feet and ran as if all the ghosts of the underworld were behind her. Except that Chang was far more menacing—and now she had enraged him. An intersection came up ahead. Da-ren's concubines lived in these parts. Ying-ying needed to go left. But she turned right. Just after the turn was a side door into the youngest concubine's courtyard.

She pressed herself into the doorway and held her breath. Chang careened past her. She ran in the opposite direction. Within seconds he had realized his mistake and was on her tail again.

"You stinking daughter of a whore," he snarled.

His voice sounded so close that all the hairs on the back of her neck stood up. Her left trouser leg had a cold, damp spot of blood. The muscles in her thighs burned. Her lungs felt ready to cave in. But fear drove her to run faster.

Another wall loomed ahead. If she took a right turn here and then the second left turn, she'd emerge onto the small plaza before the middle hall. She bore right. More barbed balls hissed after her. She was forced to run in a zigzag pattern.

Chang was close enough to breathe down her neck. He made a grab for her hair. She ripped off her heavy gold locket, almost the size of a plate, and threw it into his face.

The left turn came up. Just a few more strides. He launched more barbed balls—a vertical wall of them, blocking the left turn, leaving her no choice but to run straight on. There were no more left turns on this path, only a right turn where the path ended.

She barely avoided having her neck gripped as she made the right turn. But what was that up ahead? A person, a man walking. And not just any man, but Master Gordon, judging by the walking stick he swished—Chinese men never used canes unless they must.

"Help! Help!" she yelled in English.

He spun around. "Bai Gu-niang? What's the matter?"

Behind her Chang stopped. A foreigner was a tricky addition to any situation. They were above the law, answerable only to their own kind. But for any Chinese who trespassed against them, the foreigners demanded the stiffest penalties.

"That man's trying to abduct me," Ying-ying said, panting, pulling Master Gordon along as she continued to run. Chang wouldn't let her return to the safety of the middle hall. But a man who wished to have his head remain on his shoulders would think twice before invading a foreigner's dwelling. "Take me to your rooms."

"Abduct you?" Master Gordon was astonished. "For ransom?"

"For Young Master."

"The fourteen-year-old?"

"The other one."

"But he's in Canton."

"He's back." Alas. *Alas.*

"I see."

Ying-ying's stomach dropped in alarm—Chang had sneaked up on them and was now directly behind. She yanked at Master Gordon to run faster. Too late. He crumpled like last year's straw toy—Chang had sealed his acupuncture points.

Ying-ying's one moment of inaction, of staring at Master Gordon's body on the ground, cost her dearly. Now she had no more opportunity to run away, not with Chang's hands coming at her.

Amah had pounded into her head that she was never to reveal her martial-arts skills unless she was in grave personal danger. Everything she had done so far in her own defense could have been explained away by determination and sheer luck. After all, even a rabbit would bite when attacked. But she had no more options left to her. Unless she wished to be raped by Shao-ye, she must fight.

She threw herself to the ground, rolled to Mr. Gordon's inert body, and grabbed his walking stick. It was made of hard wood, a bit heavy, but as good a weapon as she could lay her hands on now.

She wielded it like a sword, pointing its tip at Chang's elbow. His eyes widened in surprise at the training evident in her move. Then he changed the direction of his strike and made a brazen attempt to yank the walking stick from her.

The deflating truth was that he probably could. But she refused to think about it. She slashed the stick at his wrists, forcing him to withdraw his hands. Then she aimed it at his heart. A direct hit, even with a dull weapon, would do damage. He somersaulted backward. A moment later he had his own weapon in hand, a short stick with nine thin iron chains at the tip, each ending in a metal ball the size of a quail's egg.

Nine-snake whip, a nasty weapon, yet one easy to conceal beneath bulky winter clothes. He leaped high and slashed the chains toward her. She dodged, not daring to take the whip head-on. One of the metal balls could easily catch her on a finger and break it.

She moved behind the corner of a turn in the alley. The whip tore away a section of the wall, barely missing her head: Chang was no longer merely procuring her for Shao-ye; he was out to teach her a lesson.

He advanced. She retreated, and tried to get in a jab or two while he swung the whip behind himself for another strike. He backed her into the lotus pond garden outside the Court of Contemplative Bamboo. She tried to hold her ground, to move sideways instead of always backward. But still he advanced. Closer and closer the edge of the pond came. She maneuvered left, leaped on the miniature bridge, and regretted it the moment she did.

The bridge led into the small pavilion. If Chang managed to push her into the pavilion she'd be completely cornered—the pond to either side, the artificial hill behind, and Chang holding the bridge. Time to forget such niceties as intact fingers and fight like the mangiest, hungriest dog on a snow-covered street.

She poked the walking stick directly into the descending head of the nine-snake whip and tangled it within the chains. Then she jerked the walking stick hard to her right.

He pulled the whip toward him. She pushed along, then extricated her stick to strike him across the upper chest. He whipped the chains at her. She ducked, and aimed for his knees. He jumped up, avoided her hit, and brought the chains down at her again. She parried it with the tip of the stick, aiming a kick against his stomach.

When her soft-soled boot connected with his abdomen, the wound in her leg hurt, but the pain was overshadowed by her surprise. He had been so overwhelming in his attack, and she so ineffectual in her defense, that she had not expected any success. He seemed just as surprised, and staggered a step back.

She was off the bridge, but still at the edge of the pond. If only she could topple him into the pond, she thought longingly. That would give her time to run.

The opportunity came sooner than she had anticipated. For some reason, Chang was noticeably weaker than he had been at the beginning of their fight. His footwork slacked. His whip, when it came down, had only half the force it had earlier commanded. Perhaps he really was old. Perhaps he tired easily.

Ying-ying did not question her good luck; she exploited it. Now it was she who advanced on Chang, the two of them moving along the rim of the pond. He whistled shrilly, startling her. Was he calling for help? If he thought Shao-ye would come to his aid, he must not know their young master at all.

She drove the walking stick against his left arm, forcing him to move to his right, ever closer to the edge. Now it was she who had the audacity to try to put her hand on his weapon. With her stick entangled in the whip, she reached in and grabbed the whip by the base and yanked at it. He pulled back. She abruptly let go of both the whip and her own stick. He stumbled back. Another kick to his stomach and he crashed through the frozen pond with a long, pained grunt.

"Master!" someone screamed.

It was Little Dragon, running toward them, a sheathed sword in his hand. Ying-ying leaped back. Little Dragon flung aside his sword and slid into the pond. He cursed and shivered but wasted no time in dragging Chang to the edge and lifting him out.

No wonder he handed Chang heated spirits in winter and did the latter's work in summer. They were master and disciple.

As soon as Little Dragon climbed out of the pond he set to work, raising the prostrate Chang into a semblance of the lotus position. He sat down behind Chang, in the lotus position also, held the older man upright with his left arm, and pressed his right palm to Chang's back, between the shoulder blades.

Why? She had bested Chang. But all she did was upset his balance and tip him into the pond. Why was Little Dragon treating him as if Chang had suffered some severe internal damage?

A gong clanged in her head. What had Amah said? *You don't suppose I was the only one injured that night, do you? I dealt him a heavy blow too.*

In all the fear and confusion of the night, she hadn't thought of that. Chang was the one who had fought Amah when she stole the jade tablet. What was his purpose in Da-ren's household?

What had been Amah's purpose in Mother's household? To hide from the law and remain safe. Who was to say Chang hadn't an equally long—or longer—list of crimes to his name? And what had Little Dragon said to Little Orchid? *He doesn't even dare visit his old mother—and he's desperate to see her.*

Was that why Chang had fought Amah years ago, because he hoped that by catching the flying thief trying to make off with Da-ren's treasured artifact, he would have his own crimes pardoned? And was that why he curried favor with Shao-ye, in the hope that the latter would be able to help him someday?

She shoved all the chaotic thoughts out of her head. She had a more immediate concern: Master Gordon was still out there, lying on the frozen ground.

He could be ill for days if she didn't get to him fast.

IT HAD TURNED CLOUDY. Whipped by a celestial gale, streaks of fleece tore across the sky. Shadow and light chased each other as the moon was alternately veiled and revealed.

She unsealed Mr. Gordon's chi paths and helped him to his feet. He wobbled. She moved more of his weight onto herself. Spiky pain shot through her leg. She winced but made no sound. First she'd take Master Gordon to his rooms, then treat her own wound.

"Is that Little Dragon?" he whispered as they entered the garden, which they must cross to get to the Court of Contemplative Bamboo. "What is he doing with Chang?"

She didn't answer—she was staring. In the intermittent light, a column of steam rose above Little Dragon's bare head. Was his chi that strong?

Chang's face contorted. A torrent of blood spewed from his mouth. Little Dragon shut his eyes in concentration. But it was no use. Another stream of blood burst from Chang's mouth. More blood dripped from his nostrils. Blood even seeped from his ears, blood made black by the dark of the night, a ghastly, bone-chilling sight.

"God in heaven!" Master Gordon gasped.

Despite Little Dragon's restraining arm, Chang slumped to the side, his head thumping on the paving stone as he fell. Little Dragon sobbed, knelt down, and pulled Chang's unresisting form into a hard, desperate embrace.

"Let's go," Ying-ying urged Master Gordon.

"Shouldn't we help him? That man's in great medical need."

His naivety frustrated her. She dragged him forward. "We can't help him. Let's help *you*."

Out of the corner of her eye, she saw Little Dragon scooting back some distance from Chang's body. He kowtowed three times. Chang was dead, then. Her heart quailed. She had not meant to do him any lasting damage—she only wanted to escape. Was it really so easy to kill a man?

She heard the flutter of Little Dragon's robe and moved aside without thinking. He landed where she had been standing. Without a pause, he disabled Master Gordon exactly as Chang had.

Ying-ying was outraged. "How dare you treat your master with such disrespect?"

Little Dragon's handsome face was a mask of scorn and fury. "He is a stinking foreign devil. My master is over there, dead. You killed him, you daughter of a whore."

The epithet, more than his accusation of slaughter, stunned her. Big Treasure had called her that. Chang had called her that this very night. But Little Dragon had always been polite, despite his antipathy.

"Your master tried to catch me so Young Master could dishonor me," she countered. "You know what kind of man Young Master is. You know how he treats women. Was I supposed to go along?"

"Who cares how Young Master treats *you*?" Little Dragon spat. "My master was a great man. If he wanted to beat you stupid, you should kowtow afterward and thank him for his instruction!"

"Well, too bad your master wasn't capable of it. I beat him fair and square."

Little Dragon looked as if steam were going to rise from him again. "Shut up! My master was injured five and a half years ago. If he hadn't been, he would have crushed you with his little finger."

He pulled his sword from its sheath and pointed it at her. "I am going to avenge him. I'm going to send you to the underworld as his slave."

She took a step back. She wasn't afraid of him. If she could beat the master, why should she fear the disciple? But she had a healthy respect for the sword. She was not going to fight it barehanded. Now, where was Mr. Gordon's walking stick? Had it fallen into the pond? Or was it somewhere on the ground?

"Aren't you ashamed of yourself, fighting a girl?" She needed to buy herself some time.

"Are you scared?" he taunted.

She took another step back and turned sideways, to get a better look at the edge of the pond. No sign of the stick. *Damn it.* "Not only will you be fighting a girl, but an unarmed girl. What will people say when you lose?"

That was an unwise thing to say. The tip of his sword was suddenly before her neck. She sidestepped it, but not before breaking out in a cold sweat all over. He was uncannily swift with the blade.

The sword came unerringly at her throat again. She rolled to her left. He gave her no breathing room. The blade followed her and was upon her almost before she could rise to her feet again.

Clang. It was met by another blade.

"Master Keeper Lin," said Amah, addressing Little Dragon by his surname with elaborate courtesy. "You should be ashamed of yourself, Master Keeper Lin, fighting an unarmed girl."

Ying-ying scrambled to her feet and ran behind Amah. She had never been so happy to see anyone in her entire life. Amah was in good health. Her voice was steady and strong. And she had come upon them so softly that neither she nor Little Dragon had been aware of her approach.

Little Dragon's face twisted with rage. "You! I remember your voice. You are the thief who injured my master!"

"Good memory, young man," Amah answered calmly. "Were you hiding and watching us? It's true I left a bit of Thousand-winter Chill in his blood. But he should be fine, as long as he didn't tax himself—or take cold baths."

"Your disciple." Little Dragon's voice shook. "Your disciple pushed him into the frozen pond tonight."

"Really?" Amah looked at the pond, and at the sodden, blood-spattered body at its edge. Her expression was unmoved. "Is that him then?"

Little Dragon's jaw worked.

Amah turned to Ying-ying. "Were you disrespectful toward Master Keeper Chang?"

"He was trying to force me to submit to Young Master's ignominious will."

"I see. I should have known that boy was involved somehow—when I saw the state of our rooms my mind did not immediately turn to him." Amah sighed. "Ying-ying, go and kowtow to Master Keeper Chang."

It was an incomprehensible command, something she'd have refused outright under normal circumstances. But at this moment Ying-ying was glad to do anything for Amah. She kowtowed not once, but three times.

"Master Keeper Chang was a magnanimous man. I'm sure his ghost has forgiven you, as you meant him no harm," said Amah. "You did not know that cold water was fatal to him."

Little Dragon laughed harshly. "You with your fancy words and false gestures. Fine. I'll let the whore's daughter go and kill you instead."

Ying-ying shivered. Amah looked at him steadily. "I injured your master. But he wounded me no less severely. The account was even between the two of us. Do not get involved in an old feud. Or it will never end."

Little Dragon sneered. "It ends tonight. Your disciple killed my master. I kill hers. Sounds fair enough to me."

He raised his sword and pointed at Amah. Amah unsheathed her own sword. "Ying-ying, don't stand there like a fool. Go help your teacher."

HURRIEDLY YING-YING WARMED MR. GORDON'S bed with a brazier pan. She warmed him with a half glass of spirits before tucking him in. "Stay here tonight. Don't go out again."

He gripped her hand. "What is going on? Will you be safe?"

She squeezed his palm. She knew he was confused and worried, but she had to get back to Amah now. "I'll be fine—my amah is here. I'll tell you everything tomorrow."

He had some interesting English medicines that he had shown her before. She applied a balm to the puncture wound on her leg and rushed back to the garden.

Amah and Little Dragon were fighting on the miniature bridge. The long retreat had done wonders for Amah. There was a new fluidity to her movement, a potent ease, like the glide of an eagle in the sky. Her thrusts were clean, her swings strong, and her parries secure.

They engaged in a series of attacks and counterattacks. Amah, to Ying-ying's relief, did not seem intent on killing Little Dragon. She probably planned to humiliate the young man, to wrest a resounding victory that would leave him no choice but to scamper away, licking his wounds.

Little Dragon, however, was not intimidated. Ying-ying was astonished to see how adept he was with his weapon. He was what? Nineteen, twenty at most. Strength and aggression she expected from him, but despite his murderous rage, he also displayed a surety and cleverness beyond his years.

Their movements quickened and quickened yet again. They were now closer to each other, their motions more brutal, the swords clashing closer to the hilts than to the tips. Ying-ying had her fingers between her teeth, her heart quivering with each collision of the blades. Amah must have realized she was dealing with no mere enraged, impotent child here, but a well-trained and possibly prodigious talent, for she drove her sword far forward, and followed with a somersault backward, into the pavilion.

Little Dragon followed. Amah leaped onto the stone table to give herself the advantage of height. As their blades continued to thrash and clank, she aimed a good half dozen kicks at him: One just missed the side of his head; another caught him squarely below his left collarbone. He wavered a little, but did not make any sound, and was back in the fight in no time.

Amah put her aerial capability to full and dazzling use. She catapulted over his head; her feet landed on and immediately kicked against the railing, reversing her direction, launching the tip of her blade directly at his back. Lin barely sidestepped in time, so surprised had he been by her agility and the unexpected direction of the attack.

Amah soared, twirled, wheeled. She performed impossible feats. But Lin could no longer be discomposed. He stepped up to the table at the center of the pavilion and refused to budge from the spot, an ideal place for holding defenses. At one point Ying-ying could swear he closed his eyes and used his other senses guide him, so as not to be distracted by Amah's leaps and bounds.

The situation was developing toward an impasse: Amah, once heir to the legendary skills of the Order of the Shadowless Goddesses, dominated the battle but could not subdue the resilient Little Dragon, who, despite his youth and relative lack of experience, held firm against her.

Then everything changed. As Amah again elevated and plunged toward him, he raised his sword to meet her charge, while his left arm swept up in a peculiar motion. Something small and slender shot out of his sleeve toward Amah's legs. A sleeve arrow. Before Ying-ying could even gasp, Amah cried out in pain.

Their swords met and ground against each other. Using that resistance, Amah flipped backward. Little Dragon let fly another sleeve arrow, this one hitting Amah squarely in the thigh. She fell like a bird that had been struck with a slingshot.

Amah did not lose her wits. In the narrow space between the stools and the railing, she rolled away from Little Dragon as soon as she landed. But he proved quicker on foot. He leaped down from the center of the table and intercepted her. Shifting his sword from right hand to left, he slammed aside Amah's hurriedly upraised blade.

Amah again attempted to pierce him. But her position was too vulnerable. He kicked her arm. She screamed and dropped her sword. Without further ado, he crouched down and struck her three times on the torso with his right palm.

The abrupt deterioration in Amah's fortune caught Ying-ying completely lead-footed. Mere seconds had passed from the moment the first sleeve arrow had been deployed. She stood paralyzed, her viscera quaking with each wallop of Little Dragon's hand, as Amah groaned like a beast being clubbed to death.

Then Ying-ying was racing across the bridge, screaming, "Leave her alone!"

Little Dragon looked up in disdain. She grabbed the sword that had dropped from Amah's hand and pointed it at him. "Leave her alone or you will have to answer to me."

Her hand must be shaking badly—the tip of the sword wobbled all over the place. Little Dragon regarded her for a moment. "I already said I'd let you go. Now leave."

"I won't. You will not touch her again."

His face hardened. "Fine. You asked for it."

The next moment his sword drove directly at her chest. Acting on pure reflex, she sidestepped. The blade missed her arm by a hairbreadth. She heard her own screech of fright.

He did not give her a moment to breathe. His sword slashed at her. She ducked and took another two steps back. This time, as the long, sharp edge of steel descended, her own sword came up and she was suddenly filled with an energy bordering on panic. All other thoughts and concerns, even those of Amah, were preempted by her pressing need to not be killed.

She parried his thrust. The contact was quick, but jarring—she could almost hear the bones of her forearm rattle. Circulating her chi to her sword arm to protect against the impact, she took another hit on her blade. And it hurt despite the protection of her chi.

The confines of the pavilion did not help her. She dared lean neither right nor left for fear of being trapped against the railing or the stone stools. What exercises she had with swords or the steel fans—too long ago now—certainly never included a homicidal opponent or such awkward surroundings. Barely a few moves into the battle she was already panting, and if her insides shook any harder, it would cause waves in the pond.

She must get out of the pavilion if she was to have any chance. But he must think it a good idea to keep her in, for as she backed closer to the bridge, he deliberately forced her to her right, away from her exit.

In desperation she jumped onto a stool, and then from there onto the stone table. The tabletop, being merely placed on top of a round column, shifted, causing her to wobble. He immediately swung his sword in a horizontal slash at her knees. She crouched, and with all her strength pushed his blade as far to her left as possible and at the same moment leaped forward to the railing.

Her plan was to land on the railing, and from that high vantage point to leap clear of the pond altogether to the other side. Amah had performed much more complex maneuvers, so Ying-ying figured she had a chance. But when she looked down, she discovered she had clearly overshot the distance to the railing. Her body reacted on its own, her legs kicking down, attempting, against the odds, to find some footing. But only her heels caught the outside of the railing.

She did her best to push off. But her angle was too awkward. Instead of an upward bound, she was going forward but down.

"Ying-ying!" Amah moaned. "Careful!"

She flung her arms out and caught the edge of the pond. But that was not enough to prevent two-thirds of her body from breaking through the ice. She whimpered from the cold that instantly swamped her, through her silk trousers and the several pairs of pantalettes underneath.

Fortunately the pond was not deep, only up to her waist. Pushing off with whatever slippery traction she could get, she hoisted herself out, to Little Dragon's chortles.

Without hurry he stepped off the bridge. "Why, is it already washday, Bai Gu-niang?"

Ying-ying backed away from him and picked up her sword, which had landed on a sheet of ice that still hugged the edge of the pond. She had no clever retort for him. Her shoes oozed mud. Much of her front was raw from scraping against ice that had broken jaggedly. As a stiff wind blew, her legs and bottom screamed with cold, her sodden garments sucking every last shred of warmth from her blood.

He renewed his attack without another word. As Ying-ying moved to duck his blow, the mud on her soles made her foot slip out from under her; her other knee hit the paving stone hard. But she managed to keep his sword from reaching her. As he drew back to drive at her again, she rolled sideways, toward a dwarf juniper in a large planter.

As his blade fell, she scooted behind the planter, furiously scraping the mud from her soles, and his sword slashed nothing but a branch. He came around the planter, and she scampered so as to be opposite him again. Irritated at her tactic, he swung his sword and hacked off the top third of the dwarf juniper tree in one strike.

Ying-ying gulped. They could see each other's faces clearly above the truncated tree. He struck again. But the lower portion of the tree's trunk was much thicker and did not give. Just as she was about to breathe a sigh of relief, however, he toppled the whole thing to the ground.

Now there was nothing between them but the overturned planter, which he easily leaped over, sword pointed straight at her. She crouched down and grabbed a small pot of withered chrysanthemum and hurled it at him. By reflex he parried, and the collision of his sword with the pot broke the latter and sent clumps of dirt flying.

She dashed off another clay pot. This time he sidestepped it and was directly before her. Their blades clashed and scraped. He dominated, but she held her own.

As the peril of imminent death faded a little, their combat settling into a certain rhythm, hope began to revive in Ying-ying. Given time, perhaps Little Dragon would come to his senses and see that even if he killed every person who had ever crossed his master, it would not help bring Chang back, or make his journey less lonely in the underworld.

Her hopes did not grow beyond a flicker, for Little Dragon abruptly intensified his attack. "I've had enough of this. You die now."

He raised his left arm. What happened to Amah flashed through her mind: He was going to launch a sleeve arrow at her. She somersaulted backward; the sleeve arrow hissed past her ear. But in her urge to avoid it, she forgot that she was standing only a short distance before another dwarf juniper in a large planter. Her feet landed squarely on the lip of the planter; it pitched forward, the dwarf juniper knocking her to the ground. She struggled to crawl out from underneath, but stilled as Little Dragon's foot came down on her sword.

Without thinking, she pulled out a long silver pin from her hair and jabbed the sharp end into his foot. He yowled. She scrambled out from under the dwarf juniper and threw a handful of dirt in his face.

He roared and hacked down at her. They were once again in the thick of it. Ying-ying's arm ached. The sword was getting heavier. Her lungs couldn't bring in enough air. But Little Dragon was tireless—and seemed more homicidal by the minute.

"Stop! What are the two of you doing?!"

Ying-ying nearly lost her concentration. Mr. Gordon. What was he doing out of bed? She barely ducked in time. A fraction of a second later and Little Dragon's sword would have sliced through her arm.

From the corner of her eye she saw Master Gordon raise his arm. What was he holding, aimed to the side? Was that a...It must be the pistol they had spoken of earlier in the day, an eternity ago.

Bang!

At the loud explosion, Little Dragon froze. Only for a split second, but long enough for the tip of Ying-ying's sword to sink into his shoulder. He screamed. Then he screamed again and crumpled to the ground. Ying-ying sealed the acupuncture points on his legs. She had no idea why he was bleeding from his right thigh, and she did not care. She ran for Amah.

Amah was still and silent. Ying-ying threw herself down and cupped her hand beneath Amah's nose. The slightest stirring of air brushed against her skin. Her relief was knife-sharp. But then she lifted Amah's wrist to check her pulse and cried out: Amah's pulse was that of someone whose internal organs had been damaged beyond repair.

As tears rang down her face, She put her hand at the center of Amah's abdomen and tried to aid the older woman with some of her own chi. But she was running near empty. When she tried to force out what little remained, a flash of agony struck the center of her own abdomen. She didn't care. If she had to give all her blood to Amah, she would.

At last the connection between them warmed. Something was getting through to Amah. Her eyelids fluttered. Her lips moved. "Stop," Amah whispered hoarsely. "It's no use."

"We'll find you a court doctor," Ying-ying promised wildly. "We'll find you a martial-arts master who can help save you."

"It's no use," Amah repeated, her voice thin as a ghost's breath. "You must look out for yourself now. Dig under the third pomegran..."

She did not finish her sentence.

Ying-ying's eyes burned. Her heart burned. She stood up and marched toward Little Dragon. Master Gordon was there, hunched over him, tearing strips off his own clothes to bind Little Dragon's shoulder and leg.

"I don't know what happened," he shouted to Ying-ying, his words falling over one another. "The bullet must have struck the top of the artificial hill, then ricocheted. Fortunately it only grazed him. I don't think any major arteries have been—"

Ying-ying pushed him aside and pointed her sword at Little Dragon's throat. She almost didn't react in time to the kick he aimed at her left shin. Whether he had already opened his chi paths on his own, or whether she had botched the sealing of those paths in the first place, he was mobile.

She somersaulted backward. As she landed, Little Dragon got up, his sword again in hand.

"Please stop!" Master Gordon placed himself between them and spoke in Chinese. "You are both my pupils. Must you do this?"

Little Dragon strode forward, lifted Master Gordon by the front of his tunic, and heaved him to the side. Master Gordon flew as if he were a rag doll, hit the garden wall, and fell limply to the ground.

"Master Gordon!" she screamed.

But she could not go to him. Little Dragon's sword seemed to have multiplied to become a forest of blades. And no matter how she swung her own, she could not hack her way through.

She didn't hear the footsteps at all until the garden had filled with guards, their weapons drawn.

"What is going on here?" demanded Da-ren.

Twenty-three

Aftermath

SUCH WAS DA-REN'S AUTHORITY THAT Ying-ying and Little Dragon each took two steps back.

"What is going on?" Da-ren repeated, his voice even quieter.

"She killed Master Keeper Chang!" Little Dragon got in the first word.

"He killed my amah, and he would have killed me too if Master Gordon hadn't intervened!"

"Her amah was the thief, Da-ren! She was the one who took your jade tablet. She deserved to die."

"What?" Da-ren stared at Ying-ying. "Is that true?"

"No, no! He is trying to slander a dead person!" Ying-ying shouted, half in panic. "I'll wager that Chang, *his* master, was a notorious criminal, hiding out here, feeding on your largesse. And he tried to use force to make me submit to Young Master!"

"My son?" Da-ren's eyes narrowed into slits. "He is in Canton. What has he to do with anything?"

"He is back. Chang lured me to my courtyard, saying my amah sent him. But when I got there, Young Master was in my room. I ran away, but Chang wouldn't let me go. He kept after me. I had no choice but to fight him."

"You think you are too good for Young Master," Little Dragon snarled. "You daughter of a whore."

"Shut up," Da-ren exploded. "How dare you speak so of Bai Fu-ren. Shut up!"

Tears welled up in Ying-ying's eyes. For the first time in her life, Da-ren had come to her defense. But then Da-ren's harsh gaze turned to her. "I have always wondered about last summer. I have always wondered that my son should have been so stupid as to go before Minister Chao's residence and make a fool of himself. He insisted that he had never gone there. That he had simply wakened there. I did not believe him at that time."

Ying-ying suddenly felt her icy wet garments, as if she were plastered all over in a dead man's skin.

"You and your amah did it, did you not? You did it so that you would be rid of him." Da-ren's voice was dangerously quiet. "He is a wastrel. I do not blame you for not wanting him. But what you did brought shame not only upon him, but upon this entire household."

Upon Da-ren, the man she most wished would think well of her.

She dropped to her knees. "Da-ren, please extinguish your anger. It...it wasn't like that."

Too late she saw that she should never have mentioned Shao-ye.

"So you admit it."

"Da-ren!" shouted the majordomo. "I cannot feel a pulse on Master Kuo-tung!"

Ying-ying cried out and rushed to Master Gordon's inert body, convinced that Master Keeper Ju must be wrong. Master Gordon's pulse was slow and weak, that was all.

But she, with her trained and sensitive hands, also could not find a pulse. Nor could she detect any air coming out of his nostrils. And when she placed her ear over his chest, she heard only a resounding silence.

She screamed.

And kept screaming.

YING-YING DIDN'T KNOW HOW SHE ended up in her own courtyard—there was so much roaring in her head, like a spring sandstorm, all dark, relentless clamor. She did have a faint impression of seeing Little Dragon being led away, his hands and arms bound together. And she had just as vague a recollection of Bao-shun's gentle, sympathetic voice in her ear, reminding her that much needed to be done for Amah's "after matters."

She cleaned Amah and dressed her in her best clothes, her whole head numb as she did so. After she had finished, she sat by Amah's side, holding her cold, callused hands. When she had been a little girl, Amah used to brush her hair, and those hands had always been infinitely gentle as they pulled a comb through her tangled strands.

And in the bottom of one of her trunks, Ying-ying still had all the candle-stub mock seals Amah had carved for her, the very last one of which gave her the title "Lady of the Silver Blade."

It was easy to feel compassion for a frail mother or an exiled friend. But Amah had always been so strong, so capable, and so stoic. Ying-ying had never thought about how difficult her life must have been—or how lonely. She had never wondered what broken dreams Amah held close to her heart. She had never even asked about her years in the Abode of the Shadowless Goddesses—and now she would never be able to.

She was shivering uncontrollably before she realized that she was still in her clammy and bloodied clothes. She changed out of them, tidied herself up as best she could, then crossed the entire breadth of the residence to Master Gordon's rooms.

He had been laid out on his bed, shoes and all. She stared at him in the light of a flickering candle, half hoping his eyelids would flutter. He couldn't be dead. His young friend had just found him after traveling half the world. His enemy was no more. He could at last go home again and revisit that beautiful house in the south of England where he had been so happy.

He had everything to live for.

She was bone-weary, but she could not seem to sit still for long. So she started to tidy his things: They probably needed to be delivered to the British Legation, along with his body.

Da-ren had provided him with a well-appointed suite of rooms. It wasn't until she was making piles and stacks that she realized he had brought very few possessions of his own from England—clothes and books, mostly.

She would like to keep a memento for herself. But she didn't know what would be appropriate for her to take—the boy who had journeyed ten thousand miles to see him probably had a much stronger claim on everything.

Then she came across the poem about listening to the rain that she had written out for him. Beneath it she found a translation he had undertaken. She ran her fingers over the lines of his spidery handwriting. This would be a beautiful memento—beautiful and utterly inadequate. For what object could represent kindness, understanding, and acceptance?

And how could anything embody friendship that made the soul glad?

Someone was calling her name. She looked up to see a young lackey. "Bai Gu-niang, Da-ren wants to see you."

Mutely she followed the manservant. But instead of leading her to Da-ren's study, or to the middle hall where he received callers, the lackey led her back to her own courtyard.

Da-ren was already waiting, his face hard. "Where is the jade tablet your amah took from me?"

Ying-ying trembled. In addition to all the other black marks against her, henceforth she was also a girl who had been brought up by a thief. "I don't know, Da-ren. My amah never showed me anything valuable."

"Did she say nothing to you, then, before she died?"

Ying-ying hesitated. She had wanted to find what Amah had left her in private. But that luxury was no longer possible. "She said something about a third pomegranate."

"Dig it up."

It was pitch dark outside; she lit a few lanterns for illumination. Plunging a shovel into the soil was like trying to hew granite with a spoon—the ground was solidly frozen. Only after her arms had been jarred numb did she remember to use her chi.

The digging was slightly easier after that, but it was still cold, exhausting, skeleton-rattling work. And after she had pulled the poor tree out, root and all, she found nothing underneath. She closed her eyes for a moment and started on the third one from the right.

Her arms were about to fall off from exhaustion when she at last found the buried bundle. Underneath the layers of oilcloth was a black-lacquered box the size of one of Mr. Gordon's dictionaries. She wiped it with her handkerchief and took it to Da-ren.

As he reached for the lid, something occurred to her. She slammed her palm down on the box.

He frowned. "What is the meaning of this?"

"Da-ren, please be more careful."

She turned the box around so that the lid would open away from him. Then she moved to the side.

He lifted the lid of the box. Several golden gleams shot out—Amah's needles. To his credit, Da-ren did not flinch. Turning the box around, he looked inside.

His breath caught. "You have never seen any of it?"

The contents of the box dazzled in the candlelight. Pearls bigger than apricots, jasper as green as summer grass, bangles of blood-red jade. Was this something Amah had set aside for her old age, for when she could no longer leap high walls or even lift a sword? So that she'd always have a roof over her head, money for food, and perhaps, just perhaps, an occasional string of coins for betting?

Ying-ying's throat felt as if someone had been rubbing sand inside it all night. "No, Da-ren. I have never seen any of it."

Da-ren pushed the precious jewels aside. At the very bottom of the box was the tablet of white jade—the one object that had changed Ying-ying's entire life.

"Do you know what this is?" Da-ren asked.

The question surprised her. She almost nodded before she remembered that she should disavow all knowledge of the jade tablet. "No, Da-ren."

"It is one of a set of three made by Buddhist monks in a time of imperial persecution of their religion. The monks hid their treasures, and left clues to the whereabouts of those treasures in these jade tablets. They look almost identical, except for markings on their edges."

Ying-ying had dismissed the tablets as inconsequential, because she had been convinced that they were all copies of something else. So they were *supposed* to be duplicates?

"The monasteries today are but a shadow of their former glory," Da-ren went on. "But in their heyday, during the Tang dynasty, legend has it that they had giant Buddhas made from pure gold."

Ying-ying often wished that she had lived during the Tang dynasty, when China had been at the height and breadth of its power, when art and literature flourished, ladies' garments were light and vivid, and foreigners came bearing paeans and tributes instead of demoralizing demands.

It had been a time of such abundant wealth and grandeur that anything seemed possible.

"Everywhere I go I see desperately needed reforms. There is not a single ministry that is remotely efficient or effective. The civil service examinations still test only the Confucian classics. No one knows how to make modern machinery or steel-clad warships. And it takes less time for news to travel from Moscow to Shanghai than it does from Shanghai to Peking."

Da-ren sighed, a deep, bone-weary sound. "So many have the funds, but no will for forward-looking changes. I have the will, but no funds. At one point it seemed I might track down all three of the jade tablets— a soothsayer went so far as to tell me that I would find the treasure in my lifetime. And then I found out that two of the three tablets had gone overseas—and this one here was taken from me."

Ying-ying kept her eyes on her feet, mortified at the reference to Amah's theft. Perhaps, if she could locate the jade tablet in Master Gordon's possession...

"Now it has come back to me," Da-ren continued. "It is a sign from above. I will have all three tablets in time and they will lead me to the treasure."

"Da-ren is certain to have swift and resounding success," she answered with the language expected of her.

Before Da-ren could say anything else, the majordomo rushed in, his face ashen.

"Did you find my son?" Da-ren demanded sharply. "Which pleasure house did he run off to this time?"

Shao-ye dared to leave the residence on a night like this?

"We have not yet located Shao-ye," answered Master Keeper Ju. "But the maid Little Orchid has hanged herself. She is beyond saving."

Ying-ying gripped a nearby table.

Da-ren covered his face with his hand. "Give her a good burial. Compensate the family accordingly. And disturb me no more with such news."

He rose and left, taking the jade tablet and the rest of Amah's cache with him.

Ying-ying expected the majordomo to follow. Instead he remained behind and checked at the door to make sure Da-ren had gone far enough. She steeled herself. The majordomo was entitled to scold her: He was the one who had to set everything right again.

When he came back to her, he pulled a silver ingot of at least ten taels out of his robe and pressed it into her hands. "It's a shame what happened to your amah," he said in a hushed voice. "Maybe she was a flying thief and maybe not, but she was a good woman. You buy her a decent coffin."

"I can't, Master Keeper." The silver was solidly heavy in her hand, and still warm from his body heat. She couldn't believe it. The majordomo, of all people, the man who had always seemed so supercilious and impatient. "It's too generous."

He sighed, his pointed face softening with pity. "Keep it. Things are worse than you think, Bai Gu-niang. Da-ren is the best man there is. I would scale of a mountain of knives and swim a sea of fire for him. But Young Master…"

He shook his head. "Young Master returned to his rooms last night in a rage. He screamed at everyone. And when the rest of his lackeys had left, he beat the girl. The marks on her face when we took her down just now, you don't want to know."

The beating had been the last straw for the already desperately unhappy girl.

"Mark my word, Bai Gu-niang," the majordomo warned her. "Young Master will not make things easy for you. I know you are handy with a sword but a sword does not defend against everything. For as long as you remain here, he will try to take his revenge on you. And now that your amah is no more…"

Ying-ying nodded slowly. She should have known it would be impossible for her to stay on after the events of last night. But to actually hear it, to have Master Keeper Ju's silver in her hand for when she must survive on her own—she could not think. She could not think.

"Bai Gu-niang use care," the majordomo said. "I take my leave."

Ying-ying walked him to the gate of the courtyard. And then she stood in the cold, paralyzed. There was Amah's funeral to attend to and Master Gordon to accompany to the British Legation, but beyond that the future was a dark abyss. Where would she live? And how would she feed herself when the majordomo's silver had run out?

Someone threw her down and gripped her neck. Little Dragon, strangling her with his bare hands. The guards' ropes must have been no match for his wiles.

She hit him on the head with the silver ingot. But his chokehold only became tighter.

"I can't find him, so I'll kill you first," he said, his teeth gritted. "If you hadn't been so uppish, Little Orchid would still be alive—and the baby too. That baby was mine. Mine!"

She hit him even harder with the silver ingot. She wasn't a helpless girl like Little Orchid: She fought back. Finally, on the third hit, Little Dragon cried out and let go.

Loud footsteps ran toward the courtyard, dozens of men. Little Dragon leaped up. Ying-ying, too, scrambled to her feet. Where was the shovel with which she'd been digging half the night? She would bash his head in yet. But he rushed out and leaped on top of the wall that penned in the alley leading toward the courtyard.

"You get down here, Little Dragon!" shouted Bao-shun's voice.

"That's Master Keeper Lin to you," Little Dragon shot back.

He jumped onto the roof of the house in the next courtyard.

The men rushed to follow him, but Ying-ying knew they wouldn't catch him. She rubbed her neck, her hand icy against the probably sorely bruised skin of her throat.

A huge commotion erupted in the direction of the front gate of the residence. Horses, definitely horses. Had Little Dragon stolen a mount from the stables for his escape? No, the horses were coming toward Da-ren's residence, not away.

Checking all around to make sure that Little Dragon was really gone and not about to ambush her again, she made for the front gate. Already she could hear the horses being reined to a stop. Now footsteps came pounding.

Several lackeys sprinted past her.

"Master Keepers, what is going on?" she shouted.

One of the young men turned around to answer even as he kept running. "Imperial messenger—with imperial directive for Da-ren."

No imperial messenger had come to the residence during all her years here. And so early in the morning—the sky was gray under clouds that promised more snow, but the sun wouldn't rise for at least another incense stick's time.

Da-ren himself came running, a sight she had never seen. After a moment of hesitation, she followed him, trailing some distance behind. By the time she reached the front court of the compound, Da-ren was down on one knee, and the imperial messenger had nearly finished reading his scroll.

"...appointed the governor of Ili. Out of our tender compassion, his womenfolk and offspring may remain behind. We expect our loyal servant to uphold the trust of his sovereign and to sacrifice everything for the good of the country."

Da-ren dropped his head. "This servant's unending gratitude to the Son of Heaven, and to the Old Buddha. May ten thousand times ten thousand blessings rain on them."

Ili? Ili was in Chinese Turkestan, at the edge of the world. Da-ren had been exiled. The dowager empress must have at last had enough of his relentless calls for modernization.

Da-ren stayed on his knee as the imperial messenger and his two escorts remounted and left. He seemed stuck, unable to get up. The majordomo ran out and knelt before him. "Da-ren! Da-ren! What are we to do?"

Da-ren placed a hand on the majordomo's shoulder and slowly straightened. "We are to depart as soon as possible. I leave the details to you."

Ying-ying bowed her head when Da-ren passed before her. He stopped. "Bury your amah. Pack your things. You will come with me."

Had he said this yesterday morning, she would have done everything in her power to persuade him that she should be included among his womenfolk, mercifully allowed to remain behind.

But everything had changed. Now he was the only person who could still protect her. He—and the sheer distance from Peking to Ili—would keep her safe from Shao-ye, from Little Dragon, from everyone and everything else that would descend upon a girl with no parents and no home.

She sank to her knees. "Yes, Da-ren. Thank you, Da-ren."

Twenty-four

Journeys

THE HOUSEHOLD WAS IN CHAOS. As Ying-ying rushed back and forth between her own courtyard and Master Gordon's rooms, everyone she encountered along the way seemed to be running, shouting, or weeping—Da-ren beating Shao-ye black and blue after the latter finally returned from his night of revelry only added to the pandemonium.

And yet preparations proceeded apace.

Riders had already been sent out to ready relay stages for the changing of horses along the endless road to Chinese Turkestan. Courtesy messages concerning Da-ren's appointment and departure were delivered by the gross. Carriages and wagon carts were parked in the front courtyard, lackeys pushing and shoving crates and trunks inside.

In the midst of everything that required his attention, plus seeing to the visitors calling upon Da-ren to wish him well—too few visitors, as the appointment was a decisive sign of Da-ren's ouster from the inner circles of the court—the majordomo somehow found the men and a spare donkey cart to take Amah to the cemetery. Ying-ying didn't even need to go select a coffin; a handsome one, lacquered and shiny, had already been delivered, along with several changes of white mourning clothes.

At the cemetery she took part in the digging, no longer bothering to hide the fact that she could break through the frozen soil faster and more easily than the men who had accompanied her. When Amah was in the ground, a temporary wooden grave marker erected over the fresh mound of earth—the majordomo had promised he would see to a proper gravestone—Ying-ying set fire to a huge pile of special underworld currency. Then she laid out a bowl of rice and a pair of chopsticks, poured a cup of spirits onto the soil, knelt down, and kowtowed three times.

She remained on her knees a long time afterward. She had no idea whether she would ever return from the wilds of Ili. Whether she would ever again see the grave of the woman who had shaped her into who she was.

The servants who had come along had to remind her that they must all hurry back to continue with preparations for departure.

Back at the residence, she packed all Master Gordon's belongings into two trunks: one of his clothes, the other of his books and letters. But no matter how she searched, she couldn't find his jade tablet. A disappointment, but also a relief: Now she wouldn't need to struggle between her desire to honor his wishes and her equally strong desire to please—perhaps thrill—Da-ren.

That afternoon, Master Haywood's body, in a grand casket, was sent away, accompanied by Da-ren's secretary, Da-ren's younger son, and a number of the household guards. She slipped out of the residence—there was no one to keep track of her anymore—and followed the carriages as they made their way to the British Legation.

She had never been to this part of the Tartar City—she had seen so little of her hometown in all her years. The carriages drove along the frozen Grand Canal, their wheels clacking against paving stone. The British Legation was situated almost directly on the canal, hemmed in by the Han Lin Library to the north and the Imperial College to the west.

She did not go in with the carriages, but stood on the far side of the canal, some distance from the imposing gate—the site of the legation had once been the residence of a prince of the blood. About two incense sticks later, the same carriages came out and left. There had been no ruckus or tumult; the British inside must have accepted the explanation the majordomo had crafted with Ying-ying's help: that Master Gordon, delighted from seeing his young friend, had taken several drinks too many at the Lantern Festival feast, then fallen down in a most unfortunate way.

She had been feeling strangely inanimate, as if she were made of plaster and sawdust. But as she watched the carriages drive away, the finality of his death—and Amah's—at last sank in.

Overnight, she had lost everyone who loved her.

Her tears were stinging hot in her eyes, but ice-cold upon her cheeks. She let them fall. She wept for the wonderful future that Master Gordon would never know, the threshold of forty that Amah would never reach, and the bleak days that stretched out endlessly before herself.

For the first time in her life, she feared the future, as Mother and Amah—and perhaps Da-ren, too—had always feared it for her.

LEIGHTON REACTED PARTICULARLY STRONGLY TO the dose of quinine at midday. Afterward exhaustion smothered him. He drifted in and out of sleep, seeming to grow more tired each time he opened his eyes.

At some point his throat became parched. He finished the glass of water that had been left on his nightstand, but that wasn't enough. To reach the pitcher on the table, he must get up.

It took him quite a bit of time to manage the feat and stagger across the small room. When he lifted the pitcher, his arms felt as if they were made of wet clay. He had to lean against the door for several minutes before he could gather enough strength to edge his way back to bed.

At the window he stopped to rest again. He was in an upper-story room of the minister's residence, high enough for him to see over the wall that surrounded the compound.

There was a river outside—or was it a canal?—that he hadn't noticed on the night of his arrival. The day was fading. The frozen canal glinted dully in the scattered light. The road that ran alongside the canal was empty of both traffic and pedestrians.

Except for a beautiful Chinese girl dressed all in white.

She was crying. Not bawling, not sobbing, just...weeping, her face wet with tears, the rims of her eyes red, her nose and cheeks too.

Was he hallucinating?

He closed his eyes and rested his forehead against the cold glass pane of the window. When he opened his eyes again, she was gone.

HERB DIDN'T VISIT AT ALL that day. Leighton consoled himself with the explanation that Herb did come, but was denied entrance by either Dr. Ross or Miller the assistant.

He was much better the next day and impatient to see Herb. When it was near dusk and still his friend hadn't arrived, he asked Miller for paper and pen to send a message.

The young man swallowed. "Let me speak to the doctor."

A few minutes later Dr. Ross entered the room, looking grimly determined. Leighton was puzzled by his countenance—surely he wasn't so ill that he couldn't be allowed even a brief visit.

The physician sat down. "I'm very sorry to have to inform you of this, Mr. Atwood, but Mr. Gordon passed away the same day he came to see you."

The words washed over Leighton, a jumble of miscellaneous sounds. "Can you—can you say that again?"

"Mr. Gordon is no more," said Dr. Ross gravely. "There was a Lantern Festival celebration at his employer's residence. I am told he attended in an expansive mood, took a drink or two too many, and had an unfortunate fall. I examined his body after it was brought to the legation yesterday, and I believe what I saw was consistent with the explanation of a fatal head injury."

Leighton stared at him. "His *body* is here?"

"Yes."

"I want to see it. Now."

Dr. Ross opened his mouth as if to argue, then closed it again. "All right. I'll fetch Miller."

They had to leave the minister's residence to go into a smaller house on the legation's property. It was bitterly cold outside, and yet all Leighton felt was a scalding in his chest. They had to be wrong. They had to be. Herb had been incandescent with life. And they had so many plans. The Great Wall, the Ming Tombs, the Temple of Heaven. The teahouse-theater and the candied haws. The visit with Herb's pupil, the young lady to whom he had been deeply attached.

But there was the casket, set upon a long dining table. And when Miller lifted the lid of the casket, a cry tore from Leighton.

Herb looked peaceful, as if asleep. But he was cold as marble and almost as stiff. Leighton clutched at the side of the coffin. Both Dr. Ross and Miller sprang forward to grab hold of his arms, fearful he might fall.

"Please. Please give me a minute—alone."

They did.

He fell to his knees. For what felt like an eternity he knelt with his forehead against the side of the casket, drowning in despair. Then he pulled himself to his feet, laid his hand over Herb's, and told his friend, "I'll take you home. I'll take you back to Starling Manor—to Father— and you need never leave again."

TWO WEEKS LATER HE WAS back in Shanghai with Herb's ashes and belongings. There were several telegrams from his mother waiting for him, her relief and happiness palpable in every word. The most recent message asked that he please cable as soon as he returned to Shanghai, so that she, Mr. Delany, and Marland could set out on the next steamer bound for Honolulu. *That way we will see you a fortnight sooner.*

Leighton set sail the next week. His steamer called at Yokohama before charting a course east to Hawaii. The islands came into view as beautiful as a dream, green mountains rising from a shining blue sea. And as his steamer pulled into port, he immediately spotted the fair-haired boy, covered to the ears in flower garlands, leaping up and down on the dock, waving his hat wildly in the air.

Marland.

Next to him Mother was already wiping at her eyes. And the man with his arm around her shoulders must be Mr. Delany.

When Leighton came ashore, just as many garlands of jasmine and plumeria were piled onto his shoulders. With Marland's arms banded tight about him and Mother's hands on his cheeks, he finally allowed himself to cry, too.

For everything he had lost and everything he had never lost.

THE HOUSE THEY HAD HIRED was in the hills above Honolulu, with a cool breeze on the lanai that gently caressed the skin, and a breathtaking view of Diamond Head and the azure waters beyond.

It was after lunch. Marland had gone to his room to change into clothes more suitable for vigorous activities—he'd insisted on holding off exploring the island until after Leighton's arrival. Leighton and Mother remained on the lanai.

"I have a letter from Lady Atwood for you. It reached me shortly before we departed San Francisco," said Mother.

Leighton took the still-sealed envelope from her.

Dear Master Leighton,

By now you should have learned of your uncle's passing. What you do not know is that I killed him. I have always been seen as a devoted wife, and he was no longer a young man. It was ruled as a natural death, and now I am free.

But not from my own conscience. I have committed murder and I will always be a murderess. The question is whether I go off to evangelize in the Serengeti or spend the rest of my days in a prison cell, until I am escorted to the gallows.

I will let you decide. If you choose to turn me in to the authorities, this letter will serve as a written confession.

I wish you well.

Yours,
Alexandra Atwood

"Is everything all right?" asked Mother.

"Yes, everything is perfectly fine. Lady Atwood sends her regards," Leighton answered. He rose and kissed Mother on her cheek. "I'd better go change too."

In his room, he lit a match, burned Lady Atwood's letter, and wrote a reply.

Dear Lady Atwood,

Enjoy the Serengeti.

Your servant,
Leighton Atwood

When Marland came to knock on his door, Leighton had already changed, the sealed and stamped letter in his pocket.

"I've decided what we are going to do this afternoon," said Marland, his speech now marked by a noticeable American accent. "We are going to ride to Manoa Falls and then go to the beach."

"You lead. I will follow," Leighton answered.

He ruffled Marland's hair, still not quite used to how tall the boy had become. And how old. Leighton would turn seventeen in weeks, which meant Marland was ten: He had missed nearly six years of his brother's life.

But then Marland took his hand and together they ran out of the house.

Into limitless sunshine and limitless beauty.

FOR WEEKS THE CARAVAN HAD made its laborious way along Hehsi Corridor, part of the route once used by merchant caravans to carry silk from the south of China to the great cities of the Mediterranean. North of the corridor stretched the Gobi Desert, south the Tibetan plateau. Even the oases along the way seemed dusty, their very existence—to Ying-ying at least—infinitely fragile.

But now they had finally arrived at Jiayu Pass, the westernmost gate of the Great Wall. Years ago, Ying-ying had mentioned it during her first meeting with Herb. She never would have believed that she would someday see it with her own eyes, the Gate of Sighs, much less that there were still three thousand *li* to go before they reached their eventual destination of Kulja, the administrative seat of Ili.

Da-ren descended from his carriage to climb up to the top of the great earthen fort that guarded the pass; Ying-ying followed. Beyond the pass the land was brown and desolate, the mountains in the distance equally so—this was the territory of the invading tribes, against which the Great Wall had been built.

Silently Da-ren walked from one end of the rampart to the other. Did he wonder whether he would ever see the imperial city again? Whether his bones would be buried here, half a continent away from those of his ancestors?

Da-ren exhaled. "We will proceed," he told Bao-shun.

Ying-ying remained a moment longer upon the ramparts, feeling very nearly overwhelmed by the scale and inhospitality of the land ahead. But then she squared her shoulders, followed Da-ren down, and made ready to continue the journey.

Thank you for reading *The Hidden Blade*.

- Want to know when the next Sherry Thomas novel will be released? Sign up for her newsletter at www.sherrythomas.com. You can also follow her on twitter at @sherrythomas and like her Facebook page at http://facebook.com/authorsherrythomas.
- A review at Goodreads or at a venue of your choice would be greatly appreciated.
- *The Hidden Blade* is a prequel to *My Beautiful Enemy*, which picks up the story four years later, when Ying-ying and Leighton meet at last. Read on for an excerpt.

My Beautiful Enemy: an excerpt

Chinese Turkestan
1883

LEIGHTON ENJOYED AN OASIS. But unlike the oases of the Arabian deserts, this particular oasis had no date palms. Though it did have farmlands and orchards that suddenly leaped into the view of the weary traveler, the verdant acres lively and defiant against the endlessly arid Takla Makan Desert, never far to the south.

There were also no natural springs. The crops and the fruit trees were irrigated by melted snow that had traveled miles from the nearest mountain, along an ancient and complex system of underground tunnels that had been constructed entirely by hand.

There were, however, Bactrian camels, a train of them just outside the courtyard of the open-air restaurant, feasting on grass and oats. Inside the courtyard, beneath the shade of grapevines growing on overhead trellises—he wondered what the French would think of the *terroir*—the clientele consisted mostly of traders and travelers, lured by the sizzling fragrance of spiced mutton grilling over an open fire and the yeasty aroma of freshly baked bread.

Once, great caravans had teemed on these routes, carrying precious bolts of Chinese silk across the vast steppes of central Asia to the coast of the Caspian Sea, to Antioch, and finally to Rome, to feed the empire's ever ravenous desire for luxury fabrics.

The rise of great ocean-faring vessels had rendered the land courses obsolete hundreds of years ago. The caravans that still plied the route were small, sometimes no more than a few camels, trading between towns. And most of the legendary cities of yore were either lost or reduced to mere shadows of their former glory.

Yet a sense of continuity still lingered in the air. Marco Polo had drunk the same sweet, cool wine as that in Leighton's cup, made from oasis-grown white grapes. A thousand years before that, Buddhist missionaries from India had braved the same perilous paths, carrying the teachings of the Tathagata into the western provinces of China.

Sherry Thomas

Leighton, too, had traveled to China once—alone, with almost nothing in his pocket, and little more than an irrational hope in his heart.

Now he was again in China, at least technically. But Chinese Turkestan, currently controlled by the Ch'ing Dynasty, was of a different character altogether, a place of endless desert, vast blue skies, and snowcapped mountain ranges.

A new customer walked into the courtyard, a young Kazakh dressed in a knee-length robe and a fur-lined, long-flapped hat. They were in a predominantly Uyghur part of Tarim Basin, but one encountered Kazakhs, Kyrgyz, Han Chinese, and even Mongols on the road. The diners looked up for only a moment before returning to their food and conversation. Leighton popped another chickpea into his mouth.

"Bring me soup and bread," the young Kazakh ordered as he sat down. "Mind you skim the fat off the soup. And the bread had better be still warm."

Leighton cast another glance at the Kazakh. Why did he think he had seen that face before?

The Kazakh now had a dagger in hand, scraping at the dirt underneath his nails. The weapon was six inches of deadly, gleaming blade, and he wielded it with no more care than if it were a toothpick. A man seated close to the entrance of the courtyard, who had been looking at the Kazakh with the interest of a pickpocket, turned back to his stew of sheep's brain.

The Kazakh's food arrived. He sheathed his dagger and attacked the round disk of bread, pausing only to wash it down with soup. Halfway through his meal, he flicked Leighton a hard look.

All at once it came to Leighton. Not when or where he had seen the Kazakh, but that last time he saw the face, it had belonged to a *girl*.

The memory was hazy, almost dreamlike, the kind of recollection that felt more imagined than real. Add to it the Kazakh's unfriendly bearing, grimy appearance, and affinity for sharp objects—Leighton was inclined to dismiss the notion out of hand.

And yet, now that the idea had arisen, he couldn't help but notice that the Kazakh was a tad too old to have such a perfectly smooth face. And wasn't his wrist, when it peeked out from his sleeve, a bit delicate in size for a man?

Not to mention his thick robe and close-collared shirt. At the edge of the desert, temperatures plunged directly after sunset. But now it was

2

high noon on a spring day; the sun seared, the air hot and heavy even in the shade. Most of the other travelers had loosened their outer garments, but the Kazakh kept his closed and belted, even though he must be perspiring underneath.

She stopped eating—Leighton realized that he had changed the pronoun he used to think about the Kazakh. Instead she watched him, her gaze frosty. Her dagger, which had never left the table, was now once again unsheathed, the naked blade pointed directly at him.

He was not in Chinese Turkestan to make trouble. The goal of the British was to pass entirely unnoticed on their intelligence-gathering mission. In fact, he was already leaving, on his way to meet his colleagues in Yarkand. There they would debate whether to brave the Karakoram Pass directly into Kashmir, or tackle the relatively easier Baroghil Pass, still two miles above sea level, for a more circuitous route back to the raj.

The wise choice would be to stop gawking at the girl, finish his meal, and ride out. Until he was on Indian soil, he was not entirely safe—the Ch'ing authority, who had recovered control over the territory only recently, was not kind to spies. And anything that could delay his return added to the risk of being found out.

Yet he could not shake the feeling that his seemingly unreliable memory of having seen her before was not something to be ignored. That it had not been a case of two random strangers passing each other, but an encounter of significance.

The nature of which significance just happened to elude him entirely.

He drank from his wine, then stood up, jug in hand, and seated himself opposite her—the unwise choice it was, then.

The people of these parts were by and large friendly and hospitable. It was not uncommon for strangers to sit down together and chat. "You look hot, friend," he said in Turkic. "Have some of this wine."

Up close, her eyes were the color of a desolate sea, charcoal grey tinged with blue. Her lips, greasy from lunch, were the dark red of aged claret.

Without a word, she picked up the wine jug he had pushed across the table at her, held it above her head, and poured a fine stream straight down her throat.

The grace and precision of her action, the way her throat moved as she swallowed—his awareness of her was suddenly the sort to elevate his heart rate.

"Good wine," she said, sliding the jug back to him. "Many thanks."

When he glanced down at the wine, he saw that the dagger had also found its way across the table, its tip no more than two inches from his chest. He turned it around, and with a flick at the pommel, sent it skidding directly back into its scabbard.

"Good blade," he said.

Her eyes narrowed. She slapped the table from underneath. The sheathed dagger leaped up a foot off the table, still perfectly horizontal. She knocked the dagger with her soup spoon. It flew directly at him.

He barely deflected it with the wine jug. The dagger fell to the table with a loud clatter.

One thing was clear: The show of force removed any doubt of her gender. Only a young woman traveling by herself would be so wary of being approached by a man, offering wine and friendship.

"Is this how the Kazakhs repay hospitality?" he asked.

She glanced around at the startled diners. Quickly, eating and talking recommenced on the part of the latter. She turned back to him. "What do you want, stranger?"

"Am I a stranger to you?"

"I've never laid eyes on you before. Of course you are a stranger to me," she said scornfully. But she did return the dagger to her belt.

"But I have seen you. I don't remember when or where, except that I have seen you."

"So what?" Her small teeth sank into a piece of carrot from the soup. "I have seen a thousand strangers on these roads. Passed them without a backward glance."

She was full of thorns, and just short of loutish. But strangely enough, he felt more at ease with her than with a roomful of eminently proper English misses.

"Where are you headed?" he asked.

He wasn't usually so loquacious. Though he absorbed languages with the ease of white cloth in a vat of dyes, he rarely spoke unless spoken to, in any of those languages.

"West," she answered tersely. "You?"

She was studying his face. There were places in the world where his green eyes would be a dead giveaway of his racial origin. But fortunately, in the heart of Asia, there existed natives with eyes of sky and forest, and every color in between. And he was now sufficiently tanned to pass for one of them.

"West, too." Then he surprised himself by telling something close to the truth. "Kashmir is my eventual destination."

"Lucky you."

"Have you been to Kashmir?" And was that where he might have met her?

She shook her head. "No, but I've heard it's a nice place."

There was an odd wistfulness to her voice, the way an invalid stuck at home might speak of the world outside. She lifted the wine and drank as she did before, her fragile-looking wrist remarkably steady as she suspended the heavy jug above her mouth.

He swallowed. There was nothing retiring, modest, or pliant about her. Yet for reasons he couldn't fathom, he found her blatantly, ragingly feminine, like a pearl at the tip of a knife.

She set down the jug. Their gazes met—and held. She had been wary and hostile, but now she was tense in a way that seemed not entirely related to her earlier distrust of him.

Pushing away what was left of her soup, she asked, "Where are *you* from?"

She knew, the thought came to him. She knew that he had seen through her disguise.

"Persia." He gave his standard answer—Parsi was one of his strongest languages.

"You are far from home."

There was an accent to her Turkic, and not a Kazakh one—the only thing Kazakh about her, as far as he could see, was her clothes. Perhaps Turkic wasn't her mother tongue. But so many different variations of the language were spoken over such a large territory by so many different people, it was quite possible that she hailed from an area or a tribe unfamiliar to him.

"Some of us are not meant to grow old where we are born," he said. "You, my friend, are you also far from home?"

A shadow passed over her face, something almost like pain, as if home was so distant as to be beyond reach. Then she shrugged. "Home is wherever I am."

Oddly enough, he felt an answering pang of longing. Not so much for the mortar and bricks of home, but for the idea of it, that safe, happy place he had once known. "Where will you be making your home next?"

She thought for a moment. "Kashgar."

He would reach Yarkand much more conveniently by turning south a hundred miles or so before Kashgar and following the course of the Yarkand River upstream. But he found himself reluctant to contemplate that faster path. He did not want them to part so soon, still strangers.

"Perhaps we can share the road for a few days, if you are traveling alone."

After having traversed the territory all the way to the Altai Mountains and back, another hundred miles or two hardly mattered.

If, that was, she agreed to it.

Surely she must understand the average criminal would gravitate toward an easier quarry. And she was a poor target if one were out for gold: Her blue tunic was frayed at the cuffs and the hem, the embroidery along the lapels long ago soiled into squiggles of greasy black.

She popped the last piece of bread into her mouth. A desire to kiss her, bread crumbs and all, shot through him like a bullet.

"Well, the road does get lonely," she said.

She did not move—or at least he could swear she did not move. Yet all at once she twirled a palm-size grape leaf by its stem. It was early yet in the year; the vine that spread on the trellis overhead was not weighed down by ripe clusters of fruit. He would have to stand with an arm stretched to pluck a leaf. Yet she had done it while remaining perfectly still in her seat.

As a warning, it was far more sobering than a rattling of the dagger. She was stating, quite plainly, that she could cut his throat before he even knew what happened.

He smiled, thoroughly impressed. "So you will permit me to accompany you?"

She, too, smiled, now that she had established she needed barely lift a finger to take his life—a smile as sharp as her blade. "Yes, do come along."

More Books by Sherry Thomas

Heart of Blade Series
The Hidden Blade
My Beautiful Enemy

The London Series
The Luckiest Lady in London
Private Arrangements
His at Night

The Fitzhugh Trilogy
Claiming the Duchess (short story)
Beguiling the Beauty
Ravishing the Heiress
A Dance in Moonlight (novella)
Tempting the Bride
The Bride of Larkspear (novella)

The Marsden Brothers Series
Delicious
Not Quite a Husband

The Elemental Trilogy (Young Adult Fantasy)
The Burning Sky
The Perilous Sea
The Immortal Heights—2015

Not in a series
The One in My Heart—late 2014 (Contemporary Romance)

CPSIA information can be obtained at www.ICGtesting.com
Printed in the USA
LVOW08s0212190615

442981LV00007B/581/P